The Body on the Moor

Nick Louth is a best-selling thriller writer and an award-winning financial journalist. A 1979 graduate of the London School of Economics, he went on to become a Reuters foreign correspondent in 1987. He was for many years a *Financial Times* columnist, and a regular contributor to many other financial titles in print and online. *The Body on the Moor* is the eighth book in the DCI Gillard crime series, and his twelfth thriller overall. Nick Louth is married and lives in Lincolnshire.

www.nicklouth.com

Also by Nick Louth

Bite
Heartbreaker
Mirror Mirror
Trapped

DCI Craig Gillard Crime Thrillers

NICK LOUTH

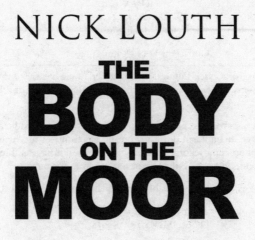

THE
BODY
ON THE
MOOR

CANELO CRIME

First published in the United Kingdom in 2021 by

Canelo
31 Helen Road
Oxford OX2 0DF
United Kingdom

A CIP catalogue record for this book is available from the British Library.

Print ISBN 978 1 80032 526 5
Ebook ISBN 978 1 80032 171 7

Look for more great books at www.canelo.co

Printed and bound in Great Britain by Clays Ltd, Elcograf S.p.A.

1

For Louise, as always

Prologue

Last night I dreamt I returned to Longstone Moor. I saw the lonely single-track road winding across the top under the slate grey sky, felt the keening wind and the stinging horizontal sleet. It wasn't the first time. Each of these recurring dreams is the same, a cold twilight and the same illicit task. I know this bony Derbyshire land, above High Rake, the straw-coloured tussocks and the blasted stones, the clack of crows scrutinising every movement from dead hawthorn branches. We've come a long way to be here. The ancient road sign by the last cattle grid is barely legible, its warning of disused shafts just a corroded etching. Beyond it, scattered tombstone fragments of dry stone wall lead off to the high top, only its crown of rusted barbed wire surviving. This is close to where I met him, that fateful day almost twenty years ago. And in the dream it is his body that we are carrying from the boot of the car. His lifeless corpse, so heavy already, gets weightier with guilt and regret at every step. In the exterior knowledge that a dreamer often has, I know this is the wrong body. It is the one that I wanted to bury for ever, but not the one that I did.

I have the legs, and she the arms, but the corpse still drags on the wet grass, his clothing snagging on the rusty wire. One hundred yards to the old lead shaft and it feels like a hundred miles. In this recurrent nightmare it is always like this, a lifetime's burden. But finally, we see the shaft and its ring of downtrodden fence, the barbs snagged with tufts of wool from errant sheep. The wooden warning board is tilted on its rotted post. We have to descend on the spongy grass for several feet until we see the shaft. It is a struggle to carry him without tripping. Finally, we feel as much as see the abyss, hear its sibilant whisper, crooning a welcome. We swing and release, and then the burden is gone, down, down, swallowed silently by the darkness.

And then I awake, drenched in a guilt that will never go.

Chapter One

Almost four o'clock in the morning. Detective Chief Inspector Craig Gillard was in the upmarket Surrey town of Esher standing in the bedroom of a third-floor flat with the lights off. The curtains were closed, except for a small gap through which he was peering with binoculars. Next to him, at a partially opened window, were two marksmen from the firearms unit with sniper's rifles. Eighty yards away, uphill, they could see the back view of a newly constructed seven-bedroom home belonging to one of Britain's most dangerous criminals.

Terrence Joysie Bonner, forty-three. Accused of murder, GBH, and trafficking class 'A' drugs.

This home had been under surveillance for a week as part of Operation Whirlwind, a coordinated attempt by the National Crime Agency to take down one of the largest drug distribution networks in the UK. In less than ten minutes' time, in more than sixty locations across the UK, police officers would be raiding the homes, offices and vehicles of those suspected of being involved.

Nothing had been left to chance. In the street on the far side of the house were eight uniformed officers in an unmarked transit van. In a cul-de-sac at the right-hand rear were two more unmarked vehicles with four officers

3

in each, and at the end of the road leading to the estate a second firearms unit. In the garden of the house a plain-clothes officer was hiding behind a shed, and a female plainclothes officer walking a dog was on waste ground adjacent to the target home. Every side was covered.

The only lights on at Bonner's house were two carriage lamps outside the back door. The interior was dark. With luck, he would be asleep. Gillard had arranged with the local authority for the streetlamps to be gradually dimmed in the minutes leading up to the raid as the police arrived, and then turned on maximum once it began.

Every single officer had been briefed about how to tackle Bonner. The sometime nightclub doorman had a well-deserved reputation for violence, brought to public attention by the horrific case of the body parts of a man being strewn along the hard shoulder of the M4 motorway. Bonner was the enforcer for the gang, and the victim of this crime was an underling. Bonner was assumed to possess a firearm, but the idea was to catch him while he was asleep.

All the officers were on the same police radio fre-quency. One of the officers, listening in on a bug placed inside the house, was ready to give the signal to move in, once the senior NCA officer in charge in Manchester, where the main raids were taking place, had given the signal.

The countdown began. Ten, nine, eight, seven, six...

A light went on in the house, upstairs.

Too late to call it off.

Gillard gave the signal. Five seconds early.

The crackle over the radio indicated the door team were on their way to the front door at the far side of the house. Gillard heard the bellowed warning of 'Armed police!', and soon after the crack of the door ram. A second light went on upstairs and a burly silhouetted figure threw open a window.

Bonner.

Gillard picked up the radio and called: 'Target emerging from rear upstairs window. Team Bravo hold position.' Three uniforms, two male, one female, were in the shadows behind the high rear fence of the house and acknowledged the order.

Bonner jumped from the upstairs window and dropped into the shadows with a soft impact. He seemed to be wearing a T-shirt, underpants and a pair of Crocs. He had a phone in his hand. A few seconds later he shot into the light of the rear lawn, sprinted down the garden and hurled himself over the fence. He landed neatly on the footpath.

Behind the three uniforms.

'Team Bravo, quarry is behind you,' Gillard said. The female officer was the first to react, but as she turned to Bonner, he picked her up as if she weighed nothing and threw her into her two colleagues. They all fell sprawling across the pathway. Bonner ran off in the opposite direction, towards the cul-de-sac where Team Charlie were waiting in two unmarked vehicles. For a man dressed in little more than his underwear he made a good turn of speed. Gillard was aware, because they kept telling him, that the armed officers next to him had a bead on Bonner. They could not open fire unless an officer or member of the public was in imminent danger. It was a finely tuned decision, constantly subject to change.

As Bonner ran into the street, eight uniformed officers emerged from two vehicles. The fugitive came to an abrupt stop, losing a Croc, and then reversed, sprinting left. From behind the officers, a motorcycle raced into the cul-de-sac, the dark-clad rider hunched over the tank as it mounted the pavement at speed, heading for Bonner. The uniforms, some brandishing Tasers, turned to the speeding bike, unsure whether it was a police rider. Once it was clear that it was not, their reactions were too slow to do anything other than scatter as it swept through. Ten yards ahead, Bonner ran alongside the motorbike, which slowed down just enough for him to climb on the pillion. With eight cops in pursuit it headed left along the alleyway following the edge of Bonner's back garden fence, and past the entrance to the block of flats Gillard was in.

Only one of the pursuers was in with a prayer. Tiana Clore – a tough Barbadian, built like Serena Williams – had represented Barbados in the heptathlon in the London Olympics, where she ran the 200 metres in just over twenty-two seconds. She left her colleagues for dead, sprinting left along the alleyway after the bike and out of Gillard's field of view.

Shouting instructions into his radio, Gillard ran from the bedroom into the next room left, which had a balcony overlooking the footpath which curved round left beneath it and after seventy or so yards emerged into a residential street. The motorcycle was thirty yards ahead of Tiana, but slowing to negotiate a cycle barrier, a pair of offset metal railings at the end of the alley. It was only five yards ahead when Tiana hurdled the barriers and with unbroken stride got almost within touching distance. The bike slewed right, to avoid a parked car blocking its exit, while Tiana slid across the bonnet, to cut off its escape.

The rider saw her approaching from the left, wobbled one way, then the other, gunned the engine, the front wheel lifted and Terrence Bonner tumbled off the back, his unprotected rear skidding on the gravel.

Tiana landed on him like a missile, and in the following thirty seconds gave as good as she got. As the motorcycle made good its escape, half a dozen officers piled in on Bonner. At least one of them was laid out by a punch before Bonner was eventually subdued, handcuffed and bundled into a police van.

Gillard was quickly into Bonner's home. The newly acquired property had been expensively furnished, but the gangster hadn't really had the time to put his own imprint on it. While he watched uniformed officers loading electronic items into clear plastic bags, Gillard already felt that the case against this most dangerous man, like all gangland prosecutions, would come down to whether key witnesses could be persuaded to give evidence.

–

Gillard got his first close-up look at the prisoner at eight o'clock in the cells at Staines police station. Through the CCTV monitor into the suicide-watch cell he saw the gangster lying apparently relaxed on the blue plastic-covered mattress. Despite the shoe-sized dressing on his grazed buttock, and the bruise on his cheek from Tiana's fist, Bonner remained an intimidating sight. Clearly gym-fit despite being overweight, he was extensively tattooed right up to his shaven head. Though arrested in just a T-shirt and skimpy underpants, he was now wearing a pair of boxers retrieved by police for him from his own bedroom. They bore a legend printed across the crotch: 'May contain nuts.'

It was down to the National Crime Agency to pursue the case, on which it had been working for more than a year, but Gillard wanted to ask Bonner a few questions about some unsolved drug-related assaults in Surrey before he was transferred up to Nottingham that afternoon to face the main charges. He was brought to an interview room, where he sat, huge arms folded, oaken thighs apart. His neck was so short that the lobes of his ears sat sideways on his massive shoulders. Vince Babbage, the desk sergeant, had already booked him in with three serious charges relating to drug-trafficking and assault.

The duty solicitor arrived, a tall, slender and bespectacled young woman named Emily Harper, who looked like she'd only woken up a few minutes ago. Ms Harper was so pale and youthful that it hardly seemed possible she'd had the time to be qualified to drive a car, let alone become a solicitor. Gillard briefed her on the charges against her client before they went in, but as they entered the interview room he was aware of her shrinking behind him as she got her first glimpse of Bonner, who looked up with a grin on his face.

'Kind of yer to offer me your daughter.' When he lifted his chin to speak his lumpy head squeezed rolls of flesh from the back of his neck.

'Don't speak to her like that,' Gillard said. 'She's on your side.'

'I'll speak to her any way I fucking well please.' Bonner then unleashed a torrent of invective at Gillard, before adding, 'Get this schoolgirl out of here before I get some ideas. I want a proper lawyer. Now, you, cunt-stable, bring me some breakfast before I get my mates to go round and give your wife a sausage sandwich through the back door.'

There was a time, back in the seventies and early eighties, before Gillard began in Surrey Police, when awkward customers like Bonner could be taken to a cell and given a right seeing-to by officers who knew where to kick, stamp and punch that wouldn't leave too many bruises. Resisting arrest, attempting to escape, assaulting an officer were all charges that were rarely challenged by magistrates when there were three or four official accounts against one from a previously convicted felon like this one. But everything was different now. CCTV, bodycams, and above all changed attitudes within the criminal justice system. Criminality was considered a disease of society, in which miscreants were not bad but vulnerable, not villains but merely 'differently moralled'. Offenders were themselves considered the victims of poor upbringing, broken homes, inequalities of wealth and background, and a lack of parental love.

All of which was often true. Gillard knew that much, but it didn't help when you were at the sharp end. Having some thug threaten to rape your wife, and then demand breakfast – which Bonner knew under the regulations he was entitled to – infuriated officers. The menu at Staines today was lamb hot pot, Caribbean jerk chicken, an all-day breakfast, pizza or vegetarian lasagne. Detainees could choose from a selection of options – vegan or vegetarian, halal or kosher – all checked for allergens. Most of the food was takeaways, which often meant some poor uniform having to go and fetch it, at further cost to the public purse. Gillard had heard tales of prisoners repeatedly sending back food because it wasn't hot enough, or was too salty – 'I've got a heart problem, see' – giving some inexperienced PC the run-around.

Sometimes it made his blood boil.

There were still things that could be done. Bonner was returned to his cell unfed. Gillard would get Babbage to post a cereal bar through the door later. Much later. That would be deemed an adequate breakfast when they were short-staffed, a permanent state of affairs. More concerning was the young solicitor, who was trembling at the lurid suggestions Bonner had made as he was being manhandled out of the interview room, about how she might more usefully earn a living on her knees in front of him.

'Are you okay?' Gillard asked her, once the prisoner was banged up again.

She nodded and blew her nose. 'I've been doing this for three months now, and never had anyone speak to me like that before,' she whispered.

'Don't take it personally. We can get you a coffee. If I were you, I'd sit down for ten minutes, because I don't think you're in any condition to drive right now.'

'Thank you,' she said. 'That's one client I'm happy to pass to the barrister ASAP.'

Chapter Two

Julia McGann was already running late when she made her final check in the hall mirror. She brushed her dark bob, applied mascara under her large blue-grey eyes and pouted for the crimson O. Looking reasonable, she thought. Thirty-nine, yes, but still as petite as when she left school. Then she spotted her tights. She groaned to herself. Straight out of the packet today. Bloody pound shop rubbish, a false economy. A small tear would have been okay until she had a chance to change at chambers. But this was a monster rip, the kind of ankle-to-thigh ladder suitable for rescuing the occupants of high-rise buildings.

Not today, of all days.

Cursing to herself, she ran back to the bedroom and rifled through the underwear drawer with the speed of a crack-addled burglar. Finally, a pair of old reliables: dark, woolly, thick and yes, a little baggy, but nothing an extra tug to the waist and an extra notch on the belted skirt wouldn't fix. A ten-second wriggle and she was ready, grabbed her briefcase and fled for the bus stop.

That two-minute delay cascaded.

She missed the bus, then caught another less direct service five minutes later. The best stop still left her a ten-minute walk. She could hardly believe that at her age, a practising barrister for almost four years, she was still struggling with the basics of earning a living. While still on the bus she rang in, hoping against hope that Hogarth wouldn't pick up. She was in luck. Receptionist Veronica answered, her vowels crisply enunciated.

'V&I Barristers, good morning.'

'Veronica, it's me. I'm running late.'

'Oh dear, filthy Duster let you down again?' she giggled, a delightful tinkle. Julia's car, an ancient and grubby yellow Dacia Duster, was still in a garage in Surbiton after breaking down a week ago. The cost of the repairs exceeded the vehicle's value, but she needed it fixed and she had maxed out both credit cards. The question was, where was the money to come from?

'No, missed the bus. The Duster's out of commission for now. How's his mood?'

'Hogsy's not a happy bunny, I'm afraid.'

The dreaded Clive Hogarth, chief clerk.

Only in his mid-forties, Hogarth had the wattles and paunch of a Dickensian uncle. He wore exactly the same grey suit and a pale blue shirt every day, with tightly laced Oxford shoes, polished to a regimental shine, his swollen ankles spilling over the top. And he had a spiteful demeanour. Never judge a man by his title. In many occupations, a clerk is a lowly creature. But in the world of barristers, the chief clerk is king. Hogarth, a great obese warthog of a man, controlled every aspect of V&I, which stood for the Latin *veritate et iustitia*, truth and justice. The staff considered it a pompous overstatement.

Loosely self-employed, barristers famously eat only what they kill, and it was Hogarth and Hogarth alone who decided which case each barrister would get their teeth into. His spreadsheets mapped out the entire legal resource of the organisation, making promises to clients and lawyers alike, and quite often breaking them. Hogarth had grown up in Enfield, that vast characterless sweep of suburbia on the fringes of North London. His father had been a legal clerk, and he'd known from the age of eleven that he would be one too. There were only two things that the junior barristers needed to know about Hogarth. One was his fanatical devotion to the local football team Enfield Town, on whose results his mood would swing. The other was his halitosis, a consequence of severe gingival disease. His teeth were stained and jumbled, his gums a febrile, swollen magenta.

Julia had been warned about him on day one at V&I. Her fellow juniors had advised that you didn't want to sit too close to Hogarth, and should never agree to go for lunch. You didn't want to make him laugh. And you certainly didn't want to make him shout. Hogarth wasn't stupid, he was aware of what only your best friend will tell you. He kept a big supply of extra strong mints on his desk and crunched them noisily throughout the day.

It was Hogarth who had interviewed Julia on the first day of her induction to V&I. Sitting her in the principal reception room, a cross between a library and a Victorian pub snug, he'd eyed her as if she was a piece of fresh meat.

'You've been chosen for pupillage by Christopher, our star barrister.'

'That's great, thank you,' Julia said.

'Don't thank me, you weren't my choice,' he said. 'We lost the one we really wanted.'

That was the thing about Hogarth. He liked to remind you of your status, and in V&I Julia had begun at the very bottom, powerless, which is where he wanted her.

Pupillage under Christopher turned out to be an even broader learning experience than expected. A blond Flashman with perfect teeth and a public-school delivery, his eloquence seemed quite capable of converting an Ulster Unionist to ardent Catholicism. Yet underneath the charm he was a hard taskmaster, expecting long hours of research and preparation from Julia for the cases she was helping him prepare. But equally, her time with him involved long boozy lunches, expensive evening meals apparently charged to commercial law clients, and finally, and with no great surprise, Julia's seduction. Later, she regretted surrendering her briefs to him so easily (his joke, which she was certain he had used before on others), but Christopher was a force of nature who could not be refused.

Ironically, it was Christopher himself who taught her in the first week of her pupillage how to assert herself in the world of men. Standing up straight, shoulders back, with a forthright chin was originally a military imperative, but, as he told Julia, it does wonders for women too. The courtroom is a theatre, and you must deliver every verbal volley with panache as well as accuracy. Hour after hour they had role-played advocate and judge, or cross-examining a difficult witness, continuing over an expensive meal at one of the many restaurants where Cadwell was a habitué. After the first bottle of Châteauneuf-du-Pape he had mesmerised her with his wide blue eyes, and said, 'How do you defend a rapist?'

'Well, it depends.'

'Very little, actually. As you are well aware, the vast majority of rapes in the age of the smartphone aren't even brought to trial by the CPS, because of the difficulties of consent. The mobiles of victims are very often full of various shades of come-hither texts exchanged between perpetrator and victim. Jurors have great difficulty in setting aside a context of banter and suggestion, for which they *do* have firm electronic evidence, to convict for an accusation of rape, for which they have no proof but the word of the victim.'

'But the law is clear about consent to an individual act, which can be withdrawn.'

'Yes. But juries, women perhaps even more men, are quicker to excuse male lust than female caprice. "Okay, he was a slave to hormones, but she was a slut."'

'That's terrible.'

'Terrible, yes, but true. And be aware, rapists are going to want you defending them, not me. If an attractive, mature woman believes him, he can't be that bad. That's the thinking, and you've got to be ready for it.'

And the very next day after Christopher had given that balanced and pretty speech, Julia became aware that he had been boasting to other men within chambers about having bedded her. James Cheetham, married and known womaniser, as well as being Christopher's closest pal, had invited her on a date. When she'd refused, he'd said: 'Oh, come on, Moggy, be a sport.' It was her playground nickname, used only by her closest friends. She had foolishly disclosed it only once, when in bed with her indiscreet and clearly two-faced pupil master.

Christopher had proved himself a slippery bastard.

–

That had been five years ago, but throwing off the reputation had involved many haughty refusals to colleagues who fancied their chances. It was probably why her status within chambers had only microscopically improved in all that time. Her workspace reflected that. Yes, she now had her own office, of Victorian virtues: character and pokiness. It was a rhomboid book-lined nook of dark wood off a steep staircase between the first and second floors of the chambers. The mezzanine nature of the space meant its grand twelve-foot ceiling, cornice and ceiling rose wasn't matched by useable lateral elbow room, which was at best six foot by nine. A big bite from one side had been taken out of the room to provide additional storage space for the second-floor chamber above, now occupied by Christopher, and on the other side the top of a first floor ladies' bathroom intruded like a three-foot-high plywood blister under a table, adding the occasional refrain of cisterns and gurgling pipes. It left her with enough room for a small desk, so long as she didn't mind being pinned against her own bookcase when the external door was fully opened. True, she did possess a tiny mullioned window overlooking an alleyway, but because of an ill-fitting frame it served better to funnel in noise and traffic fumes from outside than to allow in adequate light.

When anyone used the stairs, the entire room creaked like a galleon in a storm. It had only taken her a week to be able to distinguish the tread of each member of the chambers, from the light pattering footsteps of the junior clerk Sharon Smith and the crisp heels of Edwina Pym, to the brisk well-shod feet of Christopher, right up to the ominously slow and heavy tread of Hogarth himself.

And it was the approach of the latter that she was now hearing. Hogarth was on his way down from Cadwell's room, and stopped outside hers, his breath stentorian.

Julia had been sitting at her screen going through the details of the never-ending KL Beach Resort Investment fraud case.

'Ms McGann, may I come in?' Hogarth said, pushing open the door regardless. A sulphurous taint like a recently struck match filled the room. 'I think I've got a case for you.' His fat fingers felt into his jacket pocket and he pulled out an extra strong mint, popping it into his soft wet mouth. 'Maybe we'll finally get some fees out of you.'

'Clive, as you are perfectly well aware, I have several tens of thousands of pounds owing—'

The clerk held up his large flabby hands and smiled, having succeeded once again in getting her to rise to the bait. 'I know, but it's all about cashflow, my dear. Now, we have this huge National Crime Agency case, sixty odd villains seized all over the country. As you may have heard, Mr Cadwell has been requested to represent the head of the gang, Callum Sinnott.'

'Yes, I'm aware of that.' Julia had overheard Christopher crowing about it to Edwina. The Sinnott crime family had been untouchable for years, and the newspapers had been full of the ever-larger reach of this Birmingham-based gang. Callum Sinnott had built the business on amphetamines but had expanded into cocaine with links to the 'Ndrangheta, the all-powerful Calabrian mafia. With the NCA's huge raid bringing in dozens of hardened criminals, there were a lot of spoils for lawyers to fight over.

'Well, a certain Mr Terrence Bonner, who I understand is chief *consiglieri* to Sinnott, had also requested Mr Cadwell. They are obviously going to need separate representation, so I'm going to take the risk of suggesting you.'

'Thank you,' she said, not sure that thanks were actually the appropriate response to such a half-hearted recommendation.

'Well, we are a bit stretched. James Cheetham is booked solid until Christmas, and Edwina Pym has got a series of urgent dental appointments.'

Julia felt deflated by Hogarth's continued failure to ever make a virtue out of a necessity. 'So is this a late return, Clive?' Such last-minute substitutions were often arranged by a clerk whose big hitters were overbooked, but they were a pain to the junior barristers who were forced to take them on at short notice.

'I suppose you could say so,' he chuckled. 'But you're used to them aren't you? Plea and committal at ten tomorrow, Nottingham Magistrate's Court.'

'Nottingham! Can't the solicitors deal with that?'

'Yes, but the solicitor wants to meet you. The client had his heart set on Mr Cadwell, so you have a sales job to do.'

Her heart sank. 'Which solicitors?' she asked.

'Ropes, Peel, Deaton.'

She had vaguely heard of them, a northern firm now expanding in the south.

'They are a new client for us, and I want to keep them happy,' he said. 'They've big offices in Leeds and Manchester, so if we impress them with the depth of our talent, they'll offer us more work down the line.'

Julia was very sceptical of this, but held her tongue. If the client had insisted on Christopher Cadwell but had been offered her, whom they presumably had never heard of, they would already be disappointed. She would have a hill to climb to show that she could do as good a job as her more illustrious colleague. Hogarth had made no secret of the fact she was not even second choice.

'I'll get right onto it,' she said. 'Who am I meeting?'

'Alasdair Dicks, senior partner. He'll have a couple of juniors with him. He wants to have a quick chat with you first at nine thirty in the Primavera Cafe, near the Justice Centre.'

'In Nottingham! My car's off the road.' It would have been bad enough even if the filthy Duster been working. By train it was going to be a silly-o'clock start.

Hogarth surveyed her with a jaundiced eye. 'I'll leave the travel arrangements up to you, Ms McGann. However, I hope your timekeeping tomorrow is a little better than it was this morning.'

Chapter Three

The train grumbled and squealed its way out of London St Pancras, rocking sideways as it slid out under a still-dark sky heading for Nottingham and points north. Julia McGann clutched her polystyrene cup of black and stale coffee as a talisman against sleep. She had got up before five that morning to catch the 5.56 from Guildford to Waterloo, changing at Vauxhall, then the Victoria Line to King's Cross St Pancras. At that time of day there were virtually none of the suited commuters on the tube that she was used to seeing on her regular journeys into central London. Instead, there were exhausted-looking cleaners, middle-aged West Indian ladies, washed-out-looking young Poles and Romanians, and a scattering of building and construction workers in heavy boots and paint-stained overalls. What her late father would have called the hidden underclass, of which he no doubt would now have considered her a constituent. An Appeal Court judge, William McGann had encouraged his only child to go into law. Despite family connections, her career had moved as slowly as a spider wading through treacle. She had struggled for work since being called to the bar and had yet to pay off her tuition debts.

She opened her fat briefcase and tried to reacquaint herself with some of the details of the Bonner case. Just a quick glance down the list of charges confirmed that Terrence Joysie Bonner was a dangerous and thoroughly unpleasant individual. In addition to the charges of conspiracy to supply and distribute class 'A' drugs, which was the main outcome of the NCA raids, there were numerous abhorrent acts of violence of which he was accused. Acid thrown in the face of a rival drug dealer. Using a tracked construction vehicle to run over the legs of one of his own gang's dealers, the unfortunately named John 'Lucky' Finnegan, for being an informer. Then there was the dismemberment of one Janille Murdoch, whose mortal remains were found spread alongside a motorway hard shoulder. The conspiracy charges were supported by a considerable weight of electronic evidence. However, on the murder and GBH charges against Bonner, the evidence was less impressive. It hinged almost entirely on the word of Barry Karl Menzies, a convicted drug dealer in his own right and now under the police witness protection programme.

Much depended on the character of Menzies. If she could show that he was an unreliable witness, a man whose own past was a tapestry of lies, the jury might not be convinced by his story and clear Bonner of those charges. The other aspect of this complex case was that as each of the principal defendants had their own barrister, there might well be a lot of buck-passing between them. While there was no doubt that somebody had crushed the legs of Lucky Finnegan, the victim himself – still alive, though now confined to a wheelchair – was not listed amongst the prosecution witnesses. Perhaps it was because he believed somebody else had driven the bulldozer.

Friends often quizzed Julia about her ability to defend the indefensible. In the minds of most people, the vilest criminals should have no defence and simply accept their fate. They couldn't understand why Julia went to such lengths to get her clients acquitted. Julia's response was that the truth would out. She didn't know whether her clients were guilty or not, that was up to the jury to decide. She set aside her feelings about the quite unpleasant individuals who it was her job to defend. In this case she could be fairly certain that Bonner would be going to prison for quite a long time anyhow because of the conspiracy rap, even if she managed to get him off the murder and GBH charges.

A sharp squeal of brakes eventually confirmed Julia's arrival at Nottingham. Amazingly, despite three connections, she was nearly on time. The Justice Centre was only a short walk from the railway station, which was just as well because it had started to rain, a blustery shower which wrestled and bullied her umbrella. So it was that she arrived at Primavera Cafe near the court building to meet Alasdair Dicks, senior partner at Ropes, Peel, Deaton. It was 9.37. She was seven minutes late.

–

Dicks was waiting for Julia at a table at the far end of the large and busy cafe. Judging from the number of hefty legal briefcases, he could have been any of half a dozen besuited types scattered about the tables, but she recognised him from his LinkedIn photograph. Grey-haired, gaunt and bespectacled, aged around sixty. Undistinguished but definitely old school. As she hurried across to him he managed a perfunctory smile and indicated the seat opposite.

'Sorry I'm late,' she said, a phrase that tripped off the tongue almost automatically every working day. She sat down and placed her baggage on the adjacent seat.

'Well, you're here now, Ms McGann,' he said.

'Call me Julia,' she said, offering him her hand. His handshake was limp. They were joined by a tall young woman who Dicks introduced as Emily Harper. 'I've brought her up from the Surrey office, as she's done most of the background work so far.'

'So now you've read up on him, what do you think?' he asked Julia.

'Even without meeting him I can tell that Bonner is hardly going to endear himself to any jury. They just need to glance at him to imagine his previous convictions. Given the electronic evidence he can hardly deny the conspiracy to supply, but I think we can make tremendous progress casting doubt on the counts of murder and GBH. Yes, his DNA was found on Murdoch's clothing, but there are innocent possibilities for that. I intend to home in on the character of the prosecution's chief witness. He is very much the weak link in their case.'

Dicks pursed his lips and nodded. 'That's my thinking. Unfortunately, Bonner is minded to plead not guilty to all counts.'

'Yes, I'm not surprised. It would go better for him to accept the inevitable on conspiracy and we can make a better fist of fighting the more dubious accusations.'

'Well, good luck with that. He is quite intimidating, face-to-face, so Emily tells me.' He checked his watch. 'I'm afraid I have an appointment in Crown Court, but I wish you both luck.' As he stood, he said: 'By the way, you may be aware that we were promised Christopher Cadwell by your chief clerk, Mr Hogarth.'

Julia's answer had been prepared well in advance. 'Yes, I was aware of that. I'm afraid Christopher is in high demand these days, as you can imagine.' She hated having to act as a marketing manager for her colleague, but she had no choice.

'That's understandable, though for your chambers to leave it so late to tell us was a little inconvenient.' Julia could see that Dicks was a master of understatement. He then cleared his throat, for his own barb. 'So, Ms McGann, I've looked through your CV. I'm dearly hoping that you have hidden qualities.'

Charming. She smiled anyway. 'I promise I will do my best.'

'Let's hope that is good enough,' he muttered. With that he stood up, gathered his raincoat and briefcase, and departed.

'I'm sorry, he can be a bit cutting, can't he?' Emily said.

'Don't worry, I'm used to it. Now let's go and see our client,' Julia said.

—

Julia and Emily made their way out of the cafe and hurried in the rain down a ramp to the Nottingham and Beeston Canal. The tall glass frontage of the modern court building dominated a waterside plaza opposite Victorian warehouses now turned into bars and restaurants. In the foyer, a five storey atrium, there was a queue for bag search at the security station, but Julia walked to the front and showed the barristers' digital ID on her smartphone. After being waved through, she waited for Emily, who'd had to surrender her bag of search. They went down a flight of dark echoing stairs to the holding cells which adjoined the Bridewell Police Station.

Julia peered through the panel and saw the imposing figure of Bonner splayed across his chair, staring back at them. The custody officer unlocked the door and let them in. 'Any trouble, I'll be right here, duck, don't you worry,' she said, as she pushed the door open. Julia wondered how a seemingly unfit officer in her fifties could hope to restrain even the most slightly built schoolboy shoplifter, let alone a man with Bonner's reputation for violence.

'I'm sure we'll be fine,' said Julia. She strode in trying to exude a confidence that she didn't feel, approached the prisoner and extended her hand. 'Terrence, my name is Julia McGann, and I'll be your barrister. I think you've already met Emily.' She gestured at her colleague.

Julia hoped that Bonner might stand up for her. It was a psychological trick that worked most of the time. She had found that even hardened working-class criminals tended to have an embedded class inferiority complex, such that the presence of a confident, forthright and apparently upper-class woman would intimidate them.

But not Bonner.

'I told her I wanted Cadwell,' he said, his arms resolutely folded across his chest. 'A top scorer, not a late substitute.'

Julia sat down opposite Bonner. Emily took the seat beside her.

'I'm afraid Christopher Cadwell is unavailable,' Julia said. 'I think you've been told that already. We only have a few minutes before you are due to make your plea upstairs, so I think we could best use the time by marshalling the resources we do have to get the best possible result. Now, just to remind you that everything that is said here between us is confidential. We are on your side, but it is essential that you are utterly truthful in everything you say to us. Is that clear?'

Bonner glared at them through narrowed eyes. 'I've been banged up twenty-three hours a day for something I didn't do. No one does that to *me* and gets away with it.' He prodded himself in the chest with a fat finger.

'We are as anxious as you are to not waste any more hours of your life banged up. But unfortunately there is a long list of very serious offences that you have been charged with, so unless we start picking holes in the Crown's case they *are* going to get away with it.'

Julia was aware in her peripheral vision that Emily beside her was trying to make herself invisible, her slim legs wound around themselves at knee and ankle. Her hands were gripping each other in her lap hard enough for the whites of her knuckles to illuminate the room. Terrified, bloody terrified.

Bonner shifted his position and tightened his huge arms, making his chest bulge further, and sucked down a big inhalation as if all the air in the room was his. 'How much am I paying for a couple of skirts to flutter their eyelids at the judge, eh?' A slight smile slipped across his fat lips, and his eyes slid across to Emily.

'Forget my gender. My considerable skills and experience are all that stands between you and spending the bulk of your life behind bars, so I strongly suggest you park your prejudices and help us work together,' Julia said. 'And for the record, it's the taxpayer who is footing the bill for your defence, which is pretty generous of them, wouldn't you say? You claim not to have any money, which might come as a surprise to those who were arrested with you.'

'I'm skint, I told 'em.'

Julia had read every word of the police seizure document for Bonner's home, which included four cars and a jet-ski. Media reports suggested the house itself was worth over a million, and had planning permission for a swimming pool in a covered extension. Explaining why a professional nightclub doorman could legitimately afford all that would be a problem for another day.

'All right, be that as it may,' she said. 'We have less than ten minutes now before you are taken up, and you will be asked whether you intend to plead guilty to any of these charges. I take it you are intending to plead not guilty?'

'Yeah. That's it.'

'That is your prerogative. I would just like to point out to you that there is likely to be a certain group dynamic in operation as regards the conspiracy charges. That is to say the prosecution will be putting a great deal of pressure on some of your supposed co-conspirators, those accused of more minor crimes, to plead guilty in exchange for a shorter sentence for them and a much greater chance of implicating you.'

'Yeah, fucking Baz Menzies for a start.'

'Indeed. Given that some of these people have been shown quite clearly to be in electronic communication with you about these matters, this will be damning evidence.'

'If any of them grass me up, I'll boil their kids in acid.' He banged the table so hard with his fist that both women gave a start.

'We have to be smart, Mr Bonner. We have to wargame the possibilities rather than issuing counter-productive threats. That is why I think at some stage you should consider pleading guilty to the conspiracy to supply drugs.'

'Never!'

She glanced at her watch. She had just two minutes left before the custody officer would come for him. 'You don't have to do it at this stage, but in a month or two at the first Crown Court hearing, I want you to seriously consider what I suggest. If you admit certain crimes that some of your other colleagues are likely to confess to, your more specific denials may carry a certain extra weight with the jury.'

'But I'll still go down for years for the drugs, won't I?'

'Several years, perhaps. But better that than the decades you will certainly face if you are convicted of the more serious charges.'

'That's easy for you to say, innit? Telling me to accept years of my life inside.' The fat finger pointed at her accusingly. 'Tonight you'll go back to your big comfy house, nanny for your kids, big fucking car no doubt, whatever happens.'

If only you knew: Terrence Bonner's house and cars were undoubtedly a great deal more impressive than hers.

'As I said before, I'm on your side. It's up to you whether you want to take advantage of that.'

The scrape of boots and the rattle of keys heralded the arrival of the breathless custody officer, tasked to bring Bonner into the court.

–

Bonner pleaded not guilty to all charges, as expected, and the case was referred to Crown Court. He made regular eye contact with Julia during the two-minute hearing, which she took as at least the beginnings of trust. Given the number of days the trial might last, it could be a very lucrative case for her, and one that if she won would lift her profile enormously. After the formalities had finished and Bonner was taken down, the two women retreated to the Primavera Cafe for a well-earned coffee and slice of chocolate cake. Julia's train wasn't until three p.m. and she had hours to kill, having had to allow time in her return ticket for the possibility of court delays. More than £140 for a return train fare just for a two-minute hearing, and she'd not get a penny back for months, not until the case was finished and the Legal Services Commission coughed up. Another fiver for cake would make little difference to her ruined finances.

The young solicitor looked nervous but had regained a little of her colour. 'You handled him so well,' Emily said.

'Bonner is an exceptionally challenging individual,' Julia said. 'By contrast, most criminals you will come across are quite meek when they are facing a long jail term.'

'He was so rude to me,' Emily said, then shared with Julia the crude comments that Bonner had made during their first meeting.

After expressing her shock, Julia said: 'The point is, Emily, that you have to take control, right from the first moment. Deep down most of these offenders are cowards. People like Bonner feel at home in the realm of the physical, where they have the capabilities that they need to survive. But put them in a court setting, where the ability to phrase an argument, to follow a logical train of thought, and to convince the sceptical are the requirements for success, and they shrivel. Most of them realise they don't have the right skill set. The courts are designed to intimidate, and that is one part of the job they still do well. In the end, so long as they can see it's in their interest, most clients will defer to you because only you can help them.'

'Even as I sat there, I felt he was all over me.'

She had noticed it, as Bonner undoubtedly had. Julia had learned the hard way to assert herself. But you couldn't just make it happen, it required an inner sense of self-worth drawn from every aspect of your life. For her, the lesson emerged not from her job but from a damaging personal relationship that she had torn herself out of after fifteen destructive years, in which her personal sense of value and dignity had been shredded. On the final day she had flung a glass of wine in his face and stormed out of the restaurant. For all the satisfaction that gave her, there were scores still to be settled in that department. She had vowed never again to put the trajectory of her life in another's gift. It was a lesson applicable in her career too.

'Emily, if you stay on this case with me, I can give you a few hints that might help.'

'Really, would you?'

'Of course.' There was so much that Julia wanted to tell this young woman who was just starting out on her working life. 'If I may, can I suggest that your youthful appearance is working against you? Try dark-framed spectacles instead of the slender metal, a jacket with more definition in the shoulders and a coarser fabric, perhaps some kind of dark twill. Anything to add a bit of gravitas.' She didn't want to go on too much, but there was so much more she could have said. Emily was tall, but by choosing flat shoes she didn't get the benefit of the assertive and percussive footfall that even a one-inch heel bestows. And her make-up was all wrong, too. Emily had fair, soft eyebrows, but they needed to be darkened a little to emphasise her expression, with some eyeliner to underline those nice hazel eyes. She didn't need to be a vamp like Edwina Pym, whose thick make-up and extensive dark eyeshadow made her look like a superannuated air stewardess. For Emily just a few subtle tweaks would be enough, once she got a bit more self-confidence. *That* was the crucial issue. It would do wonders.

A crash of crockery at the far end of the cafe punctured Julia's thoughts. The only casualties appeared to be a broken glass and some scattered mugs. She turned back to Emily and shared a smile with her.

'I've got to go to a meeting with the senior partner now,' Emily said. 'It's been nice to meet you.' They both stood up to leave and Julia picked up her briefcase.

'Good to meet you too. I'll get this,' she said, indicating the crumb-filled plates.

'That's kind, thank you.'

As Emily turned to go, Julia pivoted to retrieve her shoulder bag, which had been hooked on the back of the adjacent seat.

It wasn't there.

She blinked and then scanned the table between them. And where was her phone?

She checked her jacket pockets and looked on the floor.

Nothing.

'Emily!' she called, as her colleague was just reaching the door. 'Emily!'

For some reason Emily didn't turn, or hadn't heard, and stepped out into the street. Julia, short of possibilities, ran after her and ignored the looks she was getting from the other diners. She caught up with her only after fifty yards.

'Emily, thank goodness I've caught you—'

'What's the matter?' Emily said, clearly alarmed.

'My bag's been stolen, and my phone too.'

'How awful.' Emily looked at her watch in a sense of panic. 'My meeting starts in five minutes, but come along with me, the office is just round the corner, and we can get you some cash sorted out in the office.'

'I haven't even paid for the coffee, would you mind?'

Emily blinked. 'No, of course. How terrible for you.'

Julia felt a complete fool as she made her way back into the cafe with Emily.

—

Julia sat on the train home, fuming, reviewing a day crowned by disaster. She had lost £150 in cash and all her credit cards, including one she had just received and to which she had just transferred all her balances. To begin with she couldn't even remember precisely what it was called, or which bank it was from, and fretted that the thief might have already maxed it out before she was able to report it stolen. She'd lost her flat keys, her car keys, and – because the phone was the centre of her life – the only record of the name and details of the garage where she had left the car. No one at the cafe had seen anything and a perfunctory search had turned up nothing. The only CCTV in the place was focused on the till, as if to catch out only staff pilfering. Worst of all, Julia had endured the utter humiliation of going to the Nottingham office of Ropes, Peel, Deaton and having to borrow money, which no doubt would make her the laughing stock of the firm. Her train ticket, which she'd had as an email on her phone, she was able to access by borrowing a workstation and getting a printout.

She had then gone with one of the paralegals to the police station and reported her loss. After waiting ages to be seen, the male sergeant at the desk showed absolutely no interest in the case, but simply tutted when she recounted the details, the lack of CCTV at the cafe, and the apparent diversion caused by the broken glass.

'Aren't you going to ask me if I saw anyone suspicious?' she had asked the officer, as he appeared to finish the form.

'If you want, for all the good it will do,' he muttered.

'Well, no wonder the Nottinghamshire clear-up rate is so abysmal,' Julia said crisply.

The officer gave her a dead-eyed stare and turned the clipboard he was writing on towards her. 'You see that case number? It's got 514 on the end. That's the number of reported crimes in the county so far today. As for the effects of austerity on our manpower—'

'Spare me the details,' Julia said. She copied down the incident number and walked out.

–

Back at the law offices she started the tedious set of calls to cancel cards, followed by a message to her best friend Rachel who had spare keys to her flat. The last phone call was the one she was least looking forward to making. Hogarth. With his unerring sense of timing the chief clerk picked up immediately and listened as Julia poured out her tale of woe.

'So, let me get this right. You have borrowed money from our new clients?'

'Yes. They were very sweet about it. They said that it's the kind of thing that could happen to anybody.'

'Ms McGann, I sent you up there hoping that your abilities would inspire awe and respect. But it seems that we will have to settle for pity, won't we?' He hung up.

As the train rumbled past rain-sodden estates and flooded fields, Julia allowed the dark thoughts about the theft to gather in her head. She was quite sure that the crash of crockery in the cafe had been a deliberate distraction by one of a team of thieves who had been looking for unattended bags. She hadn't noticed anyone at her end of the cafe, but because the table she had shared with Emily was up towards the till, there was constant movement backwards and forwards. She berated herself for her carelessness. She had quite a good memory and tried to think if there were any suspicious-looking characters in the cafe. Her mental idea of a pickpocket was as stereotypical as anyone else's; she pictured a hoodie-wearing youth. But there had been very few if any men below the age of retirement in the cafe. Of course, women could be thieves too, and they tended to attract less attention. She couldn't even now picture the person who had dropped the glass, though she was sure she was female.

Julia had been involved in defending criminals long enough to know what would typically happen to her stolen possessions. The distinctive bag and purse would have been ditched nearby almost immediately, the cash stuffed in a pocket and probably by now already spent. The credit cards would either be used quickly for a series of contactless transactions for booze or fags, or sold on to someone who specialised in extracting greater value from them. Her old iPhone would probably be of less use, though cracking the pin wouldn't be too difficult. Her keys and the address might well find their way onto the dark web, sold to the highest bidder. Potential buyers would use Google Street View just as if they were looking to move in, assessing from the outside of her home what kind of value might lie within, and whether it would be worth the risk to buy the keys and burgle given that the owner would already have been alerted. The thought made Julia nervous. She closed her eyes, seeking respite from the whirring of her thoughts as the train pushed on towards its destination.

Rachel was a star, as Julia had known she would be. She picked Julia up at Guildford Station, passed across the spare key and drove her home. They then walked around the flat together to be sure that nobody had broken in. Julia was sure that her address had been noted somewhere in her handbag, but agreed with Rachel that an immediate break-in with nearly 200 miles of travel from Nottingham was quite unlikely. Rachel then lent her £100 and an old dumb phone until she got herself sorted out. Before she left, Rachel gave her friend a hug and said: 'Tomorrow will be better.'

They had met as thirteen-year-olds, growing up in adjacent houses in Esher, and had cemented their friendship in grammar school. Rachel Meadows had just moved down with her parents from Derbyshire and was always the more worldly: the first to smoke and the first to give it up; shapely, with a mop of honey blonde hair, she lost her virginity at fourteen, before Julia had even been kissed. Rachel was allowed unsupervised parties at home from the age of fifteen, where she made lavish use of the drinks cabinet and sold to her friends the textured and flavoured condoms she had found in her father's bedside drawer. Rachel and her freewheeling parents were considered beyond the pale by Julia's strait-laced mother. She banned Julia from the friendship, which had the opposite effect to that intended, deepening the two girls' alliance. Julia learned to be sly, and to lie with a straight face, skills that would come in useful in her later career. Her first night of teenage drunkenness at one of those parties involved some abominable cocktail of crème de menthe and advocaat. She could still recall in her nightmares the whorled pattern and stench of the Meadows' bathroom carpet where she had woken up delirious and sick in the middle of the night. Her mother thought she was on a weekend school field trip. Even now, she was unable to stand the aroma of either constituent of that deadly drink.

Julia, the more academic, got the better A-level grades but coached her more wayward friend, whose keen intelligence was less disciplined. After exams, the two travelled around France and Italy by train, getting stuck without a place to stay in Lyons, going home with two handsome French boys to a balcony flat near the station. Julia had awoken in a strange bed to a morning of black coffee and French cigarettes, feeling sophisticated and grown-up. A woman, finally.

Rachel had remained the closest of Julia's friends, until Himself upended Julia's life.

Julia had met him, curiously enough, in the Derbyshire moors. Julia, then twenty, had been staying with Rachel's aunt, who ran a farm near Bakewell. She and Rachel had taken a couple of ponies across the moors, and come across a group of walkers, one of whom had a twisted ankle. Himself had characteristically taken charge of his fellow walkers, but his mobile phone, back then the only one in the entire group, could not get a signal. Rachel and Julia cantered back to the farm on their ponies to summon help. The two young women were later bought a pub lunch by the group, and when Himself discovered Julia didn't live far away from him in Surrey, he persuaded her to swap phone numbers. As he was unaccompanied, Julia had blithely assumed he was single, but it was the worldly

Rachel who scrutinised his hands in the pub and noticed the slightly glossy skin and indentation on his wedding ring finger.

Deceit.

Rachel hadn't liked Julia's married man from the word go, and coined the handle which the two used to refer to him. Himself was for the next decade and a half the centre of their many anguished conversations. To Rachel the trajectory of this doomed relationship was obvious from the outset, but for Julia it was true love. Until the bitter end, fifteen years later, the word murder hadn't even entered Julia's daily vocabulary. After it ended, the word ricocheted around every conversation, dark fantasies of vengeance inspired in equal measure by the two women.

After Julia had waved Rachel goodbye, she settled in with a welcome G&T and wandered around her home, relieved to find no evidence of a break-in and appreciating the quiet, solitary comforts it offered her. She surveyed the paintings on the wall, the framed photos of her with her pony, and with Rachel. Finally, she took from a drawer one of the many framed pictures of her with Himself, this one taken on a country walk about a decade ago, his arm possessively around her shoulder. She wondered how he was, and what her life would have been like if he had kept to his word and left his wife.

Chapter Four

Adam Heath closed the spreadsheet and looked up from his new Apple Mac. Out of the rain-speckled westerly windows of his third-floor office, looking towards Ledbury Lane, the late afternoon sky was the colour of a bruise. Beneath it, the year ten hockey players were making their way back towards the changing rooms from Ledbury Field, the foghorn booming of the fifteen-year-old boys mixed with the higher registers of the girls. It was the end of the day's final period. The grass shone verdantly, from this distance giving no clue that it was desperately in need of reseeding, an expense which had not yet been accounted for in the capital spending account.

As headmaster, that was just another thing on his plate: the new transgender teaching policy, which had gone down like a lead balloon in this morning's staff meeting, the impending Ofsted appeal against the miserablist verdict of 'good' when everybody knew St John's Academy was actually 'outstanding' and had been for the whole five years under his leadership, and then of course there was money. The move to academy status three years ago had released funds from the local authority, but the head of every department had become a supplicant, demanding cash that really should have been conserved for future years. Lowering expectations was an important part of his job.

He made his way across the new deep-pile carpet, to the east windows towards Twycross Crescent. It was Thursday, 16 January and almost three thirty. Parental cars were already blocking the pavements on the residential street, despite his strict instructions that vehicles must be left in Whipsnade Avenue, which was wider. It still astounded him that this had been the main subject of conversation at the parents' evening before Christmas. Protests against having to walk an extra hundred yards to the school gates. In his day, no one was given a lift to school. All pupils walked, cycled or caught the bus.

Was that Melanie Darroch?

The year nine pupil was making her way to the school gate with another girl he didn't recognise. With 1,127 pupils it was impossible to recognise everyone, especially from behind and more than a hundred yards away. Melanie was easy to spot, with the dip-dyed pink hair she had been sanctioned for two days ago. Fortunately, her pregnancy was not yet beginning to show. Adam tried to focus on the other pupil. A dark ponytail, shirt untucked at the back, skirt illicitly shortened, at least two inches less of it than stipulated by his regulations. No, he couldn't be sure. Kate Green possibly, but she was year ten and not known to be an associate of Melanie's.

The two girls were lost to view, and Adam Heath raised his eyes to the skies. There was a rainbow. Intense colours, spread right across the estate above Gilbert Avenue.

How lovely.

Adam Heath had no idea that he had less than an hour to live. Why would he? Most of us haven't a clue about the last day of our lives. That is probably how we would like it. For all that, not many people, given a choice, would choose to spend five and a half hours of their last day on earth in a staff meeting.

Adam Heath smiled at the rainbow. He didn't know that he was going to be murdered. That the shock and outrage over his killing would come to dominate the national press for the next two weeks, nor that his school would be torn apart as more of his life became known.

Murder changes everything.

—

At 4.27 p.m. Adam Heath logged off from his computer, stepped out of the office and locked the door. Mrs Truslove, the long-serving school secretary, was still working at her desk and wished him good night. He descended the six flights of open-plan stairs, exited the administrative block and strode just over a hundred yards to the staff car park. There were a few pupils about. Those staying for music tuition could be identified by their size-able instrument cases, a few others had sports bags. They all avoided eye contact with the headmaster.

There weren't too many cars remaining. Heath walked to his beloved 1985 Jaguar XJ6 saloon, manually unlocking the driver-side door, and tossed his briefcase onto the passenger seat. He put his mobile phone in the glove compartment, slid on his brown leather driving gloves, turned the ignition and listened as the big cat purred. A touch of the stereo button, and the sound of Acker Bilk's 'Stranger on the Shore' filled the car. Only when he was sitting in his classic car, with the music on, did he feel the school day had really finished. Never mind that his home was just a three and a half minute drive away, it was about psychological compartments. School over, evening beginning. He eased the big vehicle gently out of the car park, and turned right into Twycross Crescent, and then into Whipsnade Avenue. Since he had last passed this way in the morning, he noticed that somebody had spray-painted out the first part of the street name. He made a note to bring it up at morning assembly tomorrow.

Zero tolerance.

As he left the estate and made the left turn onto the main London Road, he wondered again whether it was some district council joke that so many of the newer streets around St John's Academy bore the names of zoos. Certainly, the school had originally had a reputation as nothing more than a prison camp for an ill-tamed rabble. That was in the early seventies. Much had improved since then.

As the long notes of the clarinet reached into his mind, he thought about Ingrid. The relationship he had ended earlier that week had always been dangerous, seeing as it was with someone else who worked at the school. The age gap and, more significantly, his seniority added a great deal of spice to the pleasure he had taken from it. The fact they were both married was less exciting; he'd trodden that path many times. A decade ago, he wouldn't have given it a second thought; indeed he had lived rather more adventurously when he was simply a head of department. His affair with Ingrid, kindled on a school skiing trip a year ago, had smouldered away, mainly squeezed into two hours once a week late on a Thursday afternoon, when Stella was at her exercise class. Had it been more than sex? For her, yes, obviously. She had wanted love, the love she didn't get at home. Those passionate hours, intensified by their rarity and fleeting nature, could appear to be love, but he was old enough and experienced enough to know that what was living in each of their heads was quite different. She no doubt thrilled to the embrace and the whispers and the kisses. What he saw in his mind's eye was Ingrid in the stockings and lacy black basque, straddling him in the summer house, her hips fluidly busy and an animal growl of passion escaping her throat.

He thought about it every time, or variations on the theme.

Being the school principal, he had taken extraordinary measures to keep their term-time affair secret. Ingrid would park her car in Badgers Walk and take the short but winding alleyway between the high garden fences and hedges towards his home in Highgrove Crescent. She would stop at the laurel hedge adjoining his garden, reach over the side gate to silently slide the oiled bolt, and slip through across the rear lawn into the specially insulated summer house. Whichever of them was there first would put on the fan heater, get out the car blanket and fold it over the swing seat that they used, and put out the box of tissues. All the tawdry apparatus of an illicit liaison. The blinds would already be lowered, but between the slats Ingrid would be able to see if Stella's little Citroën were parked on the hardstanding at the side of the house. Only twice had the emergency plan been triggered, each time because the Zumba class had been cancelled. Once was when Ingrid was alone and saw the little blue car come back early. On that occasion, because it was spring and some of the bushes were in leaf, it had been relatively easy for Ingrid to slip out of the summer house and dart the ten yards to the side gate unobserved. The second occasion, in November, was much worse. They were already at it, halfway through when the glare of the headlights shone through the slats. Adam was all for carrying on for the final few seconds, but Ingrid was already off him, scrambling for her clothes.

Probably the most important part of their secrecy was their studied indifference to each other at school. She was a newly qualified history teacher, attractive but not flashily so, he the absolute ruler of the school. They needed to minimise their interactions, because Stella could smell out an affair at 500 yards. Adam and Ingrid never phoned, emailed, or texted each other. Instead, they would post coded messages beneath crime news stories in the town's online paper on the Wednesday evening before their trysts. Most of the other messages were of the hang 'em or flog 'em type. Theirs, under suitably anonymous usernames, started with some anodyne message about the article above, and ended with question marks and exclamation marks which encoded their plans. Usually, it was the simple double exclamation mark which indicated their normal arrangement. The code had been his idea, and he was very proud of it. He had never mentioned to her that he'd used it before with someone else.

It was a week since he had terminated the affair, and Adam Heath was now feeling reasonably confident that the potential emotional damage from doing so had been limited. He had taken the risk of meeting Ingrid for lunch at an obscure country pub twenty miles away to explain the situation, and she had been mature, understanding and, most important of all, composed throughout the meal. Only when he had been driving away did he spot her in her own car in the pub car park, her face slumped on her arms over the steering wheel. Adam even took a little bit of satisfaction from that. If she hadn't been upset at all, he would have been quite miffed. Women often got addicted to him, it had taken him years to realise that. But now, even though he was fifty-five, he expected it.

The Jaguar took the turning into Highgrove Crescent. All the houses here were substantial mock-Tudor homes, built in the 1930s and with extensive gardens. Fortunately, there had been very little of the garden infill developments that had ruined some parts of the town. He had, under Stella's name, objected to some of the planning applications which would have marred the crescent, and had a quiet word with a councillor friend on the planning committee just to make sure. Here there was no graffiti on the street signs, the dog bins were emptied promptly, and the pavement parking epidemic which made parts of the town look like a council estate had been nipped in the bud. Some leaflets under the windscreen wipers of the offending vehicles had seen to that.

All in all, Adam Heath was feeling fully in control as he turned into his secluded drive at number nineteen. Stella's car wasn't there, but the little dry patch on the drive showed that she hadn't long departed. He pulled up next to her slot, hit the remote button for the roller door on the garage, and watched with satisfaction as the metal shutter slid soundlessly upwards. He never left his precious big cat at the mercy of the elements.

There was a slight noise from behind him.

A glimpse of a gloved hand, then something looped around his neck. Before he had a chance to utter a sound, he was pulled back hard against the Jaguar's seat. Adam Heath's hands shot to his neck, to ease a constriction that was already agony. But the ligature was cutting deeply into his throat, his cries of alarm emerging as nothing more than a low animal growl. The last act of his life was to glance into the mirror at his assailant.

He saw. But there was no one there to tell.

Chapter Five

It was nearly half five in the afternoon when the call came through from the control room. Detective Chief Inspector Craig Gillard was sitting in his unmarked grey Vauxhall in a layby near Leatherhead taking advantage of a lull in the caseload to catch up with some paperwork on his iPad. It was also the first day back at work in the control room for his wife Sam after an absence of several months. The post-traumatic stress disorder she had suffered after being kidnapped the previous year had been slow to ebb, but in the last month she had made huge progress, and a short break in Portugal just after New Year had done them both a world of good.

He recognised her on the radio alert, and picked it up, delighted to hear her voice. He soon realised there was a ragged and breathy edge to what she was saying. Was she having a relapse? With the required formality, she described that a hysterical woman in West Oakham had reported her husband sitting dead in his car on their drive. Minus his head. She'd had to get the caller to repeat that aspect several times, and then urged her not to touch the car or the body.

The detective acknowledged her, then added: 'Are you okay, Sam?'

'Yes, fine.'

The report seemed almost impossible to believe. 'I'm on my way,' he said, starting up the car, activating blue lights and sirens, and headed out into traffic. West Oakham was a fast-growing commuter belt town just a few miles away towards Woking. Sam said she had dispatched a patrol car that was only two streets away, and paramedics were en route too. 'The victim has been identified as Adam Heath, principal of St John's Academy. His wife recognised the clothing and his car.'

'Thank you, Sam,' he said. 'Take care.'

It took Gillard less than ten minutes to reach Highgrove Crescent, which he turned into just ahead of the CSI van. The two uniforms already there were busy. One was trying to help a middle-aged woman, who was sitting on her own doorstep bawling her eyes out, the other was still putting up crime tape around the car, an aged Jaguar. A small gaggle of neighbours had gathered at the end of the drive. He was glad that en route he had called in family liaison officer Gabby Underwood. If what Sam had told him about the body was true, the wife was going to be in terrible shock.

As he emerged from his Vauxhall, another patrol car and an ambulance pulled into the crescent. The CSI van was driven by Kirsty Mockett, a relatively new but diligent young officer, who wriggled into her Tyvek suit, booties and gloves while Gillard was at the boot of his own car doing the same. Kirsty, already practised at the quick change, was ahead of him, taking copious pictures around the car, whose driver-side door was open. They couldn't approach within two feet of the vehicle because of fresh-looking bloodstains on the tarmac, but it wasn't hard to see. The victim was still wearing his seatbelt, his gloved hands by his sides. There was plenty of blood on the leather seats, and a little spattered on the driver-side window. Still, it was nowhere near as gory as Gillard had expected.

None of it was yet dry.

'This has only just happened,' Kirsty breathed.

'I'm going to call in an immediate search of the surrounding area,' Gillard said, reaching for his radio. 'We're definitely in the golden hour. It's getting dark, so we need some arc lights too.' It was so rare to get to a murder crime scene in that vital first hour, when the perpetrator may not yet have made their escape, when evidence was fresh and unsullied and witness memories still unclouded. He noticed that there was an alleyway which ran along the side of the back gardens. He spoke to a sergeant from the second patrol car and asked him and a colleague to start a search of the gardens and alleyways.

'I need you to start right now. What you'll be looking for is a murder weapon, which is probably a knife, and which may have been thrown into a garden, along with discarded blood-covered clothing. And a human head, obviously.'

'Righto, sir.' The sergeant went slightly green.

'Watch out too for drops of blood on the path, smears on gates or fence panels in the alleyway. Make sure you wear gloves. Photograph everything.'

The sergeant acknowledged the orders and hurried off to brief his men.

Kirsty Mockett and one of the uniformed officers were meanwhile erecting an enormous white tent which completely covered the car. Gillard nodded at the wisdom of that. Rain was forecast, and they couldn't take any chances. Before the tent was fully in situ, he knelt and looked under the car from the passenger side. There seemed to be no blood on the tarmac here, and he was able to get close. There were a couple of drips of fresh oil underneath the vehicle, not unusual for a 1980s Jaguar, and he could hear the tick of the engine cooling down. He rested a gloved hand on the bonnet and could still feel some warmth. It was a short trip from St John's Academy, so the car wouldn't have got too hot. The fact there was still heat to feel was yet more evidence that the attack had taken place immediately after the ending of the journey, which was not long ago.

Gillard made way for the final installation of the CSI tent. He got to his feet and saw that the front door of the house was open, and a female uniform had been posted there. The witness, no longer visible, was presumably inside. Before going in to talk to her, he made his way into the back garden. A closed and bolted side gate in a high hedge on the left appeared to give access to the alleyway. He examined the latch, which appeared to be clean, and retrieved two small plastic evidence bags from his Tyvek suit. One he taped around the latch and the other high up over the bolt. On the other side of the gate he could hear the heavy tread of constabulary boots. He called through and got a reply from the sergeant. 'Can you tape an evidence bag over the outside of this gate latch?' Gillard asked. The officer acknowledged him and complied.

At the front door, Gillard slipped off his Tyvek, and switched his booties for a fresh pair before stepping into the carpeted hallway. He followed the sound of sobbing. There in the kitchen he saw PC Zoe Butterfield making a cup of coffee for a dark-haired middle-aged woman who was sitting on a stool by the kitchen bar.

'Mrs Heath?' Gillard asked. He got a wordless nod from the woman, who was in the middle of blowing her nose. He was happy to wait a couple of minutes before asking her anything, and spent his time observing. Clean hands, no nail varnish, no apparent signs of blood on her clothing.

'I know you probably don't feel ready to say anything, but our best chance of catching whoever did this is to ask you a couple of questions now. Is that all right?'

The woman nodded. Zoe passed her a mug of black coffee, and she held it in both hands as if she were cold.

'Can I ask you what time you discovered your husband's body?'

'Half an hour ago,' she said, her voice thick with emotion.

Gillard nodded. That would be 5.15 p.m. and accorded with the timing on the emergency call.

'And where had you been?'

'Zumba.'

'Is that a regular class?'

She nodded and continued to cry into a wad of paper handkerchiefs that Zoe had given her.

Gillard squinted at the kitchen clock. 'What would that be, four until five?'

She nodded, and said something, her mouth so loose and uncontrolled that the words could not be discerned.

'Is that every Thursday?' It was his best guess of what she'd said. 'And did it run on time?'

The woman nodded again. Zoe put her arm around her shoulders, which triggered a fresh bout of crying. Gillard exchanged a look of sympathy with the young policewoman. This was going to be slow, for understandable reasons.

'Your husband's car was parked in front of the open garage door. Would he normally drive it inside?'

'Yes.' Haltingly, over the next few minutes, he managed to extract from her the detail that Adam Heath was a creature of habit. Thursday was his early departure day – on most others he would still be at school until six. He would drive the short distance to their home, go inside, then deal with emails for a further two hours. Today had been a normal day for them both, and she had seen nobody in the drive or garden on her arrival. She always parked her car outside on the hardstanding, and on this occasion had assumed Adam was going to wash the car because of its position in front of an open garage door. So she had gone into the house to drop off her bags, before coming out again to find where he had got to. All this had only taken five minutes after her arrival.

And only then had she looked into the car, and seen the horrifying spectacle of her husband, sitting neatly at the wheel, without his head, blood everywhere.

–

Once family liaison officer Gabby Underwood arrived to look after Mrs Heath in the kitchen, PC Zoe Butterfield joined the search of the house. Two male uniformed officers headed for Adam Heath's home office, while Gillard concentrated on the downstairs. There were plenty of framed photographs on the wall from which it was possible to trace a rough history of the relationship. The young Adam and Stella Heath looked to be outdoorsy folks who had met when they were still in their early twenties. There were plenty of pictures of social gatherings and then a single baby boy, who by the latest picture had turned into a robust student-age male. Heath had clearly played competitive rugby as a youngster and was pictured in later years on what looked like a fell running or cross-country course. He was clearly a physically capable individual, which made Gillard wonder about who it was that could have overpowered him in his own car with so little resistance evident.

He looked up as the two male uniforms began to ferry out electronic devices in clear plastic bags. They included two laptops and a desktop workstation.

There was a rear lounge which had been turned over to an enormous collection of jazz from early New Orleans, all the way through the great female voices of Ella Fitzgerald, Billie Holiday and Nina Simone, right up to Charlie Parker, John Coltrane and Thelonious Monk. Much of it was in wall-mounted CD racks, but there was a plentiful supply of original vinyl too. Bookcases lined the far wall. Much of the reading matter was on the subject of education and administration, but there was plenty of modern fiction from both sides of the Atlantic. Within the bookcases there were a couple of niches containing small black-and-white arty photographs of a semi-naked woman, clearly a young Stella Heath.

Gillard was holding up one of the pictures for a closer look when Zoe Butterfield walked in.

'What did you find?' he asked, replacing the photo.

'Nothing unusual. They appear to have separate bedrooms, the son I understand is away at university, and there's the usual amount of clobber in his private office. He seems to have plenty of hobbies.'

'Jazz?' Gillard asked, indicating the CD collection.

'I was thinking of photography,' she replied. 'He's got a big collection of cameras, slide projectors, a screen. All that old-fashioned stuff.'

'We'll see if any interesting pictures emerge from the computers,' Gillard said. He turned away, aware now that he could no longer hear sobbing. Perhaps Mrs Heath might be amenable to giving a more detailed statement.

–

'Can you think of anyone who might have wanted to do this to your husband?' Gillard asked. Stella Heath was slumped opposite him in an easy chair in the rear lounge, staring vacantly out of the window. She was a handsome woman. Her large dark eyes were bloodshot and her small delicate nose reddened from the clump of tissues she had worked through. She shook her head absent-mindedly, then for a brief moment her lips were distended as if miming a word, a bitter and angry one.

'Sorry, what was that?' he asked.

Her eyes flicked back into focus. 'No, I can't think of anybody.'

Gillard was convinced that she had thought of somebody.

'It's such a horrible thing they did to him,' she said. 'I can't get the image from my mind.'

'Try not to think about it,' Gabby Underwood intervened, stroking the woman's arm. 'Think of the good times.' That failed immediately, as Stella Heath burst into fresh tears.

Gillard waited for a few moments, then asked gently:

'Mrs Heath? Can I ask if either you or your husband have any money troubles? Was he in debt? Were you open with each other about these kinds of issues?'

Her reply took a minute to emerge. 'Adam is very careful with money. He is certainly in charge of our finances, but we have a pretty good pension pot on top of the schoolteachers' scheme.'

'Do either of you gamble?'

'No. Perhaps just a flutter on the Grand National once a year.'

'Was your husband ever threatened by a pupil at the school?'

She nodded and blew her nose. 'In fact he was assaulted more than once, most recently a year or two ago. But he can look after himself. Or so I thought. Do you think it's a pupil?'

'We're keeping an open mind, Mrs Heath.' He took a deep breath for the next part. 'I want you to think carefully about the question I'm about to ask you. I understand that St John's Academy is a Church of England school, and is also multiracial. Are you aware of any controversial remarks, teaching, assemblies or anything like that in recent weeks?'

'Adam hadn't mentioned anything. I mean, there are always controversies. They were having to think very carefully about the gender transitioning of some boy who is currently in year ten, but nothing had been implemented to my knowledge. I think it would be better if you were to ask the deputy head, Mrs Squires.'

–

After another five fairly fruitless minutes with Mrs Heath, Gillard went outside to see how the investigation of the victim's car was proceeding. CSI had now finished erecting bright lighting and a wedding-sized marquee over the Jaguar, which left a good three yards of space on all sides within the tent to move around the vehicle. CSI chief Yaz Quoroshi and a male technician were crouched down looking at the body through the open driver's door. The seatbelt had now been disconnected and a large clear plastic bag had been pulled over the torso, to prevent any further spillage of bodily fluids from the open neck contaminating the seat. CSI wanted to be sure that anything they found in the fabric got there before they began to work on the crime scene.

Quoroshi looked up as Gillard, now clad in fresh booties and latex gloves, crackled his way towards them.

'Have you found the head?' Gillard asked.

Quoroshi shook his own. 'No. Nothing from the alleyway and garden search so far. But we have a few clues here. As you suggested, it's pretty clear that the victim was dead before the head was removed. There is a fair amount of blood, but far too little for a beheading. There is also this,' he said, indicating a series of parallel gashes in the sides of the leather headrest.

'That's where the knife was used,' said the other CSI technician, a newish recruit by the name of Joe Alvarez.

'You mean cutting through the neck from the front?' Gillard said.

'That's one possibility,' Quoroshi said, less eager to draw conclusions than his junior colleague.

Gillard carefully eased the torso forward, pushing down the plastic bag so he could see the seat. The cuts didn't continue along the front of the headrest, which is what he might have expected if Alvarez was correct. He returned the body to its previous position, then opened the rear driver-side door. Two deep indentations were visible in the headrest rear, though not enough to cut the leather. These grooves connected to the cuts on the side.

'I think I know how he was killed,' Gillard said. 'I'm just going to release the headrest. Can you grab me a large evidence bag?'

Alvarez walked off to get a bag, while Gillard carefully pressed in the two catches on the twin metal supports for the headrest, which allowed him to slide the whole assembly out of the seat below. Carefully he backed out of the rear seat and showed it to Quoroshi.

'See this long encircling incision? A pound to a penny that was caused by a wire, not a knife.'

Quoroshi blinked, not quite following Gillard's reasoning.

'My best guess is that the assailant was hiding in the rear footwell, having perhaps got into the car at school. The moment our victim got home and stopped the car, the assailant reached forward with a cheese wire or something similar, looped it round the victim's throat and pulled him back against the seat. You wouldn't actually need to be that strong. The pressure against the front of the throat would be irresistible once the assailant leaned backwards to use his weight. A couple of twists, one between the neck and the seat, would hold it firm. He could then have looped the wire around the back of the headrest, which is where the indentations at the back come from. To complete the murder, he could then tighten the wire with a twisting rod inserted between the wire and the headrest. You would only need a screwdriver, turning it round and round a few times to complete the asphyxiation. Adam Heath would have been absolutely helpless.'

The CSI chief's eyes widened at Gillard's interpretation.

'I think the headmaster was garrotted first, and only then beheaded,' Gillard said.

Chapter Six

Four months earlier

If the bag snatching was the first of September's strange events, others soon followed. Julia arrived early at chambers the day after the theft, having barely slept. Living alone, it was easy to imagine danger behind every night-time sound. She had taken every precaution, with the mortice key turned in its lock and the snib up on the Yale, but it hadn't eased her fear. Her garden flat was the only place she had been able to afford in Guildford even with the assistance of her father's inheritance. It had been burgled two years ago, the intruder forcing open the louvred kitchen windows, and removing the glass slats. Those had since been replaced with uPVC. Nevertheless, with one claim already, her insurance premium was steep. Replacement locks would be just one of the many expenses of the previous day's disaster.

The first two hours at work was spent ringing round the remainder of the lenders whose various cards had been in her purse. So far at least the damage hadn't been too bad: less than £200 on various contactless transactions up to the point of cancellation, including petrol and in a mini-mart in Nottingham. Two other credit cards, close to the max, hadn't been touched at all. She still had to deal with many of the other cards: various discount and points cards, a legal-library card, a key card for the gym. Annoying and time consuming.

And there were bigger worries. The theft may have added little to Julia's mountainous debts, but the loss of £150 in cash had drastically worsened her cashflow crisis. It was infuriating that the snail's pace of the court system was keeping her from thousands earned but not yet paid. On top of that, the sheer mendacity of some law firms was infuriating. Just a month ago, she had taken on a defendant for a big London firm. They had told her that legal aid was granted but had failed to forward the certificate. She was halfway through the case, a fraud which involved reading 1,183 pages of documents, when she discovered that no certificate existed. Legal aid had actually been refused as the client, supposedly bankrupt, was thought to be hiding assets. Julia would have to join a long list of creditors with a chance of being paid of approximately nil.

Looking at the full horror of her bank account, Julia realised she was running out of all options but one. To borrow once again from her mother. She picked up the phone, and with a due sense of dread listened to it ring out. Elspeth McGann, eighty-one but ferociously independent, had lived since widowhood in South Devon in a five-bedroom clifftop rectory, which she would by tradition only heat between All Saints' Day and Epiphany. Come rain or shine, Mrs McGann would take an eight-mile walk each day, accompanied by her spaniel Winstanley. She had plenty of money stashed away, and that's where it stayed. Elspeth was an austerity throwback: not the mild recent version, but the original post-war thrift. Unfranked stamps were still steamed from letters, all meat bones boiled for soup, sheets sewn sides to middle when worn, even threadbare tea towels continued to be used, while years of Christmas and birthday present replacements piled up untouched in the linen cupboard. *Make Do and Mend*, the wartime bible, had become her life's philosophy. Elspeth had broken a spectacle frame in 1993, and after a shocking quote for a replacement at Specsavers, returned to her tubes of Araldite and rolls of sticky tape. Likewise her hair, last cut commercially at shocking cost in 2002, was now confined within an ever-larger bun.

Elspeth answered the phone by reciting the entire number. After recounting the story of the theft, Julia said: 'I need to borrow some money, Mum.'

'What a surprise, dear.' Elspeth had a fine line in sarcasm, and never hesitated to deploy it. 'And like loans in the past, they will not be repaid, I presume.'

'I've got thousands of pounds earned but tied up in this fraud trial which never seems to end, and as soon as it does, I *will* repay you.'

'Is this the same trial you told me about last year?'

'Yes. They had to empanel a new jury in July, and they're only just getting going again.'

'My word, by the time it's over I'm sure I'll be dead.'

'Sometimes, Mum, I think that by the time it's over I'll be dead!'

'Well dear, I'm a bit short at the moment, because I've got to pay for the buildings insurance next week. But I could let you have £50.'

In Elspeth's words, Julia was a 'wastrel and a dilettante'. Though she would grudgingly advance her money, it was always in small amounts, by postal order with a covering letter. Those missives, and the preceding phone calls, constituted an extended lecture. The subject matter was always the same; the disappointment that Julia represented not only to her but to the memory of her late father. Not only a failure in her career, in which she had dithered for almost a decade before trying to become a barrister, but more particularly her extraordinary lapse in failing to snare a suitably solvent husband. While Julia certainly shared those disappointments, oh boy did she, she always found it profoundly depressing to endure an hour-long monologue in exchange for less than £250, which was the maximum value of a postal order.

Julia was born like a marital afterthought when her mother was forty-two and her father already sixty. He lived for another thirty-four years, masking his obvious disappointment over his daughter's progress with a fatherly affection for his only child. Eventually, of course, on her mother's death, Julia would presumably inherit the remainder of his wealth. That could be a long time coming. She loved her mother dearly, despite everything, but the woman looked likely to make it to her century.

'I'm sorry, Mum, these dribs and drabs are not going to do the job. Let's just bite the bullet and make it £50,000. Then I won't have to keep pestering you.'

Elspeth gasped. 'You think I'm a millionaire? I don't have that kind of money.'

'Of course you do, Daddy's investment account had much more.'

'Julia, that money is *his*. You'll be robbing his grave.'

They had been through this before, years ago. 'Mum, he's not Tutankhamun, he doesn't need it to go through to the nether world.'

'I will not have you pillage your father's memory.' She slammed the phone down.

Not for the first time, Julia imagined her mother meeting with an accident. Everything would be so simple then.

–

It was typical that something unnerving should happen after a stressful day. With three outside meetings and an hour on the phone to the locksmiths and her insurers, Julia had been trying to dodge Hogarth almost all day. It was five o'clock when the heavy tread of his footsteps announced his arrival outside her office. The big man was known to work until seven or eight o'clock in the evening, poring over his spreadsheets, but taking long breaks prowling around the chambers, lurking outside doors, his breathing audible within.

Julia held her breath, wondering if there was a quick phone call she could make. But before she had a chance to think, he knocked twice, then entered. His glowering bulk seemed to fill the room along with the stench of matches.

'Ms McGann, I need you to substitute for Ms Pym at Chelmsford Crown Court, ten o'clock tomorrow morning. Nothing onerous, defendant accused of wounding with a knife.'

'Yes, but it's the far end of Essex. Look, Clive, why can't she do it?' The last thing Julia wanted now was an expensive commute across London for which she wouldn't be repaid for months.

'I'm sorry,' Hogarth said, with a shrug. 'Female judge.' He explained that the case was in front of the redoubtable Mrs Justice Perkins. 'Female judges never seemed to like Edwina,' he said. Julia had heard the stories many times. Edwina was pinned down on points of law, interrupted from the bench, berated even for assertions that from a male barrister would pass unchallenged. Hogarth's spreadsheets showed Edwina's rate of success depended on the gender of the presiding judge. With men, her vampish looks and easy charm went down a dream, but women sniffed out the chancer that she was. Consequently, Hogarth, ever the hands-on manager, would sometimes switch Edwina out of cases if a female judge was announced. And as usual, he had waited until the last minute before letting Julia know.

So tomorrow, Julia would be up early once again to pick up somebody else's case. Unlike Edwina, Julia performed equally indifferently with judges of either gender. Mrs Justice Perkins was quite a stickler and had a terrifyingly incisive mind. She would be no barrister's first choice. But then Hogarth wasn't so intent on preserving Julia's reputation as that of his second-best fee earner. Edwina may not have been quite as luminous a star as Christopher Cadwell, but she brought in a steady stream of income. If only I had more like her, Hogarth had been heard to say within Julia's earshot.

It was that October evening that Julia arrived home with a stack of paperwork to read through ready for the next day. It was dark when she got in, and she had let slip from her mind the fact that she hadn't yet changed the locks.

At a quarter to nine she looked up from her desk and stared at the curtains. Behind them, cast on the material, was a shadow, lit by the neighbours' movement sensor light. It was a hooded face at her window, peering in.

Chapter Seven

Julia gave a start and knocked over her wine, her third glass of the evening and thankfully almost empty. After she rescued the drink, the face had gone. She parted the curtains and stared out into the garden. Had anyone been there at all? The light was off now, the darkness unremitting. She dithered about whether to call the police but decided against. A visit tonight from an officer was most unlikely, especially as she couldn't be absolutely sure what the shadow was. With her caseload, she certainly didn't have the time to endure a telephone lecture about better locks and security lights, which was almost certainly all that would happen. Besides, if her stolen keys had already found their way down here from Nottingham, a burglar was much more likely to choose a time when nobody was in. She turned on the exterior lights and stood at the French windows but could see no one. She did not have the courage to pick up her torch and step out into the garden in the darkness.

After another hour, she went to bed, but took ages to fall asleep. The night passed uneventfully, and as soon as her alarm sounded and before it was properly light, Julia went out into the garden with a torch to quickly check for signs of intruders. She saw a crisp packet and a drink can, half concealed in a mulch of sycamore leaves down by the compost bin. At first she thought the litter had been chucked over the wall from the street, but then she saw a footprint. Some kind of training shoe, smallish size. There was mud on top of the wall too, which would indicate someone clambering over. It wasn't too difficult if you were nimble and didn't mind squeezing through the gaps in the hawthorn hedge on the other side. Confirmation of last night's fears made her nervous. What could she do if they returned? Having a leasehold on the garden flat gave her exclusive rights to the garden, which made up for the semi-basement outlook at the front. Briony Winters' flat upstairs was more spacious and secure. Briony seemed to be spending more and more time at her boyfriend's place, which had kept down the incessant clacking of high heels from above but now meant there was only elderly Mrs Drake on the top floor to go to in an emergency.

Julia headed off to Chelmsford feeling nauseous with anxiety. She had left two lights on and the radio on low, with the forlorn hope that it would make the place seem occupied. She left a telephone message for Briony, asking her to keep an eye out on her return. The case turned out to be straightforward, was over in forty minutes with a guilty plea and Julia was soon back on the train. When she got home that evening, she checked in the garden again.

She found two cider cans and some cigarette ends that had not been there that morning.

Someone had definitely been there. Again.

–

For several weeks nothing happened. There was no fresh litter in the garden, and Julia began to forget about the nocturnal visitations. Besides, she had plenty to keep her busy in the day. Nottingham Crown Court had by the end of October finally published a schedule for the trial of Callum Sinnott, Terrence Bonner and other members of his gang. First was the pre-trial preparation hearing at Crown Court in November, with the trial itself provisionally set for late January 2020 and expected to last for six weeks, under the well-known hardliner Mr Justice Oakeshott. Julia needed to visit her client and prepare his case, assuming he intended to deny all charges. She and the solicitor, Emily Harper, travelled up together to Strangeways, as HMP Manchester was still universally known. Bonner was being held there on remand in a high security unit.

Julia was pleased to see that Emily had taken her advice. She had on a herringbone jacket with dark trousers and a pale blue blouse. Her earrings were pearl studs rather than the dangly ones she had won previously. She had perhaps gone a bit too heavy on the eye make-up, but that together with a darker lipstick instead of the tangerine shade she had used before added half a dozen years to her and just the beginnings of gravitas. Having secured table seats in first class they spread out their papers, discussing the case using the code letter K in place of their client's name. It was a sensible precaution. Cases had in the past been compromised when the other side had overheard strategic planning on the train.

The main worry as Julia saw it wasn't the prosecution case against the sixteen defendants, which was quite overwhelming when it came to conspiracy, it was that other defendants could justifiably blame Bonner alone for the many violent acts. The enforcer's track record made him an easy target. That would mean the various defence barristers squabbling amongst themselves, rather than opposing the Crown. It was a prosecutor's dream.

The first glimpse of the prison showed a new and modern extension built on to the original hub-and-spoke Victorian lockup. Strangeways, one of the few prisons to have its own gallows, had been a place of execution and horror well into the twentieth century. A riot and rooftop protest there in 1990 led to reforms, but Julia could see it still hadn't quite lost its forbidding atmosphere. The security check was far more intrusive and thorough than anything that she had experienced at even the Old Bailey, and required the two women to leave their mobile phones and even ballpoints behind. The metal detecting wand wielded by a female security guard traversed slowly and closely over them. It was set off by the zip on Emily's trousers and Julia's underwired bra as well as somehow detecting a spare plastic button in a side pocket of her jacket. Emily, who had seemed quite confident on the train, looked younger and more lost with every security door and corridor they passed through. There was a rising jeer of prisoners in the distance, sensing somehow the approach of women, and a smell like men's changing rooms. After a labyrinthine journey with a large and friendly male custody officer, in which they were largely spared the sight of felons, they were finally brought to a modern bright interview room in what was clearly a new extension of the jail.

Bonner was already there, sitting athwart a fixed metal chair at a fixed plastic table, his head so closely shaved it looked almost oily. His expressionless countenance did not alter on their arrival.

'This looks a bit better than I expected,' Julia said cheerfully as the door was locked behind them. She glanced up at the skylight through which sunshine poured.

'Yeah, but it's the people that make it really special,' Bonner replied with half a smile.

'How have you been treated?' Julia said, sitting down, opening her briefcase and bringing out a sheaf of court documents.

'I've been banged up twenty-three hours a day in isolation. The food is shit, the screws are sadists, and the cells are freezing cold. So yeah, it's good.'

Julia looked up. 'Terrence, have you had any chance to consider how you will plead?'

'Not guilty, all charges.' He folded his arms and tightened them across his chest, a full stop to every assertion.

'That is your right. As I mentioned, I would have preferred to take a more nuanced approach—'

'I'm not here to make your job any easier.' Bonner stared at Julia, then let his eyes wander slowly up and down Emily's body. The young solicitor folded her own arms across her breasts and stared back at him. *Good. She's challenging him.*

'You should be. When my job gets easier, your chance of liberty improves.' They locked eyes. Julia passed across a printout of a thread of texts between Bonner's phone and two of the other defendants. It was an extensive discussion of the supply of something to a known mid-level dealer called Dev Linton. Julia pointed to a particularly incriminating message from Bonner. 'Hold the gear until you get payment.'

'This, Terrence, is going to be very hard for you to deny,' Julia said.

'It was a mixing desk I was selling him.' Bonner stuck his chin out belligerently, daring them to contradict him.

'For £40,000?' Emily said. 'That seems quite a lot.'

'It was good gear, top of the range stuff. He had a mate who was a DJ.'

'And according to this thread it was wrapped in bin bags,' Julia said.

'Yeah, and?'

'I'm sorry, that's not going to convince anyone. If sound equipment is that expensive, it's hardly going to be lugged about from one vehicle to another in bin bags, is it? The prosecution will take you to pieces.' Julia stared at him. 'It may be my job to believe you, but twelve jurors will have their own opinion. I suggest, Mr Bonner, that you think again.'

While Bonner's face tightened in contemplation, Julia glanced at the wall, where a fresh coat of paint covered some extensive graffiti. Level with the edge of the table was one long and neat sentence. In this light it was still legible, the correct grammar and use of adjectives even more chilling than its pornographic lucidity. It was exactly what Emily said Bonner had threatened to do to her. The image was now in Julia's head, irrevocably, the writer's gift. As Julia turned back to her client, his slight smile and inflected brow told her he knew she had read it. An almost imperceptible nod, and his eyes slid sideways to Emily.

The meaning was clear. *When I get the chance, I'll do that to her.* Julia didn't doubt he was serious.

Chapter Eight

January, the day of the murder

Home Office forensic pathologist Dr David Delahaye was at the scene shortly after six, by which time there was a sizeable public and press presence at the end of the street. Uniformed police had blockaded both ends of Highgrove Crescent, allowing access only for residents and police. PC Zoe Butterfield had spent the last hour and a half answering the ever-ringing Heath landline. Word had clearly got out, and teachers, parents and of course the press were doing all they could to find out more.

While Delahaye examined the corpse, Gillard went around to visit Mrs Priscilla Squires. The deputy head of St John's Academy lived just a few streets away in a semi-detached house behind a gnome-infested garden. The woman who came to the door had clearly been expecting him, as she was formally dressed in blouse, jacket, court shoes and pearls. Mrs Squires was in her late fifties and matronly, with a firm jaw and a steady gaze under a helmet of dyed dark hair. Her husband made coffee and brought out slices of cake, while Mrs Squires professed her shock and horror at what had happened. Gillard knew this venting process would be a necessary precursor to almost every witness interview before any useful information could be obtained. It was ten minutes later when they finally sat down across the dining table from each other, and he was able to ask her some questions.

Mrs Squires said she had worked with Heath for nine years, from his arrival at the school.

'Was he well-liked?' Gillard asked.

'By staff, reasonably. Some found him a little bit over-bearing. But then there are only two types of head: the overbearing but effective and the consensual wet fish, who pupils take for a ride.'

'What about pupils?'

'They respected him, which is rarer than you might imagine. Adam could be quite terrifying, which is good for discipline, although unfortunately those that we would most hope would be intimidated by him always had bigger shadows looming at home.'

'Did you like him?' Gillard asked.

'He was good at his job, and I like to work with people who are good at their jobs. Look, you will discover that I applied for the headship at the same time as he did, and considered I was much better qualified and more experienced than he. For quite some time I resented the fact that he leapfrogged me, but he eventually earned my grudging respect.'

Gillard's eyes widened at such disarming truthfulness. 'Thank you for your honesty.'

'There's no point wasting your time, you've got enough to do as it is. We should get everything out in the open.'

'On that subject, were there any controversies that he was involved with at the school?'

An almost imperceptible eyebrow lift did not escape Gillard's notice. 'A large school is inevitably a microcosm of the society in which it is embedded. So everything that troubles society as a whole will be expressed in some measure within the school. Political or linguistic fissures, inequalities of wealth or opportunity. Even, you may be surprised to find in a Church of England school, religious differences.'

'How so?'

'We average twenty per cent of our intake from non-religious or other religious backgrounds, obviously so long as they understand that Anglican teaching will constitute most of the religious input. In fact, because of our Ofsted performance, we could easily double that percentage. We are always oversubscribed. We already have a thriving South Asian ethnic intake of Hindu and Muslim students. At St John's Academy we think of this as a very good thing. All pupils take part in making food for Eid and Diwali as well as Christmas and Easter. We build bridges, not walls.'

Gillard realised that this was a long-prepared speech, presumably aimed at parents. 'I'm really thinking about any disputes with pupils or parents, particularly with the Muslim community.'

'We haven't been showing any *Charlie Hebdo* cartoons, if that's what you mean. It's worth noting that the most devout Muslim or Hindu parents would obviously not choose a C of E school for their child. We tend to get those who value superlative education above faith. I'm absolutely certain that this tragic event was unconnected to anything that was taught at the school.' Her expression dared Gillard to disagree.

'Were you aware of any arguments involving the principal in recent days?'

She smiled. 'Acrimonious debates are par for the course, but there was nothing unusual in any of the recent meetings that I attended with him, and I didn't hear about any other particular problems.'

'I understand that Heath was assaulted on at least two occasions by pupils?'

Mrs Squires rolled her eyes. 'Well, technically. A year ten boy pushed him in a corridor, in an argument about uniform. That was two or three years ago. And a sixth former, on his final day at school, ran past and flicked his ear, presumably for a dare. If you're looking for potential assailants amongst the pupils, I have some better candidates. We had a budding arsonist who was excluded in the summer term two years ago after setting fire to the changing rooms. He is almost certain to have a criminal record. There is also a disturbed young lady who had been rather stalking him. She now attends a different school.'

'Thank you, I'll need the details of those individuals.' Gillard was considering asking Mrs Squires about whether there were any rumours or speculation about the head-master, but decided that this lady would probably be the last to receive the confidences of more junior staff. He settled for a more open question: 'Is there anything else about the principal that you would like to tell me?'

'Only that he will be greatly missed.' It was at this point that her chin finally trembled, and tears filled her eyes.

Gillard thanked her and returned to his vehicle. As he drove back the short distance to the crime scene, he took in the tidy, well-cared-for homes, the high-end vehicles and the whole suburban edifice of this well-to-do area. What had happened to one of their neighbours was utterly alien. Not something you would expect outside Middle Eastern battlefields. It just did not fit in at all.

–

Back inside the CSI tent, Gillard saw DS Vikram Singh, who told him the forensic pathologist had departed and the corpse had been moved carefully into a body bag before being taken to the local hospital's mortuary.

'Anything fresh emerge?'

'Not so far, sir. It's pretty dark out there now. I've noted down who has been spoken to.'

The golden hour was long gone, and from the clipboard that Singh showed him, the hurried door-to-door enquiries seemed to have produced little useful information. Plenty of uniformed schoolchildren had been seen on the normal post-school routes through the alleyway leading between Badgers Walk and Highgrove Crescent. The only CCTV cameras were at the off-licence on the main road and some recently installed on the pedestrian crossings, but these didn't capture vehicles turning into the crescent. The nearest ANPR camera was two miles away. Uniforms were currently trying to catalogue whether any domestic CCTV footage was available, although expectations were not high. Privacy rules stipulated that home cameras that covered public thoroughfares were liable to the onerous GPRD data requirements. A proper search of gardens and alleyways would have to wait for first light the next morning.

In the meantime, there was no sign of the missing head, nor of the murder weapon.

–

Gillard was back at Surrey Police headquarters at Mount Browne by nine p.m. Hopes for an early breakthrough had been dashed. There were now fifty uniformed officers on the case, of whom twenty had been dispatched to take witness statements from key members of staff at St John's Academy. He didn't expect that to throw up anything, but these were evidential boxes that needed to be ticked. From the information that had trickled in, Adam Heath had left school at his normal time for that day, well after most of the staff had departed, though no one saw him get into his car.

Electronic proof of that journey was going to be difficult. There was no satnav in the car, and there were no ANPR cameras covering the short route between school and home. There was a CCTV camera at St John's Academy which covered the staff car park. However, it was mounted on the roof of the changing block for the swimming pool and the cabling to the camera had been damaged in the arson attack two years ago. It was on the extensive list of equipment to be renewed. If someone had managed to get into the headmaster's car, there were no witnesses to it. Research intelligence officer Rob Townsend had put the headmaster's mobile phone through the Aceso Kiosk, a portable investigatory timesaver which quickly stripped out all of the electronic data. Previously, it could take many hours or sometimes days to retrieve the same data with the help of the service provider. The Aceso showed that the phone had been switched off at roughly the time the principal had left the school and was not turned on again during the journey.

Gillard was less surprised that the door-to-door inquiry had thrown up nothing. It sometimes took weeks for people to review in their heads what they had seen and come forward with crucial information. He was now hoping for some results from the fingertip search which would take place in Highgrove Crescent and Badgers Walk at first light tomorrow.

He had set the first incident room meeting for nine a.m. He was really hoping for some kind of forensic discovery by then, not least the discovery of the missing head.

—

Gillard got home just after Sam. He had picked up a takeaway pizza, and after quickly embracing his wife, they wordlessly devoured it from the cardboard box while sitting on opposite sides of the kitchen table. These were the kind of meals that they had been used to having in their early years living together. They grinned at each other and fought over the little cheesy scabs stuck on the inside of the packaging. It was one of the little games they enjoyed. Sam was particularly pleased to find a hidden chunk of pineapple, and doubly so when her husband pouted at her for eating it all.

'So, greedy, how was your first day back?' he asked.

'Busy,' she said, hooking a hank of dark wavy hair behind one ear. 'I forget how hectic it gets, and how you don't have a moment to yourself.'

'It helps to be busy.' He knew that his wife was still struggling with flashbacks. She was tough, but the trauma of being buried in a garage inspection pit, locked inside a freezing steel box, was not one easily forgotten. He'd known her only six years, but the last one had been the most testing of their young marriage. She wasn't yet forty, more than a decade his junior, and still had the girlish figure which he'd always found attractive. The ordeal of the last year had deepened their connection, even as it had infused it with moments of melancholy.

'And of course quite a day for you,' she said, reaching across to stroke his hair, now a greying fuzz which had once been fair. 'Dead headmaster and all that. The media are all over it.'

'They are, but it's a shocking crime and that keeps everyone buzzing. The school is closed tomorrow, so at least I'll be able to take a closer look without getting under everybody's feet. I'm convinced there was a stowaway in the car, who must've got in when it was parked at the school.'

'Did he stop anywhere on the way home?'

'We don't know. It's not far, and if he did stop at the shops, for example, the assailant must have known he would do so. The chances are that whoever killed him knew him well.'

'Why do you say that?'

'It's just a question of knowing his habits. The attack happened on a Thursday, the one day of the week his wife wouldn't already be there when he drove home. Whoever it was, was either invited into the car, or he was able to break in without difficulty and hide until the principal got there. If there was an escape car parked near the house, nobody appears to have seen it. Someone running away on foot with a bloody head in their arms would stand out a bit.'

'That all makes sense,' Sam said.

'Our murderer must have known the crucial details of Heath's life, or undertaken some meticulous research. I think we will find the answer to this in his personal life.'

Chapter Nine

Two months earlier

It was in early November, a couple of weeks after the trip to Manchester, when strange events at Julia's home resumed. One night, an hour or two after she had come home from work, she thought she saw movement in the garden. She had taken to peeking out from time to time; it had become a nervous tic that disrupted her evenings. She was convinced that she had just seen a dark shape behind the bushes. It wasn't completely dark yet, so she slipped on her wellies, donned her Barbour jacket and grabbed a heavy torch, then made her way out through the French windows and across the lawn.

'Is there anyone there?' she called out loudly, more for the benefit of her own self-confidence rather than because she was expecting to have the question answered.

There was no reply. She pressed on, advancing with her torch, and triggering next door's dazzling movement sensor light. Behind the shed she found a plastic carrier bag with a grubby sleeping bag inside it. Gingerly, she lifted the bag up and thought about throwing it in the dustbin. Should she call the police? She could predict what they would say, that someone had just tossed it over the wall. She was well aware that getting the police to come round even for a burglary was difficult, so there was no chance for this. But what should she do?

She settled for taking the trip upstairs to see if Briony was in. She was, and was aghast that there was evidence of someone sleeping in the garden.

'How did they get in?' Briony said, offering Julia a glass of chilled chardonnay, which she accepted. 'The wall's nearly six feet high.'

'But there are trees and bushes on the other side, and some thick old ivy stems. Kids could easily climb it to make a den.'

'Do you think it's kids?'

'Probably. Any genuine criminal would have broken into the shed by now, it's not that hard.'

'I could borrow Roger's dog, Max, for the weekend and let you have him. He is a sizeable beast with a good bark on him.'

Roger was Briony's sometime boyfriend, and the dog was a boxer. 'That might be useful. Would you ask Roger for me?'

'Of course.'

Julia had no great expectations that she would. Briony was one of those breezy women who made grandiose promises and then forgot all about them. There were dozens of offers of having lunch together which had never transpired. Pleasant but flaky. Still, if the dog was available, that would make her feel safe. She didn't know it yet, but things were about to get worse. A lot worse. And it coincided with trouble at work.

–

Having turned down James Cheetham, Julia thought she had finally dealt with all the unwelcome advances at work.

But she hadn't counted on Clive Hogarth. The chief clerk was unmarried, always came to staff parties unaccompanied, and never mentioned his home life. The only known change since his youth had been moving from his parents' home in Enfield across the M25 to the more salubrious Hertfordshire village of Cuffley. Three miles, but another world, thanks to the financial success of V&I. It was rumoured that he had tried it on a couple of years ago with one of the junior clerks, a young woman who inexplicably fled from chambers after just three months of apparently good work. There was never any proof.

And now Julia was in his sights. He had asked her to lunch several months ago, one of the warning signs that even Edwina had been kind enough to share with Julia in her first week. Hogarth had a nearby pub that he frequented, but always made his seduction attempts at a more upmarket place, according to Edwina: 'If he ever wants to take you to Le Manor Blanc, refuse. Make an excuse, feign period pain, anything.' Submitting to Hogarth, Edwina suggested, would be like being rogered by a Komodo dragon. So Julia made an excuse to avoid Le Manor Blanc, and then again for the next two occasions he asked, until she was sure the message had got through.

It had. And in the months leading up to Christmas the trouble really began.

Hogarth began to punish her: allocating trivial cases in distant courts, failing to chase overdue payments for her, giving her late substitutions, and perhaps the cruellest of all, cross-courting. This was a scheduling torment, available only to clerks, which required Julia to shuttle between two cases at almost the same time. Eventually, faced with an impossible commitment the next day, she rounded on him right in the main corridor of chambers.

'What is it you want me to do? Fly?' she asked.

'We're short of bodies, and I've got several clients I need to keep happy.'

'Why does it always fall to me? Why don't you ask Nilish?' He was a new barrister, young, sharp and energetic, who had just emerged from pupillage under Edwina. The general view was that Nilish was headed for great things.

'Because Edwina wants him with her today.'

'James?'

'Busy.'

'Christopher?'

'Do me a favour, Ms McGann.' Hogarth had always made it clear that as their chief earner, Christopher was never to be stretched on pifflingly trivial cases like these.

'You're setting me up to fail, and I want to know why.'

'Not at all, I have every confidence in your abilities.' Hogarth managed to say the words and undermine them with his expression. The final exhalation almost choked her with sulphur.

Julia had stormed out, slamming her office door behind her, inspired for revenge. She waited a week to make sure she got it right. She slipped into work early, on a day when Veronica had a dental appointment. She filched from Veronica's desk the spare key to Hogarth's office. She had with her a small toolkit and it took just five minutes to sabotage the chief clerk's chair, a glorified typist's job that skated around on five casters. It was the matter of a few moments to remove one of the casters, and partially unscrew a second so it barely engaged in the thread. For good measure she unscrewed part of the chair's base and removed the large clip which limited the seat rake. Without the clip, and the return spring it connected to, the seat back would fold almost flat with enough weight. Hogarth had a habit of leaning back and putting his feet on his desk while on the phone.

Julia made sure she was on the phone shortly after nine thirty when Hogarth arrived. His office was a floor below hers. She heard his voice, the slam of the door and then a minute later the unmistakable crash of twenty-five stones of unsightly fat toppling backwards into the old fireplace behind his desk. The bellow of pain delighted her. Others ran to his aid, for what turned out to be a nasty gash on the back of his head.

Hogarth was far from stupid, and in subsequent weeks cast suspicious glances at Julia, though he never asked her for another date. Nevertheless, although the punishment diminished it did not cease, particularly when it came to chasing payments. She was in a bind, and he knew it. Time and again she had considered resigning from V&I to find a home in a different chambers. The trouble was that her debts were still too pressing, and Hogarth would probably not chase money owing for her once she'd left. She couldn't afford to spend six months or a year as a relative unknown starting from the ground floor with somebody else.

If she was going to change things, she wondered whether perhaps she should sell her flat. When she had first bought it, she loved the garden, entirely hers under the lease, and the freedom to sit out when the weather was nice. She liked Weldon Road, even though she was usually forced to park her car under a hawthorn tree full of nesting pigeons, the only space left by the time she got home. The burglary two years ago she had taken in her stride, but by November, with fresh worries about intruders, she was getting stressed. She found that even during court hearings her concentration was corroded by worries about whether she had fully locked up, or whether somebody might get in. She couldn't afford to be distracted like this. Very soon, the pre-trial preparation hearing for the Bonner trial would take place. Easily the biggest case she'd ever been involved with, and one of the most complex. It would require a hundred per cent concentration.

–

The following Saturday, Julia shared her concerns with Rachel during a walk in Stoke Park with her son Jack. Rachel had been to hell and back when her City career collapsed and took her marriage with it, but always managed to maintain the robust common sense needed to deal with an energetic three-year-old.

'You're just going through a bad patch, Moggy,' she said. 'It's like with my gardening business, I had two clients default on payments last year in the same month that Neil stopped paying maintenance. You just have to get past it. You love that flat and wouldn't be so happy anywhere else... Jack, what are you doing now?'

Rachel was looking at her son, who had thrown his scooter down with a yell and was now dragging it across the grass.

'Jack, watch out... Oh for goodness' sake, you've got dog poo all over it.'

The little boy looked up, his face angry and pink. He was wearing a little blue anorak, and a cycle helmet, knee pads on his trousers and hi-vis tags on his ankles and wrists. Jack abandoned the scooter, then ran away across the path with his arms out horizontally, making his favourite whooshing noises.

'Racing cars?' Julia asked Rachel, who was bending down, trying to clean the scooter wheels.

'Space fighters, that's the current favourite.' Rachel used nearly a whole packet of wet wipes for the disgusting task. 'I'm only a gardener to get me into practice for this kind of thing,' she said with a laugh, saving the last wet wipe for her own hands, and finally finishing off by dragging her fingers backwards and forwards on a clean stretch of grass. She then bundled up the besmirched tissues into an old Tesco bag, which she sealed with a knot and dangled from one finger.

'Come on, Jack,' she called out. 'Are we going to go home or are you going to stay here?'

'Staying.'

'Ooh, remember you've got your lovely new dinosaur research station at home from Granny.'

'No! Staying. I want my slime.'

Rachel rolled her eyes. The reusable Slime Lab was the bane of her life, smears of the home-made goop turning up everywhere on carpets and curtains. Julia laughed and made her way over to the boy while Rachel lifted the scooter back onto the path. 'Come on, Jack,' Julia said. 'I think we're going home. Mummy needs to wash her hands.'

Jack peered back at his mother, clearly considering whether to throw a tantrum. He scrutinised Julia for cues, to see whether she was on Mummy's side or not. 'Staying,' he declared, grabbing the scooter from his mother and heading off down the path. Julia ran with him, careful not to smile nor endorse his rebellion. The negotiating skills of a three-year-old should not be underestimated.

Julia then made the mistake of seizing the scooter handlebars, bringing him to a halt. It brought an immediate yell of anguish from Jack. 'No!'

Rachel had arrived by now, and said: 'Well, Mummy and Aunty Julia are going home for a lovely cup of coffee.' Mummy had clearly had enough. Though she still retained the bright cheerful tone, all singsong cadences and encouragement, Julia could detect the brittleness of her mood. It would be dark in half an hour, but Jack's obstinacy was unrelenting. He was testing her.

'Staying here!' he yelled, all furrowed forehead and red pouting lips.

Rachel turned to her: 'One three-year-old, going cheap, one careful owner. Any takers?'

'Yes please,' Julia said, with a smile. She'd swap with Rachel in a heartbeat. She knew that motherhood was no pushover, she had seen that it required extraordinary patience, bottomless love and a cajoling, mock-delight to inspire and ultimately sway a capricious toddler. But she'd give it a go. The magma of motherhood glowed unrelentingly in her entrails. Hidden from exterior view, it smoked and steamed through her dreams, and erupted unpredictably in little frustrations at her lack of purpose. It boiled over while sitting on trains to pointless hearings for criminals whose life was already ruined and wasted at fifteen, it simmered while she read dull legal text in Archbold, or even while listening to Edwina or Christopher holding forth in the pub. *This is all pointless.* That's what she felt. It had no meaning. She was meant to have a child. Yes, she was. And why didn't she have one? And why could she never have her own little Jack? Like cross-examination, never ask a question to which you do not know the answer. She had the answer, it had weighed on her for five years.

I don't have my own little Jack because of one hateful man. Himself.

–

The following Friday, Julia finally had something to celebrate. She had for two weeks been busy on a case, an apparently impossible defence brief which she had won. Hogarth was pleased enough to volunteer to immediately chase various client solicitors for over three grand owed to Julia for cases stretching back months. To celebrate, Julia invited Rachel out for a post-work drink, on her.

'What was the case?' Rachel had asked.

'Domestic abuse. I won on a technicality and the CPS offered no evidence.'

'Were you defending some brute of a wife beater?'

'Well, it is my job.'

'And you got the bastard off?'

'Yes, somewhat surprisingly. The wife had retracted her testimony initially, when she forgave him. It happens a lot. However, on this occasion the police, thinking there wouldn't be a prosecution, then mislaid much of the evidence, including CCTV footage which may have supported his alibi, when she later reinstated her accusations.'

'Oh Moggy, how do you sleep at night?'

'I don't, at the moment, as you know.'

Julia wasn't under oath, so hadn't dared tell her friend the whole unsavoury truth. The defendant was a six-foot-five-inch unemployed builder accused of striking his wheelchair-bound wife repeatedly in the face with a heavy glass ashtray. She'd said her crime had simply been to turn off the TV when England was playing. His story was that he hadn't been at home at all, but in the pub with a mate watching the game. The mate backed his story. Given her injuries, pursuing an acquittal had seemed an uphill task until Julia found the pub manager's statement. It mentioned he'd passed CCTV evidence backing the defendant's story to the police. However, the evidence log showed it was either lost or deleted and had certainly never been examined. Police negligence had undermined the defendant's defence, and without it no conviction could be considered sound. It was, if she said so herself, a brilliant piece of detective work.

When she won such cases, Julia used to feel guilty about it. No longer. As Hogarth had reminded her, a victory is a victory. And a bank draft on its way is money to spend.

Finally.

Julia had dressed up in a little black dress and what she called her ten-minute heels, while Rachel was in a king-fisher blue sheath dress and ankle boots. They had swept into one of Guildford's trendiest and most crowded bars determined to have fun. They got talking to two young men at the bar. One was Aaron, a very boyish late twenties, with trendy purple-framed glasses and one dangly earring. She didn't like the earring and wasn't overly fond of his plaited beardette either. She just couldn't imagine running her fingers through it. But she enjoyed the attention. Rachel, who could flirt for England, was cosying up to the other guy, a muscular self-confident fellow in his mid-thirties who clearly went to the gym. But to Julia's mind Faz, as he called himself, was more in love with his own body than any woman could be. The turning point for the evening was when Rachel recounted the timeworn story of how she got fired from her City job for smashing a phone into a senior director's face.

'Why?' Faz had asked.

'Because he was asking for it. The guy was twice my age, earned millions off our backs, and was always making comments to the female staff. I'd put up with it many times before, but this time I was under a lot of stress. I just snapped.'

'Sounds like you have a temper,' Faz said, shaking his head reproachfully.

'Listen. I was on two phones to New York and Hong Kong and standing up trying to shout currency orders through to the dealer opposite. It was a big deal, tens of millions, and the tosser groped my arse. He walked away with this big smirk on his face. So I swung the phone by its cord, a bit harder than I intended.'

'Ouch,' Faz said.

'I broke his nose. There was blood everywhere. The client in New York, who was on that line, was mystified at the sudden uproar, especially as I'd just got him a two-point narrower spread on the deal than he expected.'

'Wow,' said Aaron, looking at Rachel with a certain amount of wonder.

'Never upset a Derbyshire farm lass,' Julia said, nudging Rachel playfully in the ribs.

'I never grope on a first date,' Faz said, with a wink at Aaron. 'But women do like to be shown they are attractive.'

'Not in caveman style,' Rachel said.

'A consensual kiss might be a better idea,' Julia said. 'Groping is always a high-risk activity.'

'Huh, you sound like a lawyer,' Faz said.

Julia laughed. 'I'm a barrister. And I've defended gropers and worse. But I helped advise Rachel on her employment tribunal case, and got her payoff increased.'

The two men definitely cooled towards them from that point and chilled further when Rachel revealed that her new career was as a landscape gardener.

'So after you've killed the gropers, you bury them?' Aaron asked.

'That's it,' Rachel said, with a wink at Julia. 'Cavemen belong underground.'

Aaron went to the toilet, while Faz scanned the bar for fresh and less chewy prey. Julia and Rachel rolled their eyes at each other and decided to move on. They said a casual goodbye to Faz, who was leaning forward on a barstool, thighs apart, to talk to an attractive barmaid half his age. That left a hefty gap at the back of his white cargo trousers revealing the waistband of his underpants, printed with the word 'Stud'.

Julia was in a mischievous mood and couldn't resist. A couple of After Eight mints had arrived earlier with the bill. While Faz was otherwise engaged, Julia slipped the slender chocolates out of their paper sleeves and dropped them down the back of Faz's jeans between the two layers of clothing.

The moment they got outside the bar the two women leaned on each other, roaring with laughter. 'Moggy, you are so wicked!' Rachel exclaimed.

'Well, he is a complete shit,' Julia chuckled. 'And in five minutes, with a bit of body heat, he'll look it.'

Whatever happened at the next bar was a bit hazy, and by the time she got home, Julia was quite the worse for drink. A Rusty Nail and a Sex on the Beach had just been the start of it. She'd lost count of the number of vodka shots they had consumed by the end. The alcohol had done its job. It had stopped her worrying about the flat. And that was how she came to be surprised.

–

It was gone midnight. She was sober enough to know to hold the railing as she carefully descended the metal stairs to the basement entrance. She fumbled in her bag for keys, then struggled to fit them into the lock. She muttered to herself and leaned against the wall, so she wasn't blocking the glow of the streetlamp.

Only then did she see.

Five yards away, a child was sitting on her recycling bin, chin on knees, hunched up like a gargoyle.

'Can I help you?' Julia said, the middle-class way of saying: *who the hell are you and why are you on my property?*

It was wearing a filthy brown anorak, hood pulled tight around its face, dark jogging bottoms, scuffed trainers. It wasn't clear what sex the creature was. 'I thought you was never getting home,' the urchin said, snot running down its top lip. 'I'm hungry.'

Julia stared at the girl, for girl she was. Thin, pasty-faced, shivering now she came to look at her. Probably no more than thirteen or fourteen.

'How long have you been here?'

'Fucking hours.'

'Why are you waiting for me?'

The girl shrugged, her mouth a gash of misery. Julia was unwilling to open the door and risk letting this street creature into her home. She might be on drugs, or armed with a knife.

'Whereabouts do you live?'

'Nowhere.'

'Have you run away from home?'

There was the semblance of a laugh.

'Look. This is *my* home. Would you please be kind enough to leave?' she slurred.

'Kind enough?'

'Are you going to leave?'

No answer.

'Look, I'll let you have a pound,' Julia said, stepping away and reaching into her handbag. 'You better be gone before my husband gets in.'

The girl laughed. 'You ain't got no husband.'

'I have, and when he gets in you better be gone!'

'You live all alone. I know that much.'

Julia's hand froze, coin suspended in her fingertips.

'What do you know?'

'I can see that you're well pissed.'

The girl was right, she was drunk. 'What business is that of yours?'

The girl's hands remained stuck in her anorak pockets. 'I don't want your money. I'm hungry, and I ain't got nowhere to go.'

'You've been sleeping in the garden, haven't you?' Julia said, rapidly trying to sober up.

'What if I 'ave?'

'I'll call the police.'

'Oh yeah? I thought your job was to help people like me. Lawyer, innit?'

Julia was horrified the girl knew this. 'I'm a barrister, and I defend or prosecute as required.'

'I seen you in the court. Objection, your honour!'

91

Julia snorted. 'I'm afraid you've been watching too much television. It's rather less gladiatorial than you imagine.'

'Not when you get to prison, it ain't. But you don't know much about that, do you?'

'It's time for you to go, I'm afraid. If you don't want the pound that's up to you.'

'Twenty quid, Miss unmarried McGann. Then I'll go.'

Now Julia was really frightened. How did she know her name? She felt her phone in her bag and wondered how she could defend herself if this girl tried to mug her. She was a tiny thing, the same height as Julia but a lot skinnier. But she could be strong, she could be wiry and she could be armed. The girl would never believe that twenty quid actually mattered quite a lot to Julia at the moment, until the case money came through. She probably imagined that all barristers were rich.

'I could let you have some food,' Julia said. 'But I'll not let you in.'

The girl just stared at her. 'Okay,' she said eventually. Only now did Julia notice that the girl was missing the top two incisors, and some of her other teeth were black. It made her look both dangerous and vulnerable at the same time.

'I'll bring you some soup.'

'You got any fags?'

'No. I don't smoke, and neither should you.'

The girl looked down and inspected her heavily bitten nails, which in the streetlight still showed fragments of glitter varnish. Julia took advantage of the opportunity to open the door, jump inside and close it behind her. Her first impulse was to call the police, but the moment the door was shut she felt less endangered. She glanced out through the glass panel of the door and saw the pathetic specimen shivering Gollum-like outside, now off the bin and slouching by the door. Perhaps she should call Rachel, at least to let somebody know what was happening and that there was someone on her doorstep. She looked through the cupboards for a tin of soup. She knew there was a Waitrose tub of Indian sweet potato and coconut dhal in the fridge, but she wasn't having that. Bachelors' lentil soup from the pound shop would do the trick if she could find the tin. Ah yes, there it was. She opened the can, poured the contents into a dish and set the microwave for three minutes. While it was heating, she rang Rachel and left a message.

'Rachel, it's me. I just want to let you know in case anything happens, that I discovered who it was who appears to be camped in my garden. A little waif of a girl. I'm just heating up some soup for her. She needs to go to social services.'

Julia finished leaving the message, waited for the ping, then poured half the soup into a bowl. What a way to sober up.

When she opened the door, the girl was gone.

Chapter Ten

For four days Julia saw nothing of the waif. She lay in bed at night listening for clues that her intruder was back in the garden. The autumn gales ensured that there was plenty to hear. The hammering of the rain on the flat roof of the back extension, the scratching of the rose bushes on the bathroom window, the loose fence panel rattling on the house opposite. It wasn't just sounds. The neighbours' confounded movement sensor lights, triggered by waving branches when it was windy, seemed to go on every couple of minutes and bathed the left-hand side of her garden in light. Never a good sleeper, Julia's thoughts were constantly drawn to that young vulnerable girl.

She had thought again about calling the police, but dismissed the idea. What would they do? It was really social services that she needed to call, because that was where the police would take the girl. But she didn't have a name for her, and no clue about her age. Under that tightly drawn hood she looked perhaps fifteen, but could have been a few years younger or older. This wasn't some random piece of begging, though. The girl knew her name, knew she worked at court. She racked her brains to think if she could have been a relative of one of her local clients over the last year or two. It was impossible to say. She had been involved with 119 cases in the last three years.

This couldn't have come at a worse time.

The fraud trial was resuming on Monday and would take most of her attention, but she still had plenty of preparation to do for the Bonner case. The plea and trial preparation hearing, delayed at the request of the CPS, was in a week, but she still had to win Bonner round. She wanted him to plead guilty, because she felt the weight of evidence against him was so overwhelming, but he seemed to think he could get off scot free. Amazingly, in his entire criminal life he'd only ever served six months inside. A combination of luck and some judicious witness intimidation seemed to make him believe that he would never go down for a serious stretch. Julia was convinced that was about to change. But the man had God-given self-confidence, and in front of a sceptical jury that smug expression would add weight to their probable dislike of him.

And here she was, lying awake at four in the morning, worrying about some young girl.

The next thing she knew she had woken up, hearing a noise. The sound was real enough, a tapping at her bedroom window. She sat bolt upright in bed. The wind was keening, and the movement lights opposite flicked on, silhouetting a figure on the other side of the curtains. Julia screamed, and reached for the phone. Now she really was going to call the police.

–

The police came, but not until late the following after-noon, having established that the intruder was probably the young girl and concluding that Julia was not in imminent danger. Still, it turned a bad night's sleep into a terrible one and ruined the following day's work. She had to get a colleague to cover a court appearance so she could be in the flat when the police arrived to check it over. Two young officers, both female, went with Julia on a rather cursory tour of the garden as it was beginning to rain. She couldn't point to any damage, the sleeping bag was nowhere to be seen, and the litter Julia herself had cleaned up on a previous occasion. The policewomen talked about securing the shed, making sure tools capable of forcing entry into the house were under lock and key, and recommended speaking with neighbours about security. All right and proper, but nothing she couldn't have got from a website had she not known it already.

'You say you spoke to this young lady on a previous occasion?' asked the slightly older of the two, rubbing her gloved hands together against the cold.

'I did, and it really concerned me that she knew my name and that I was a lawyer. I kept thinking: why me?' Julia brought the two officers back inside, then explained that she had tried to discover if this young woman was associated with any of her clients and had come to no firm conclusions. 'She clearly recognised me,' Julia said. 'To be able to do that she's almost certainly been in court herself.'

'You really should get her name and address, then we can make some further progress,' said the other officer.

'I rather think that's your job,' Julia said. 'I don't want her punished, I simply want to make sure that she is all right.'

'And to stop pestering you,' the older one said, with a wry smile.

'Exactly.'

Once Julia had seen the two policewomen off the premises and made herself a coffee, she checked her watch to see whether it was worth going back to chambers. No, it wasn't. Not at four p.m. The rain was lashing down now, on a squally wind.

The doorbell chimed again. Assuming it must be the policewomen again, who had barely had time to leave, she had a coffee in her hand when she pulled open the door.

And there she was, bold as brass. The filthy anorak, its hood shadowing her features, soaked joggers and scuffed trainers.

'Could do with a coffee,' the girl said. 'S'freezing out here.'

Julia tried to close the door, but only succeeded in spilling the coffee over the doormat. The girl's foot was stopping it closing. 'Stop panicking,' she said. 'I'm not going to hurt you.'

'What do you want?'

'I'll have that coffee.'

Julia kept the mug out of her reach. 'Actually, I just want you to go away and leave me in peace.'

The light from the hall caught the girl's face. She looked upset. 'Got nowhere to go, have I?'

'Where were you last living?'

'Nowhere.'

'Let me call social services then.'

'Fuck that! I'll get killed if I go back there.' She removed her foot from the door, allowing Julia to close it. The conversation continued through the glass.

'What's your name?'

'What do you care? I'm just a nuisance, ain't I?'

'What about your family? Where are they?'

97

'Ain't got no family. Kicked out years ago, I was. When my old lady got a new fella.'

'Where did you sleep?'

'In the park, on the street, in a squat.'

'Where was that?'

'Round here for the last couple of weeks.'

'Are you local?'

'No.'

'So why here? Why me? Where did you see me in court?'

The girl shrugged. 'I won't get found in a rich town like this. And your garden was better than the park. No perverts creeping about in the night.'

'So where had you been, before the park?'

'Merstham.'

Julia knew the place, a dormitory suburb at the junction of the M25 and M23. Not poor, but run down. 'Is that where your family is?'

'Who cares about them? They didn't care about me.'

'So where did you stay?'

'Some blokes offered me a place.'

Now she was safely behind the door, Julia's fear was displaced by pity. 'You've got to be very careful. There are some bad people out there.'

'You really think I didn't know that? Sometimes you don't have no choice.'

'Were you abused?' Julia could hear it in the girl's voice.

'Yeah. I was abused. Pimped out, raped, beaten up, given drugs, pimped out again when I was high enough to smile, raped, beaten up... round and round for months.'

'That's awful.' Julia could hear her own handwringing tone. But what could she do? 'Did you go to the police?' she asked.

'Nah. The coppers aren't interested. They'd much rather nick me for shoplifting or possession than take on the big boys. It's the easy life, innit?'

'The police are better now. And I could make sure that you speak to someone sympathetic, someone who will help you.'

'Right, sure you would.'

'It's my job to pursue justice. As a barrister.'

'Is that right?' The response dripped with sarcasm.

Julia turned to the telephone table by the front door, scribbled down a phone number for the best criminal solicitors firm that she knew, and pushed it out through the letterbox to the girl. 'Ring that number, they will look after you, I promise.' Through the dimpled glass Julia could see the girl scrutinising the paper.

'So, shall I go now, then? Shall I just fuck off into the rain like a bad dream? Sleep behind a skip, find something to eat in a bin?'

Julia didn't say anything, but her heart was in her mouth.

'Yeah. I know your type,' the girl said. 'Thousands like you, ain't it? Happy to read about it in the *Guardian*. All sympathetic, yeah. Put some money in a tin, even pay a bit more tax, feel a bit better. But you don't want it on your own fucking doorstep, do you? Too uncomfortable. Face-to-face. Oh no, can't have that. Lower your house prices, won't it?'

Julia was dying inside. Everything the girl had said was true.

She watched the girl slowly climbing the stairs up to street level, hunched against the downpour. Julia was moved by pity, and part of her was considering whether to let the girl sleep in the spare room. But then there was the issue of dirt, of filth, possibly lice, on her sheets. And theft. Maybe she was just scoping out the place for a burglary for somebody else. One of those blokes, as she had said. Maybe there was a Nottingham connection. The liberal curse: a heart that dies a thousand deaths, torn between empathy and self-interest, principle and hypocrisy. The girl had opened the gate in the railings at the top of the stairs, and carefully closed it after her, resetting the latch. That was more than the postman ever did. Somehow that tiny touch tipped the mental argument.

Julia opened the front door a crack and called to the girl. She turned around, her hands thrust deeply into the anorak pockets.

'Here is a key, to my garden shed,' Julia dangled it from her fingers. 'I'll give you a spare duvet, and you can stay there for tonight. At least you won't get soaked and frozen.'

For a moment the girl just stood there and looked at her.

'Are you hungry?' Julia said.

'Yeah.'

'I'll get you some soup.'

'All right.'

Was that a thank you, or had she imagined it? Julia directed the girl around the building through the side gate and into the back garden. She said she would follow in a moment with bedding and some soup. Julia looked out through the French windows and watched the girl making her way towards the shed. *What am I doing?* Just inheriting a problem, a responsibility. She had never done anything like this before, but she just didn't feel right kicking this child out into the rain. This time, she did open the posh Waitrose soup. She also cut her a chunk of the ciabatta to go with it. While the microwave was droning, she dug out an old blanket, her spare duvet, and a pillow. The pillow was stained, and she'd been meaning to throw it out. But it would do for the girl. She opened the French windows, slipped on her wellies and headed to the shed with the bedding. The rain had stopped, but it was overcast and damp, with a chill wind from the north.

The girl was waiting by the door of the shed, shivering. It was a solid structure but the window frames were rotted and the insides were covered in cobwebs. It took several minutes to clear the inside enough for the duvet to be put down. Julia felt the spongy wooden floor. It was clearly damp, rotting probably. She found a bin liner to insulate the blanket and duvet from the wood.

'Is that going to be all right for you?' Julia said, hoping the answer was a definite yes. Instead she got a shrug, and a slight smile. For the first time, the girl slipped her hood down. She had greasy shoulder-length mid-brown hair, but rather fine features. Her brown eyes were large and her dark eyebrows expressive.

By the time Julia got back to the shed with the food on a tray, the girl had wrapped herself in the duvet, and put the blanket round her shoulders. She looked almost photogenic in a refugee camp kind of way. The sort of picture you'd get in *National Geographic*. Afghan child bride, perhaps, plucky teenage Yemeni breadwinner.

Julia wouldn't dare take her picture.

'I have one condition for letting you stay,' Julia said, as she passed the tray across.

'Yeah?'

'Your name. I need to know who you are.'

'I'm a nobody, best you don't ask.' The girl spooned some soup to her mouth.

'I'm sorry, I'm going to insist on knowing your name.'

'Dezzy.'

'Dezzy what?'

'Don't remember.'

'Come on, everyone's got a surname.'

'Flynn. Destiny Flynn.'

Julia was appalled. Destiny? Dear God.

—

As soon as she got back inside, Julia went straight onto the Missing People website. She had used the charity before when researching evidence for a case. The volunteers there did a fantastic job of connecting those who had gone missing with those who were seeking them, without the heavy-handed involvement of officialdom. Those who had run away could send word to their families, and there were guides to action for all involved. She searched the name Destiny Flynn and it came up straight away. Aged seventeen, last seen in Forest Gate, East London.

She had been reported missing by a children's home early in 2015, aged twelve. Julia cross-checked on the National Crime Agency missing persons database, and found an identical record, this time with a photograph. She was just a child, in a pink top with a cheeky face. It was heartbreaking.

Julia considered reporting a sighting but remembered what Destiny had said. That she would be killed if the children's home found out where she was. Instead, she rang Rachel.

'You know that girl I mentioned?'

'You mean the urchin burglar?'

'She's not a burglar.'

Rachel laughed. 'You don't know that. You of all people should wait for the evidence, before jumping to conclusions. Anyway, what was it you wanted to tell me?'

'She's been missing from a children's home since 2015.'

'Have you rung them?'

'No. She says if the children's home knows where she is, she'll get killed. So I'm letting her stay in the shed for tonight.'

'Oh, Moggy. I'm not sure that's a good idea.'

Julia sighed. 'She's an adult, technically, in that she's old enough to leave home. Seventeen, but she looks more like fourteen or fifteen. There's no statutory duty for her to go back.'

'What about her family?'

'It's a sad tale, Rachel. The girl is destitute. I can't leave her out in the rain. It's just for one night.'

Rachel laughed. 'Come on, Moggy. It starts with one night, and as she watches the pity crystallising in your mind, she will be sizing up what she can get out of you. Pretty soon you'll be giving her a home and paying her pocket money. You, who have so much spare cash. Not.'

'If that's what she expects, she'll get a shock.'

'Look, you're being really kind, but it's best to get the professionals involved. Social services, start with them.'

'Rachel, she's incredibly scared. She says she'll be murdered if her whereabouts is known.'

'God, don't you think you've got enough on your plate as it is without inheriting this responsibility? You do your good work through your day job. You defend the criminal underclass.'

'That's a bit pejorative,' Julia said.

'Excuse my lack of woke awareness, I'm just telling you how it looks to me. I'm your best friend because I tell you the truth, and the truth is you're potentially getting in deep waters here. Even assuming she's harmless, she might have some drug dealing boyfriend or pimp who gets to know where you live. When you're out, they'll burgle the place. You read the papers, you know what can happen. I mean, didn't you just get your bag stolen in Nottingham?'

Julia knew Rachel was right. She always was. She had a mind like a barrister, but unlike Julia's, it didn't switch off in the personal realm.

Chapter Eleven

Rachel was right. It took just a week for Destiny to move in.

Julia had suffered a god-awful day at work. Clive Hogarth had thrown at her a combination of cases which once again left her trying to be in two places at once. She had made the first one in good time but was held up by an hour-long adjournment called by the judge which left her hopelessly late for the second case. She was only needed for five minutes in a plea in mitigation to make the case for a persistent drug offender, but the judge, Mr Justice Walker, a gammon-faced traditionalist whose nickname was Klingon for his heavily ridged forehead and trenchant views on punishment, berated her for two minutes solidly at the bench. Utterly humiliated, she stumbled her way through her mitigation presentation and had it roundly dismissed. The defendant got three years and made sure he swore at her as he was taken down.

On the way home from London, having already downed a mini bottle of wine on the train and feeling in need of a more substantial drink, Julia headed off to join her colleagues. The run-up to Christmas for V&I was a series of ever-heavier drinking nights, starting in the middle of November and working up like an alcoholic advent calendar to a grand meal and piss-up in the week before the actual festivities. It was something of the character of the legal profession that the strictures of day-to-day formality led to an almost outrageous level of childish misbehaviour once the socialising began. In Julia's belief much of this could be laid at the door of the barely grown-up public schoolboys who dominated the profession. Though to be fair it wasn't just the boys. Edwina Pym had boasted of seducing at least a trio of the male trainees over the years after having first drunk them under the table. However, those female staff of lower standing, like Julia, were more likely to end up as prey than predator.

Tonight's drinks, the second on the list, was by long tradition at Vine Bistro and Grill, just round the corner from chambers. Tiny, noisy and atmospheric, it was already packed with legal professionals by six when Julia arrived. Edwina and Veronica had been there a half hour and were already on their second bottle of Prosecco. The principal rule was no work talk, and since making yourself heard in this packed venue involved raising your voice, it was certainly sensible. Edwina was giving the latest instalment of the Algarve villa renovation saga, this time over the delay in having the swimming pool retiled. Veronica interspersed snippets about her new hedge fund manager boyfriend and his yacht. Julia, who didn't know where the next car repair bill was coming from, could hardly get a word in. When she did, she blurted out the tale of her night-time visitor.

'But where on earth had she come from?' Veronica asked.

'That's the point, I haven't been able to find out,' Julia said.

'Julia, my dear,' said Edwina. 'You have to draw a firm line with these unfortunates. Your job is to speak up for them, but not tuck them up in bed at night.' She then told the story of how a decade ago, she had run into a rough diamond of a fellow in a gastropub used by barristers near the law courts. 'He was handsome and charming, but his accent rather gave him away, along with the fact that he was like a fish out of water in the bar. His interest in me turned out to be professional rather than personal. He was the son of an East End crime boss, whose brother I was prosecuting. Once I discovered that I had to surrender the case.'

'Lucky escape,' said Veronica.

'Who had the lucky escape?' The call from the doorway came from Christopher Cadwell, standing there looking sophisticated and louche with his cashmere coat over one arm.

'Edwina did,' Julia called. 'I haven't escaped yet.'

Christopher slid through the crowd like a knife, issuing roguish smiles to one or two women with whom he was clearly acquainted, and indicating with a raised eyebrow to a passing waiter that a fresh round of drinks was required. Even Edwina was silenced by his presence. At Christopher's request, Julia summarised her story.

'Oh Moggy, why didn't you bring her along, you spoilsport?' he said. Christopher enjoyed using her nickname, to remind everyone that he had once slept with her.

'Christopher, it sounds like the girl's barely house-trained,' Edwina said.

'She drinks cider from the can, apparently,' Veronica said, making it sound as exotic as a hummingbird sipping from an orchid.

'Her name is Destiny,' Julia added.

The chorus of braying laughter suddenly embarrassed Julia. She hadn't mentioned the girl in order for her to be ridiculed.

'Well, well, you do have an exotic pet,' Christopher said. 'I thought Mark's boa constrictor was impressive enough.'

'Perhaps she's the throwback daughter you never had,' Edwina said.

Even Veronica scowled at this cruelty. Julia was suddenly angry. She was aware that her choice of career meant she skated gaily across the lives of others less fortunate, never plumbing the dark and terrible depths of circumstances hidden beneath that fragile crust. But she at least knew that that world beneath was real, the suffering and predicaments happening to real people, not simply illustrations of points of law to end up dry and dusty between the leaves of textbooks.

'Anyone could end up like her, you know,' Julia said. 'Accident of birth, bad luck. It could be any of us. Being in the wrong place at the wrong time.'

Christopher laughed gently and rested a patrician hand on Julia's shoulder. 'Oh dear, oh dear, Moggy,' he said. 'And, speaking of wrong place, wrong time, here comes Hogarth.'

Julia used the arrival of the chief clerk as a diversion to exit via the ladies. She'd had enough for tonight. She had been planning to tell her colleagues about Destiny's life: the sexual slavery, the abuse, the endless fear. But she realised that they didn't want to know. They needed the ice to keep them above those frigid waters.

But what if it broke? That's what she wanted to know. If any of them were in the girl's position, who would sink and who would swim?

It was pouring with rain by the time Julia got home at 9.45 p.m., having sobered up considerably. She descended the steps, opened the front door and shook out her coat and umbrella. Once she had turned up the heating she glanced into the garden. A faint bluish light was visible through the grimy shed window. Light from a phone.

Destiny.

Julia had left her some food this morning, in a plastic bag. A four-pack of sausage rolls which had been on offer in the local convenience store and a carton of orange juice. The girl was so pallid, Julia wondered whether she ever had any vitamins. Probably wouldn't know what to do with broccoli. She had found herself lying awake at night wondering where Destiny went to use the toilet, where she washed, if she managed to change her clothes at all, even how she managed to keep her phone charged and in credit. Finding herself caring about this young waif, Julia realised that Rachel had been right. She was beginning to inherit a responsibility. A form of displaced motherhood, standing in for the real version she had always yearned for.

If that was the case, she might as well do it properly. Julia dug out her wellies, slid into her jacket and padded down to the shed. The night was not only wet but now bitterly cold. She hadn't quite reached the shed door when the light inside went off and the door was pushed open from the inside. In the faint glimmer of her torch, Julia could see in the shadow right at the back of the shed the reflection of a pair of narrowed, determined eyes. Beneath them was the curved blade of a knife. 'Oh, it's you,' Destiny said.

'You scared me half to death,' Julia said. The blade disappeared from view.

'I thought it was him,' she said.

'Who?'

'The bloke I'm trying to avoid.'

'I'm sure whoever it is doesn't know you're here.'

The girl nodded and flicked on her phone. The bluish light cast a ghostly glow on the bottom of her face. 'Hope not,' Destiny said. 'Or you're dead too.'

Julia wanted to know who this man was, but felt she would have to tease it out of the girl. Out here, she was on edge, too nervous to admit to anything.

'Have you found it possible to sleep?'

She shrugged. 'It's wet in here. The floor's all rotten.'

'Look, I was just going to say if you'd like to sleep in the house, it's okay.'

Destiny eyed her suspiciously but said nothing.

'It's all right, honestly. You'd be able to have a shower and a warm bed.' Even as she made the offer, Julia was thinking nervously about the knife. Maybe it was just because the girl was scared. But she wasn't happy about sharing her home with a girl who had a blade.

'Who's in there?' Destiny asked, pointing at the house with her chin. She clearly still suspected a trick.

'I'm quite alone. No husband, as you rightly pointed out.'

'Did you call the social?'

'No. And I won't so long as you are straight with me. I can help you.'

'Yeah?'

Julia explained what she had discovered about her on the missing persons websites.

Destiny looked like she was going to panic. 'Don't you contact them, right? The only people who are looking for me want me dead.'

'I'm sure that can't be true.'

'Have you ever had anyone pour petrol on you? Put his boot on your chest and stand over you with a lighter? You are one click from being dead.' There was no doubt that her fear was real.

'Who did that?'

She shook her head. 'No. I can't even say his name.'

–

Julia led the girl inside, got her to shed her filthy trainers by the French windows, and showed her to the bathroom, while she dug out a fresh fluffy towel. 'Have you got any spare clothes?'

'Nah. I've got some dirty ones in the sleeping bag. Can you charge my phone for me? I need to borrow your cable.'

'Of course,' Julia said.

The girl fished in her trouser pocket and hesitantly handed across the phone. Julia could see in Destiny's face that this was an enormous piece of trust. The device was in a terrible state. The screen was cracked in numerous places, partially repaired with sticky tape, bits of paint had flaked off the casing, giving it an odd marbled texture of glossy black and dull grey. Julia rooted through her cardboard box of electronic bits and bobs and soon found a cable that worked. Only then, when Destiny had seen where it was being charged in the kitchen, did she go into the bathroom and lock the door. Julia could soon hear the water going, and for the first five minutes waited outside the door. The water continued to thunder, so she left Destiny to it and returned to the kitchen.

It was forty-five minutes later when the girl emerged wrapped in the towel. She looked like a different person, and curiously, less young. Now, Julia would have put her at eighteen or nineteen instead of fourteen or fifteen. Her hair, which had previously been lank and flat, was thicker and lustrous, even though parts of it were still wet. Her face had a pink healthy sheen, which revealed a delicate bone structure and a slender neck. Only her dark watchful eyes were unchanged.

'That was great,' she said. 'I helped myself to your shampoo and skin cream.' Her expression said *I hope that's all right*. There was courtesy there, not in words but in intonation. It didn't matter. A bridge had been crossed. Julia sat the girl in front of the gas fire in the lounge and put it on maximum. Sod the arrears.

–

The washing machine and tumble dryer were left running until midnight. Destiny's clothes still weren't particularly clean, but they didn't smell quite as bad. The brown quilted anorak seemed quite beyond saving, and its rank odour ensured that Julia left it hanging in the external wheelie bin cupboard. A trip to the charity shop for clean clothes seemed a good idea.

Julia showed Destiny to the spare room, lent her a hairdryer and another towel. She had mentally run through a checklist of whether there was anything in that room that was worth stealing and come to the conclusion: probably not. Nevertheless, she would still have been uncomfortable to discover evidence that the girl had been going through her possessions. She slid her own limited collection of jewellery into a sock and hid it in a training shoe in the bottom of her wardrobe. Her purse she hid in a coat pocket, hanging above.

It was gone two, and the girl's taciturn nature hadn't changed. They were sitting by the fire when Julia made another attempt to initiate a conversation.

'Are you going to tell me who's been threatening you?'

'You don't need to know.'

'I might be able to help.'

'Black belt in karate are yer?' She sniggered.

'Legally, I mean.'

'Ah, yes, the law. Justice for the little person. Where's your TV?'

'I don't have one.'

Destiny's face distorted as if she'd been told that Julia existed entirely without breathing. 'You're having a laugh, aintcha?' She wouldn't leave the subject alone until she had been escorted around each room in the house to prove there was no TV. 'You're weird,' she said, finally convinced.

'My TV was stolen in a burglary two years ago. A friend lent me an old one, which was always on the blink, and then I realised I didn't spend much time looking at it anyway. So I chucked it out.'

'What you do of an evening?'

'I read, a lot of it is for work.'

Destiny reappraised her. 'No boyfriend, no social life, no TV. No wonder you drink.'

Julia felt like she been slapped. To have her drinking criticised by a down-and-out. It would be funny if it wasn't so sad.

–

Julia was astounded at Destiny's ability to avoid saying thank you. Offering gratitude was so deeply ingrained in

Julia's upbringing that she couldn't get her head round the kind of people who could take and take again without acknowledgement. She supposed that after all the years of defending criminals, she shouldn't be surprised. But that was work, a separate compartment in her head. In court, in cells, in prison interviews, offenders were judicially tweezered from one set-piece to another, without touching the professionals who dealt with them. You didn't have to interact with them as people. They were cases. Intellectually stimulating because of some arcane point of law, or more often boring because of their inevitability. Only rarely did these cases cross the line and touch her.

This was different. Destiny was inside Julia's home, a middle-class temple where the constructs of social etiquette prevailed. She fed the girl some leftover lasagne that she'd defrosted, then watched in fascination as her guest used her fork to carefully lift the pasta lid to check the contents before consenting to eat it. The broccoli Julia had served as a side dish was completely ignored, but it didn't stop her asking for ice cream.

'I don't eat ice cream,' Julia replied. 'Sensitive teeth.' *Why was she having to give excuses?*

The girl looked at her as if she were a creature from another planet.

'Look, Destiny, this isn't going to be a permanent thing, you know. You're going to have to find somewhere to live.'

'Cos I want ice cream?'

'No. Because I can't have you around here when I go to work.'

'Afraid I'm going to tear the place to pieces? Steal all your stuff? Shit in your bed?'

'Not at all.'

'What, then?'

'Quite simply, I don't know anything about you, who you are or where you come from. This is my home, and when I'm at work, I need to know it's safe.'

Destiny smirked at her. 'Maybe your husband or boyfriend could come and look after it?'

'Stop being a smartarse.'

'So why haven't you got anyone? You're not that ugly.'

'Charmed, I'm sure. Especially coming from a girl without her two front teeth.' Julia felt she absolutely had to counter-attack.

'Yeah, well. That was the drugs. Methadone. You stop caring about yourself. So anyway, why don't you have a boyfriend?'

'Maybe I have.'

'Nah, you don't. I'd know.' She tapped her nose. 'No one comes round, and you drink a lot on your own. You're lonely. That's the only reason you let me in. For a bit of company.'

Chapter Twelve

January, Friday

The alarm went off at six, its annoying chirpiness carving its way into Gillard's dreams. He had been lying in a close embrace with Sam, spooned around her from behind, her long hair fanned across the pillow. He gently extracted himself, trying not to wake her, and tapped the phone to stop the racket. He slipped out of bed to the en suite, yawning as he flicked through emails while peeing. There was one from the lab, with the results he had hoped for. Several DNA traces were found in Adam Heath's car. One, unsurprisingly, matched the victim and another his wife. Three others were unidentified, none on the national DNA database.

He finished his ablutions, rapidly showered, and returned the first of the overnight messages from the uniformed inspector who was in charge of the crime scene and today's search. Inspector Jim Lucas was assembling thirty officers at first light for the fingertip search of the alleyways and gardens around the Heaths' home. If the murder weapon or the victim's head had been casually disposed of, they would soon find them. The biggest disappointment so far was that the public appeal for witnesses had thrown up very few sightings of unidentified adults in the area. All they had so far was a Tesco delivery driver, a window cleaner, two plumbers and a builder working on a garden wall in Badgers Walk. Not very promising leads.

Gillard gobbled down a bowl of cereal and a mug of black coffee before heading for the car. Sam was on a later shift, so he left her a note with a smiley face and a kiss, saying he was hoping to be back by eight o'clock that evening. While he drove to Mount Browne, he listened to local radio, which gave extensive coverage to yesterday's murder. He had wanted to keep out of the public domain the fact that the principal had been beheaded, but inevitably the news had leaked out. One local radio disc jockey was already discussing with callers the 'previously hidden Islamist threat within Surrey's school system'. To Gillard that seemed to be jumping to conclusions. Having an agenda was always the enemy of detective work.

He arrived at the CID building at Surrey's police headquarters to see DC Carl Hoskins working the phones. Hoskins, shaven-headed, overweight and a bit of a joker, could always be relied upon to uncomplainingly tackle the worst of the drudge work. Normally it was CCTV, but so far that hadn't played a significant role in this invest-igation. Still on the phone, he turned to face his boss, and indicated with his finger at the headset that there was some significant information coming in. Two minutes later, after the call was finished, he turned to Gillard and said: 'I've just been told that Adam and Stella Heath were hosting a Syrian asylum seeker on and off for the last year.' He looked triumphant.

'Was that from Mrs Heath?'

'No, an anonymous tip to the helpline.'

'I'll ask her when I speak to her later,' Gillard said.

The nine a.m. incident room meeting brought together DI Claire Mulholland, DCs Rainy Macintosh and Michelle Tsu along with research intelligence officer DC Rob Townsend. Gillard, who had just updated himself with the latest from the search from Inspector Lucas, began by laying out the facts of the case. Adam Heath's name was written at the centre of the whiteboard, encircled by the categories of his life: family, colleagues, friends and the as-yet unnamed asylum seeker. 'We will gradually populate these categories with names, but this will probably not be the essential core of the investigation. That remains evidence at the scene: witness sightings, the missing murder weapon and body part, plus forensics. They will be the sieve through which all other evidence will pass.'

There were nods of agreement.

'Rob, where are we with the various phones and laptops from the Heath household?'

'Nothing much so far. As you know, Heath's phone was found on the body, and had been turned off. There's a fair bit of search history on his laptop and desktop PC to go through. Mrs Heath has an iPad, and her phone at a quick glance doesn't look incriminating. It will take a few more days to get anything certain. I've only just got the equipment from the headmaster's office.'

Gillard nodded. 'Uniforms have finished searching Heath's garden and the alleyway behind. They've not turned up anything so far. Michelle, how are you doing with the rest of the family?'

'I've spoken to Matthew Heath, the son. He is on his way back from Liverpool University,' she said. 'He seems to have an alibi, attending a class, but has agreed to give a DNA swab locally. He said his father gave him a lift to the station at the start of term, so his DNA may well turn up in the car. I've just started looking through bank statements and credit card bills. There are no obvious signs of financial difficulty.'

'That's quick work, Michelle,' Gillard said. 'The school is closed today, but I have arranged for every teacher to attend and requested that every pupil over the age of fourteen provide an elimination swab. This is a fairly hefty forensic burden, and I'm sure many of the kids or their parents won't comply immediately, but it is justified by the fact that the murderer almost certainly got into Heath's car at the school.'

'What about the asylum seeker, sir?' Hoskins asked, a little too eagerly for Gillard's liking.

'I'm re-interviewing Mrs Heath later, I'll see what we get.'

—

Tariq Afwan was picked up at six a.m. from his Home Office-provided accommodation with the help of G4S which provided the shared terraced house. The uniformed team which had gone in there seemed to treat it like a drugs raid. When Gillard got to the premises in Reading, he could see that the door was severely damaged with the characteristic indentations made by a ram. There was by then just a single female officer by the door, but a group of half a dozen other dark-skinned individuals were congregating there too.

The detective chief inspector greeted the officer, but was immediately surrounded by some of the other residents. 'Sir, can you tell me what's going on?' asked a tall man with a neatly shaved beard and moustache. 'Are we being deported today? Because I still have a case before the tribunal.'

'Don't pay any attention, sir,' the female officer said, indicating the asylum seekers. 'They've been going on about this all morning.'

'I'm not surprised, seeing as you lot knocked the door off, constable. We only wanted to talk to the guy.'

'I wasn't here at the time, sir. Came on shift at ten,' she replied smugly.

'I don't know what the Home Office plans are,' Gillard told the assembled group. 'I'm here to find out what you can tell me about Mr Afwan.'

'He's from Syria,' said one of the other men, a short fellow with a pockmarked face.

'How many of you share this house?' Gillard asked.

'Nine,' came the chorused reply. Gillard was surprised that a standard terraced Victorian house could accommodate so many people.

'Lots of little rooms,' said the tall man.

'Are any of you his friend?'

'I am,' said the short man.

'Perhaps you would tell me about him.' Gillard guided the man, whose name was Mahmood, to his car for some privacy. Over the next fifteen minutes he got a reassuring picture of Tariq Afwan, topped by an alibi. Mahmood said they had travelled together by coach to Oxford on the day of the murder. He had no evidence, but Gillard noted the times so he could check some of those details with the man himself.

Gillard arrived with DC Shireen Corey Williams at Staines police station at ten a.m. Shireen spoke some Arabic, although their understanding was that the asylum seeker who had been arrested this morning had reasonable English. Desk Sergeant Vince Babbage showed them down to the basement, where Tariq Afwan was waiting, evidently distraught, in an interview room.

'He's spent the last hour crying,' Babbage said, indicated through the glass panel. 'Thinks he's going to be sent back to Syria. He says he'll be tortured.'

The two detectives entered the room and Afwan looked up with a mixture of fear and hope in his dark, red-rimmed eyes. He was a dapper man, in his late thirties, with spectacles and a neat beard.

'I am not Isis,' were his first words. 'I did not do this thing.'

'What thing is that?' Gillard asked as he sat down at the table.

'This beheading.'

'Who told you there was a beheading?'

'I saw it on Facebook. I am friends with many other people who are friends of Mr Heath.'

Gillard exchanged a glance with Shireen. 'Look, Mr Afwan, we just want to find out a little bit more about your relationship with the Heath family.'

'Please, I want lawyer.'

'Don't worry, Mr Afwan,' Shireen said. 'I spoke to Mrs Heath this morning, and she told me you had a great friendship with them. We are simply trying to eliminate you from our enquiries.'

'This is not a formal interview,' Gillard added. 'Please, relax.'

'Relax? Police kick down house door at six in morning, shouting, running through house. How can I relax?'

'I do agree it sounds a little heavy-handed. It wasn't what I intended,' Gillard conceded. 'I apologise for that. Perhaps you can tell me where you were on Thursday afternoon?'

'In Oxford. My friend Mahmood paid for us to visit.' He showed an e-ticket on his aged smartphone. 'We went to see dreaming spires.'

Gillard nodded. It looked a solid-enough alibi, and the times matched those given by Mahmood. Mrs Heath had already said that Afwan had not been to visit them for some weeks.

Over the course of the next hour, Afwan told them his life story. How he had lived in Homs in western Syria, qualified as a paediatrician, and settled down with his wife and two children. Then came the civil war in 2011. At first his family was not involved, then his brother was picked up by the Syrian police, his body dumped in a river, with signs of torture all over it. The house was damaged when the Syrian Air Force dropped a barrel bomb nearby, and they were forced to leave for Idlib, where a cousin made room for them. Afwan became involved in emergency care in the local hospital. 'I saw little ones, poisoned by gas, foam all over their faces from the lungs. Children of two or three years old,' he said. 'It was then that I decided to escape to Britain, because in my life there was no other hope.'

He described how he had bribed smugglers to get over the border into Turkey, and then with dozens of others on a small inflatable boat to a Greek island. 'My wife and I walked carrying our two young children for six weeks, until we got stopped at the border with Croatia. We slept in the cold and the rain with just two plastic sheets to protect ourselves and went hungry for many days.'

Gillard's questions gradually dried up as the immensity of the man's odyssey emerged. There were tales of kindness, of a Macedonian taxi driver who would let the whole family sleep in his car overnight when he didn't need it, and who then smuggled them right across Croatia to the border between Slovenia and Austria. Kind people from a local church gave them shelter near Vienna, but people were not always friendly. Afwan left his wife and two children, one of whom was sick, with his Syrian neighbour's cousins in southern Germany, and made his way to England, being smuggled inside a container lorry with many others from Afghanistan.

'Why here?' asked Shireen. 'Weren't there many places in Europe where you could ask for asylum?'

He shook his head. 'I speak English, and learnt all the English words for my medical speciality. The English people are kind, I was told. They have many medics from other countries, so I thought I would be welcome.'

Gillard was touched by the man's naïveté, but also by his dogged determination. He could only imagine the effort required to get here.

'How did you meet Mr Heath and his family?'

'Through Embrace. It is for respite, where we stay with families. That is how.'

Shireen had told him about it on the way over. Embrace was a charity with a website which offered single refugees temporary placement with host families in the vicinity. Through weekends away, it sought to address the loneliness, hidden mental health issues, and poverty of refugees caught in limbo while their cases were considered by the Home Office. This could take anything up to five years, during which refugees could neither work nor receive benefits. Gillard had been surprised to hear that to avoid communal strife, the Home Office deliberately mixed up refugees in their official accommodation. Afwan lived with two teenage Sudanese boys, a blind Libyan academic of seventy, an Afghan from the minority Hazara tribe, an Iranian Christian and a gay Albanian who in contravention of the rules always had his English boyfriend over. With only a smattering of common words between them, sharing a kitchen and a bathroom was a nightmare.

'You know how much spending money they get each day?' Shireen had asked him. 'A fiver.'

'For everything?'

'No, they have a card for food up to a certain amount per week. But it doesn't cover toiletries, bus fares or anything else.'

Afwan said he'd met the Heaths two years previously, and had stayed at their home with the family a dozen times, the last being three months ago.

'Did you like him?' Shireen asked.

'Mr and Mrs Heath, I love them,' he said wiping tears from his eyes. 'This terrible thing, terrible.'

'I understand you are a practising Muslim,' Shireen said.

'Of course.' He shrugged. 'But not fanatic. No pork, no alcohol, but also no prayers in the middle of the night, no jihad nonsense.'

'Have you ever travelled in Mr Heath's Jaguar?'

'Yes, many times. He picks me up from the bus station.'

'I hope you understand that we do have to check this out,' Gillard said.

'Of course.'

'We will need you to volunteer a sample of your DNA for us to compare against what was found at the scene of the crime.'

'Now I know what will happen,' he said throwing up his arms. 'My DNA will be in the car, and police will say "Yes, he's Muslim, he must have done this thing".'

'There are many other pieces of evidence we would consider,' Gillard said levelly.

'May I look at your phone?' Shireen asked.

'Why you want see my phone?' he asked.

'It will help us verify your story,' Gillard said. 'You can have it back in half an hour.' He knew there was an Aceso Kiosk upstairs which could do it quickly. Shireen should be able to see if there was any evidence of extremist websites, or incriminating conversations in Arabic.

Gillard's gut feeling was that the refugee was not involved. As he had suspected from the start, the call to Crimestoppers may have been from someone who had an agenda. However, the next piece of evidence was more intriguing.

–

Back at Mount Browne, research intelligence officer Rob Townsend briefed Gillard on what he had found from the computers seized at the Heath household. 'I haven't had a chance for an in-depth look as yet, but there is a fair amount of pornography on one of the laptops, which from its other contents we assume to be his.'

'Not kiddies, I hope.'

'Haven't really looked through it, but based on the search terms it seems to be standard commercial stuff. Bondage, cuckold...'

'Can you remind me what that is?' Gillard asked. 'It was years ago when I went on the illegal image course.'

Townsend coloured slightly. His pale complexion and gingery hair made it easy to spot. 'It's where a guy videos his wife being… done by someone else.'

'Okay, I get it. Was it recent?'

Townsend nodded. 'It was a pretty regular search. And usually involved… males of another ethnicity.'

'All right, I get what you're driving at. I suppose we need to keep an open mind about whether stuff like this was just a fantasy or acted out for real. If it were the latter, that could be an active line of inquiry.'

'I suppose you should ask Mrs Heath,' Townsend said.

Gillard snorted with scepticism. 'I'm not in a hurry to do that, given the shock she has already endured. Just because her husband was interested in it, doesn't mean to say she was.'

Townsend nodded. 'I see your point.'

'Keep me posted on anything else of interest. Shireen is looking at the phone of their asylum seeker friend at the moment. I'll ask her to keep you in the loop.'

Once Townsend had left, Gillard looked at the log of other items found at the house. Slide projectors, cine film cameras and so on. There could be more to find.

–

Stella Heath had stayed with friends nearby that night, and it was late on Friday morning in the dining room of that neighbouring house that Gillard next spoke to the head-master's widow. Family liaison officer Gabby Underwood brought her in and went to make a coffee. Mrs Heath looked drained and pale, and said she had not slept a wink.

'Have you found anything?' she asked Gillard.

'Not so far. But these are early days. The house-to-house is really only getting going now, and the school staff interviews will take a few days too.'

Gillard had been fed a wealth of intelligence by the liaison officer. Having spent all yesterday evening and this morning with Mrs Heath, Gabby Underwood had gleaned a huge amount about her marriage. There had clearly been hints about infidelity in the past, though she said that the promotion to headmaster from head of department had made him tighten up his act. 'Those were the words she used,' Gabby had told him. 'And in the past, there was a woman, Maggie, that she hated. I think it's long over, however.'

He needed to proceed in a sensitive fashion and couldn't afford to refer to what Gabby had heard. In cases like these, where an empathic liaison officer had been used as a confidante, trust was extremely delicate. All he could hope to do was to tread a similar path and hopefully elicit similar confessions.

'Were you happy in your relationship?' he asked Mrs Heath.

'Yes, reasonably. We had our ups and downs, of course, but in the last few years things had been good. Adam was very focused and was doing a fantastic job at the school.'

'He was a head of department previously, wasn't he?' Gillard said, looking down as if checking his notes.

'Yes. English.'

'And he'd been doing that for four years, having transferred from another school in the area?'

'Yes.'

'What about your own work, Mrs Heath?'

'I teach Italian and Spanish at the local sixth form college. With Adam being so busy, I went down to three days a week.'

'And which of you is the photographer?' Gillard asked with a smile. 'I couldn't help noticing some rather good portraits in your home.'

'That was Adam.' She gave a wistful smile.

'And slides, home movies?'

'Yes. Mainly holidays, that type of thing.'

'But not exclusively?' Gillard slipped out the hint of greater knowledge, and sat back in the chair.

'It's not relevant, is it?'

'You tell me,' he said.

Stella Heath sighed and inspected the ceiling. 'This is all private.'

'The more fully informed we are the better the chance we have of catching your husband's killer.'

'I'll tell you this,' she said, leaning forward, her face suddenly animated and full of passion. 'Find that bloody woman who tried to ruin my marriage. She's the one you need. She'd been trying to take him away from me for well over a decade. It would be just like her to arrange something like this.'

Gillard sensed the deflection. Stella Heath certainly didn't want to talk about Adam's photographic hobbies. That of course didn't prove that they were significant to the crime; perhaps they were simply embarrassing. 'Do you have a name?'

'Maggie. Presumably Margaret. I don't know the surname. Adam was incredibly secretive about her. It was years before I found out. I overheard him on the phone to her.'

'What do you know about her?' Gillard asked.

'Next to nothing. I found this letter, unfinished, inside a suit jacket he had asked me to take to the dry cleaners some years ago. It was written to her from school when he should have been working.' Gillard was surprised when she reached into a pocket and produced a weathered piece of paper. She unfolded it and handed it over to him.

June 4, 2014

My dearest one,

The cacophony of 4B is just outside the door, but I'm blocking it out. I should be marking home-work, but this is a better moment to send you my love than comb through their execrable efforts to understand Shakespeare's sonnets. For all the noise, when I write to you there is a little capsule of peace, and longing for the next time we can spend some precious moments together. Finding the opportunity to write to you is increasingly hard, because home is no longer a safe space for me. I know Stella has been going through my desk ever since she found the phone message. She is on the warpath, and I count the days to when I can finally be out of this horrific marriage. And I can be with you forever, my darling.

In the meantime, I think we need to make the precautions a little tighter. I shall get a new phone, for a start, because she is suspicious of me hiding my current device from her.

Gillard read it and looked back at her. 'It's not exactly incriminating, and it is six years old.'

'Well, it's probably not the most recent one, but it's the one that I found. Obviously, there will be others in her possession.'

'Are you sure the relationship was still continuing?'

She shrugged. 'He promised me on his life that he had finished with her in May 2013, seven years ago, which as you can see is a year before this one was dated.'

'Did you confront him about this?' Gillard asked.

'Yes, we had an enormous row. We separated for a while over it.'

Maybe it wasn't the same woman. Gillard was wondering whether to ask this inflammatory question but settled for a different one. 'Do you know where this Maggie lives? What she did for a living? We would certainly like to ask her a few questions.'

The semblance of a smile passed over Stella Heath's handsome features. 'I know she lived in Guildford.'

–

While Gillard was interviewing Mrs Heath, DI Claire Mulholland and Michelle Tsu took over a classroom at St John's Academy, and with the help of the school's office staff were working their way through the list of current and former pupils who might have had a grudge against the headmaster. The interviews were brisk and brief, and mostly conducted with parents in attendance. The two boys who had theoretically assaulted Adam Heath looked utterly chastened to be interviewed by the police. Claire was absolutely certain from the moment she saw them that neither would have been capable of the horrific act that the headmaster had endured.

Kerry-Anne Phelps, the girl who had been excluded from school, was something of a different matter. Claire had read the school's notes about her, which detailed a long campaign of stalking: waiting for Heath outside his office, leaving notes on the windscreen of his car, and finally hanging around outside his home. Kerry-Anne had originally sought help over the breakup of her parents' marriage.

Escorted into the classroom by Mrs Squires, the girl strode across to the policewomen as if she was on a Paris catwalk. The faux leopard skin coat, high heels and her thick wavy blonde hair added more than a layer of glamour. The make-up was on the heavy side but looked professionally applied. It was hard to believe that she was just seventeen.

'Thank you for coming in,' Claire said, offering her a seat. After they had double-checked the dates of her attendance and later exclusion from the school, the two officers got down to business.

'I understand you are studying fashion and design now at college, is that correct?'

'Yes. I have my own YouTube channel, and 18,500 followers there and on Instagram.'

'You will be aware of what happened to Mr Heath,' Claire said.

'I'm utterly shocked,' she said. 'He was precious to me.' There were tears in her eyes.

'Do you have any idea who might have committed such an act?'

'Well…' The girl pulled out a packet of cigarettes, and languidly fitted one to her lipsticked mouth.

'You can't smoke here,' Michelle said firmly.

She lit up anyway and blew a thick plume of smoke towards the ceiling, then locked gazes with Michelle. 'I have a few ideas.' She took another drag on the cigarette

and held it out languidly to one side between long mani-
cured fingers.

Claire reached forward and took the cigarette from her
hand.

'You only had to ask for one,' the girl said, with one
shapely raised eyebrow, as she watched Claire tread out
the fag on the floor.

'If you've only come here to waste our time, you will
regret it,' Michelle said.

'I may have mentioned Adam to subsequent
boyfriends, some of whom were really quite possessive,'
Kerry-Anne said. 'They aren't schoolboys but grown
men. Who knows what they may have done? They do
tend to get rather obsessed with me, unfortunately.'

'I'm sorry, can you be clear? Subsequent boyfriends,
you say?' Michelle asked.

'Yes. But I keep their details confidential.'

'We'll get them if we need them,' Michelle said.

'Adam loved me. He used to write letters to me.'

Claire could see from the record that this accusation
had been made before.

'Do you have them?' Claire asked.

'I wouldn't sleep with him, you know,' Kerry-Anne
said. 'He wanted to, of course. They always do. But he
was married, and I wouldn't permit it.'

'But do you have any of these letters?' Claire asked,
again a question that had been asked in the past, according
to the school investigation.

'I burnt the originals, to protect him, but I learned
them off by heart.' She looked up towards the ceiling.
'"Darling Kerry-Anne, I find it so difficult to see you
every day in school and not be able to possess you, to
make love with you—"'

132

'All right, that's enough,' Claire said, exchanging a glance with Michelle. 'We'll need to take a DNA swab from you to eliminate you from our enquiries.'

The girl smiled. 'I'm happy to help.'

After the swab was taken, the two detectives watched as Kerry-Anne slowly made her way to the classroom door: tall, poised, shapely and quite deadly to the career of any male.

'A fantasist,' Michelle said.

'And no less dangerous for it,' Claire said. 'Clever enough not to make the ultimate accusation, but the potential for blackmail is quite apparent.'

Several psychiatric assessments had been made of the girl around the time of her exclusion, but the school had never been allowed to see them. Claire's initial request had also been informally rebuffed. A warrant would doubtless be required.

'Right,' said Michelle. 'The only one left to see is the arsonist, but he's got a pretty good alibi. He's in jail.'

–

Nineteen-year-old Gerald Corbett was actually in HMP Coldingley, an open prison just west of Woking, and was in the last three months of a two-year sentence for burning down a derelict warehouse. When Claire and Michelle arrived see him what they saw was a whip-thin bespectacled boy, afflicted by acne and with a half inch fuzz of dark hair which did nothing to hide his prominent ears.

Claire's immediate impression was that Corbett was almost designed to be bullied. He looked several years younger than his age, fidgeted constantly and radiated vulnerability. There was nothing in his record to indicate that he was capable of violence, not even when surrounded by baying enemies on a school playground. In his case, because of the conviction, the psychiatric reports were already available for the officers to read. A broken home, death in a road accident of an older sibling, and a very weak academic record.

The two policewomen had pretty much decided that Corbett was not their man even before they had asked the first question. When the prison governor said the prisoner was logged onto one of the jail's computers at the time of the attack, they felt their work there was complete.

Gillard was working on the whiteboard in the incident room. Around the central figure of Adam Heath he had drawn several spokes. One was labelled family, and at its centre was Stella. The other two were labelled school and private life respectively. Interviews with staff and pupils had been proceeding all day with no great insights. They now had a pretty comprehensive collection of DNA samples, which should at least start to narrow down the possibilities a little. Initial results from the car had shown half a dozen different DNA traces in the car apart from Heath's own. They included that of his wife and son. The other four were unidentified. However, the samples from staff and pupils were a good twelve hours behind those from the car and the crosscheck had not yet been made.

A more interesting email arrived in the early afternoon, from the fingerprint facility at Lewes in Sussex. CSI had submitted a series of prints found on the car. Most of these matched those of Adam Heath on the driver side and boot lid, and Stella on the passenger side.

There were a few other unidentified partial prints, but it was the next section that really attracted his interest. Glove prints on the top of the rear driver-side window showed how the perpetrator had got in, the old trick of flexing out the glass enough to slide down a wire to hook around the door release knob. But those gloves had been elsewhere. All over the rear of the driver's seat and particularly the headrest, the inside panelling of the rear driver-side door, and on the door handle both inside and out.

This was a huge piece of forensic evidence that supported Gillard's hunch that the assailant had sat in the back seat and garrotted the headmaster. Not only was the positioning of the assailant perfect for the suspected mode of attack, but the prints of the gloves themselves were of two types. There were partial latent prints, relatively clean and faint as they were on the glass, which might have been made before the attack, as well as much clearer prints which had a deep series of transverse impressions across the palm which indicated wire or some other ligature had been wound tightly around them. Bloodstains on the index finger and thumb of the left hand further identified the movements of the assailant immediately post-attack. There was one single bloodied thumbprint on the driver-side front door handle, which matched two fingertip marks on the underside lifting flap.

It was clear that the team at Lewes had done a terrific job, as had CSI in spotting and recovering such a clear series of marks. Gillard was aware that Derbyshire Police and Nottingham Trent University had together with the Home Office begun a project for a national database of glove types. He wasn't particularly expecting that these gloves might have been used in another crime, but he forwarded the email anyway to see if there was any extra information that they might extract.

He then called up Yaz Quoroshi, head of CSI, and congratulated him on his team's work.

'Thank you. I'm very impressed with what the technicians at Lewes have managed to do,' Quoroshi said modestly. 'It's almost possible to see the timeline of the attack, putting together each hand movement from whoever was hiding in the back right up to the garrotting and subsequent escape.'

'It's terrific work, but one part of it puzzled me for a while,' Gillard said. 'Why the attacker needed to open the driver's door at all.'

'Yes, it's not obvious, is it? Once he's killed the victim, and then used the knife to cut off the head, why open that door?'

'I think I got it eventually. It was to retrieve the head. It would be slippery with blood and quite heavy and might well have fallen into the victim's lap.'

'That's a good point. I had assumed the head would have been retrieved by reaching from behind the driver's seat.'

'I don't think there was enough blood on the rear seat to account for that,' Gillard said. 'But the front of Heath's shirt and his trousers were absolutely drenched.'

'Either way the logistics of this exercise are quite grisly,' Quoroshi said. 'I don't understand why they would go to the trouble of taking the head. There is no practical purpose, because the body was going to be easily identified, sitting in his own car in his own drive.'

Gillard too was aware that almost all cases of mutilated bodies in British crime were gangland associated murders where by removing the head and sometimes hands, the perpetrators hoped to delay identification of the victim. 'Perhaps it was a trophy?' he said.

'What about the terrorism angle? Is there any connection between Heath and Islamists?' Quoroshi asked.

'I put in a request to the Met's counterterrorism unit and have been told informally that they can't find any connection. There are half a dozen notionally Muslim pupils at the school, but according to the staff there is no evidence of any contentious issues around teaching, images of the Prophet, controversial documents or assemblies. The biggest issue the school was facing was over a transgender pupil, and they were scrambling to put together a policy that made sense. Again, that is simply what I've been told by the staff,' Gillard said.

'So probably nothing to do with the pupils then,' Quoroshi said.

'I'm not so sure,' Gillard replied. 'Those gloves weren't large. Medium, or small even.'

Gillard heard the sharp intake of breath at the other end. 'Could a child be capable of a crime like this?' Quoroshi asked.

'A psychopath child certainly, a clever and determined one. But the killing method is so foolproof, he wouldn't have had to be particularly strong.'

–

Matthew Heath, son of the victim, was met at Reading Station by his mother, accompanied by family liaison officer Gabby Underwood. Matthew was a strapping lad of at least six foot two, with hands to match. The gloves would not have been his. His upset was palpable, he had an alibi and Gillard decided there was no rush to interview him.

Gillard was much more concerned by the lack of progress in getting a description of anyone in the vicinity of the Heath home at the time of the attack. It didn't help that so many of the homes in his street had large front gardens and high hedges. The profusion of alleyways between crescents, closes and cul-de-sacs behind his home was an even bigger obstacle. If the murderer had left on foot, which was the best way to avoid standing out, there were no less than four different residential streets that could be reached in five minutes' walk via the alleyways. Statements had now been taken from fifty schoolchildren who lived in the surrounding areas, but the overwhelming majority of them claimed already to have been home by the time that Adam Heath left the school. While the school was big enough that no pupil would know every other attendee, no one reporting seeing unknown adults or children who weren't wearing the school uniform.

As the statements came in gradually over the course of the afternoon, Gillard's frustration mounted. DCs Carrie 'Rainy' Macintosh and Carl Hoskins, the Laurel and Hardy of the team, came in at half past four, having already sent in a further twelve statements to the major inquiry system.

'No one saw anything,' Hoskins said, as he slumped down his crumb-flecked chair, and set his tablet computer on the desk.

'There wasnae much light and the alleyways are so overgrown that a lot of the parents tell their kids not to use them, though I wouldnae expect that to make much difference,' Rainy said.

'It beggars belief, doesn't it?' asked Gillard. 'The culprit might well have been drenched in blood, and carrying, presumably in some kind of bag, a heavy human head.

But we can't find even a single drip on the pavement or tarmac.'

'CSI is still working up and down that alleyway,' Hoskins said. 'There's over a hundred yards of it, so it'll be taped off for a while yet.'

At that moment Gillard's phone pinged. It was a text from Kirsty Mockett, with a photograph attached. *Look what I've found! It was at ankle height at the narrowest part of the alleyway behind Adam Heath's house.*

The photograph was of a sprig of privet hedge, with a faint red smear across the myriad tiny leaves.

Blood.

So the perpetrator *had* exited via the alleyway.

Chapter Thirteen

The bloodstained leaves were sent off for DNA analysis, and the remaining uniformed cops revisited all the homes that bordered the relevant alleyway, asking once again for witnesses, and permission to search the gardens behind the hedge. Gillard reckoned Kirsty Mockett had been very clever to concentrate on that part of the alley where untrimmed edges closed in so it was little more than three feet wide. It was logical that this was the place where the assailant might not be able to pass through without contact. The fact that the smear was at ankle height might indicate the severed head was being carried in some kind of bag, and the flank of that receptacle would be the widest part of the fleeing perpetrator.

Gillard emailed her his congratulations and copied the photograph to several others on the sprawling inquiry. Tomorrow was Saturday, and as soon as it was light he wanted to be back at the crime scene, looking more closely at the various residential streets which the alleyway led to.

–

Dr David Delahaye rang Gillard just after he finished the post-mortem on Adam Heath. After exchanging pleasantries, the forensic pathologist said: 'I don't suppose you happen to have a spare head lying about the place? It would make the toxicology report a little more comprehensive and a look at his eyeballs for petechiae would be useful.'

This dry comment was the nearest Delahaye ever got to making a joke.

'Sorry, David, we are doing all we can to try and find it,' Gillard replied.

'Well, there is nothing I have found to contradict your theory that the victim was garrotted. There are distended veins in the lower neck, petechiae in the chest and lungs, along with some foam. These are all symptoms of asphyxiation. As you are no doubt aware, a good chunk of the neck was removed along with the head, the cut having been made at the C2 vertebra, so we don't have the part of the throat that was constrained by the ligature. His left hand shows deep indentations across the index and middle fingertips, which could be evidence that he managed to insert them under the ligature.'

'Any ideas what was used to garrotte him?'

'Something quite fine. Possibly fishing line, but more likely picture wire; there is some evidence of twist texture on one of the fingers, which would have me lean towards the latter.'

'Anything else come to light?'

'Marks on the remaining vertebrae indicate a serrated knife or possibly a small saw was used as well as a more conventional blade. It must have been sharp because the cuts were quite clean.'

'Evidence of professional skills would you say?'

'It's hard to be sure. A strong stomach, certainly. There would have been plenty of blood.' The pathologist sighed. 'Otherwise not much to report. Slight enlargement of the liver, indicative of prolonged alcohol consumption, nothing too unusual for a man of his age. Basic toxicology shows nothing untoward. He was generally in quite good condition.'

'That fits in with what we've heard about him. He was a keen cyclist and had played rugby for a couple of amateur teams up until his forties.'

Gillard mentally ran through what they knew so far about the killer. 'Whoever it was had an interesting collection of attributes: not noticeable in a school environment, yet able to get into the car and hide there waiting for the victim. Small to medium hands, the good sense to wear gloves, and enough strength and determination to go through with the killing.'

'I agree with you that from the vantage point of the rear seat, the victim would very quickly have been helpless even against someone much less strong when he was,' Delahaye said. 'Have you got anything from the DNA?'

'Nothing conclusive. Apart from the family, there are quite a few traces inside the car. We're expecting the matches for various school colleagues and some of the pupils to come back in the next few hours. That should give us a little more to go on.'

'Are you thinking it might be a pupil or ex-pupil?' Delahaye said.

'Reluctantly, I am being dragged in that direction,' Gillard said. 'It is the gloves that worry me most. We have so many glove prints we're really quite sure. A man with big hands cannot squeeze them into child-sized gloves and still do the job. Which leaves a couple of possibilities. A small woman or, just possibly, a child.'

–

Fresh from her discovery in the alleyway, crime scene investigator Kirsty Mockett had picked her way through Adam Heath's garden. It was now getting too dark to see much, and as she was finishing her shift in half an hour, there seemed no point in setting up artificial lights. Most of her colleagues were now shrugging their way out of their Tyvek suits and getting ready to knock off. But in her case one discovery prompted a new line of thinking. The back gate from Heath's garden into the alleyway was a solid six-foot-high hardwood construction, which fitted snugly into the seven-foot box hedge. It was secured with a hefty padlock, seemingly new and uncorroded. The padlock was at waist height, with an older but carefully oiled bolt at the top. She had managed to get prints from both these and had sent them off to Lewes for analysis.

She next turned her attention to the small and secluded summer house, a Swiss-style structure 6' x 10' with its own mini balcony and mildewed glass windows in wooden frames. It too was padlocked. A path of flagstones led from the kitchen door to the summer house and then on to the back gate. Kirsty went back to find Yaz Quoroshi, who would have the key. She would just have time to do some DNA samples and collect a few prints from inside.

-

It was six o'clock on the Friday evening when Gillard got a phone call from Chief Constable Alison Rigby. One of the new wave of assertive female bosses, she had a stellar reputation from her time at the National Crime Agency, where she had broken open a major drug ring. She had taken a keen interest in Operation Whirlwind and the arrest of Bonner, but this was the first call she had made to Gillard in relation to the beheading case.

'How's it going?' Rigby asked. Gillard described the main leads so far and the lack of obvious motivation. 'Adam Heath looks to have had something of a past, but I'm holding off looking into that too closely until I get the full cross-match results of DNA from staff and pupils, which should come in the next few hours.'

This was exactly the same report that he had given to his direct boss, Detective Chief Superintendent Brian 'Radar' Dobbs. Tall and moustachioed, he was considered diligent if unimaginative. Gillard had reported to him for several years, but still didn't know what exactly his superior did all day besides push paper.

'Could it be the wife?' Rigby asked.

'I can't entirely rule her out. There is plenty of potential for motivation, but there would be much easier ways for her to have murdered him. The beheading makes it logistically complex and messy, and somebody must have really wanted to do it that way.'

'I quite agree. However, I'm concerned about the press coverage, which has played very heavily on the potential Islamic element. I want you to make sure that your team are all on the same page about this – there's enough minority community alarm about this already. Even though there's no one in the counterterrorism branch involved in the investigation, I wouldn't be surprised if they are feeding information to the press on the quiet. Reporters have been besieging Mr Afwan.'

'I'm very sorry to hear that, ma'am. I can only speak for my officers, but I'll make sure that we're singing off the same hymn sheet.'

–

As soon as he'd finished the call, Gillard rang Sam. 'I can be away by 7.30 p.m. tonight. Shall we go out to dinner?'

'That's great!' she replied. She'd only been back at work a few days but was already beginning to get into her stride. Her kidnapping ordeal the previous spring had cast a shadow over the entire year, and only now were her energy and enthusiasms beginning to return to those of her old self. With a big case like this, it was extremely rare for her husband to get home at a reasonable time. Sam had now restarted exercise classes and had begun an Open University course in criminology. When they had first met, Sam had been a community support officer, but the work she now did at the control room made her feel at the centre of activities.

They hadn't been to the Palace Tandoori for over a year, but the owner, a chubby Indian who went by the name Sid, short for Siddharth, remembered them well. They ordered the Friday Feast, which included onion pakoras, shami kebabs, poppadoms and pickle tray, and a mixed tandoori platter of lamb, chicken and king prawns, which arrived sizzling and smoking on a cast-iron dish. They both ate as if starving and were given a complimentary mango lassi each by Sid. As Gillard thanked him, Sid leaned close and said: 'I'm mortified about this beheading down the road. It's not good for us.'

'Why, has something happened?'

'Dog mess through the letterbox. Flyers returned with racial stuff and "go home" scrawled on it. I've been here fifty-two years, and I'm still treated by some people like I arrived yesterday. I'm Hindu not Muslim anyway, but they don't seem to care.'

'We're really sorry to hear that,' Sam said. 'People can be so horrible.'

'What was the response when you reported this?' Gillard asked.

Sid rolled his eyes. 'I didn't report it. Racial hatred works in cycles, and I've seen a few of them, I can tell you. But I also know from experience that unless someone is hurt, I don't get much joy from the local bobbies. Even though I've got CCTV which shows a bloke in a baseball cap, jacket and trainers shoving stuff through the letterbox.'

'If you can email a section of video to me, I can forward it, and then I promise you, there will be some action.'

Once Sid had departed, Gillard shook his head. 'I know that we've had severe staff cuts over the last few years, but this kind of thing really annoys me.'

Sam reached forward and rested her hand on his. 'I know. But you can't do it all yourself.' Then she smiled at him and shook her head.

–

First thing on Saturday morning a great stack of DNA results came through. It indicated that three members of staff had been in Adam Heath's car, each in the front seat. The traces found in the rear driver-side seat didn't match anyone at the school, nor the two troublesome ex-pupils, Kerry-Anne Phelps and Gerald Corbett. Neither of them showed up in any of the DNA or fingerprint matches.

Gillard sat at his desk at Mount Browne with mounting disappointment. He had hoped for some clear evidence. A second sheaf of results from a different lab showed that the bloodstains on the privet hedge sprig matched those in the car. That was something, at least. With them was a series of DNA matches from the summer house in Adam

Heath's garden. Here, as well as Adam and Stella Heath, there were traces that matched a member of staff, Mrs Ingrid Taylor. Looking back to the first results, he saw that her DNA had also been in the car, the only member of staff apart from the deputy head Mrs Squires, and the head of geography, Thomas Murphy.

He called up a staff photograph taken from an online school yearbook, which had kindly been captioned for him by Mrs Squires. Ingrid Taylor was standing on the back row of three, and only her face could be seen. Zooming in as much as he could, Gillard reckoned the woman was in her thirties. Looking back through the statements and background material, he established that she lived some distance away, and was quite a junior member of staff. He didn't want to jump to conclusions, but this looked significant. One thing he didn't want to do at this stage was to upset Stella Heath by asking her if she knew why Ingrid Taylor had been in their summer house.

Instead, he rang the woman herself at home.

After introducing himself, and explaining that he was following up on her statement and samples he asked: 'Mrs Taylor, your DNA has turned up in Mr Heath's car and in the summer house in the garden.' He didn't ask a question, but left an expanding silence at the other end.

'Is there something you want to tell me, Mrs Taylor?'

'Adam gave me a lift home a couple of times.'

There were questions enough about this considering where she lived, but Gillard pressed on. 'Why were you in the Heaths' summer house?'

'Gosh, I can't think. Perhaps last summer, when they had a garden party.'

'Do you remember the date?'

'No, I'm sorry.'

'I can tell you that there was more of your DNA found there than that of Stella Heath. And none of any other members of staff at the school.'

'I can't explain that,' she said coolly.

–

Gillard called an incident room meeting for 9.30 a.m. with an enhanced whiteboard diagram. He had added Ingrid Taylor and 'Maggie' to the spokes emanating from Adam Hogarth's box. Red dots showed where a DNA connection had been made, and green had been added for those, like Kerry-Anne Phelps and Gerald Corbett, who seemed to be in the clear.

It being the weekend there wasn't a full crew gathered there. DCs Rainy Macintosh and Carl Hoskins sat side by side, sharing what smelled like bacon sandwiches. Research intelligence officer Rob Townsend was there with DS Vikram Singh, who was the evidence officer. DI Mulholland and DC Michelle Tsu were off duty until the evening shift.

'Okay everyone. We've made some good progress forensically. There's not much mystery now about how Adam Heath died. The post-mortem pretty much confirms what I suspected, that he was garrotted with a wire from behind by someone who was presumably hiding in the footwell of the car.'

'Someone with tiny wee hands,' Rainy said.

'But who knew how to break into a 1985 Jag,' Hoskins said.

'Maybe they had a key,' she replied, taking another bite of her sandwich and looking at her colleague. 'Or made one, like an evil wee elf.'

'No, the glove prints seem to indicate it might have been a wire loop break-in,' Gillard said. 'As far as we can tell, this person must have been in the car for some time, probably getting in when it was parked at the school. This strongly suggests that whoever did it was not worried about being identified.'

'Och, are you really suggesting the culprit is a schoolkid?' Rainy asked incredulously.

'Or a member of staff, possibly,' Townsend added.

'Yeah, but how many schoolteachers know the wire loop trick,' Hoskins said.

'No, I'm not saying anything—' Gillard began.

'What if Heath had stopped to give someone a lift?' Singh asked.

'It's only a two- or three-minute journey home,' Hoskins said.

'Yes, but we don't know that he went straight home, do we?' Singh replied.

Gillard nodded. 'We haven't had any reports of the vehicle being spotted off its normal route. Indeed, the only corroboration of that short journey we have is the periphery of a piece of CCTV from a parade of suburban shops, which shows the car passing. That footage shows no sign of any passengers, front or back.'

'It's the beheading that gets me,' Townsend said with incredulity. 'Why would anyone do that?'

'They'd really have to hate him,' Hoskins said. 'And they must have had a strong stomach.'

'There might be a message there,' Gillard said. 'Based on the original name of the school.'

He had everyone's attention. 'Has everyone heard of Salomé?' Gillard asked.

Hoskins whispered something to Rainy. 'Not salami, yer wee bampot,' she muttered back at him. 'It was only sliced once.'

Gillard continued. 'It's the biblical account that Herod was so impressed by Salomé dancing, he offered her anything she wanted. And she chose the head of John the Baptist, on a platter.'

Hoskins chuckled. 'Call me weird, but I would have gone for the prawn dhansak instead.'

'The school these days is called St John's Academy, but four years ago it was still called St John the Baptist,' Gillard said. There was an 'aah' of recognition across the assembled detectives.

'And Adam Heath was the head,' said Rob.

'So they didnae just want the head, but the head of the head,' Rainy said.

'It's a very dark sense of humour,' DS Singh said.

'Aye, I'm laughing my head off,' Rainy said.

Gillard held up his hands for quiet. 'The point of all this is: if this is a deliberate message, who is our Salomé?'

–

Later that morning, DS Singh arrived back from a trip to the Heath household with a stack of evidence bags and boxes on a trolley. 'What have you discovered, Vikram?' Gillard asked.

'I've been documenting the paperwork and non-electronic evidence from the house. I also went into the loft and found a whole treasure trove of other stuff including Adam Heath's photo collection, and it's very interesting.'

'Tell me more.'

'It's clear that the Heaths had a very free and open relationship. There are lots of pictures of them at what looks like a naturist camp when they were young, and there are hundreds of pictures of Mrs Heath in the nude. I guess you would call most of it artistic, and he's certainly a pretty good photographer. But I also found a box of Polaroids, in which Mrs Heath is in compromising positions with a number of different black guys.'

'You didn't find any videos, did you Rob?' Gillard asked.

'No. There's nothing digital like that. I think this stuff is quite old, late 1990s or early 2000s maybe. Pre-Internet most of it,' Singh said.

Gillard sighed. 'Well, I guess I will have to tackle Mrs Heath about it, because it's an obvious line of inquiry. While I'm at it, I'm going to ask about Ingrid Taylor. That might come as a bit of a shock to her.'

'Poor woman,' Townsend said.

'Did you find any love letters, Vikram?' Gillard asked.

'No. I was looking out for them, after what you said about Mrs Taylor. Of course, he may have hidden them carefully to avoid his wife finding them.'

Gillard became aware that Rainy Macintosh was waiting to speak to him. He had asked her to look in more detail at the idea that the killer was classically educated, and trying to make some sick joke.

'I've looked up the biblical reference, sir. New Testament references say that St John the Baptist was imprisoned by Herod because he had condemned the king for divorcing his wife and marrying his sister-in-law. Salomé was, through this relationship, Herod's stepdaughter.'

'Most of what I remember is from the Dance of the Seven Veils,' Gillard said. 'Like an early version of striptease in the Hollywood film, I recall.'

'Aye, that was based on an Oscar Wilde play from the 1890s.'

'If the murderer is trying to tell us something, apart from how clever they are, what is it?'

'That the killer is a woman, perhaps?' Rainy said.

Gillard pursed his lips. 'Hmm. Salomé ordered the killing, but didn't carry it out.'

'Och, maybe there's a better connection with another biblical beheading. Judith seducing then killing the Assyrian general Holofernes, who enslaved her people. I was gobsmacked when I saw the painting by Artemisia Gentileschi in the National Gallery in London a few months ago. I've just emailed you a copy.'

The two detectives called up the image on his screen. 'Good God, it's incredibly savage,' Gillard exclaimed. The Baroque painting unflinchingly depicted two women holding down a struggling man while one of them pulled a sword through his throat. These women were not passive, submissive creatures but powerful and determined, centuries ahead of their time.

'Aye, and the woman who painted it was just seventeen, destined to become the most famous female painter of the seventeenth century but already a victim of rape. She gave evidence in a trial, but despite conviction her accuser went free with the backing of the Pope.'

'So she painted her revenge,' Gillard breathed. He looked at Rainy and said, 'We're getting the impression that Adam Heath was a lecherous individual. I just wonder if any of this is connected?'

Gabby Underwood had fed DCI Gillard plenty of useful information about Stella Heath in the two days since the murder. The family liaison officer was looking for details of her marriage which might give a clue to the killer, but her main observation, relayed to Gillard by phone, was the wave of anger breaking through the woman's grief. 'There is fury with her late husband, but even more focused on this Maggie woman, whom she is convinced is the killer.'

'That sounds reasonable.'

'She is also getting very impatient about not being allowed to return to her home and keeps asking how much longer she will have to wait,' Gabby said.

At three p.m. on Saturday Gillard joined Gabby in visiting Mrs Heath at the neighbours' house where she had been staying. Her son Matthew answered the door, and asked if he could sit in on the interview.

'No, I'm sorry, I can't allow it,' Gillard said. 'I need to speak to your mother alone.'

'If she's a suspect, she'd like a solicitor to be present.' The lad was clearly trying to support his mother, but the last thing Gillard wanted to do was to ask about her sex life in front of him.

'She's not a suspect, and this isn't a formal interview.'

In the end Gillard interviewed Mrs Heath in the chilly sun lounge of the house, where the closed uPVC doors gave them some privacy.

Mrs Heath had made herself up and done her hair. She was a handsome woman, and from the couple of photographs he had seen, she'd been quite something when she was younger.

'Mrs Heath, I need to ask you some questions of a delicate nature to at least close off some possible lines of inquiry. I will only be making notes by hand, and I can assure you that if this turns out not to be relevant, it will go no further.'

Her face tightened, and she lifted her chin to prepare for the revelation.

'We have found some intimate photographs. Perhaps you'd like to tell us about them, and when they were taken.'

There was a long silence. 'There was a brief period in our lives, more than a decade ago, when our marriage was on the rocks. I had suspected that Adam was having an affair, and he admitted to a brief fling, although as it turned out it was more than that. Far more.' She paused and examined her nails. 'He said that he needed more adventure in our love life. We talked about things, what he wanted and what I wanted, and with some trepidation I agreed to some threesomes. I'm sorry, this is very embarrassing for me to talk about now.'

'That's why I wouldn't let Matthew sit in.'

She looked up at him. 'Thank you, I appreciate that.'

'How did you find the new partners?'

'Adam found them. He subscribed to a specialist magazine and website. I really didn't want to know the details, but I did insist that we meet the... candidates in advance at a neutral venue.'

Gillard said nothing.

Stella looked out of the window. 'I had thought that all three of us would be in bed together, but in the event Adam just watched and took photographs. I think I had some sixth sense about it, because my one insistence was that nothing digital would ever be recorded.'

'Very wise. Did you keep in contact with any of the men?'

'There was one very handsome guy, an absolutely charming Trinidadian, who made it clear he wanted to have an affair with me. He approached me a couple of times after it was all over, but I'd gone into this thing to save my marriage, not to destroy it. It was a means to an end, but it was clear that Adam was getting a lot more out of it than I was. He would look at the Polaroids quite a lot and constantly wanted to talk to me about it afterwards, while we were in bed. It really turned him on, and just knowing that turned me off.'

'You have the guy's name, the Trinidadian?'

'Only his first name. Charles. We only used first names. I've no address or anything, unless you can find it amongst Adam's paperwork.'

Gillard finished writing his notes and looked up at her. She was staring levelly at him. 'That's really everything I want to say about that subject,' she said to him. 'It all finished in 2005 or 2006. I can't see it's relevant to what happened to Adam.'

'Perhaps I can also ask you about Kerry-Anne Phelps…'

Stella rolled her eyes. 'What a nasty little piece of work she is.'

'Do you think your husband had an affair with her?'

'No. He vehemently denied it, and on this occasion I do believe him. Adam may have been a philanderer, but he wasn't stupid. To have sex with a pupil would be an idiotic thing to do. But it's certainly true that she used to hang around the school car park to speak to him, wait for him outside his office, send letters to the house. She wrote him poetry which, annoyingly, was quite good. She's very bright but very disturbed.'

'How long did it last?' Gillard asked.

She rounded on him. 'You make it sound like "a thing", detective chief inspector. But it is not a single thing, it is two quite separate things, and those things are a long way apart. First thing: a crush, existing only in her head, and probably still there. Second thing: Adam's awareness of it, as a career headache, dealt with and over, many months ago.'

'All right, let me rephrase. When did Adam say he was first aware of her interest in him?'

'About two years ago, Adam found her in tears behind the science block, self-harming with a pair of compasses. She gave him some heart-wrenching tale of the breakup of her parents' marriage, and begged him not to refer her through the formal channels. She'd had a bad experience with a school psychologist. If Adam made an error of judgement, it was to see her twice more, alone, at the girl's request, because she felt suicidal. However, he told me about it right from the start, and kept a formal log which Mrs Squires retained.'

'Sounds squeaky clean.'

'Oh my goodness, he had to be. Kerry-Anne is very clever, and I think she was trying to blackmail him into having a relationship. I suppose you would say that Adam was a father substitute for her.'

'Did he ever give her a lift in the car?' Gillard asked.

'I'm pretty sure he didn't, because he knew it would have been stupid. However, the log he left with Mrs Squires would give all the details. He had prepared his defence against Kerry-Anne well in advance, anticipating that at some stage she would claim he had abused her. The whole thing was like a game of chess. He had to choose the moment to exclude her from school very carefully, knowing that she was capable of making some very detailed and believable allegations.'

'I have a few other details to put you,' Gillard said. He and Gabby glanced briefly at each other, knowing that this was the critical point of the interview. 'Do you know Mrs Ingrid Taylor, from the languages department?'

'Vaguely.' Her eyes narrowed, trying to work out what was coming.

'Has she ever been to your home?'

'We had a garden party in the summer, to which she and her husband were invited. Why do you ask?'

'A lot of her DNA has been found together with your husband's inside the summer house.'

Stella Heath gave a sharp cry and let her face fall to her hands. Gillard had often been required to reveal unpleasant truths within relationships. To hapless women, usually. Mrs Heath was a big girl emotionally, and she had clearly made huge personal sacrifices to try to save her marriage. For her to discover that for all her efforts it was not enough must have been shattering.

Gabby put her arm around the woman, who was now sobbing uncontrollably. 'I'll go and make some coffee,' Gillard said, watching while his family liaison officer fed tissues one after another to the distraught woman.

As the detective made his way from the sun lounge into the dining room, letting Stella's howls of anguish fill the house, Matthew Heath appeared in the kitchen doorway, braced as if for a fight, fists flexing. His stare of hatred directed at Gillard didn't quite mask the tears in his own eyes.

'What have you said to her?'

'I have brought her the truth. I do accept it is the messenger's job to be shot at.'

Matthew pushed past and went in to comfort his mother. Gillard left the house and walked three doors up to the Heath house, where a female PC was on guard. 'The family are going to be allowed to come back from tonight,' he told her.

Gillard returned to his car for the journey back to Mount Browne. He closed his eyes, stretched and sighed. He had immersed himself in the murder of Adam Heath for almost forty-eight hours and was already at the stage where he couldn't quite see the wood for the trees. There were motives, yes. Two spurned lovers, at least, only one of whom had been identified. Even she was saying nothing. The wife, even. She had a good reason to hate her phil-andering husband. Certainly, the likeliest motive in the case seemed to be love or jealousy. Money seemed not to be a part of it. If this had been a stabbing, even a poisoning, it might all make sense.

But a beheading?

The biggest mystery of the entire case was the sheer savagery of the killing, a grotesque, unnecessary and risky MO. Where was that head? Two nearby canals had been dragged, underwater search teams had begun to grope their way through ponds, reservoirs and gravel pits as far away as Hampshire. No disembodied head had so far been found. No one had seen the assailant, but he or perhaps she had left clues. DNA, in all likelihood, too. The one so far unidentified trace found in the rear footwell. Then there were the smears of the victim's blood on the alleyway foliage, and the glove prints.

He'd love to find those gloves.

Chapter Fourteen

Peter Welland was a long-standing friend of Adam Heath's. They had played rugby together until their mid-30s when Welland was posted abroad, working in Dubai for a British multinational. In latter years he had kept contact with Adam mainly online, but they had met for the odd drink in London when Welland was passing through. DI Claire Mulholland had taken Welland's call and offer of help as it was passed through to the incident room, and noted down the details of their friendship. Welland was en route from Dubai to New York but was staying in a Heathrow hotel. She arranged to see him that evening in the hotel lounge.

Welland was instantly recognisable to her from the LinkedIn profile she'd seen and waved to her from a secluded table at the far end of a very quiet bar. Fiftyish, tall and heftily built, he had a cauliflower ear partially hidden under a thatch of snowy hair, presumably testament to time served in the scrum. A florid face, together with the already drained pint glass in front of him, hinted at his drinking habits and perhaps some high blood pressure too. He offered to buy Claire a drink, but she declined.

'I'm absolutely astounded that this has happened to him,' he volunteered, as she was getting out her notebook. 'I've worked in Saudi, and in the Kurdish oilfields of Iraq in the past. Not during particularly dangerous moments, but if anyone had said that it was him, a Home Counties schoolmaster, who was going to get beheaded rather than me, I would have said they were mad.' He then made several clumsy attempts to try to find out non-public elements of the investigation, ending with: 'I suppose it was some Muslim kid at the school.'

'As I said, I can't share anything with you that hasn't been cleared by my boss,' she said. 'But again, the fact that the counterterrorism branch is not involved should give you some idea which direction we're leaning in.'

'Fair enough,' he said, scratching his head. 'Poor Stella, she must be in a terrible state.'

Claire nodded. 'Would you say you were a friend of them both, or just him?'

Welland waggled his hand and creased his face into a sceptical grimace. 'Him, mainly. I think in later years she imagined that I led him into bad ways, on our occasional pub crawls. But actually it was all quite innocent.'

'Did he ever say to you that he thought his life was in danger?'

'No. His career, yes, once.'

Claire raised her eyebrows quizzically.

'A year or so ago, there was this hot girl in school pursuing him.' He shook his head and blew out his cheeks. 'Deadly stuff, these days. Particularly for a schoolteacher.' Welland couldn't repress a grin, which seemed to indicate he would have preferred the old days. He saw Claire's expression, and explained himself. 'I saw a photograph of the girl she had sent him. Any red-blooded male would have been tempted. But school-wise he was squeaky clean, was Adam.'

'Did Mr Heath confide in you about his marriage?'

'Yes. I think it's fair to say that he wasn't happy in recent years. He wanted out.'

'We understand he did have affairs.'

Welland nodded. 'Yes, quite a few, over the years. Not so much recently, not once he was promoted to headmaster. He quietened down all-round I suppose. There was this long-standing relationship, totally top-secret, however. He even had a false name for the woman.'

'Do you remember what it was?'

He squinted into the middle distance. 'Nope. Always been hopeless with names.'

'Maggie?'

'Ah yes, that could be right. Or Kat, Katherine perhaps? Something to do with cats sticks in my memory.'

'Did you meet her?'

'Once, briefly. I thought she was nice. Very clever, great sense of humour. Nice legs too.' He grinned.

'Can you tell me anything else about her? What she did for a living, where she lived?'

He shook his head. 'It was a long time ago now.'

'So what happened to that relationship?'

'Same as happened to them all. He got bored and ended it. She was getting a bit clingy. Oh God, but it went on for years and years. A right old drama, in one hundred episodes.' Welland shook his head and stared at his empty glass. 'You'd never have guessed it all, to look at him. He didn't look like the kind of bloke who would have a complicated love life.'

'Can you think of anyone who would want to harm him?'

He shrugged. 'Only Stella, if she ever found out everything he'd got up to. No, seriously I don't believe that. She's a nice woman. I'll be honest with you, I used to fancy her like crazy at one time. She was hot stuff. Some of the things I could tell you.' He shook his head in disbelief. 'Christ, I can't believe he's dead, you know?'

'Was he ever in debt? Cross someone in a property deal? Get threatened by the husband of a girlfriend?'

Welland shook his head. 'Not that he told me.'

'Did he ever take drugs? Recreational cocaine, anything like that?'

'If he did, he didn't tell me.' Welland pointed at his pint. 'That was his poison in the early days, and it remains mine. In fact, if you'll excuse me, I'll get another one in.'

Claire waited for the big man to return from the bar, by which time half the new pint was already gone. 'Can you pass my details across to Stella?' he said, passing her a business card. 'I only had Adam's email, and want to know when the funeral is. There weren't many like Adam Heath.'

'Well, he will certainly be remembered,' she said. 'If you have the contact details for any of his other friends, would you forward them to me? I got a list from Mrs Heath, but you never know if it's complete or not. Sometimes secret friends know the most.'

Welland nodded, and as she stood to leave shook her hand.

'The secret friend Maggie is the one you want to find,' he said. 'And as I remember now, she was a professional. Accountant or something. The only woman in the office with a bunch of stuffy men. If I can dig up any more details, I'll email you.'

—

Stella Heath was on a mission. The moment her house keys were returned to her, she took her own home apart.

Matthew was out for the evening with some friends, so she would have several hours to herself. She ignored the phone, which rang every few minutes. The police had been through and taken all the obvious stuff. Photo albums as well as computers, boxes of slides as well as iPads. But she had the advantage of knowing her husband. From the stacks of pornographic magazines she had found under a suitcase on top of a tall wardrobe in the early years of her marriage, through to the condoms she had found in a grimy old chest of drawers in the garage seven years ago. She knew every cavity of depravity. The Ingrid Taylor news had been a slap in the face. Why had she ever believed that leopards change their spots? Stupid of her, absolutely stupid. She been a fool for the full twenty-seven years of their marriage. Swallowing the lies, believing the promises, hoping that Adam had a better nature to appeal to.

Where to look? She had been through Adam's office on many occasions, the garage too, which he kept deliberately filthy to keep her away. She had steeled herself to investigate almost everywhere. There was only one place left, and the police had already been there. The loft. She had an idea what she was looking for and exactly where she would find it. But first, to get up there. She had always been a little scared of heights, but if Adam had installed a proper pull-down aluminium ladder, she would have tackled the fear. The fact that there was still only a rickety stepladder made her believe that any secrets that remained in his life she would find up there, where he thought she wouldn't go. The police had brought their own ladder and taken it away again after they had finished rooting around.

Stella dressed in overalls and old trainers, went to the spare bedroom, and pulled out the grubby wooden stepladder. With some difficulty she manoeuvred it out onto the landing underneath the wooden hatch. She spread the steps and climbed as far as she could. This was the third step from the top, and standing on it her head touched the hatch. She knew that Adam had never hinged the heavy blockboard lid. She braced her hands against the lid, and pushed. A draught of cool air, laden with dust, swept her face as the lid lifted off the architraved sill. She now needed to mount another step before sliding it to one side. As she lifted the lid to the right, the stepladder creaked, and she could feel it slightly off-balance, one of its forefeet no longer in contact with the carpet. She had no hand free to steady herself and settled for just pushing the lid halfway onto the rafters. Hands now free, she clambered up to the top step, sliding her torso through the restricted space, easing the hatch further to one side. There was supposed to be a light, but in the darkness she couldn't see where the switch was. She retreated down the steps and into the garage, until she found a torch.

Once back on the stepladder, she ascended to the highest step and shone the light within. The loft looked surprisingly clean and well organised, the floor boarded out and holding many boxes. The light switch, she now saw, had been mounted in almost deliberate awkwardness on a high timber almost directly above the hatch. It would have been easy for Adam to reach, but for her almost impossible. It would require her to stand with a leg each side of the open hatch, on tiptoe.

Stella reached up to the lip of the hatch, took a deep breath, and pulled herself upwards. Once she was propped with her arms locked, her feet dangled, unable to reach the top step of the stepladder. Only by gingerly placing each foot on the two higher hinges of the ladder was she able to climb any higher. She did so carefully, and then eased her bottom onto the edge of the hatch. Then she was able to roll to one side, place the torch down, and slide the hatch back into its hole for safety.

Finally able to safely explore the loft, she looked through many boxes containing dull school materials. At the far end of the loft she caught within her torch beam a framed portrait 4' x 3'. It was a black-and-white enlarged photograph of her, naked but for stockings and suspender belt, sitting on the edge of a canopy bed, with her legs apart, breasts jutting and only her down-stretched hands barring the view of her sex. She had forgotten just how erotic that picture was, and how beautiful her body had been at the age of twenty-five when it was taken. Adam had wanted to put a smaller print of it in the downstairs bathroom, but she had refused to have it hung anywhere visible to guests. Adam had finally agreed, keeping that smaller print in his bedside drawer. This giant version had been printed about three or four years ago, when she had finally seen off her rival Maggie. Adam said he'd had it done to remind himself of what a prized beauty his wife was. It was meant to be complimentary.

Now, she wasn't going to take that at face value. Adam was very clever indeed, and she suddenly thought that this would be exactly where he would hide them.

Stella turned the picture around. The back was sealed with brown paper, but there was an outline beneath, an A3 rectangle, somewhat smaller than the picture. She used her fingernail to cut through the paper and tore open the backing. There, close against the back of the photograph, was an envelope bearing the legend: *letters from M.* It was a treasure trove.

Chapter Fifteen

My dearest Adam,

I think about you every day, every hour of every day. I have so little of you and want so much. I dream of the time when we can be together twenty-four hours of every day, when I don't have to share you. Thank you so much for the diamond earrings for our fifth anniversary. They look beautiful on me. Adam, it's such a shame that you cannot come with me to see The Marriage of Figaro, even though we planned it so very long ago. I offered your ticket to Rachel, though I am not sure she is a great opera fan. I shall think about you during the performance.

Your ever loving
M

(Surrey Police evidence docket XK4567/19
– letter dated September 2006)

Ian Ferguson was in the remand wing at Strangeways, a place full of the fidgety and anxious, constant new faces, short tempers and suicide attempts. His trial on a single count of wounding with a knife was due in a month, and he thought about little else. But the arrival of big Terry Bonner as his cellmate changed all that. Bonner, on remand for murder, GBH and various drug charges, took over the cell from the first minute. 'These are the rules,' Bonner said, standing over his cellmate. 'You'll now have the bottom bunk, I've got the top. Give me your pillow, because I need two. No using the toilet while I'm here, understand? Don't speak unless spoken to, and anything you see or hear stays up there,' he said, tapping Fergie's temple. 'Do what you're told, and you'll survive with both balls.'

With the man's reputation, already being whispered from cell to cell before his arrival, Fergie was not going to quibble. In the following days, Fergie felt like an unwelcome guest in his own home. The cell became a royal court, where other prisoners came to pay homage to the gangster, and to offer tribute in the form of drugs or phones. One particular female screw was a regular visitor. Young and seemingly inexperienced, she was always nervous, as well she might be. Ferguson knew not to hang around while Bonner entertained. He assumed this was how Bonner got no less than three mobile phones, which he had been seen playing with on his bunk. The phones were farmed out to accomplices to store in their cells and returned when Bonner needed to use them. Curiously enough, the cell was never raided during the time Fergie shared with him. Bonner seemed to have it all sorted, except for one thing – a woman on the Out, the outside, who had something he wanted and couldn't be found. Fergie overheard one phone call.

'Where is she? You've had weeks. I don't care how difficult it is, I want a fucking result. Get it back, understand? I chose you, mate, because we ain't known associates. It's your big chance. But if you let me down you know what will happen. Yeah, think on.'

Let back inside the cell after the call had finished, Fergie avoided eye contact with the big man, but it didn't stop him demanding: 'What the fuck's up with you?' After Fergie spent the next ten minutes apologising for whatever it was he'd done, he slid quietly onto his bunk, aware of the huge muscular calves of Bonner dangling over the side from above. The big man cursed silently to himself as he tapped away on the phone, presumably giving orders to various contacts on the Out. There was just one final comment that Bonner made out loud as he finished up on the phone.

'You can run, bitch, but I'll track you down. And I'll burn your face right off. No one thieves from Big Tel and lives.'

–

It was Saturday morning two weeks before Christmas. Julia and Destiny were in Guildford town centre together on a charity shop clothing expedition, but with a first stop to pick up a reconditioned smartphone for Destiny, whose old one had virtually died. Things had changed. Julia was letting Destiny stay in her flat overnight and when she was around, but wouldn't let her have the keys. Julia kicked her out in the morning when she went to work. The shed had been kitted out with a chair, a battery-powered light, a new sleeping bag and some pillows. Destiny could go there any time.

Destiny was still very nervous about being out in public, even though Julia thought she was well disguised. She was swaddled in a big white winter coat Julia had lent her and had the faux fur-lined hood up over a blue woolly hat. She had ditched her old trainers and was wearing some high heel boots they had found for three pounds in the British Heart Foundation shop. The boots had a paint stain down the back, but Julia reckoned a little white spirit would restore them. A second-hand pair of jeans, a zipped suede skirt, and child-size rugby shirt cost less than a tenner in total. New purchases, for less than twenty pounds in total, included a complete set of new underwear from Peacocks, along with a pair of pyjamas and some thick colourful socks.

When Julia picked up a pleated skirt at Age UK and held it to the light, Destiny said: 'I'm not wearing that.'

'It's for me, what do you think?' Julia held it against herself and sidled up to a mirror.

'S'all right, I spose. Why don't you buy new stuff?'

'I can't afford it, Dezzy.'

'What do you mean? You're a rich lawyer, aintcha?'

'You might be surprised how little I earn. I did a trip up to Woolwich Crown Court a couple of weeks ago, for which I worked out I was paid forty-seven pence an hour, after expenses.'

'Huh? That's shit pay.'

'The basic rate for a plea and mitigation is okay, but takes no account of overheads. It took me over four hours to get there and back, and I had to deduct my train fare.'

'You should work in Tesco's. The pay is better, and you can nick loads of stuff.'

Julia gave her a withering glance. 'I went into this to uphold the law.'

'I'd never bother to steal any of this crap,' Destiny muttered, flicking through a rail of jumpers and cardigans. 'When I was on drugs, me and Caz went up to London and did perfume. She did the distract, and I grabbed the stuff.'

'Were you caught?'

'A few times.' She chuckled. 'But generally it ain't hard, most of the security guards can't even run, big fat blokes about as nimble as a three-legged sideboard. By the time they caught me, I'd usually passed the gear to me butter—'

'What's that?' Julia had heard a lot of street slang but this was a new one on her.

'Butter wouldn't melt. We always go in with someone who kept a big open bag that we could drop stuff in on the sly, as soon as possible after we filched it. You never talk to your butter, never look at them, but you have to know where they are. Caz's gran was the best one we ever had. Nice little old lady, with a massive zip-up bag.'

Dear God, Julia thought. This is the girl I have invited to live in my house. 'If you're staying with me you have to go straight. I mean it.'

She shrugged and continued to flick through the rail. 'Will you buy me lunch?'

'Destiny, for goodness' sake…'

'It's Dezzy. And you're not me mum, okay?'

'I'm not your bank either.'

After a long grumbling conversation that lasted for the next two shops, Julia gave in and took Dezzy to a cafe.

'Can't we go to Caffè Nero?' Destiny said, looking at the slightly tired interior of The Coffee Pot.

'No. The coffee here is just as good, and comes in a proper mug. None of that plastic that gets washed into the sea and ends up inside baby turtles.'

Destiny rolled her eyes. 'Bloody hell, got a right one here.'

'Don't you care about the planet?'

'I can't get much beyond caring about me. Seeing as I'm gonna get murdered any time.'

'If that's really true, we have to go to the police.'

'Forget it.'

'Come on, Dezzy,' Julia hissed. 'Who's going to protect you? I can't.'

'Can't you? You don't know what you can do, until you try.'

That evening, Rachel responded to Julia's heartfelt plea and came over with Jack. Destiny seemed to be on her best behaviour and enjoyed playing with the three-year-old.

'Where's your teeth?' the boy asked Destiny.

'I lent them to a friend.'

The comment produced gales of laughter in the boy. 'Did the tooth fairy pay you?'

'Yes, she did,' Julia shouted from the kitchen, where she and Rachel were deep in conversation.

Rachel looked out at the girl. 'Honestly, she seems much nicer than I expected,' she said, leaning in close to Julia's ear.

The girl must have overheard, because she hugged the boy to her and said: 'Haven't killed anyone yet have I, Jack? No I haven't.' She continued in a singsong voice, swinging the child around. 'I've been so good, haven't I, Jack?'

Julia and Rachel exchanged an alarmed glance. 'Perhaps leave him to calm down, Destiny?' Rachel called. 'You'll make him sick.'

'It's Dezzy,' she said, pressing her mouth against the boy's cheek and blowing a loud raspberry, which sent the child into paroxysms of laughter.

They had eaten a large supermarket-bought tea, including cake and chocolate biscuits, and there was a thick rime of chocolate around the boy's mouth. Julia could see that Jack was getting overexcited.

Rachel said: 'Okay, everybody, I think we have to go now, because Jack's daddy is coming to see us later on.'

'Daddy!' Jack exclaimed. 'I want to see Daddy.'

Rachel and Julia rolled their eyes. Jack's father Neil rated himself a hands-on dad, but since the divorce he had only sent money sporadically, despite promises. Last year he'd even forgotten Jack's birthday until Rachel reminded him the day before. Certainly the ties between father and son seemed to be inexorably slipping.

Julia watched her friend. Habitually with one eye on Jack, Rachel was much harder to reach than she had been before his birth. Julia knew that her friend cared deeply about her, but calls that once would have been returned within half an hour now often took several days to be acknowledged, and thank yous for gifts that Julia had sent Jack only came by text, if at all. Rachel was stretched more and more, and Julia sometimes felt a little left out. 'Rachel, I think I am going to try to get out of V&I—'

Rachel's attention was elsewhere. 'Dezzy, can you put him down please, and don't do that.'

Julia watched as Rachel scooped up her child and turned away from Destiny. Jack was laughing and holding out one arm to the girl. 'My chocolate.'

Julia saw the furious look on Rachel's face, and mouthed to her the words: 'What's the matter?'

Her friend closed the kitchen door. 'Did you hear all those slurping noises? She licked all the chocolate off his face.'

'Oh dear,' Julia said. 'That's a bit icky.'

'God, I hope she hasn't got anything. You know, infectious.' Rachel said. She then made her way out of the kitchen and permitted Jack a quick kiss from Destiny as she hurried off to the front door. The high-pitched cacophony of gabbled goodbyes, all addressed to Jack, didn't hide the tension in the atmosphere. While Julia and Destiny stood side by side waving them off, the departure of the vehicle left a dark silence behind.

'She doesn't like me,' Destiny declared.

'She does. But mums are a bit possessive, you know how it is.'

'I'd love a kid like Jack,' she said softly. 'Always wanted one.'

This was the first crack Julia had noticed in Destiny's emotional armour. Julia risked resting a hand on the girl's shoulder. 'Don't worry, there's plenty of time for you.'

The young woman stiffened at the contact. She turned to Julia and said: 'You can't have 'em, can you?' Her dark eyes were a little softer than usual. Sympathy. Somehow it got to her. Julia's throat was thick with emotion, and she felt her face flush. 'I'm a little old now,' she said finally. It was half the truth. But the whole truth she had not shared with anyone but Rachel. No one knew the despair she had been through, least of all the man who had caused it.

Himself.

Julia turned away. When she next looked up Destiny was wearing the borrowed coat. It looked good on her, as did the smudge of eyeshadow and mascara she had put on earlier. 'I'm just going out for a bit,' she said.

'Will you be long?' Julia caught herself sliding into a fussy maternal role and expected Destiny would pick up on it.

'Nah. Back soon.' Maybe she had already got used to Julia's fussing.

It wasn't late. Only seven o'clock. As soon as the girl had gone, Julia started on the clearing up. In the time that Destiny had been staying with her, she hadn't lifted a finger to help. She left wet towels on the floor, dirty clothing on the bed and plates exactly where she finished with them. There were few discernible signs of gratitude for anything Julia had done. This, particularly, made Julia seethe, but it seemed as pointless as getting cross with a cat for being a cat. Destiny was a product of the upbringing she had endured.

Julia caught herself wondering whether Destiny would now disappear for days like she had done previously, and she realised the concern she felt about that was partly for herself. Being alone. She realised she didn't even have the number of Destiny's new phone and made a mental note to ask her. In any case, the girl had to go, and soon. There needed to be a clear plan, and an objective.

The girl was back in fifteen minutes, sporting a litre bottle of Grey Goose vodka.

'Time for a bit of a celebration,' she said.

'Where did you get the money for that?' Julia asked.

'Keep your hair on. I always keep a bit by for emergencies.' Destiny made her way into the kitchen, unscrewed the top and poured a generous glug into two tumblers. 'There you go, get that down you.'

'You didn't steal it did you? I told you. Any theft, and you'll have to leave.'

The girl's face tightened. 'I bought it you as a present, but I shouldn't have bothered, should I? Ungrateful bitch.'

Ungrateful? Me! Julia's jaw hung open at the sheer brass neck of the girl. Destiny swigged down half her drink in one go.

'Would you like some orange juice to go in it?' Julia asked.

'No. It ain't one of the essential food groups.'

'Yes, it is! You need vitamin C, vegetables, fruit.'

Destiny sat on the kitchen barstool, leaned back and chuckled. 'You don't half make me laugh.' She took another swig. 'The essential food groups are chips, saveloys, cider, ketchup and pork scratchings. Everyone knows that.' She belched loudly.

'You'll have lost all your teeth by the time you're sixty,' Julia said. 'Fruit and vegetables protect you against cancer.'

'Who cares? I'll be happy to get to me twenty-first.' She took another glug. 'Look. Do you think a greenfly cares about climate change?'

'Of course not.'

'I mean even if a greenfly had the brains of Einstein, he wouldn't give a monkey's about any of those things, would he? He wouldn't live long enough.' She leaned forward on her elbows. 'I mean, does it bother you that in millions of years the earth will be swallowed by the sun? All them whales, fucking dolphins, koala bears and stuff. All barbecued. So why bother to save them now?'

'That's a very grim philosophy.'

'Not really. Aren't you lot going to demonstrate outside the Houses of Parliament, get them to do something about it? Move the earth a bit further away or something?'

'Destiny, I mean Dezzy, things don't have to be as bad as you say. If you want children you have to believe in a good future, for them to live happily and enjoy.'

'So why didn't you have a child?'

Julia took a deep breath. 'I was pregnant once. I was with a man I adored, my first love really. We had been seeing each other for nearly fifteen years, but things were very complicated.'

'Married, was he?'

Julia was astounded that Destiny had such a finely tuned emotional radar. Offered the vodka, Julia slid her own glass across. 'I shouldn't, really,' she said watching Destiny filled the glass halfway to the brim. 'Whoa, that's plenty.' Julia sipped the vodka, then went to the fridge for some orange juice. 'Yes, Dezzy, he was married, he is married, will always be married. For years he kept me on the hook, telling me that once a certain thing happened, he would leave his wife. First he wanted to get his son finished at junior school, then it was getting him past his GCSEs, then A-levels. Whatever it was, there was always some reason why he couldn't break up his marriage quite yet.'

'You're a mug.' Destiny offered her glass in acknowledgement. 'To idiots and mugs the world over.' They clinked.

Julia shook her head in regret. 'Yes, I was a fool to believe him. But the time we had together was so precious, because it was so constrained. I didn't realise at the time that seeing each other only once a week for a one or two hours made it so much more exciting. All the anticipation ahead of the big night, and then the longing and missing him afterwards.'

'What happened to the baby?'

'I was stupid. It was a few months before his son did his A-levels, and I told him. He said all the right words, made all the congratulations, but I could tell he was terrified. He felt cornered, because I'd used the big lever. Then he said:

"Look, honestly Julia, now is not the greatest time. I can't leave her now. Her mother has just died, and her father has Alzheimer's. I need just a few more months. He'll go into a home. If I tell her I have a baby by another woman, she might commit suicide. She's threatened it before, and this time I think she really might do it.'"

'So you got rid of your precious baby?'

'I agonised about it for weeks, almost leaving it too late. Rachel, who never liked Himself, said I should have had the baby regardless. But what was I going to do if he didn't give me any money? I was in my barrister training, and I was relying on him lending me some more money to finish it. He told me that if I blackmailed him about it, he would finish with me.'

'Typical male bastard. I'd know what to do to him.'

'I thought about it, believe me. Why should I get rid of my poor innocent unborn child, in order to save the embarrassment of a conniving manipulative married man?'

'That's it, you said it right.' Destiny took another slug of vodka. 'But you didn't do it right, did you?'

Julia shook her head. The alcohol was really taking hold now. 'I did the wrong thing. And it was my bad luck that I got pelvic inflammatory disease after the procedure and had to have a partial hysterectomy.'

'Sounds shite, whatever it is.'

'Well, it means I can't have children at all now.'

'Disaster.'

'I should have had the baby, but I so much wanted to believe Adam. I couldn't believe that having sunk fifteen years of my life into our relationship, he could treat me like that.' She could feel tears pricking her eyes, but had enough sobriety left to realise she really didn't want to be crying in front of this girl, this near stranger.

Destiny nodded sagely. 'It's like one of these frauds.'

'What?'

'You know, you get emails from these people saying they've got money they want to deposit in Britain. Lots of money, millions, and they seem stupid and bewildered. They're in Nigeria or the Philippines or somewhere like that. My foster mum fell for it. You think to yourself you could do with some of that, seems easy money. But to get it, you have to wire some money, so they can afford the bank draft. It's not much to start with, but there's always more. Solicitors' fees, all that shit. It's psychology. You get so mesmerised by the imaginary sum at the end that you keep shovelling ever larger amounts of cash to them. And they sweet talk you all the time, keep going on about the golden hoard of cash at the end of it. They become your friends, and you don't even realise how much you've been ripped off.' She took a swig of her drink.

'That's advance fee fraud,' Julia said. 'I prosecuted a case last year.'

Destiny nodded. 'Your bloke, exactly the same. Held out the dream of spending your life with him, and you fell for it. First you went out with him, then you let him shag you. Then let him do you every week, whenever he felt like it. Changed your life to fit round his schedule.'

Julia nodded. 'Yeah, I never got cross when he didn't show up. Never had a headache when he felt like sex.'

'That's right. All the time, you were making sacrifices and he was withholding the final reward. Because there never was any final reward. He never had any intention of leaving his wife. It was always a scam.'

Julia was feeling woozy, but not so woozy that she couldn't see the brilliance of this metaphor, the clarity of the girl's thinking, some hint perhaps of her own experience. 'What happened to your foster mum?'

Destiny shrugged. 'She got into debt, started drinking. Her old man blamed me. I got kicked out. Ended up on the streets again. Same old shit. I've not seen her for three years.'

Julia nodded. 'Bloody men.'

Destiny looked up at the ceiling. 'Sometimes I think I should grab a child from some pushchair. That way you know you could get a good one, one that isn't always bawling its eyes out.'

'I know you're just trying to shock me. You wouldn't do that.'

'I might.'

'You wouldn't.'

'You don't know what I would do. If you had faced the aggro I've had to face, you'd realise that there's always more possibilities than just the right thing to do. All the best options, the ones that feel right, are illegal.'

'Give me an example,' Julia said.

'Right. I was sixteen, a runaway from the children's home, and me and Caz were being kept in this filthy flat on Upton Terrace. They'd bring in these blokes; horrible old ugly guys. We were so off our faces on the drugs they gave us that we were hardly aware what they were doing to us. But every so often you get something, like a beam of sunlight through the window, and you can see it all clearly. You ain't high anymore, but you ain't so down that you are going to slash yourself up. And there was this moment, this opportunity, when I realised that Janille wasn't my boyfriend like he said he was. Like a glimpse between dark curtains. Then I knew I had to get out.'

'Who's Janille?'

'He was the zookeeper. That's what they called him. And we were the animals. He had three or four houses on the same street with different girls in, maybe a dozen of us in total. All locked up, so you couldn't get out easily, and he had to get round all of them, with food and the tablets we were all addicted to. He said the local copper was in his pay, so no use calling them. There were cameras, inside and out. He said they were monitored, all the time. We were too scared to attempt to escape, because this one girl, Siobhan I think she was, she tried and they caught her. We heard them knocking seven bells out of her in the next room. Then they did something to her that made her scream like I've never heard in my life. We never saw her again. Janille said they had called the chemist to deal with her, and after that he'd thrown her in the canal. But we never knew it for a fact.'

'The chemist? You mean a pharmacist?'

'No. He was the man who kept the hydrochloric. That's what Caz had heard. When she was in another house, the same bloke came and burned the face off some girl for trying to escape.'

Horrific. Julia took a big slug of her vodka and orange. She couldn't recall anyone having been brought to trial in such a charge. Could such a thing happen in Surrey? In the leafy Home Counties? She was appalled and fascinated in equal measure. Her heart and her legal mind were squeezed side by side on the same mental sofa, fighting to get the remote for the next episode.

'So how did you get out?'

'It wasn't that hard once I had decided, once I had conquered the fear. That was the point, that was where the light came from. Like I say, Janille was out at one of the other houses. He had his own room in the house which was locked, but I just kicked the door down and ransacked it. I needed money and I knew he had it, but I also got something else that was very valuable, that he was looking after for Big Tel. I squeezed out through an upstairs window, shinned down the drainpipe and just ran.'

'And is that why they are after you?'

'Janille isn't after me. He's dead. Big Tel killed him and cut him up, for being too soft on us. That's what Caz told me. I cried about that, stupid me. I met Janille when I was thirteen, introduced by another girl at the children's home. He was a good-looking guy, with his dark skin and sharp haircut. He had a big fast car and took me and this other girl round town. He bought us some nice clothes and introduced us to some of his friends and to a private room at a club. If you live in a children's home, it impresses you, believe me. I remember he took us to a Chinese restaurant. I had never been to a restaurant before, and he seemed to know the manager. It made me feel very special. He offered us wine. After the meal, Janille dropped the other girl off, and drove fast to a park in the countryside. It was the middle of summer, and there was a warm breeze through the leaves of the trees. He kissed me. He didn't do anything else. Just kissed me and held me and told me he was falling in love with me.'

'He swept you off your feet.' Julia remembered having read the official report on the child abuse ring in Rotherham. It sounded identical. Easily impressed unloved girls from a children's home, enslaved and trafficked.

Destiny nodded. 'The stupid thing is, even after everything that happened, I still remember that fondly. It was one of the only times in my life that anyone was kind to me. He just held me for the longest time. I was absolutely desperate for someone who didn't think I was a waste of space. And he was the first. He seemed to care.

'He didn't give me any drugs for the first week, just some wine, the odd can of cider. And on the Saturday he put me up in this luxurious flat, a penthouse in the centre of the city. There was champagne there, and flowers on the table, and he had this girl called Stacey dress me all up in a white dress and did my make-up. I was so happy, I thought it was going to be my first night with Janille.'

Julia watched Destiny's hands gripping the glass so hard the knuckles showed white.

'Janille went out, and came back with this ugly scary guy, big and muscular, no hair, but with a massive long black beard with a red stripe dyed in it. Stupid me, I didn't know why he was there, but I later realised he was Janille's boss, Big Tel. I had some champagne and then went very dizzy and faint. But I still remember what happened. First, Janille left, saying he would be back in an hour. Big Tel went at me like a starving dog at a bowl of meat. I was thirteen, and there was no private part of my body he didn't use. He was rough and really hurt me.'

'Oh, Dezzy, I'm so sorry for what happened to you.'

'I was sore and bleeding for days. I never got to see the penthouse again. Most of the time after that I was back in the cage either alone or with one or two other girls. And I was too scared to say anything to them because some of them would snitch for privileges. But they'd all heard of Big Tel.'

Chapter Sixteen

My dearest Adam,
*   Here we are together, one of my most precious*
photographs, all woolly hats and scarves standing
in snowy pastures, our breath pluming into a clear
blue sky. A stolen hour, with the school closed, I'm
so glad I was able to get out at short notice. Must
rush now. Crown Court calls!
*   Your ever loving*
*   M*

(Surrey Police evidence docket XK4567/16
– letter dated September 2012)

The conversation descended into an alcoholic fog over the course of the evening. Julia hauled herself out of bed just before eleven on the Sunday morning, was horrified to see they had polished off two thirds of the vodka. She had a screaming headache and was wandering around with her eyes screwed up against the light as she rifled the drawers for ibuprofen. There was definitely the smell of toast and bacon. Having downed the tablets, she staggered into the lounge to see Destiny fully dressed, sitting cross-legged, with earbuds in, looking at a slim and silvery laptop, the remains of a bacon sandwich resting on the keyboard.

In her befuddled state, Julia thought: how can she afford a MacBook Air?

She then realised. *It's my laptop. My earbuds.*

'What on earth are you doing? Get that object off the keyboard!'

Destiny popped the remains of the sandwich into her mouth. There was a great greasy mark across the top of the keyboard. Julia knew that almost her entire working life was on that machine. She couldn't imagine what had lured the girl, but it couldn't be good.

'I was watching TV on it,' Destiny said, turning round the screen. 'Seeing as you ain't got a proper one.'

The screen was showing some glitzy ballroom dancing. Of course! *Strictly*. She seized the machine and plucked the headset away from the girl.

'Oi, I was watching that!' Destiny exclaimed, following Julia into the kitchen.

'That's for my work, and my work only. That machine cost over a grand, and I'm still paying for it.' Julia scrubbed at the greasy mark with a sheet of kitchen paper.

'I could get you seven hundred for it today from someone I know, and you could claim back the full cost on insurance. You'd be quids in.'

'I am not a fraudster. And I don't want you to touch my work stuff again.'

'I got bored waiting for you. I went out for some break-fast. I used your card, seeing as you didn't want me nicking anything.' The girl produced Julia's debit card from the back of her jeans. 'It's all right, it was just on contactless.'

'You're making free and easy with my money,' Julia said, taking the card back. It was greasy.

'Yeah, but I bought you some breakfast, so it wasn't theft.' Destiny pointed to a packet of white processed baps and some cheap bacon resting on the countertop.

'Your idea of what constitutes stealing is pretty narrow,' Julia said.

Normally, Julia would not eat bacon because of the salt, and certainly not with pappy white bread, but something about the alcoholic evening before made her change her mind. She turned on the grill, and put a couple of rashers in. She was surprised at how Destiny seemed entirely unaffected by the heavy night they had shared.

'You got really funny last night,' Destiny said, giggling to herself. 'You really hate that bloke. don't you? The one who wouldn't leave his wife and strung you along.'

'I try not to, but he closed off something that was precious to me.'

'Yeah, you said. Motherhood.'

While Julia was cooking her breakfast, Destiny played with her new phone, showing Julia a couple of selfies they had taken together, arms around each other's shoulders. God, she had been drunk. She looked terrible, and old. Destiny had taken some videos as well. Julia was too embarrassed to look at them but could hear her own slurring speech. She did catch one phrase. 'Adam Heath, I hate you, and I wish you were dead.'

'Why don't you kill him?' Destiny said.

'Don't think I haven't thought about it,' Julia said. 'Well, fantasised about it.'

'Make your dreams come true. It wouldn't be that hard. You've just got to dare to do it.'

-

Julia thought back with horror to the account that Destiny had given her about the rape by the man called Big Tel. When she was feeling better, she made a mental note to try to check up if there had been any convictions. She would also need to ask Destiny for some more facts and make some notes. She had contacts in the CPS who would certainly look favourably on any kind of prosecution against child sexual exploitation. But even in her woozy state, she realised that until Destiny felt safe she wouldn't co-operate as a witness.

After they both finished breakfast Julia suggested a walk in the park. Destiny agreed, but wanted her full disguise kit. So Julia once again lent her the white hooded coat, the woolly hat, and this time a big handknitted maroon scarf. They made their way along Recreation Road, across Stoke Road and into Stoke Park. Destiny wanted to get away from the paddling pool and ornamental garden areas, where there were quite a lot of youngsters, and into the more open parkland beyond. The trees were largely bare but there were piles of dried leaves to kick through.

'That's where I slept, before I came to your garden,' Destiny said, pointing to a secluded thicket in the ornamental garden.

'Well, you can't go back to that.' Julia then brought up a subject that had been swirling in her mind in the two weeks since Destiny had come into her life. 'We haven't really got into this in detail, but we do need to find a safe and secure place for you to stay. And for that, you have to get back on the grid. Get some proper ID, utility bills in your name, a bank account, all that stuff.'

Destiny was shaking her head emphatically. 'No. Big Tel has got people out all over looking for me, and they have a habit of finding who they want.'

'Why are they looking for you so hard?'

'Because I nicked his gun, and I still have it. Janille was looking after it, and I got it from his room when I scarpered.'

'Good grief.' Julia was aware that the stack of crimes that Destiny was involved in would complicate any attempt to persuade her to go to the police. 'Why not let him have the gun back? Or get a message to him to say where you have left it. You don't need the weapon, you probably don't know how to use it. Then he would leave you alone.'

Destiny barked a short ironic laugh. 'You've no idea how it works. You cross Big Tel, you stay on the list for life. It's a matter of honour in the gang. I humiliated him.'

'How can you be so sure?'

'He sent me a video, in which he described exactly what he was going to do to me.'

Julia seized on this revelation. 'Brilliant! That is strong evidence, easily enough to convict.'

'I ain't got it no more. It was on my old phone, and I deleted it because it scared me so much.'

Julia sighed. 'Never mind, it will be on a server somewhere. It's evidence of intent.'

Destiny turned around to her. 'You don't get it, do you? I'm never giving evidence against him. It would be suicide.'

Julia's brain was still a little befuddled, but this was exactly the kind of difficulty that she so often faced at work, persuading witnesses to testify. 'He has to be put away, behind bars. It's the only way.'

'I know, but it's not just him, there are dozens of them in the gang. They all know to get me. Even if he's sent down he can still run the gang.'

'Maybe he's already in prison.'

'He is. But just for a while, like.'

'Where?'

'Strangeways.'

A realisation was dawning in Julia. 'What is his real name, Dezzy?'

She looked carefully around, as if someone was listening, then squinted into the distance. 'Terry Bonner.'

'Bonner! I'm representing him.'

'I know you are. That's why I'm here.'

'But I'm defending him, do you understand? It's my job to get him off the charges.' This was terrible news. Bonner was the most high-profile client she'd ever had, and now she had a conflict of interest.

'I know. That's really why I came here. Because I can't get to him, but you can.'

'Get to him?'

'Yeah. I give you the gun, and you shoot him.'

—

Julia had to sit down at a bench to try to explain the sheer impossibility of what Destiny wanted done. 'You can't just take a gun to court. There is security, and besides, I couldn't… For goodness' sake, Dezzy, why are we even discussing this? You should be talking to the Crown's legal team, giving them evidence. You shouldn't have come to me.' She held her head in her hands.

'No, you've got to. You're my only chance.'

'How did this start, Dezzy?'

'I saw you in Nottingham.'

'In Nottingham!'

'Yeah. Caz was with me, and she went into the public gallery while I stayed outside. I couldn't risk him seeing me in the court. And she came back and said that you were his brief, and we followed you. I thought that if I told you what he'd done, you'd do your job badly and he'd go down.'

'And you stole my bag and phone!'

'No, Caz did that. I just knocked a couple of glasses off the table.'

'That caused me so much trouble.'

'But I needed to know how to find you. How else was I going to?'

Julia looked into the sky and counted to ten. 'For goodness' sake, Destiny. Why didn't you tell me all this straight away, instead of lurking in my garden?'

'I needed to get you on my side. Tell my story, so you could fit him up in court.'

'Well, that's a lot more of a possibility than me shooting him.' Julia laughed and shook her head. 'But I'm still not going to do it. Absolutely not. It's perverting the course of justice, which carries a maximum sentence of life in prison.'

'But it's my only chance.'

'No, I really can't. And don't ask me again.'

'Well, fuck you.' Destiny stood up and walked away. Julia did not go after her. She'd been targeted, cynically, right from the start. And now she was furious about it. Destiny was wearing Julia's coat, hat and scarf, which she wanted back, and charity shop boots that she had paid for. She had made herself fully at home in Julia's garden, and had inveigled her way into her home, her life. It was outrageous, and it was going to stop. Rachel was right, she'd been a fool. Things were going to be different from now on.

Destiny did not come back. On returning home Julia went through the flat to see if anything had been stolen. She immediately found a library book in the room that Dezzy had been staying in. *The Brothers Karamazov* by Dostoyevsky. She was astounded, then immediately felt guilty for her snobbery. The book was well-thumbed, long overdue, and heavily but illegibly annotated in pencil. Still mulling the many surprises of her guest, Julia got back to checking for theft. It was hard to say with the cash what was missing because she never really knew how much she had anyway. If any was gone it certainly wasn't a lot. However, when she checked her debit card online, she found that quite a few items had been put on it, phone credit and a series of transactions from the local convenience store. That would include the Grey Goose vodka. What a nerve the girl had!

Still angry, Julia rang the police, and told them that she had come into contact with a missing person. She gave them Destiny's name and said that she had given her a roof over her head for a few days. 'The girl sounds like she has been exploited by a gang since she was a young teenager. I'm more concerned about her welfare than anything, but don't feel quite safe having her in the house.' Julia decided to make no mention of Bonner.

The female officer on the other end of the phone was sympathetic. 'You've taken a bit of a risk, madam. You should have called us straight away. Reuniting vulnerable runaways with their families is a priority for us.'

Julia gave a detailed report over the phone but decided that she would draw a veil over the thefts. Destiny would have enough problems without being labelled a thief. She also emailed Missing People to say she'd been in contact with Destiny. Julia then rang Rachel to tell her. As usual, she was supportive of a tough line. 'Good for you, Julia. I don't mean to say I told you so, but...'

'Yes, I know, I know. You're always right.' Julia told Rachel everything, including discovering that it was Destiny and her friend Caz who had stolen her bag in Nottingham.

'I'm not in the least surprised. So are you going to give up the Bonner case?'

'No. In theory, I should report it to the Bar Council. But there's been no attempt to intimidate me, I mean, how could she? There is absolutely no way I'd do what she asks.'

'Good for you, girl.'

Julia finally felt she had done the right thing. But it did not stop her feeling very guilty about the way she'd treated Destiny and wondering where the poor girl would end up sleeping that night, and where she would go over Christmas. Still, it was absolutely clear to her that Destiny had now begun to intrude into her professional life. That she couldn't allow.

—

On Monday morning, Julia sat in her room in chambers reading up as much as she could on the Bonner case. So far there had been very little evidential disclosure from the Crown Prosecution Service, but one of the charges was the murder of Janille Murdoch, and the strewing of his body parts along a motorway hard shoulder. Destiny had described Bonner as having a huge black beard with a red stripe dyed in it, but he had been relatively clean-shaven both times she had met him.

She was flicking through the various supporting documents when she got a phone call from a woman at the Missing People website. 'Thank you so much for your email yesterday,' she said. 'Destiny has been missing for such a long time, and we were really glad to pass on the news to her family.'

'Good,' Julia said, feeling a little surprised. Destiny had told her that her birth family had shown no interest in her whatsoever.

'Her uncle has asked to talk to you about her, and how she is. Would that be all right?'

'Yes, I don't mind at all,' Julia said, and passed across her phone number. 'Do tell him that I don't know her present whereabouts, though.'

No sooner had she got off the phone than the police rang her. A detective constable called Michelle Tsu wanted to follow up on her statement about Destiny.

'There has been no sign of her, I'm afraid,' the detective said. 'We are quite concerned for her safety.'

'So am I,' Julia said. 'She is absolutely terrified of the authorities who, on her account, have let her down time and time again.'

'Well, rest assured we will find her and look after her. Every uniformed officer in town has her description, and we have alerted churches, homeless charities, refuges, local authority park departments and so forth.'

That sounded like a pretty good list to Julia. She thanked her and hung up. She had still made no mention of Bonner to the police.

The next phone call made her jump. It was from a withheld number, and she answered it cautiously. 'Hello, is that Ms McGann?' The voice seemed muffled, and there was background traffic noise.

'Julia McGann, barrister at law,' she said. 'How can I help?' Calls from clients often sounded like this: hesitant and nervous.

'I heard that you found my niece, Destiny.' The man had a slight Caribbean lilt to his voice.

'Yes, that's right.'

'How is she doing?' The man sounded quite young.

'Well, she is healthy enough, but she'd been sleeping rough, until I gave her a roof over her head for a few days.'

'In London?'

'No, here in Guildford.' The moment she said it she wished she hadn't. 'I'm sure she'll be very pleased that you got in contact. She always said her family didn't care about her.'

'We always look after her, I don't know what she's saying.' The slight laugh, and an echo as if someone else was listening in, suddenly made Julia suspicious. The man's voice had diminished slightly, as if he had turned to another person.

'Can I ask your name, caller?'

'Her uncle, I told you.'

'Uncle what? Are you her mother's brother, or her father's brother?'

'What do you care? Where is she now, lady?'

'I really don't know.' Julia now knew this was no relative of Destiny's. Certainly he didn't seem to radiate much relief or warmth at knowing she was well. Julia had an idea. 'Look, I will make some enquiries, and if I can get an address, can I call you?'

The call was cut from the other end. Her sudden turn-around from guardedness to co-operation must've been too rapid. She rang Missing People back and told the advisor of her suspicions. The advisor agreed the call sounded suspicious, and after checking with her supervisor found that this person's details had been forwarded through social services. 'Only verified family members would normally be forwarded to us,' the woman said.

'My worry is that the people who are masquerading as her family are in fact those who kept her prisoner,' Julia said.

Julia was tied up in case meetings all afternoon, but at a quarter to five decided to make a break for it and work from home. If Destiny had returned she needed to tell her that she was still being pursued. She still felt some responsibility towards her.

–

When she got home, Julia was relieved to discover nothing out of the ordinary. No one had tried to break in, and the shed was securely locked. Looking around the garden, she found no evidence of the filthy sleeping bag or any litter which might indicate that Destiny had been there.

She put on the kettle and made herself a cup of tea. Then she did a thorough inventory inside the house, to see if anything had been stolen or disturbed. Her jewellery was still there, in a sock inside her training shoe. Apart from a great pile of dirty bedlinen, towels, and some discarded underwear, it was as if Destiny had never been there. So where was she? Julia had no idea. But the alarming phone call she had received from the girl's supposed uncle made it clear that Destiny's terror was well founded.

If only she had got the girl's new phone number. The only time she had remembered to ask for it, they had been shopping. Destiny had taken Julia's mobile number and said she would send her a text.

The text had never arrived.

Julia made herself a Spanish omelette for dinner, using up some ancient potatoes and some broccoli she had bought for Destiny, but which the girl had refused to eat. While she ate, she opened her Mac and clicked through the latest news headlines. Casually, she clicked on the bookmark for St John's Academy. The website had a beautiful leafy picture on the home page, curiously devoid of students, as if it had been taken during the school holidays. There were tabs about values, about safeguarding, academic record and staff. She selected that drop-down menu and clicked through to the headmaster.

Adam Heath.

Himself.

She was familiar with this photograph, which was taken from below, making him look like a bull-chested Mussolini, chin lifted, eyes to a glorious horizon. To read the glowing, presumably self-penned, description of the principal, the casual reader would assume that here was a man embodying courage, consistency and a farsighted dedication to the enlightenment of society. When in fact, as Julia knew, he was a deceitful, vain, selfish and arrogant predator, a man who had browbeaten Julia to terminate the life of her unborn child to fit the convenience of his home life. A man who cared for little except his own pleasures and preferences.

Julia wasn't sure why she had kept the bookmark for the school website, nor why she looked at it every couple of weeks, usually when she'd had a few glasses of wine. The self-torture of gazing at his imperious photograph was the opposite of catharsis. It made her angry, not so much with him but with herself, for being a fool to have believed him for so long. It was a kind of self-flagellation.

The secret life of a headmaster.

If she had been a different person, it would have been so much fun to reveal that.

She sighed, pushed the dish away, and checked her emails. There were two from the bank, those auto-generated messages that she usually ignored. But this time she had a hunch she should open them. The oldest said that two unsuccessful logins had been attempted on her account, and the second was about access attempts from an unauthorised device.

What on earth was that about?

She re-read both messages. The unsuccessful logins had been attempted around nine thirty on Sunday. That was nonsense, because she hadn't got up until nearly eleven.

Destiny.

The little bitch. It soon dawned on Julia what had happened. Destiny had made two attempts at the password but didn't dare try a third because the account would be locked, and Julia would be alerted. Destiny then presumably had used her own phone to try a number of other times on another day.

Julia was furious. The ungrateful little bitch. Pretending to watch TV on the laptop when in fact she was trying to steal everything Julia had. After everything she had done for her. Julia spent the rest of the evening checking all of her bank details and other online financial records, changing passwords, checking access attempts. Of course, if Julia actually had any money this would be a much greater problem. If Destiny wanted to steal her overdraft, she would find it unrewarding. She considered reporting all this to the police. However, to detail how closely connected Julia had become to the young woman might jeopardise her chances of hanging on to the Bonner case. If she ever hoped to leave V&I she needed a good solid case like this under her belt. From what Destiny had said, she would never testify against Bonner. If so, good. That would give Julia much less of a conflict of interest. It was a risk that was worth taking.

As so often, Julia rang Rachel to bounce her conclusions off her friend.

'Well, I think you got your fingers burned on that one, didn't you?' Rachel said.

'Yes, you were right. You're *always* right. Don't torment me about it.'

'Do you know where she's gone?'

'I have no idea, and I'm trying not to care.'

'That's a good start, Moggy. Sometimes you just care too much. If she didn't get into your bank accounts, you've escaped lightly.'

'I'm getting two additional locks fitted tomorrow,' Julia said. 'Five-lever mortice, which they tell me are the only ones that even amateur burglars worry about.'

'Yes, but you've got to use them,' Rachel said. 'I know what you're like. You can be so dippy sometimes. In fact, I'm amazed that in your day job you can be the cool-headed legal professional, and the rest of your life is just a swamp of absolute chaos.'

'Thanks a bunch, Rachel!'

Rachel laughed. 'I just think you got off lightly. I mean, what if she'd actually stolen your Mac? Then you'd be stuffed, wouldn't you?'

'Well, it's all backed up into a data stick. When I remember, that is.'

Rachel laughed again. 'Well, with any luck you'll never hear from her again.'

Chapter Seventeen

My dearest Adam,

Last night I dreamt that we were in Derby-shire, on the moors where we first met. I was running towards you, and the setting sun, which made your coppery hair look like a halo. You were striding away from me, a rough dry stone wall between us. But I didn't get any closer, my feet kept getting caught in the mud, and there was only one rickety ladder stile I could use to get across the wall. Finally, I reached the stile, but the wood was fragile, and as I began to climb, it shattered. When I looked down at the pale sun-bleached wood, I could see it was made of human bones. As I fell, I called out to you. You turned, and your eyes looked past me.

I woke up feeling profoundly sad, because I know what this is about.

For so many years now I have been waiting, and I really can't wait any longer.

Do let me know, my darling, when that moment will be, because my heart is crumbling away like those steps.

Your ever loving

M

The locksmith arrived forty minutes late on Tuesday, leaving Julia fretting. She had arranged to work from home in the morning, but had a plea in mitigation to do in the afternoon in London, which would mean leaving by 11.30 a.m. She was hoping to pick up the filthy Duster too, now that some court money had finally come through. It was always going to be quite tight, especially as Darren from HomeSecure seemed quite leisurely. He tried to do a perfect job on the woodwork, when an adequate one was all that Julia required. She tried to avoid watching him or hanging around, firstly because he might get the wrong idea and secondly because in her experience a watched tradesman simply chats. On the other hand, the fact he was whistling cheerfully to himself and taking calls every two minutes on his mobile began to annoy her and inhibit the preparation that she had to do on the afternoon's case.

So in the end, even though she had already mentioned her departure time, she was forced to remind him. He sucked his teeth and said he had another hour's work to do. 'There are plenty of people about who will do you a rush job, but a rush job won't keep the thieves out,' he declared.

'I agree, but if I don't get to Snaresbrook magistrates by two p.m. a different thief will go free.' It wasn't quite true, but Darren took the point. He said he'd just finish the long brass bolt for the French windows and come back to do the second mortice lock another day.

As they were negotiating this, standing by Darren's van, she noticed a black BMW parked opposite. There were two men, one black and one white, sitting inside wearing sunglasses, looking at her. It wasn't sunny. She did her best to memorise the number plate and went inside to write it down.

She had a feeling that Destiny's so-called uncle had come to find her.

-

On the train up to London Julia fretted about the two men in the BMW. Logically, as they had seen the HomeSecure van, there was a decent chance that they would be put off from attempting to break in, if that had been their intention. But logic somehow didn't put her mind at ease.

Just before the court case began, Julia called her upstairs neighbour, Briony. She had never brought her boyfriend's dog round despite the promises, so Julia's expectations were low. Fortunately, she was in, and Julia was relieved to hear that the BMW had gone. But then she realised that didn't prove anything. She knew from her criminal bar work that a typical burglary takes less than five minutes.

The case went badly, and her client was unexpectedly remanded in custody. To make matters worse, the train from Waterloo was delayed for more than half an hour. She rang Briony again, to ask if she would just quickly check the doors and windows.

'Oh for goodness' sake,' Briony said. 'Can't it wait until you get home? I'm halfway through eating and I've got to go out in half an hour.' She finally agreed to take a quick look, and returned with the good news that both doors were intact and fully locked.

-

Julia was in a better mood when she got home. She finally had her car back, though the bill was even bigger than expected. At least the Duster was no longer filthy. The garage people had put it through the car wash three times to get the crusted pigeon mess off the roof, and the yellow was now shining through. On the way home she had picked up a ready meal. She set it in the microwave and was just looking in the fridge for a half-opened bottle of white wine that she knew was there when the doorbell went, long and insistent. Assuming it was Briony, Julia opened it and found herself staring at a short and slender black man in a leather jacket, with a matchstick in the corner of his mouth. He smelled faintly of cannabis.

'Where's Dezzy?' he asked, resting an arm against the door frame. 'I know she's been here.'

'She doesn't live here, and I've no idea where she's gone.'

He seized Julia's face in one hand, pushed her inside and shut the door behind them. She couldn't make a sound, so tightly was she gripped. With that hand he then lifted her almost off the ground. She was paralysed with terror. Years ago she had been on a self-defence course, but she was already completely helpless, and couldn't think what to do but beg for her life. From his other hand the man showed her a knife, small, wicked and glinting as he rotated it in front of her eyes. It was clearly very sharp. He then held the flat of it to her neck, put his mouth to her ear and whispered: 'Give us her new mobile number.'

Julia's heart felt like it was about to explode. She heard her own whimpering, like a beaten dog, and could only get a few gasping words out. 'Don't. Have. It.'

He released her jaw a little, but rotated the knife so the blade rested exactly on her jugular. She could feel her pulse tapping against the cold sharp steel. 'Don't disrespect me again. Where's your phone?'

Julia indicated the kitchen with a free hand, and was frogmarched in, the blade still against her neck. She unlocked the phone. He grabbed it, looked through the listings until he came to Destiny's name, clicked on it and waited for it to ring. An automated voice responded, loudly enough for her to hear: 'Number disconnected.'

The assailant shrugged his assent. 'Little bitch is going to pay, understand?'

Julia nodded, and felt the blade scrape the surface of her skin as she did so.

'You call the cops, I'm coming round to slowly and without anaesthetic carve you a new—' he then whispered in her ear the worst word in the English language.

The man stepped away and said: 'Tell her, we made an appointment for her with the chemist. And if she turns up, keep her here for a few hours and hang a red cloth in the bedroom window. We'll see it.'

He opened the door and climbed leisurely up the stairs to the street as if he hadn't a care in the world. Julia slammed it behind him, shot the bolt across and turned the key in the mortice lock. Shaking, she sank to the doormat, leaned back against the door and fought hard against tears. Eventually she stood and pushed the hall table against the front door. She took five attempts to unlock the phone, and her hands were trembling as she tapped out three nines, his threat repeated endlessly in her mind.

-

The first patrol car was there in two minutes with two uniformed male officers, followed shortly by an unmarked vehicle containing the detective constable she had spoken to previously. DC Michelle Tsu was a petite and smartly dressed woman, who made rapid and detailed notes in a neat script. The officers stayed for an hour, empathic and reassuring. The uniforms assured her that an officer would pass her home at least three times a day, and a squad car would be parked nearby from time to time. Questions were asked about local CCTV, burglar alarms and Neighbourhood Watch. Weldon Road had the latter, run by an elderly lady a few doors down, but Julia was unaware of any recent meetings. After Julia had told them everything she could, the detective put away her notebook.

'In your experience, will he come back?' Julia asked.

The detective shared a glance with one of the male officers. 'We obviously can't rule it out, and for all our precautions we can't be here all the time. Do you have somewhere else you can stay?'

'Yes, thank goodness.' Just the thought of Rachel's comfortable house and the welcome she'd receive made tears of gratitude spring to her eyes. 'He made a terrible threat against me.'

DC Tsu rested a reassuring hand on Julia's arm. 'We just need to get you somewhere safe, then you can try to forget about it.'

'It's all right,' one of the male officers said. 'We'll keep a good eye on the place.'

—

Julia arrived with a couple of suitcases, and embraced Rachel and Jack on the doorstep.

'You poor thing,' Rachel said, handing her a glass of chilled white wine even before the door was closed.

'This is so kind of you, Rachel,' Julia said, taking a hefty swig. 'It's all come at the worst time. I've got a hearing for this big case in January, I have so much work to do. I just can't afford the worry.'

Her friend rested a hand on her wrist. 'Moggy, please don't fret. You've always got a place here. That's what friends are for, right?'

'Aunty Julia, do you want to play with slime?' Jack asked, his face expectant.

'Gosh, let her get in first, Jack,' Rachel said.

The boy repeated his question, and Julia laughed, her eyes on Rachel: 'Why not? I've had fifteen years' experience with Himself to prepare me,' she said.

Julia remembered so clearly in the days after the abortion how she had spent several nights at Rachel's house, monopolising her. Then-husband Neil, tasked with preparing meals and clearing up, had resented her presence and was clearly envious of the closeness of the two women. He often ended up going to the pub with his mates to avoid Julia. His frostiness to Julia had, according to Rachel, precipitated the final slide to divorce. Julia felt very guilty about that, but Rachel said she would have discovered his possessiveness anyway, eventually – Julia had merely saved her a lot of time.

Once Julia had got her bags to the spare room, she joined Jack briefly at the Slime Lab toy, making alien glow-in-the-dark faces. Only when Jack went to bed, and the glasses were topped up with chilled New Zealand sauvignon blanc, did she tell the full story.

'He really had a knife at your throat?' Rachel asked.

She nodded.

'Your kind heart has really got you into trouble,' Rachel said.

'Okay, I'm going to be horrible in future, I promise!'

The next few December days passed in a haze. Julia tried to distract herself from worry by playing with Jack, watching cartoons with him, and rushing round the house as a space fighter with him on her back as the pilot, shooting aliens.

Much as she loved it, the reality of living with a three-year-old child made a big dent in her ability to work. Jack began ricocheting around the house before six o'clock in the morning, and that always included a high-speed visit to Julia's bedroom, where he would throw himself onto the duvet making the sound of explosions. Any momentary irritation was instantly dissipated when Jack declared, 'I love you staying with us, Aunty Julia.' Once, sitting on the sofa making a work call to client solicitors, Jack had burst in to blow raspberries into her ear.

She had given him a bright red metal tractor with trailer and an assortment of plastic sheep and cows for an early Christmas present. She had discovered the farm set in a charity shop during a hurried lunch break at Woolwich Crown Court the previous week. The shop assistant had been gobsmacked to see a barrister in wig and full regalia burst into the shop and pick the box from the window display. For Julia, having Jack in her life was not quite the same as having her own child, but it was a joy all the same.

Only in the quiet moments did she peer between the curtains, looking for a dark BMW, or listen out for strange noises at night. Follow-up calls to DC Tsu by Julia revealed that her attacker had not been identified, nor his car found, and there was no sign of Destiny. So, despite the distractions, she was in no hurry to leave.

Julia went to her mother's place in Dorset for Christmas and had a dull New Year's Eve watching fireworks on the

TV. She hadn't looked forward to the inevitable lectures, but in the end survived almost without argument. Elspeth was horrified that her daughter had suffered such a terrifying ordeal at the hands of a knife-wielding maniac. 'I just don't understand why you defend them, dear,' she said.

'I wasn't defending him, Mum,' she answered.

'Well, others of that ilk you do.'

The pleasures of taking Winstanley for long country walks persuaded her to remain in Dorset a few days longer than she had in previous years, returning with some trepidation to her own flat in January. The place was cold and unwelcoming, but at least she was finally up to date on work. Julia couldn't sleep for the first few days, waking up to every slight noise, every flash from next door's movement sensor. There was no sign of the black BMW, nor its occupants. The only unexpected visitors were police officers, who would ring the bell to see that she was all right. After jumping out of her skin the first couple of times, Julia got them to phone from the car before coming to the door. For the next few days, she finally began to sleep through the night, and the terror of being attacked receded. Then, two weeks into January, the world tipped on its axis.

–

It was Friday, 17 January when the locksmith was due to return, yet again. The ornate security grille for the French windows, ordered well before Christmas, had finally arrived. Julia had spent the previous night at Rachel's to celebrate her birthday, and as usual had overdone it on the wine.

She arrived back at Weldon Road just after 9.30 that morning to discover that somebody had broken in. The bolt across the French windows, fitted before Christmas, had been torn from its moorings, and there was mud from the garden traipsed into the carpet. Julia let out a wail of anguish and rang the police. A squad car arrived within five minutes with two large male officers inside. One of the officers, a handsome youngster with brown eyes and a gorgeous smile, looked around outside, while the other took down the details of her movements.

When handsome came in he said: 'It's a pretty crude break-in. There are footprints on the outside of the French windows where they kicked their way in.'

The older officer looked at his iPad. 'You'd reported two suspicious males waiting outside a month or so ago, and I wouldn't be surprised if this is connected.'

'Is anything missing?' handsome asked, donning a pair of blue neoprene gloves.

'I don't know. I haven't looked, in case I ruined any fingerprints. Have you got a spare pair of gloves?' Julia asked.

The younger officer passed across a pair and then followed Julia as they carefully made their way around the flat. The wardrobes and chest of drawers seemed undisturbed. Her jewellery was still in the sock inside the trainer. All her other valuables she hadn't yet brought back from Rachel's.

'I can't see anything that's been taken,' Julia said.

'There are muddy footprints into the kitchen,' said the handsome officer. 'I'll see if we can spare someone from CSI.'

'That would be great,' Julia said, taking photographs of the muddy marks with her phone.

'Look. There's blood!' said the older officer. It was true. There was a thumbnail-sized smear on the door of her fridge freezer.

'Must've cut himself, kicking open the door,' handsome said.

'Right, we'll definitely get you a CSI,' the other said. 'It might not be till tomorrow, because we're all backed up with this West Oakham case. Just make sure you don't touch it, okay?'

'I'll stay with a friend tonight,' she said. She offered the two officers a coffee, but they refused. 'Another time, perhaps,' said the older one with a smile. After thanking them, she watched them depart, suddenly feeling alone and vulnerable in the flat. Luckily, Darren the locksmith was due any time to patch up the doors from outside and make them secure. She had a busy day ahead, and at least she wouldn't need to wait in.

She looked again at the muddy footprints. It was pretty hard to make out the shape of the footwear, but one thing was clear. The mud wasn't dry. Whoever had been in had come in recently. She went upstairs to see if Briony was there, but there was no reply to the bell. She then climbed up to the top floor flat and gave three heavy raps on the knocker. Mrs Drake was known to be deaf, and Briony had often complained about the noise from her television. Julia could hear the sound of a TV from the door, and after receiving no reply knocked heavily again. Mrs Drake finally shuffled to the door and opened it as far as the chain would allow. She was in her late seventies, and quite sprightly. She recognised Julia and disconnected the chain. She said she hadn't heard anything or been aware of any activity.

By the time Julia got back that evening she was exhausted. Yesterday's case at Woolwich Crown Court had resumed and taken most of the day in abstruse legal argument before witnesses had been called and had now been adjourned for a month. She had dozed on the train on the way back, gone back to chambers for some paperwork, only to be pinned down by Hogarth on a scheduling mix-up. She got back to her flat at six, but didn't go in. Darren had done an excellent job patching up the doors, so she felt reassured enough to take up Rachel's invitation to spend the weekend with her and Jack.

The welcome, as always, was noisy. As Julia pushed her way in through the door with briefcase in one hand and laptop bag in the other, Jack shrieked with excitement and cannoned into her leg. He enjoyed the novelty of besieging Julia, who was more indulgent of his boisterous antics than his mother was. Rachel was preparing Jack's tea, which he would have early so he could be asleep before seven thirty and leave them the evening to talk.

'You've clearly not heard the news,' Rachel said.

'What news?'

'Okay, Julia. Sit down, I think you'd better have a glass of wine.'

Julia? Rachel never used her name. It was always Moggy. Julia placed her bags on the floor and retrieved her Mac.

'Is this about my client, the savage Mr Bonner?'

'No.' Rachel poured a generous glass of sauvignon blanc. 'Did you hear about the teacher who was murdered?'

'Just the headline. Wasn't he beheaded or something?'

'It was in West Oakham. A headmaster.' She looked at Julia meaningfully.

'Oh no, it can't be. Surely not.'

Rachel pulled her into an embrace. 'It was. I'm sorry.'

'I don't believe it.'

'I'm really sorry, Moggy. I knew you hadn't heard. But it's true.'

Julia began to cry, big gulping sobs that just didn't seem to end.

–

The next hour for Julia was a haze. She remembered reading and re-reading the BBC website story, which now gave his name but made no mention of how he was killed. She then flicked to some tabloids which gave more detail and suggested it might be a terrorist attack on the school.

'His wife found the body sitting in his car on the drive,' Rachel said.

'Oh God, I wouldn't wish that on my worst enemy,' said Julia, for whom Stella Heath had for fifteen years been that very thing. Finally, after Julia had read everything that she possibly could, she resumed crying.

Jack, who'd been watching TV in the other room, came up to Julia, climbed onto her lap, and cuddled her. He pressed into her hands his favourite one-eared teddy bear, Mr Yelp. When that did no good he offered her his tractor, pushing it onto the kitchen table together with his blue forklift.

'You're very sweet, Jack,' Julia managed through a thickening throat. She ruffled his thick blond hair. Rachel came up and held her too, stroking Julia's hair.

'Mummy, why is she crying?' Jack whispered.

'Because, darling, she has had some very sad news. Someone who she loved very much for a very long time has gone away to join the angels.'

Jack looked at Julia sombrely, his huge brown eyes reflecting the magnitude of the news. He then turned them to his mother, seeking further explanation.

'Come on, Jack, I think it's time for your bed now. Bring Mr Yelp with you.'

Once Jack had been taken to his bedroom, Rachel came over and sat with Julia at the kitchen table.

'It's been the worst day,' Julia said thickly. 'A break-in at the flat, now this. I really can't believe it. This is Surrey, not Syria.'

'It's the end of an era, Moggy. That's the way to think of it. You can turn your face to the future now. Himself is finished. It's all over now.'

The trouble was that with Adam a part of her had died too. A huge chunk of her life, one full of regrets and pain but also of moments of passion and happiness, had passed through to an unreachable place, a cemetery of the mind. Even though she never had any intention of going back to Adam, the fact that the possibility was now completely eliminated froze a part of her heart.

'You're right,' Julia said eventually. 'I really must completely rebuild my emotional life.' She reached for her glass and drained half of it in one go. 'Do you know what? They'll probably think I did it.'

Rachel actually laughed. 'You? You couldn't knock the skin off a rice pudding.'

That evening, Julia got a text from the police to say that a technician from the crime scene investigation department would come round to her flat at two p.m. tomorrow afternoon, to take a sample of the blood on the fridge door, but also to check for any fingerprints. She was asked to stay out of the flat until that time.

Then she got another text, just before she was going to bed.

It was from an unknown phone and simply said: *Like the Xmas pressie?*

Chapter Eighteen

Rachel was just cleaning her teeth, and when she emerged from the bathroom Julia told her about the text. 'I think it's from Destiny.'

'Does that make any sense?'

'No. Not that I can think of. Maybe I should ring her back.'

Rachel put a hand on her shoulder. 'Don't you dare! It will encourage her. You've not heard from her for a month, so you've got to break the connection. Ignore it.'

'What if it was her that broke into the flat?'

'Well, what if it was? You said nothing had been stolen, so presumably you would have noticed if she left a present for you.'

'Well, I didn't exactly search thoroughly.'

'The police told you not to go back until the CSI technician gets there. Wait until the morning, when you're fully sober, we'll discuss it over breakfast. You'll make a better decision that way. Besides, you've just had a huge shock. Turn off the phone until the morning.'

Julia nodded. Rachel was, as always, full of good sense. She had enough to think about for now without worrying about Destiny.

'One other thing, Moggy,' Rachel said. 'You've now got the girl's phone number, and if you give that to the police they'll be able to trace her through the phone. She'll soon be out of your hair.'

—

On Saturday morning the two women had a leisurely breakfast watching Jack blasting imaginary aliens across the kitchen, running round and round the table. Finally, Rachel persuaded him to go and watch one of his favourite DVDs in the other room.

'Ah, a bit of peace!' Rachel said. 'How are you feeling this morning?'

'I couldn't believe it when I first woke up. It was like going through things all over again. I've been looking at the news, they say there was a Syrian asylum seeker who may have been involved. He spent some time with the family.'

Rachel shrugged. 'Maybe that's the answer.'

Julia was examining her phone, looking again at the text. 'I'm really baffled by this. The girl was completely ungrateful the whole time she was staying with me.'

'Maybe she finally felt some guilt?'

Julia shook her head emphatically. 'No, she's wired differently, somehow. It was always take, take, take. She is utterly self-centred.'

'Don't ring her back,' Rachel warned, seeing Julia's hands poised above the keys of her phone. 'Leave it for the police.'

'All right, but I'm going back to the flat now. I really need to have a proper look around.'

'Can I come with you? We could look around together. I worry about you, you know.'

Julia rested a hand on her friend's arm. 'Look. That's very sweet of you, but I know you've got lots to do. I've monopolised your home, soaked up all your sympathy as well as most of your white wine. I need to check around the garden too. She might have left something in the shed, which she could at least get into.'

'All right, if you're feeling up to it. But if you need a hand just give me a bell. The childminder's here soon and doesn't have to go home until late afternoon, so I could be right over.'

Julia left Rachel's house feeling she had the best friend in the world. Someone who would do anything for her. She took her legal briefcase and the laptop bag, and the new keys for the locks that she'd just had installed, stepped out onto the street and unlocked the Duster. The car rumbled into life first time.

As she pulled away, she couldn't help thinking of the time that Adam had come with her to help her purchase the vehicle, persuading the garage to knock £300 off the price. Her eyes smarted at the memory, and she had to stop and wait a couple of minutes for them to clear. It would be so much easier if she could just hate him and let him go.

—

Julia arrived at the flat, retrieved from her bag the neoprene gloves she had been given by the PC and after donning them let herself in.

The flat smelled stale. She looked around and couldn't see any sign of a gift. She was careful to avoid the yellow-tagged areas where the mud had been trodden in, which meant pretty much staying out of the kitchen. She went to the bathroom and both bedrooms but could see nothing that had obviously been disturbed. She set up the laptop on the dining room table as usual, and made herself a cup of tea, being careful to avoid touching the lower fridge door where the bloodstain was, tagged with a yellow evidence marker. Throwing away the teabag, she flipped open the kitchen bin and saw what she imagined was the source of the smell. A bag of frozen broccoli florets, only recently started, had been tossed into the bin where it had now defrosted.

That was very peculiar. She hadn't done it.

She gingerly opened the lower fridge door by its edge and pulled out the big bottom drawer in the freezer compartment. It was very heavy and contained a white plastic carrier bag, its edges brown with what looked like dried blood. Her first thought was a joint of beef, but she couldn't remember buying one recently, certainly nothing that big. She lifted out the heavy bag and placed it on the kitchen table. She pulled apart the crackly plastic, which seemed to have frozen to whatever was beneath. The first thing she saw was a pair of blood-flecked gardening gloves, which she recognised. They had the same elasticated green wrists as a pair she kept in the shed. She gingerly pulled them out. What she saw beneath made her shriek in horror.

It was Adam's head, wrapped in cling film, eyes wide in terror. He was staring at her.

Chapter Nineteen

Julia came to on the floor. She had only been unconscious for a few seconds and struggled with the nightmare image. Surely she had imagined it. She pulled herself to her feet, rubbing a bump on the back of her head. The plastic bag was there, on her kitchen table. She hadn't dreamt it at all. A bilious feeling rose through her throat.

Her first thought was straightforward. The gangsters who had been looking for Destiny must have tracked down Adam as a way of punishing Julia for having the girl stay with her. Even as her mind raced, that stretched credulity. She and Adam had kept their relationship totally secret, at his insistence. Almost nobody knew about it. Stella Heath suspected, but didn't know who Julia was or her name. Only Rachel knew everything.

Destiny.

Julia had told her quite a lot the other night when they were both drunk. But the girl was not capable of this. Adam was a very strong man and could surely not be overpowered by a girl who weighed a hundred pounds or less. It just wasn't possible.

But there was the text message. *Like the Xmas pressie?*

Julia felt the room swimming and lurched off to the bathroom. She knelt down and managed to get her chin over the edge of the lavatory rim before the first dry heave. Then came the rest. Breakfast and more. Before she was finished beads of sweat were standing out on her forehead, and somehow she seemed to be disembodied, looking down upon herself from high above. She could see her arms embracing the toilet bowl, dark hair loose around her shoulders. They would think she had done this. She hated Adam. His disembodied head was sitting on her kitchen table, slowly defrosting, sweating moisture as it did so. Her own gardening gloves, or a very similar pair, were there too. They were covered in blood. If they were hers, they would almost certainly have her DNA inside them.

Her first thought had been to call the police.

But second thoughts crept in. This whole thing was totally incriminating. Her mind was racing. Examining the possibilities, thinking about how this would look from the outside. Her barrister's brain, looking down soberly from above at her prostrate, terrified self, leaning over the lavatory bowl, examined the evidence laid out in the defendant's home. The motive was enormous: a broken heart, vengeance, the anguish of an unwanted abortion. The defendant's story by contrast was utterly implausible. That a feral child who she barely knew, and who didn't know Adam at all, had committed the crime on her own initiative and dumped the evidence at Julia's home before disappearing.

Any jury would convict her.

–

It must've been half an hour before Julia felt ready to get vertical. She washed her face and sponged the spattered front of her sweatshirt. The squeaky sound of the street gate and footsteps down to her front door made her panic. Through the dimpled glass of the front door, she could see a dark uniform with yellow hi-vis patches.

Oh God, the police! It must be someone from CSI. The doorbell rang, a long accusatory noise that demanded attention. As quietly as she could, she scrambled into the kitchen. A sweat had already begun to mist the plastic bag in the kitchen warmth, as if Adam himself was sympathising with her predicament. She slipped the gloves back in the plastic bag, and shoved the heavy thing back in the freezer, closing the door.

The doorbell sounded again.

She stood in the middle of the kitchen, realising her feet were exactly on the muddy footprints. She stepped away, and then stared around to see if there was anything else she needed to hide. She couldn't see anything.

The doorbell went a third time, longer and more insistently. Julia didn't know what to do. She had been told that CSI might not arrive until late morning, so she could pretend not to be in. But actually, a quarter to eleven *was* late morning. She took a couple of deep breaths, and walked slowly towards the door but then realised something important she absolutely had to do.

'Just be a moment,' she called out. She turned around, scampered back into the kitchen and with a dishcloth scrubbed off the bloodstain from the fridge door, and removed the sticky yellow police evidence tag next to it. She then took off her neoprene gloves and stuffed them in her pocket. She took a quick look around the kitchen for anything else incriminating, then made her way back to the front door which she opened to reveal a smiling female officer.

'Hello, my name is Kirsty Mockett and I'm a Surrey Police crime scene investigator. I take it you were expecting me?'

'Yes, I'm sorry. I was just cleaning up in the bathroom.'

'Never mind. I got away a bit earlier than expected today.' The woman was in her mid-twenties, strawberry blonde, pretty and friendly. 'This should only take about half an hour.'

Julia showed her in and pointed out the markers on the kitchen floor where the remains of the mud was.

The woman checked with her own records on the iPad. 'So it was a burglary? According to this nothing was stolen.'

'That's right.'

'Now they've marked out some footprints for me, I can see that.' She crouched down. 'These aren't very clear, actually.'

'No, it's quite a warm flat and I think the mud has turned to dust.'

'That's a shame.' She looked up towards the fridge door. 'I'm supposed to be looking for a bloodstain on here. Can't quite see it actually—'

'Ah, no. That's a bit of a misunderstanding,' Julia said hurriedly. 'The PC thought that the burglar might have cut himself, but in fact that mark was from my own hands, some liver I was preparing. No glass was actually broken, as you can see from the windows.'

The CSI technician nodded and stood up. 'So you wiped it off?'

'Well, not deliberately. I inadvertently brushed against it when I had wet trousers.'

The look she gave Julia was quite odd. 'I thought you weren't staying here? So that the evidence would be preserved.'

'Well, it was principally to keep me safe, but yes, absolutely. I went to stay with my friend Rachel. But I had to pop back a couple of times for various things.

I'm a barrister on the recent gang case from Operation Whirlwind, so things have been a bit hectic.'

'Yes, of course, madam. There's never a good time to suffer a break-in, but still.'

Julia was pleased to hear the word 'madam', an extra notch of deference from the young technician. 'Well, if I'm not getting under your feet too much I shall just nip around and see if I can pick up any fingerprints. I'm afraid we will have to get yours for elimination purposes.'

'That's perfectly all right,' Julia said. She placed her fingers on the officer's iPad when prompted, and then submitted to a cheek swab for DNA.

She then showed the young officer the French windows which had been kicked in, and the presumed route of the burglar through the house. She could feel perspiration on her forehead and her heart was hammering in her chest. She felt her guilt was beaming out like a searchlight, but for the young technician this was clearly a little light relief from the other case she had been working on. Adam's beheading, perhaps? She wasn't going to ask about it, and nothing was volunteered. Julia left her to it and retreated to the lounge, praying that the woman didn't open the freezer door. It was almost forty minutes later when the CSI technician popped her head in and said she was finished.

'Did you find anything?'

'Plenty of your fingerprints, I think,' she said with a smile. 'However, I've got a couple of excellent latent glove prints.'

'Oh, can you do anything with those?' Julia asked, her heart starting to thump again.

'Sometimes. I've just been on a case where the gloves look like being really important, and of course we can sometimes pour in the resources to make a difference. But with something like this, well, we'd need to be pretty lucky. If there was a whole string of burglaries, for example, we could tie them together with glove prints.'

'Ah, right.'

'Never mind,' she said brightly. 'I take it you were insured, for all the damage?'

'Er, yes. That's right.'

'And being a lawyer at least you'll get a chance to put someone away for this, put the boot in for justice, eh?' She swung her own leg for emphasis.

'I'm a defending counsel on this occasion.'

'Ah. Right. One of the enemy, then!' she grinned. 'Just a joke!'

Julia smiled tightly. 'That's all right. We've each got our job to do.'

–

What she did next she knew would be pored over in the trial that would surely come at some stage. If she confessed the truth to this friendly officer, then there was at least some possibility that the situation could be retrieved. It looked awful, but it wasn't impossible. It would be the right thing to do, and in her life Julia had always done the right thing. It had been dinned into her from the youngest age. But as Kirsty Mockett prepared to leave, Julia simply escorted her to the front door, and with some relief closed it behind her. She then sat at the kitchen table, letting her heart rate return to something like normal. She picked up her phone and turned it on.

There had been an email from Destiny. The subject line was simply a question mark, and there was an attachment. It was a video. She hit play. She recognised her own lounge with loud music playing. It was the drunken Saturday night before Christmas. Gloria Gaynor. *I will survive*. Julia came into shot, dancing, badly but exuberantly, with a glass of white in her hand, the odd slosh of wine going over the rim. She recalled this, which Destiny had tried to show her the morning after. Destiny, holding the phone, was dancing too, and her arm reached for Julia into the image. This embarrassing video selfie went on for a good minute. In it, Julia disappeared for a moment, and reappeared with a glass-framed photograph of Adam Heath. 'This is him. Himself,' Julia told the camera.

'He's old and ugly,' Destiny said off-camera.

'He wasn't always,' Julia slurred. 'I wasted so much of my life with that bastard.' She took the photograph. 'Adam Heath, I wish you were dead,' she said to the picture, before smashing it on the corner of the dining table. Julia had remembered the incident and had cleared up the glass in the morning.

'Do you know what?' Julia announced to the camera. 'Adam Heath is now a headmaster, tasked with the moral guardianship of a whole host of young impressionable people. St John's Academy. Formerly St John the Baptist. What a fucking hypocrite.'

Julia could hardly look at this image of herself: drunk, vindictive, angry and spiteful. But it was what she said next, her face pressed close to the phone, her voice almost a whisper, that made her blood run cold:

'Will someone bring me the head of St John the Baptist?'

Chapter Twenty

'But I didn't mean it like that!' Julia was on the phone to Rachel. 'It was a drunken joke.'

'So let me get this right,' her friend said breathlessly. 'You have the head of your ex sitting on the kitchen table?'

'Well, it's back in the freezer now. I hid it when the police technician person came round to look at finger-prints.'

'And you didn't give it to her! Oh my God, Moggy!'

'Of course not! What do you think it would look like, me saying: "Yes, here it is in my house, the head of my ex whom I hate, with bloodstained gloves – my gloves, by the way, from the shed – but it's nothing to do with me." How do you think that would have gone down?'

'But Destiny killed him, not you. She appears on the video too.'

'Yes, yes, I know,' Julia said impatiently. 'And I was in Woolwich Crown Court at the time it happened. But that doesn't matter. There I am on screen, apparently requesting the killing. Under the law of joint enterprise, which God forgive me I've spent enough time tangling with in court, I'm as guilty as the person who wielded the knife. I've got a fantastic motive haven't I? I daresay Adam has got my old love letters stashed away somewhere at home. And I've got a few of his, laden with his promises to leave Stella, going back to the year dot.'

'But I know you didn't want him killed. You wouldn't harm a fly.'

'Well, I know that and you know that, but the presence of the evidence would seem to indicate otherwise.'

'So what are you going to do?' Rachel said. 'You can't leave it in the freezer.'

'I know that! But what can I do? I mean, that's why I rang you. Rachel, you are the only person whom I dare trust with this information.'

'Don't do anything. I'll be there in ten minutes.' She hung up.

Julia put the phone down, and thanked God for friends as good as Rachel. If she had been entirely on her own, she would have gone insane with the injustice of the situation. She still could not believe it, and the timing was the worst possible, with the biggest case of her life coming up next week. Just thinking about it felt like she was having a heart attack.

It was only midday, but she felt she needed a drink. She reached up into the kitchen cupboard where the remains of the Grey Goose vodka still sat. Only a couple of inches left in the bottom, less than a quarter. Her trembling hand reached for the bottle, poured herself a generous measure, and drained it in one. She then refilled it. No orange juice, no mixers. Destiny would be proud.

So, what to do with Adam's head?

Options: One, bury it in the garden. Two, dump it in a canal, river or lake. Three, drive far out into the countryside and bury it there. Four, toss it in a big bin on the industrial estate. Five, oh God, could she really ask Rachel to do that for her? Each and every one of the possibilities had a definite downside. She knew just how incredibly good forensic techniques were these days.

Things had a habit of being found, and once they were, an awful lot could be discovered about them. But above all, the simple act of hiding or destroying evidence was just so incriminating.

She had to keep a clear head. Rachel would be bound to have some good ideas. Julia had barely voiced the thought when the doorbell rang. She crept up to her own front door as if she was a burglar. 'It's only me, Moggy,' she heard Rachel whisper through the letterbox. 'Let me in.'

Julia opened the door and Rachel slid through, her eyes almost glittering with fear and excitement. She looked around the flat as if seeing it for the first time. Then she looked at her lifelong friend, put her arms around her, and held her close.

'You're shaking, my God. Look, we'll think of something,' Rachel said, then looked pointedly at the almost empty vodka bottle. 'Don't you worry.'

Julia could feel herself tearing up in sheer gratitude. 'Rachel, I don't know what I'd do without you.'

'I've been thinking. Everything depends on Destiny. She is bound to want something from you.'

'I already know what she wants,' Julia said. 'For me to botch my defence of Terrence Bonner, to make sure he goes down for a long time. She had even suggested that I kill him.'

'I'm sure you can make some legal mistakes, can't you?' Rachel asked.

'What, and throw away my career entirely?'

'Better that than going to prison,' Rachel said.

'If I'm caught I *would* go to prison. Perverting the course of justice has a maximum sentence of life!'

Julia set her phone shakily on the table, and the two women then looked at the video and the text from Destiny. 'It is pretty incriminating, I suppose,' Rachel said. 'Even though to me it's obvious that you were drunk.' Rachel pointedly took the bottle of Grey Goose and put it back in the cupboard.

'It's no defence. Most violent crime is committed by people who are under the influence of drink or drugs,' Julia said. 'It doesn't stop them being sent to prison.'

'So what are we going to do with Himself?' Rachel said, inclining her head towards the fridge freezer. 'If there is any way we could get him to the police anonymously, that would be best.'

'You mean dump him in a bin bag in a field and ring Crimestoppers? Something like that?'

'Yes, why not?'

'I'm not sure, Rachel. There might be some microscopic particle from here that got onto him. And these days they'll certainly find it.'

'Well, we should certainly burn the gloves. That's something obvious.'

Julia nodded. 'Yes. I thought of dropping the head in a canal, but I'm not sure. It might float.'

'You could weight it down before throwing it in.'

Julia shook her head. 'I'd constantly be worrying about some angler finding it.'

'Bury it in the garden? Or under the shed? I mean, you have sole rights over the garden, don't you?'

'I do, under the lease, but I'd have to live here forever to make sure nobody else digs it up.'

'Not if you cast it in concrete before burying it.'

Julia could see that Rachel was really trying to help. 'My DIY skills aren't a patch on yours, Rachel. I tried cementing my own front doorstep once, where it was cracked. My repairs didn't last a year. And I can hardly get a builder in to do it for me.' She waited for her friend to offer. She didn't.

'Hey, I read a true crime book last year about how some bloke got buried at night in wet cement when they were building the Westway in London.'

'We're not the Kray sisters, Rachel. I'm not going poking about a building site late at night, dragging my boyfriend's head in a bag.' Seeing the slight smirk on her friend's face, she added. 'It's not bloody funny, this is my life going down the toilet.'

'Well, you've got to do something. You can't leave it here, can you?'

'I was thinking about going on a cross-channel ferry, and halfway over, dropping it over the side,' Julia said. 'What do you reckon?'

'That's pretty good. But you'd have to go on one of those overnight crossings, to make sure that nobody sees you do it.'

'I suppose so. And I'd be sitting in a cabin with the festering thing staring at me for hours.'

'And, God, it would stink.'

'There is one other option, if I dare ask you…' Julia whispered, her eyes sliding sideways to assess Rachel's reaction. She watched the slow change of shape of her friend's face, eyes widening, jaw slackening then tightening again.

'No way, sorry. No way.' Rachel shook her head. 'I'm not burying that fucking thing on one of my sites, I'm sorry.'

'You are in the perfect position. You've got that big redesign project on all those acres—'

'I've also got two employees, Julia. How can you even ask me?'

'I wouldn't if I had any other options,' she said tearfully.

'I love you, Moggy, but I'm not going to prison for you, you have to understand that.'

'I'm sorry, really I am. I just don't know what to do. I've got to get it out of here today. I just can't stand knowing it's here. I mean, what if Destiny comes back…?'

'To get her pound of flesh,' Rachel muttered. She didn't say anything for little while, then seemed to have an idea. 'You know those gangsters that were looking for Destiny?'

'Christ, yes. I can't believe I'm beginning to forget about them, with everything else that is going on.'

'Well,' Rachel said carefully. 'It might well suit you if they found her, wouldn't it? If she was never heard of again.'

Julia looked at her friend in horror. What had they become? Even to consider this. She felt tears well up but wiped them away angrily. She just had to think clearly, to be detached and logical, and imagine it as if it was a court case for someone else. Detachment and logic. Something to retain her sanity.

—

Rachel reminded Julia she had to leave before half three to relieve Jack's childminder for her next job. Julia had stacks of work preparation to do for the Bonner case. But she couldn't begin to concentrate, and she was trembling like a leaf in an autumn gale. 'So what have you decided to do?' Rachel said as she slung her bag over her shoulder and prepared to leave.

'I'm going to post it somewhere.'

'What?'

'I have a cousin, called Hilary, who works for the World Health Organisation, she's been all over the world vaccinating children. She was in Afghanistan, northern Pakistan, Angola, everywhere.'

'Sorry, I don't get it.'

'The year before last she was in Turkmenistan. Not even in the capital, but hundreds of miles further, the back of beyond. My mother wanted to send her a Christmas present. I offered to do it for her and went to the main post office in Guildford. My mother had been bellyaching that it should be dispatched in plenty of time, so I took it down early in September, if I remember rightly. Bags of time. Hilary emailed in the following January that the parcel never arrived.'

'You're not going to post her the head, are you?'

'Not *her*, no. Especially as she is now based in Geneva. But if I parcel it up properly, make a mishmash of an address that is close to where Hilary used to be based in Turkmenistan, I could send the bloody thing off and never see it again.'

'I don't even know where Turkmenistan is,' Rachel said.

Julia went to a bookshelf and pulled down the big heavy *Times Atlas* which had been her father's and set it down on the table. She then flicked through to the Central Asian pages. 'There. North of Iran and east of the Caspian Sea.' The country was huge, shown as an almost blank beige patch with few towns, cities or roads.

'Wow, that really is obscure. Would you have to send it by courier?'

'No, definitely not. It has to go the basic post office way. Not tracked or anything, that's crucial. And the return address has to be fictitious of course, just in case. The point is to choose somewhere where the police are corrupt and useless. So even if it's found, it wouldn't be investigated.'

'I'm not sure about this,' Rachel said. 'It would start to honk a bit, surely, in a few days?'

'Yes, but if it come straight out of the freezer, and is well wrapped, and put in a polystyrene box, you'd get a good few days before it began to whiff.' Julia could see the strange look that Rachel was giving her. 'Look. My mother made me make a complaint to the post office about its non-arrival, so I got to find out a bit about what happens on that particular route. There's a flight from Gatwick three times a week which goes to Ankara with all the UK post for Central Asia. It reckons to get there in a bit less than a week from posting. Then it gets sorted and sent by plane to Ashgabat, the Turkmen capital. That's a once-per-week trip, they told me.'

'They might X-ray all the parcels. Turkey's had a lot of terrorism.' Rachel looked at the time. 'And the main post office in Guildford closes in a couple of hours.'

For a moment Julia looked stumped. 'I know, I'll wrap it up in foil.' She opened her laptop, and googled X-rays and aluminium foil. 'Hmm. It says here I would need a heck of a lot.'

'Lead would work,' Rachel said.

'Where am I going to get lead?' Julia asked. The two women looked at each other for a couple of minutes.

'Ah!' Rachel clicked her fingers and asked where Julia kept her stepladder. The folding aluminium steps were found in a cupboard by the front door, which Rachel opened.

'What are you doing?'

'I'm nicking lead flashings off your roof.' Rachel set the steps by the wheelie bin enclosure that served the three flats. A small flanged section of lead 2' x 4" wide was fixed into the brickwork from the edge of the tiles, to prevent rain getting in. Directed by Julia to her toolbox, she took out a Stanley knife, switched the blade for a new sharp one and climbed up the steps. It took only a couple of minutes to cut it from the edge of the cemented section. Using a long screwdriver she gradually bent and pulled the flashing until it came away from under the edge of the tiles.

'You might get wet bins, but needs must,' Rachel said.

'That's brilliant!' Julia said.

Back inside the kitchen with the door locked, Julia laid newspaper over the kitchen table. She took a strong cardboard wine case, removed the bottle spacers, and lined it with kitchen foil. She and Rachel then cut the lead into a dozen thin bendable strips using the Stanley knife on a chopping board. Finally, when everything was ready, Julia said to Rachel: 'Are you ready for this?'

She nodded. Julia knew her friend had an enthusiasm for horror thrillers but didn't expect her to be quite so gung-ho about involvement in their real-life equivalent. Julia pulled open the freezer door and slid out the heavy lower tray. She then heaved up the heavy plastic bag onto the table.

'Can I take a look?' Rachel asked.

'If you want. But whatever you do, don't scream. Briony will be back any time, and she mustn't hear us.' Julia pulled out the two frozen bloodstained gloves, and dropped them in a fresh freezer bag which she then sealed. She swivelled the main package until the neck faced Rachel, and then pulled back the flap.

Rachel's hands shot up to her face, her eyes wide. 'Oh my god,' she hissed. 'He's recognisable.'

Julia checked the time. 'I'd better get a move on.' The two women lifted the head out from the freezer, stripped off the carrier bag which they carefully stuffed inside another carrier for burning. The head had already been wrapped in cling film, and they added an entire roll of kitchen foil. Over the top, they wrapped the thin lead strips. There wasn't quite enough for a complete layer, but Julia felt that it would make any X-ray hard to interpret. Finally, a layer of bubble wrap. Julia filled the box with polystyrene chips left over from a Christmas gift, and the two of them carefully eased the package inside. Copious layers of parcel tape finished off the package.

'There, that's not too bad,' Julia said.

Rachel hefted the box. 'It's really heavy. Do you have kitchen scales?'

'No.' She took the package from her friend. 'Do you think it weighs more than ten pounds?'

'I would say it weighs the same as our Christmas turkey, which is normally eight to ten pounds.'

'Good, because the weight limit for basic non-tracked international parcels is five kilograms, just over ten pounds.'

A few more minutes and the parcel was complete.

'Right, now I have to get my disguise,' Julia said.

'What?'

'Rachel, this has got to be foolproof in case the return address is ever checked. It's essential they have no idea who posted it. There are CCTV cameras in every post office, and I'm a regular in the Guildford branch.'

'Moggy, you've been drinking. And you're in no state to drive.' Rachel picked up the parcel 'I've got to go to Woking anyway, so I'll give you a lift to the post office there. Nobody there will know you.'

—

It was almost a quarter to five, and Julia was in the queue at the main post office in Woking, which was inside a branch of WHSmith. It was a cold afternoon, but inside the stuffy building, with her thick calf-length leopard print coat, she was roasting. She was wearing a blonde wig, big hoop earrings and a baseball cap. She was glad she had not thrown out all the charity shop junk she had bought for the chambers fancy dress party two years ago. The ankle boots were particularly good because they added three inches to her height. For all that, she was terrified. Her throat was dry and her heart was thumping, pressed hard against the heavy cardboard box she was cradling in her arms. The same head that in years past had lain gently on her breast and promised time and again that he would leave his wife. Now to be dispatched to the back of beyond. She couldn't believe that she had been pitched into this utter nightmare.

The queue moved forward, until the big man that Julia had been hiding behind was called forward. She was now standing alone at the front of the queue, the box which must surely be transparent held in her now aching arms. Finally, she heard the queue system announce: *Cashier number two, please.* She stepped forward.

'I'd like to send this to Turkmenistan,' she said to the young woman behind the glass screen, as she heaved the object onto the scales. It weighed 4.8 kg.

'We don't get many parcels going there,' she said with a smile. 'You'll need to fill out a customs declaration.'

'I've already done that,' she said, passing across the label.

'You'd be best using the international signed service, to make sure it has a decent chance of getting there,' the cashier said. 'What would you say the value was?'

'It's less than £20,' Julia said. 'So I'd like to send it international economy.'

'I really wouldn't advise it. You can't vouch for the basic post in places like that. Use a courier service, you won't regret it.'

Julia wanted to scream but managed a thin smile. 'How much?' she muttered.

'Ah, it's a bit more than I expected. For that weight, £96.40.'

Julia shook her head. 'Can't afford it. Just the basic, please.'

'Okay, but it may take more than a month,' she warned. 'Still, it is a lot less expensive. That's £32.90. You say on the customs declaration it's books and papers, is that right?'

'Yes, don't worry, it's not fragile.'

The post office clerk copied across the address details, including the fake return address with its false name, and passed across a sticky label for Julia to attach to the parcel. She was then directed to take the parcel to a Perspex cubbyhole.

As Julia walked out of the post office she was elated.

With luck, she'd never hear anything about it again.

As soon as Rachel dropped Julia back home, she scrubbed the flat from top to bottom. She used bleach on the kitchen floor and on the shelf and basket from the freezer. She wondered if her friend was aware that even helping her wrap the parcel made her an accessory, easily enough for a five-year prison sentence. Yes, she probably would have guessed. A true measure of friendship.

She recalled just a couple of years ago defending a man of nineteen who had disposed of a knife used in an assault, a serious one but not fatal. Even though he was of previously good character, and had pleaded guilty at the first opportunity, he still got two years. He had said: 'I was just helping out a mate, that's all.' At the time Julia had thought: well, it serves him right.

What a prig she had been.

And then she got a phone call from Destiny.

–

The call came from the same number as the text and Julia answered it with trepidation.

'It's me.'

Julia recognised Destiny's sibilant voice, and her anger poured out. 'Did you do that? Was that what you meant by the gift?'

'I did you a favour. It was what you asked for.'

'You're being crazy. I didn't ask for that!'

'It's well right what you asked for. And as a favour to you, I done it.'

'No, Destiny, it's simply a biblical joke. Salomé and the dance of the seven veils. John the Baptist. Don't you understand?'

'I dunno what you're talking about.'

'Destiny, it was a terrible thing you did, just terrible.'

'Whatever.' The girl actually laughed. 'So, what have you done with it?'

Julia hesitated. She certainly wasn't going to tell her. 'I've had the police round, after you broke in. They've taken fingerprints and footprints. They will be on your trail.'

Destiny clearly didn't believe her. 'If they catch me, they'll catch you. You'll go down for years. For me, I don't give a shit. At least I'll be safe from the gangs. But you. Soft, middle class, privileged. You'll be surrounded all day by people like me, or worse. The noise, the banging on the walls, especially when they discover you're a lawyer. You won't be able to hack it. You'll be carving your initials on your wrists in no time, believe me.'

Julia had no answer to that, but she thought of Rachel's suggestion. 'So where have you been hiding, Destiny? Whose shed have you been living in?'

She laughed softly again. 'I'm not going to tell you. But I am doing all right, thank you for asking.' Her voice dripped with sarcasm.

'You'll not get away with this,' Julia said.

'I'm going to get away with a lot more than this, Ms Julia McGann,' she said. 'I've been reading the papers. It seems the cops don't yet know about you and Adam Heath. No mention of it. All those years.'

'We worked very hard to keep it secret.'

'Well. Just think what the cops will do when I post them a data stick with that video on. You were ordering an execution. They'll be all over you in a heartbeat.'

'Please don't, Destiny. I mean Dezzy.'

'Yeah, that's what I'm gonna do.' She laughed.

'Please, don't, please. I'm begging you.' Julia closed her eyes. She had feared this. The blackmail she had known must be coming. And she really didn't have any alternative but to buckle before the threat.

238

'I'll say you paid me to do it. Gave me the address, all that.'

'All right, Destiny, you win. The case begins on Monday. I will make sure that Bonner goes down for a long time, even if I have to screw up my job, my entire career to do it. You have my word. I'll make you safe, if you destroy that video.'

'Oh no, no.' Destiny laughed again. 'No, no, no. You're not getting off that lightly.'

'What do you mean? That's the best I can possibly do.'

'Look. Terry Bonner is going down for years already. That's done and dusted. But he'll live like a king inside, and he'll still run his empire outside. All the spice he wants, mobiles, bent screws at his beck and call. I want to get him back proper. For all the girls like me, that he used and abused. It's not gonna happen again. Because you're gonna stop it.'

'Look, Destiny, I will concede that you are very clever, tracking me down, stealing my purse, getting my address. I admire your tenacity, and I do like you, believe me. It's just—'

'Fuck off. Don't insult my intelligence. You don't care anything about me, you just want me out of the way.'

'No, Destiny. I know that you don't trust people, but I do have connections. I can make representations to my contacts in the prison service. To make life tough for him.' Even as she said it Julia knew she was exaggerating her influence. 'Take my word for it.'

'No. If you've lived my life, you'll know it goes better when you don't trust anyone to keep their word. Incentives. The other person's shoes. That's what works. I've learned that, long and hard.'

'Well, there's nothing more I can do.'

'Is that right? No, there is something you can do, something that only you can do. Go to your garden shed. Under the rotten floorboard in the middle of the floor you will find something. I'll ring you back in five minutes.' She cut the call.

Julia considered not going, refusing to be given orders by the girl. But she saw that was pointless. She heaved herself up from the kitchen table. She was dizzy with terror, but she dug out her wellies and peered into the garden. It was dark and damp and not very inviting. She slipped into her Barbour jacket, and donned the rubber boots. She pocketed her phone and the shed keys, and to avoid the faff of unlocking the new security grille on the French windows, she exited from the front door. She then made her way around the alleyway outside of the house into the back garden. Light rain was just beginning to fall, slanting across the light from the phone as she approached the shed. She had a suspicion about what she was going to find but kept praying that it would be something else. Her hands shook as she undid the padlock on the shed and went inside.

The spiders had been busy in the weeks since it had been vacated by Destiny, and Julia had to brush webs aside. There were a couple of drinks cans and a triangular package from a supermarket sandwich on a shelf. Julia crouched, found a loose plank and levered it up with a trowel. There were a couple of grubby plastic bags under the wood. She lifted them out, feeling a significant weight in one that confirmed her fears. She tipped the heavy bag and out slid a greasy cloth within which was a black pistol little bigger than the palm of her hand. She just stared at the evil thing, sitting there on the rags. The second bag, lighter, contained a serrated knife covered in dried blood and a coiled length of bronze picture wire with loops tied in the ends. She bundled up the bags and took them back into her flat.

She had barely closed the front door before the phone rang. 'Have you got it?'

'Yes. Is that the wire and knife you used…?'

'It is. Worked very well. But the gun is what you need.'

'But I told you before, you can't get a gun into the court. I'm liable to be searched, even as a barrister. I've never even fired one.'

'Neither have I. Just know this: I'm not interested in your excuses. Hide the gun up your arse if you have to. I know that lawyers can see their clients alone, and that's all you need. Blow his brains out and when the screws come in, call it suicide.'

'That's ridiculous.'

'No. Put the gun in his hands straight after. They'll believe what you have to say. A lawyer's word in a court of law. Sorted.'

'Destiny, please, I have to make you see that it's completely and utterly unworkable.'

'Fine, suit yourself. Monday evening, nine o'clock. The data stick goes to the cops.'

Julia was trying all she could to keep herself together. Her heart was hammering, all she could think of was that if she could give Destiny a viable alternative, something that would punish Bonner sufficiently without killing him, she could save herself from this hopeless scheme.

'If I try to shoot him, I'll probably miss. Or he'll grab the gun from me.'

'There are seven shots in the magazine. Go somewhere and practice.'

'Destiny, I'm not going to do it. What you have on video is not enough evidence—'

'Listen. Go to your laptop and look up the search history, and then tell me you'll get off scot free.' She hung up.

—

Julia let her head fall into her hands. She had a horrible feeling as she flipped open the Mac. She knew exactly where to look. The search history on the Sunday morning, the morning after she and Destiny had got drunk together. She took a while to narrow it down, but the Google search terms recorded in the history list for the hour immediately before Julia got up told a story of their own.

Adam Heath headmaster. St John the Baptist school. St John's Academy. Foolproof murder. Death by strangulation. Garrotting. Disposal of human remains. Unsolved murders. Getting rid of forensic evidence. Weight of human head.

There were typos and grammatical errors in the search terms, and some of the information there about Adam's location Julia would be able to argue that she already knew. But with the Google maps Destiny had used and satellite pictures of the area around Adam's house, it was totally incriminating. It was tempting to delete the entire history file, but that would be even more incriminating. She knew full well that deleted or private search histories were about the first thing that detectives looked for in the forensic examination of computers. They were all

242

retained on the servers of service providers and could not be deleted by users. Explaining how these terms had innocently got there was an impossibility. No one but Rachel had ever seen Destiny inside Julia's flat, and Rachel would hardly count as independent. Trying to prove that this mythical girl even existed, let alone that she had been living in the flat with her and had used Julia's laptop, would strain the credulity of any jury. No, Destiny was absolutely right. Combined with the video, this was compelling circumstantial evidence of Julia's determination to murder or arrange the murder of her former boyfriend. She suddenly understood the power of blackmail. Destiny had alluded to it when she said she would never trust anyone's word. With the kind of life experiences the young woman had suffered, that made perfect sense. Hers was a transactional adolescence. Pimped out, drugged up, rented away to the highest bidder. A wasting asset. All she had to rely on were her own wits, her own sense of cunning, and an understanding of the motivations of others. A Machiavellian ABC course, with homework.

Julia was in a corner from which she could not escape. She was due to return that evening to stay with Rachel and little Jack. Right now that seemed a world out of reach. A place of softness, of affection, of friendship and love. She realised that this latest turn of the screw would make it impossible for her to do what she most wanted: to confide in Rachel. It was one thing for her best friend to know that she had covered up evidence for a murder she did not commit, and even to help dispose of that evidence. It was quite another to plan a real killing, even of someone who perhaps deserved to die. There was moral space between the two positions, and it was not fair to Rachel, or to Jack's future, to ask her to cross that rubicon.

Julia rang Rachel and after apologising for the late notice said she wouldn't be coming over. She had lots of work to do before the case on Monday.

'It will be good to get your head into that, as a distraction,' Rachel said. She wished her good luck and hung up.

There were going to be no distractions. Because the die was cast. There was no point preparing for the trial, because there wasn't going to be a trial. Julia was going to murder Terrence Bonner, or at least try to. She simply had no choice. She didn't have time for tears, and she had to park somewhere the nervous breakdown that was hovering somewhere on the edges of her consciousness. She simply couldn't allow herself to think about anything except herself and survival.

For the first time she was experiencing a life constrained by horrible choices, a set of narrowing and dangerous alternatives, not one of which was legal. She realised she was now living the fugitive girl's life. Forget the public school education, the pony, the privileged life of a judge's daughter. Julia was becoming her own Destiny.

Chapter Twenty-one

Gillard was sitting with research intelligence officer Rob Townsend and CSI specialist Karen Desai from the Met who they had borrowed for a few days. Karen was an expert on gloves, and indeed had worked on the national glove database at Nottingham Trent University before joining the Met. They were looking at a high-resolution screen which showed side-by-side images of the glove prints taken from Adam Heath's car and the burglary at Weldon Road in Guildford. 'The prints from the car are about as good as you ever get from a set of gloves,' she said. 'Fabulous clarity. Unfortunately, those from the Weldon Road burglary are much less impressive, and we really only have one thumb tip blood stain to make that connection.'

'So how confident can you be that it is from the same pair?' Gillard asked.

'If it was just the latent impression of that thumb, there would be grounds for error. However, the shape of the bloodstain transferred on the thumb tip is unique. Kirsty said that the marked bloodstain on the fridge was lost, but she discovered this print on the underneath of a catch on some French windows. It easily makes the ninety-five per cent confidence interval.'

'So you are ninety-five per cent convinced?' Townsend said.

Karen nodded. 'More than that, actually. These aren't particularly common gardening gloves. The studded rubber pads are used in only a tiny minority of the products sold in garden centres and elsewhere.'

Gillard nodded. 'Then perhaps we should try to corroborate that with other evidence.'

'Sir, could the Heath killing really just be a burglary that went wrong?' Townsend asked.

'No. I really can't see that. Professional burglars are risk-averse individuals, while amateurs, those on drugs for example, might be messy, but they go straight for what they want. Cutting off then stealing Adam Heath's head would be a bizarre thing for any burglar to do, even if he was as high as a kite.'

'Yes, it sounds crazy to me,' Karen said.

'The most bizarre coincidence to me is who the killer chose to burgle,' Gillard said. 'A barrister, one who, come Monday, is going to be very busy defending Terrence Bonner.'

'Kirsty met her, when she did the CSI,' Rob said. Kirsty Mockett was Rob's girlfriend. 'Seems a very nice woman.'

'That was Michelle who interviewed her, wasn't it?' Gillard went to a separate desk and logged on to the local police computer. He found the report on the burglary, and the victim's statement. 'There's not much detail here. Something about a runaway from a children's home.'

'I can't see what connection there might be between the two cases,' Townsend said.

'Neither can I. But I'm going to ask Michelle to take another look, when she has a moment.'

–

Julia had just over thirty-six hours until the court came into session on Monday morning. She would be alone with Bonner in the cells for a few minutes before that. Emily, who might have accompanied her, was at Julia's request going to prepare their paperwork in the courtroom instead. That was all very well, but Julia still had to learn how to use the gun. The easiest way was to search on YouTube. There were always hundreds of videos on how to do anything. As she had just a few bullets, she didn't want to waste them even on practising until she knew what she was supposed to be doing. Googling for gun videos compounded her already incriminating web search history. Perhaps in the end she would simply have to dispose of or hide her precious laptop before killing Bonner. That was something else to look up. Could the police retrieve search records even when they didn't have the device in question? All the commonly asked questions she could find online simply referred to deleted files.

The police would expect her to have a laptop, and she would have to hand something over to them after shooting Bonner. Fortunately, she had an old Hewlett-Packard which she'd used when she was training as a paralegal. It was slow, but still worked. She would have to transfer her work data across to it to make it appear the HP was her current machine, but she couldn't build an old search history to cover the time of Adam's killing. Maybe she wouldn't have to destroy the Mac. She could wrap it carefully and bury it under the shed floor. Yes, that's what she would do, last thing on Sunday night after she'd finished doing any incriminating searches.

Julia made herself a strong cup of coffee and sat down at her kitchen table with the gun on some newspaper. She then looked through half a dozen how-to-shoot videos, starting with the basics. She discovered that the pistol in her possession was a US-made Rock Island Armoury 'Baby Rock' .38 with a full seven-round magazine in the handle. She found the safety catch, and made sure it was definitely on. She watched the body stance and handgrip used by the instructors and acted it out in front of her bedroom mirror. She felt silly doing it in her grey cardigan and slippers, which brought home the sheer absurdity of what she was planning to do. Totally hopeless. She realised you have to look the part to feel the part. She changed into a pair of leather trousers a tight white T-shirt and an old denim jacket that she had picked up from a charity shop. She brushed her hair, put on some eyeliner, added bright red lipstick, and the final touch, a pair of black elegant high heels.

Now, in front of the mirror, she *did* look the part. In fact she had to admit she looked pretty sexy. She'd always had good legs, and still had a decent figure despite the intermittent exercise of recent years. She tried her appearance sideways, with the gun barrel pointing vertically, placed against her lips. Very much the Bond girl. She dug out some Bond-themed soundtracks on YouTube and played them as she cavorted about with the gun. She *had* to feel the part, the confidence had to come from somewhere. The man she was planning to kill was one of the most terrifying gangsters in Britain. Just thinking about that seemed to make her insides liquefy.

'Come on, girl, you can do this.' She paced backwards and forwards in the flat, then decided she could not avoid going out to practise with the gun. She double-checked the safety was on, released the magazine and slid it back in, which it did with a satisfying click.

She found a suitably sized shoulder bag for the gun, zipped the weapon inside, changed into a pair of trainers for driving, picked up her keys and a pair of wellies and headed for the front door. She was going to drive deep into the Surrey countryside, and fire off three practice shots. The remaining four should be enough to do the business. It was eight o'clock, and dark, but all she would need was a wooden gate to practise on from short range.

The doorbell rang.

Through the dimpled glass panel she could see the giveaway hi-vis of a police uniform. She opened the door, her heart hammering. She recognised the officer, the older and less good-looking of the previous pair. 'Sorry to disturb, Ms McGann. We thought you were staying with friends.'

'I did for a few weeks, but you can't do it for ever. I'm sorry, I should have notified you.'

'I saw the light on when I was driving past and thought I'd just give a quick check. Given the burglary last month, you know.'

Julia exhaled for the first time in a minute. 'Thank you very much for looking after me, constable.'

'I hate to think of you all alone. Is there a Mr McGann, or a boyfriend, that can stay with you, now you're back?' The question was so naturally slid in she almost missed its significance.

'No. I have a good friend, Rachel, who sometimes pops back with me.'

The PC, who was in his mid-thirties, okay-looking but not a patch on the other one, peered over her shoulder into the flat. 'Got all your new locks fitted, now? Had no further trouble, I take it?'

Oh, the story she could tell. This would probably be the last chance for truth, for confession. But she couldn't do it.

'No, it's been very quiet fortunately. Any progress on the fingerprints and so forth that your colleague took from here?' She couldn't resist the question.

'Nothing on the fingerprints or footprints. But...' He looked at her and smiled. 'We have good reason to think your intruders were involved in another very serious crime.'

'My goodness,' Julia said. 'What crime?'

'May I come in for a minute? I don't want to say this outside.'

Julia backed up a few feet and allowed him into the hall. They were quite close to each other and she was aware that his eyes hadn't stayed on her face but had made brief forays further down to the tight white T-shirt. 'They've made some very good progress on glove prints, from your fridge door, apparently.'

'What kind of progress?'

'Just between you and me, right? The glove matches one used by the bastard who beheaded that schoolteacher over in Reigate.'

Julia didn't have to feign her shock. 'Oh, that's terrifying. And he's been in my home?'

'Yes. I really do think it's a good idea for you to go back to staying with friends for now, just until we catch him. You shouldn't come back alone. In the meantime, we'll be keeping up the patrols.'

'Did you manage to trace the car that I reported?'

'Yes and no. It's got cloned plates, copied from some perfectly innocent motorist who lives in Bradford. But we're looking out for them, don't you worry. Your break-in is now part of a much bigger operation, so rest assured your safety is a priority for us.'

'Thank you, I much appreciate that.'

The PC then asked for the address where Julia would be staying. 'I might pop round in a day or two, to see if you're okay.' He raised one eyebrow slightly, so the additional meaning was clear.

'Okay. What did you say your name was?' She tried to keep her expression neutral.

'PC Geraint Howlett.'

'Thank you, Geraint. I was just leaving actually. I'm on my way to see a friend.'

'Then I'll wait until you leave, just so I know you're safe.'

After locking up, Julia followed the policeman up the steps to the street and closed the wrought iron gate behind her. She made her way to the car, which was parked in its usual position, under the hawthorn tree. The roof was already spattered, the filthy Duster once again. Her throat was dry, thinking about what was in her bag. She looked across to the police patrol car on the double yellow at the corner. The interior light was on.

Geraint was angling for something, that was clear. But this was no time for an entanglement. After what was going to happen on Monday, he wouldn't want to touch her with a bargepole.

–

Julia drove away, past the police patrol car, and pipped her horn in thanks. She drove east out of Guildford towards Polesdon Lacey, then onto Ranmore Common Road. She found a nice hilly area with no nearby habitation. It was very dark, and the nearest streetlamps were miles away. She parked by a farm gate, then took the gun from her bag and a torch in the other hand. There was a dead tree just a few yards into the field, with a big expanse of missing bark at about chest height. Perfect. It was quiet, and only the faint drone of distant traffic could be heard.

She stood six feet from the tree, lay the torch on the ground so it illuminated where she was aiming for. She flicked the safety catch off, braced herself as she had learned from the videos, right-hand index finger through the trigger, left hand on top of right, and aimed at the centre of the tree.

The gunshot tore open the night sky. It was so much louder than she expected and echoed in her ears for several seconds. The gun had jumped in her grip, but she didn't know how badly until she peered closely at the tree. It was absolutely undamaged. She spent a good minute and could not find any sign of a bullet hole. She returned to her aiming position and picked up the spent cartridge. It was hot. The second shot was little better. This time she managed to keep her eyes open, but the tree was still undamaged. She had five shots left in the magazine. She didn't want to spend more than two more minutes doing this, in case the noise attracted someone. She wanted to be in the car and away.

'Come on, it doesn't have to be so hard. I'm going to be much closer than this,' she muttered to herself. For the third shot she stood within four feet. This time she heard the bullet splinter part of the tree. It had buried itself at least three inches in but was still too far to the right. The fourth shot was the best, near enough in the middle of the tree. That left three bullets to do the job. She couldn't risk another practice shot.

She looked up, and heard a vehicle coming along the lane. It was still a long way off, but she could see its headlamps. She hurried back to the car, stowed the gun and torch in the bag, got in and drove off briskly. The following vehicle never actually caught up with her, and she was able to circle back into Guildford.

In her mind she ran through everything she would have to do. It still seemed impossible.

–

Sunday night was wet and windy. Julia had driven up the M1 to Nottingham and had checked into an anonymous Travelodge not far off the motorway. She lugged her bags up to the room, a small beige rectangle with a window over a car park. There didn't seem any point splashing out more money given her mood. This could well be the last night of her life. On her four-hour journey in heavy traffic she'd had plenty of opportunity to think through the course of action she had decided upon. And she was still far from sure that she was capable of pulling that trigger.

But she was planning everything as if she would. Getting through security was crucial, and her biggest obstacle. A lot of that would be about projecting authority. Normally, she would arrive wearing civvies, then dress in the robing room. This time she wanted the full magisterial arrival: flowing robe, heels, wig already in place. The risk of being frisked was not quite as high as she had made out to Destiny, thanks to the smartphone app. The scheme, which had only been going for a year or two, was for registered barristers, and allowed them to show their app to staff on entry to the court building. It allowed her to take her legal briefcase with phone, laptop and other metallic items in without submitting to the metal detector. She'd used the app a dozen times already, and it seemed to work fine, allowing her to jump the queue which had hitherto been a major source of irritation to her profession. In theory, there was still a chance of a manual search. However, in practice the poorly paid and outsourced security staff at most court buildings were extremely deferential and relied on entirely predictable class and racial prejudices in whom they chose to pull aside. You could guarantee that anyone black would be assumed to be a defendant and searched, even if they were wearing a suit. Black barristers regularly complained about it. Anyone wearing a hoodie, jogging trousers, baseball cap, with visible tattoos, whatever their ethnicity, tended to be treated the same way. By contrast, South Asian legal professionals were often given the benefit of the doubt, unless they were heavily bearded, in which case they might be treated like suspected terrorists. Smartly dressed, confident white men in their fifties and sixties who could conceivably be judges were rarely troubled.

The gun she had put in a small freezer bag, sandwiched between two slices of bread and a thick layer of coleslaw. The sandwich was tight inside a plastic food box within her legal briefcase. It wouldn't fool a metal detector, but she couldn't imagine the kind of cursory hand search that might occur would ever require a peek at her lunch.

She carefully unpacked on the bed, checking everything was in order. By the time she was satisfied that everything she could have prepared was, it was eight o'clock. She had packed a small bottle of gin and some tonic but it seemed too depressing to sit in her room and drink it.

She powered up her ancient HP laptop, and looked online for pubs in the vicinity. There were a couple nearby as the crow flies, but which would necessitate using the car or crossing some major roads. But on the same side of the road, 200 yards down, was a hotel with a bar. That would do for starters. Having the previous night worn the leather trousers and high heels, she felt motivated to do so again. She spent some time getting dressed. Mascara, eyeliner, lipstick and a fashionable bolero jacket over a lacy black blouse. Part of her wanted to take the gun, for its empowering effect, but that would be utterly stupid. She tidied up the room and stowed her luggage carefully.

Just in case.

It being a Sunday night the hotel bar was stone dead, so she walked on, heading for the big chain pub that was the next nearest. A quick glance through the big window showed that it was a raucous scrum of sports screens and noisy young men. Not what she wanted. Finally, she arrived at the Windmill, a more traditional pub with food, and a roaring fire. She sat at the bar and ordered a G&T. She knew immediately she was being watched, and tonight, for once, she wanted to be. Something had clicked inside her since she became entangled in the blackmail threat. Tonight she wanted to throw caution to the wind. A man in his sixties, with a pastel shaded pullover and a ruddy face under his grey thatch, started to chat her up and offered to buy her another drink. She thanked him but told him she was waiting for somebody and swivelled slightly away. There was a better prospect sitting at a table opposite. The man she could see was tall, fair haired and probably late twenties, sitting with an overweight mate who had his back to her. Straining her ears, she could detect they were discussing neither football nor cars, another plus point. Her eyes connected with the fair-haired man a couple of times, and they exchanged a slight smile.

It was only ten minutes before he was next to her at the bar, ordering a round for his friend.

She could feel his eyes on her, so began the conversation by asking him about the menu. It was good, apparently. They got talking, the mate's drink sitting there undelivered. He was Mike, a radiographer at the local hospital, due on shift at midnight.

'I expect you can see right through me,' she said.

'The old ones are the best,' he replied.

She raised an eyebrow at the apparent reference to the age gap, and he was quick to reassure her he meant the vintage of the joke. It was soon clear that once the drink was delivered, Mike was happy to abandon his mate. He did little to disguise his interest in her. He bought her another drink, and then sat with her at a nearby table while she ate the panini she had ordered. She steered the conversation away from her occupation, but disclosed she was single. He wasn't, but said he was separated. She didn't quite believe him, but tonight she didn't actually care. Her interest was narrower.

Mike's story was that he was on duty in three hours, which is why he'd been drinking orange juice. She had assumed it was vodka and orange. 'I'm in a hotel five minutes away, I'd be happy to entertain you for those three hours,' she whispered.

The man looked like all his Christmases had come at once. He drove her back to the Travelodge, and the moment they got into her room she seized his hair and pulled him to her, ripping off his shirt. She couldn't believe what she was doing. It was as if she was a different woman. She took the lead in bed, undressing him, caressing him and demanding of him what she needed. Somewhere along the way, while riding him, all the stress and worry of the last week detonated in the most explosive orgasm of her life. Someone next door banged on the wall and uttered a muffled complaint. She and Mike laughed, and that shared humour was even better than the pleasure she had extracted from his body. When he left to go to his midnight shift it was without an exchange of phone numbers. They tacitly agreed it was a self-contained moment. She lay back on the bed and felt an utterly selfish sensation of taking without apology or thanks. It was almost as if Destiny had given her some kind of virus.

–

Next morning Julia managed a quick breakfast with a large coffee before heading off by taxi to the court building. She arrived at 9.15 in gown and wig, with a heavy briefcase in each hand. She felt sick, faint and sweaty even though the day was cold. She wasn't just nervous about the impossible act she had committed to undertaking, but also what she would do if, as expected, she bottled out. She had done only the minimum of preparation for this the most important case of her life. Mr Justice Oakeshott, a notorious stickler, would tear her to pieces if she made any mistakes, but it would be surprising if the case even got to dealing with her defendant on day one.

There were two security staff chatting to each other, one a middle-aged Asian man, and the other the same large woman she had seen on her previous visit. Julia stood around outside, pretending to be on the phone, until a gaggle of other obvious legal professionals headed into the main entrance. They were talking loudly and laughing together, although none were yet in wig and gown. She joined them in the queue for security. Of the four ahead of her, only one had his bag searched, and that was perfunctory. A woman further up the queue seemed to be using the same app as Julia and was able to take a briefcase around the metal detector. The two minutes waiting to get to the front of the queue seemed to be the longest of Julia's life. Finally, she was at the front and displayed her phone to the woman. 'Hello again,' Julia said, with as much confidence as she could muster.

It wasn't clear that the woman remembered her, and she asked if she could look in her briefcase. Julia gulped, but managed to croak out, 'If you must.'

She hefted the document case first, slamming it onto the desk and clicking open the catches. She lifted the lid, to reveal hefty stacks of folders and paperwork. To her horror, the woman lifted two or three bundles, to look underneath. If she did this on the second briefcase, the one with the sandwich box, Julia thought she might faint. She tried to seem casual, and not watch the security officer doing her job. Instead, she looked at her phone. A text had come from Rachel, wishing her the best of luck. 'Kisses from Jack too. xx'

It was like a ray of sunshine, and made her smile.

The security woman indicated the other case, but someone further back in the queue called out, 'Come on, Marjorie, she's proved she's a barrister.' It was a familiar voice.

Marjorie squeezed out a thin smile, and waved Julia through. As she lifted her briefcases and stepped around the metal detector, she looked back and saw Christopher Cadwell smiling at her. Of course, she had completely forgotten that her star colleague was defending the head of the gang. How typical of him to have learned the names of the security staff. Attention to detail. He was known to chat up the female clerks at court, sometimes getting a slightest procedural edge or a little bit of extra knowledge. Relieved to have got past the first barrier, Julia hefted her briefcases and headed off to the ladies'.

'Hold on a second, Julia,' Cadwell said. She waited for him. He was dressed in the sharpest and darkest of suits, his shave perfect, even to the dimple in his cleft chin.

'Good luck today,' he said. 'Frankly, I'm expecting the whole lot of our clients to go down. Did you see last night's disclosures from the CPS?'

Julia had not looked on the case system since midday yesterday but wasn't going to let Cadwell know. 'Last-minute job, typical,' she said.

'Yes, but extra witnesses at this stage. Going to be particularly tough for you, I imagine.'

As they were technically adversaries, Julia had every reason to say nothing. 'We shall see, Christopher, we shall see.' She wished him luck and slipped into the bathroom.

–

Julia had been sitting in the chill cubicle for ten minutes, her head in her hands, staring at the gun that she had retrieved from its greasy plastic bag. She wiped it carefully with toilet paper, slid the safety off and held it in her hand. She knew the easiest thing to do now. To press the snub barrel against her temple, to end it all. A simple click, a one-inch finger movement and it would all be over.

She felt an overwhelming wave of sadness that it would end like this. She thought she was rid of Adam five years ago. She had done everything she could to put her life back on the straight and narrow, to forget him and her ruined motherhood, to move on. Thanks to Destiny, he had come back from the grave to haunt her.

She had thought a lot about how to execute Terrence Bonner. She imagined that if she could rustle up the courage to fire, then she could kill him. But that wasn't enough. It had to look like suicide, a single shot to the head. She, a woman who couldn't kill a spider, had to kill one of the most terrifying murderers in the country. All she had on her side was surprise. A single second, possibly even less than that. He was a man who was used to action, the catalogue of the accusations against him made that very clear. He wouldn't hesitate to kill, or cause pain. She needed a little bit of what he had, a little bit of what Destiny had learned in the trials of her own life. On Saturday night, during her practice, and last night in the hotel, she had felt tough enough, determined enough to be able to do what she had to do. Now, five minutes from the act, it seemed an impossibility.

She heard two women enter the bathroom. They too were discussing the big case. Presumably defending, as the late disclosure was mentioned with a certain fatalistic humour. They'd both read it, to Julia's dismay. *I'm a useless barrister, a pathetic person, and I deserve everything that happens to me.* Once the women had left, Julia rested the gun against her temple, slid her finger into the trigger, squeezing her eyes shut.

And waited.

Nothing happened. She couldn't do it. She let go a huge shuddering sigh, finished up, repacked her bags and slid the gun into her trouser pocket under her robe. As she was leaving the cubicle, Emily entered the bathroom. The young solicitor looked as nervous as Julia felt. They greeted each other warmly.

'Your first big court case?' Julia asked.

Emily nodded. 'I checked at the desk and Serco's already delivered Bonner. Interview room six.' She blew a ragged sigh.

Julia smiled. 'Look, I'll speak to him. There's no need for you to be there. I'll spare you that. It would be better if you just laid out the documents in the court as we discussed, I'd like to re-examine yesterday's CPS disclosures before we get going.'

'Yes, I wondered whether they'd ever get John Finnegan to testify. It looks a powerful testimony too.'

'Yes, it does,' Julia lied. She was confident that with such a large and unwieldy trial, there would be plenty of time for her to skim-read the statement while the Crown was making its initial case.

The two women made their way out of the bathroom, Emily heading upstairs to court one, taking one of Julia's two document cases, while Julia headed to the interview rooms that faced onto the canal that ran along the back of the building. She descended the short staircase and signed in at the security desk. The custody officer was a bored-looking middle-aged male with his nose in a doorstop-sized Stephen King thriller. If he wanted excitement, he was looking in the wrong direction. He made no move to search her. Julia scrutinised him obliquely. Slow, fat, not interested. Perfect. He would in theory be the first witness on the scene, and presumably not too rapidly. The man peered at the log, and led her towards room six. Julia looked through the smoked glass panel, and saw Bonner, exactly as before, arms folded, bald head glossy, chin jutting. He seemed to be glaring at the ceiling.

The custody officer unlocked the door and let her in.

Chapter Twenty-two

'Good morning, Mr Bonner,' Julia said, pulling back the plastic chair, and sitting opposite her client. Bonner's eyes flicked at her, then returned to examining the ceiling.

'I'm being stitched up,' he said.

'On the contrary, today begins your opportunity to put forward your side of the story.' Julia then went through a series of standard questions about how the client had been treated in custody. On this occasion she wasn't interested in the answers, but simply wanted time to elapse, to wait for the custody officer outside to settle down. She opened her briefcase and removed a small stack of documents. She had a lump in her throat. She pulled the gun from her pocket and slid it onto her lap under the table.

'Police interviewed me on Friday,' Bonner said. 'A new witness. I know who it is, Lucky Finnegan. Should have killed the bastard when I had the chance.'

'Well, you had a good go running him over in the JCB, didn't you? Take a look at those.' Julia laid down a sheaf of documents in front of him, thick with legalese.

Bonner leaned forward, just as she had hoped.

'Just there,' she said, pointing with her left hand. He looked closer, his head only a foot from the table. With her right, she aimed the weapon at him, less than two feet away. The bang was colossal in the small room. Bonner's head flicked towards her, his hand already reaching for the weapon, his face contorted. The wordless bellow.

She had missed.

She gave a panicky scream.

The next shot was less than a second after the first. Julia's eyes must've been closed, because when she opened them, the back half of Bonner's head was missing, a gory mist sprayed on the beige wall behind. Her screams were planned, but involuntary too. She rushed around the table, and as Bonner toppled backwards off the chair, she leapt on him, pushing the gun into his right hand. There was plenty of blood, but she needed more of it. 'Help me, please. Help!' she yelled. She had far more time than she expected, time to feed Bonner's right index finger into the trigger guard, time to rub the palm of her own right hand on his, aware that gunshot residues needed to be found there. There seemed to be blood absolutely everywhere. It could only help.

It seemed like an hour before she heard the thundering of feet, the rattle of keys, the door opening, but it was probably half a minute. The overweight custody officer was simply gawking from the doorway, apparently already out of breath.

'Don't just stand there, get an ambulance!' Julia yelled.

–

It was three hours later when Julia consented to be interviewed about the suicide. She had been checked over in hospital, cleaned up and found to be unharmed. Now, wearing clean clothes retrieved by the police from her suitcase in the car, she was sitting on a brand-new sofa in the rape suite of Nottingham City police station. She was surrounded by potted plants and children's paintings pinned to the wall. It made her think of Jack. A middle-aged female officer called Tracy had been with her for an hour, reassuring and comforting. 'You'll be all right, duck,' she said. 'It's been a terrible shock for you.'

At one point in the hospital, Julia had laughed uncontrollably, before starting to cry. The officer had been alarmed, but a nurse assured her it was down to shock. In fact, it was the simple relief, the lifting of intolerable stress. Julia was convinced she had carried out her task perfectly but was aware she now needed to feign something more appropriate to her story.

The arrival of a detective seemed a good moment to start. DCI Bob Knowles was straight out of 1970s casting: a balding, shrewd-eyed fellow with the remnants of a comb-over, plus pockmarked skin and bad teeth. Julia could smell the taint of tobacco, and she noticed that Tracy could too, her nose wrinkling.

'Thank you for agreeing to talk to us so soon,' Knowles said. 'If any of it becomes too much just let us know. We'll take a formal statement later, we're just after a few pointers for now.'

The detective ran through the details of Julia's arrival and entry to the interview room with Bonner. 'Did you see any indication during the early minutes of the interview that he was armed?'

'No. He was always belligerent, in previous interviews he had made offensive remarks to one of my female colleagues. But it never occurred to me at any time that he had a weapon.'

'So, talk me through it, Ms McGann. Take your time, slow it down, as if it was a TV crime thriller.'

Julia blew a sigh. 'Well, Bonner had said he was very concerned about the new evidence. And he asked what kind of sentence he might get if it all went badly. I told him he might be looking at a whole life tariff. Mr Justice Oakeshott is one of the old school crime and punishment brigade, as I explained to him.'

'What was his reaction?'

'He said: "There's no way I'm doing that. Absolutely no way." And that's when he pulled out the gun.'

'From where? He was wearing a sweatshirt and track-suit trousers, neither of which had pockets. Did you see where he'd stowed it?'

'No. I was looking at the documents, so my head was down. I must have just caught sight of it in my peripheral vision, because the gun was already close to his head.'

'Like this?' Knowles said putting two fingers against his right temple. 'Or some other way?'

'No, pretty much like that,' Julia said. 'I jumped at him, to stop him. I think the first bullet must've missed, but we were struggling for the gun. Then the second shot went off.'

'Did he fire it, or did you?'

'To be honest, I don't know what happened in those few seconds. I don't think I got my fingers into the trigger.'

Knowles shook his head. 'All I can say is that it was extremely courageous action, Ms McGann.'

Tracy was nodding her head vigorously in affirmation. 'I'd have rolled up in a ball on the floor and screamed my head off.'

'Well…' Julia demurred.

'You tried to save his life, Ms McGann, even though he was one of the most violent and sadistic criminals in the country,' Knowles said. 'He's certainly one of the worst that I've ever come across.'

'You're forgetting something,' Julia replied. 'I believed this man's account. It was my job to defend him. It is not surprising that an innocent man faced with life behind bars might feel suicidal.'

Knowles snorted. 'Innocent? I know you had your job to do, but let's not pretend that he wasn't an evil bastard.'

'That was up to the court to decide, and sadly it has been robbed of its opportunity to do that. Whatever you think of Bonner, justice was the loser here.'

'Fine words, indeed.' Knowles closed his notebook and put his pen away. 'Just one thing. At what point did Bonner fall over? Was that before or after the second shot?'

Julia knew she had to be careful. She'd read quite a lot about ballistics during her web searches and it was a minefield, so like any good barrister she turned the tables. 'To be honest I couldn't say. What I do want to know, for my own future safety, is how he managed to get a gun into the court building. He could have shot me, he could have shot anyone.'

Knowles nodded. 'Rest assured, that is absolutely the focus of our enquiries. Frankly, from my point of view, I couldn't give a toss that he killed himself. But I'm very concerned that he either concealed a weapon all the way down from Manchester, or was supplied with one here. Neither of these possibilities are anything but alarming.'

Just as Julia was getting up to leave, Knowles called out, 'There is one last thing, Ms McGann, I do have to ask you. You'll think it's absurd, but nonetheless.'

She raised her eyebrows. 'Yes?'

'Technically, the easiest way to get the weapon in to that room would be if you had smuggled it in. Perhaps you wanted to kill him yourself?'

Julia tried to laugh. 'You are joking, right? This was going to be my biggest earning case ever, and now I won't even get fully reimbursed for hundreds of hours of preparatory work I've already done.'

Knowles spread his hands wide and smiled. 'Just thinking outside the box.'

'Detective chief inspector, I can't even kill spiders.'

He nodded and let her go.

–

Detective Chief Inspector Craig Gillard was halfway through Monday's incident room meeting when DC Carl Hoskins, who had been casually looking at his phone, said, 'Bloody hell. Terry Bonner has committed suicide. Blown his brains out at Nottingham Crown Court.'

That stopped everyone in their tracks. DCs Rainy Macintosh and Michelle Tsu crowded round Hoskins to look at his phone, while everyone else got out their own devices to check.

'Seems he was in the cells with his brief,' Hoskins added. 'I've got a mate at the NCA who was due to give evidence later this week, but he says it's all been adjourned.'

The news distracted them from the lack of fresh clues on the Adam Heath case. Ingrid Taylor remained the only one of Heath's former girlfriends identified, and she was still denying everything. Forensic examination of the victim's computers and those of Mrs Heath had revealed little so far, while CCTV at Oxford railway station had backed the asylum seeker's alibi.

'Someone must've been very lax on searching him,' Gillard said. 'Came all the way down from Strangeways by prison van, presumably.'

'Och, I feel sorry for the barrister,' Rainy said.

'Wasn't that the woman who'd had a break-in, Michelle?' Gillard asked.

Michelle nodded. 'Yes, Julia McGann, lives just ten minutes down the road.'

'She'll be glad to be shot of the case then,' Hoskins said, putting his phone down.

Gillard rubbed his chin. 'Michelle. Have you had a chance to take another look at that burglary as I asked?'

'Not yet. I left a message with Ms McGann, as I mentioned. But as you know she was defending Bonner. With all this kerfuffle in Nottingham, I can't imagine I'll get to speak to her for a few days.'

'Can't we get into her house? Is there a key with the neighbours, anything like that? It would be a bit heavy-handed to seek a warrant.'

'I left that request as part of the message, sir. She's not got back to me. Understandably.'

Gillard nodded. 'There is something not right about this, Michelle. It just seems too much of a coincidence. First the same gloves were used in the Adam Heath murder and in this burglary, and now she's caught up in Bonner's suicide.'

The young female detective shrugged. 'Maybe there's a connection, sir.'

Gillard nodded, and switched his attention to the Internet. 'What chambers does Julia McGann work for?'

'No idea,' Michelle replied. Gillard rolled his eyes and typed the barrister's name into Google. He soon found out, jotted down the phone number and rang them up. A woman with a cut-glass voice answered the phone and put Gillard through to a man called Hogarth who described himself as the chief clerk. 'How can I help?' Hogarth asked.

'First off, I'd like you to pass on Surrey Police's best wishes to Ms McGann. She's obviously had a horrible shock with what happened in Nottingham. We'd also like her to give us a ring about the incident she previously reported to us, as soon as reasonably possible.'

'I'm afraid I don't know anything about what that incident is, but I will pass on the message.'

Gillard thanked him and then came to the real reason he had rung, although he couched it as an afterthought. 'And could I ask you a final favour? Can you send me Ms McGann's appointments list for the last month? We're trying to cross check where she might have been.'

'This is a little irregular,' Hogarth said cautiously. 'Have you asked her?'

'Not had the chance, yet. Don't worry, it just saves us asking her a load of questions when she's still in shock. Nothing to worry about.'

'I shall email it immediately. It's not client privileged information, but I must let her know that I have done so,' Hogarth said primly.

'That's fine,' Gillard said, passed on his email address, thanked Hogarth and hung up.

The email reply came almost immediately. It took Gillard just ten seconds to find the answer he wanted. He then made a couple of quick phone calls, and threw the receiver back onto its rest.

'Oh well, that's one hunch that bites the dust.'

'What hunch was that?' Michelle asked.

'It was a pretty wild one. What if Julia McGann had been Adam Heath's girlfriend? Her gardening gloves, perhaps, which is why there's an imprint on her fridge. A long relationship, which ended badly for her, and she nursed a grudge.'

'What? You think she could have beheaded him?' Michelle said incredulously.

'The butchering barrister of Guildford slays again,' muttered Hoskins, smirking at Michelle.

Gillard shrugged. 'Well, like I said, it was a wild theory, and now it's kaput anyway.'

'How so?'

'At the exact time that Adam Heath was being murdered, Julia McGann was at Woolwich Crown Court, representing a client. It says so on her schedule, and I've just double-checked it with the clerk of the court.'

'That's a cast-iron alibi, I suppose.'

'Yes,' Gillard sighed. 'Like the Forth Bridge. So back to square one.'

–

For Julia, most of the rest of the day was a haze. Her phone was jammed with messages, including half a dozen from Rachel, hoping she was okay. She had even sent an image of a drawing from Jack, all lurid colours and scribblings, which according to Rachel's translation was a get-well card. It made her smile, as did the accompanying photograph of Jack, his tiny fist full of crayons, smiling up at the camera. She sent quick acknowledgements to messages from Surrey Police, Hogarth and finally solicitor Emily, who had been worried sick when she heard the news.

After the end of the police interview, Julia had made her way to the client's solicitors Ropes, Peel, Deaton to brief them on what had happened. She was received with kindness and concern by all, principals and staff. Someone found her brandy, and a minion was sent out to fetch top-of-the-range coffees. Over the next few minutes, it dawned on Julia that she was now something of a legal celebrity. Scattered among the many messages from colleagues on her phone there were more than a dozen from various reporters who wanted to interview her. How they had got her number, she had no idea. Emily persuaded her to go to the ladies', where she could point out one or two specks of Bonner's blood that had survived the shower.

'What about all your legal kit?' Emily asked, as Julia rinsed and dabbed at a hank of hair over one ear.

'The police have it all. Wig, gown, right down to my underwear. Blood got everywhere.'

'You should stay in your hotel tonight,' Emily said. 'You're in no state to drive.'

Julia nodded. She had a few phone calls to return, but she was already feeling better now than she had for days. Finally with a moment to herself, she rang Rachel from the solicitors' disabled toilet, the only place where there was no chance of being overheard.

'You poor thing, Julia. How are you?'

'I'm fine, really. It was just a bit of a shock,' she whispered.

'What a weird thing, him killing himself. Just what the girl Destiny actually wanted you to do to him.'

Julia just sighed. She wanted to tell someone, but didn't dare. But Rachel knew her better than anyone, and could read the silence.

'Oh my God. Don't tell me that you...'

'Rachel, I had to,' Julia hissed. 'She'd hidden a gun in my shed, and I had to learn how to use it.'

'I don't believe it,' Rachel gasped. 'Oh God, this gets worse and worse.'

'No, it doesn't, not anymore. It's over now, I carried out my side of the bargain. I know it's terrible, but Destiny told me the things that this man had done to her.'

'Moggy, you committed a murder!'

'I was compelled to. Look, Rachel, I love you so much, and I can never hide anything from you, but you've got to swear to me on Jack's life that you will never, ever let even a hint of this slip out.'

Julia was horrified at the long silence.

'I promise, Moggy. But this has got to be the end of it.'

Chapter Twenty-three

Gillard had got home at a reasonable time that Monday evening, and was just settling down to Sam's home-made *carbonade flamande*, when his phone pinged. His message to ballistics in Birmingham had been returned. They had now established that the weapon Bonner used was one known to have been used in a previous incident by his gang back in 2017.

'Anything important?' Sam asked, as she sat down to dinner with him.

'Not really, just confirmation of what we expected. There were some wild theories circulating in the NCA that rival gangs who wanted Bonner dead might have got a weapon in through a bent barrister. But it was definitely his own gun.'

'So it was suicide.' Sam took a forkful of beef and chewed it thoughtfully.

'That's what it looks like.' Gillard's first mouthful creased his face into an appreciative shape. 'Oh, this is delicious.'

'It's ox cheek and beer, has been in the slow cooker all day while I was on shift.'

'Absolutely lovely.' He looked up at her. 'I fancy a beer.' He went out to the kitchen and came in with an open bottle and two glasses. 'Fancy sharing a Hobgoblin?'

She laughed. 'Sounds like a Tolkien threesome.'

'Funny girl,' Gillard muttered, pouring the beer. He was glad to hear Sam in high spirits. He had sorely missed her bubbly self in the last few months.

'You know, Sam, this thing about Bonner still doesn't quite add up. He knew there was more incriminating evidence coming, but there was a stack against him already. And I just don't see him being the depressive kind. His anger was always projected outwards. That's his psychological profile. Most prisoners who kill themselves manage to do it in their own cell, by hanging usually, a belt or something similar. Why come all the way down from Manchester to Nottingham, concealing a weapon, risking all those searches, in order to kill yourself in front of your barrister?'

'When you put it that way, it does sound odd.'

Gillard shrugged. 'It's not my case, anyway. My old mate Bob Knowles of Nottingham CID is in charge. He's a shrewd bloke. I think I might give him a call tomorrow. They should have their post-mortem in by then. It's really odd that so much of this is swirling around the same barrister.'

'Maybe he was trying to shoot her?'

Gillard laughed. 'And ended up dead himself? She's a small woman, according to Michelle. No, if he'd wanted to shoot her, for whatever reason, she'd be dead. In fact, if he wanted to kill her, he'd probably have been able to do it with his bare hands. No gun required.'

–

Gillard managed to get hold of Bob Knowles by phone on Tuesday afternoon. Knowles had briefly been his boss during a short stint at the Met twenty years ago, and had made a deep impression on him for his refusal to take anything at face value. They had kept in occasional contact ever since, often bouncing ideas off each other in their respective cases.

After greeting each other warmly, Gillard asked: 'Do you reckon Bonner really killed himself?'

'It's hard to believe. He wasn't the suicidal type, if there is a type. But the fact it was his gun is pretty conclusive.'

'That's what I would have thought,' Gillard said. 'Have you had the post-mortem results?'

'Only verbally, so far. It raises more questions than answers. The shot that killed Bonner entered the left-hand side of the head behind the ear and exited through the back on the right, taking a saucer-sized chunk of skull with it. It's not where you would normally shoot yourself, and if Bonner fired the shot, he could only have done so with his left hand. But he is right-handed.'

'Then he was shot in the struggle,' Gillard said.

'That's what we've assumed, yes. There are roughly equal amounts of gunshot residue on the hands of the barrister and on Bonner's right hand, so at the very least it indicates that her hand was near or on the gun for at least one shot. We're having just as much trouble explaining the bullet which passed through the palm of Bonner's left hand, exiting through the knuckles at the back.'

'There were only two shots fired, right?'

'Yes. Two bangs heard in very quick succession, according to all witnesses, and two bullets and casings. One shot left in the magazine.'

'Let's play devil's advocate and pretend that Ms McGann wanted to kill him and had the gun,' Gillard said. 'The first shot, let's say, he partially blocked with an upraised hand, and the second hit him in the head.'

'Yes, I can't get that scenario out of my head. Ballistic-ally, it's certainly the easiest explanation. Everything else is tricky. If Bonner had the gun, how come he shot himself through the palm? Through the back of his hand, okay, if he was trying to hold her off with his left, but not the palm.'

'Hmm. But what if her hand was already on the gun, and he brought his left across to try and remove it, while his right was still in the trigger. That might be through the palm.'

'Yes, that's possible,' Knowles conceded.

'However, if Ms McGann did kill him, then someone in the organisation must've supplied her with Bonner's gun.'

'And that seems a stretch,' Knowles said.

'Agreed. Though we both know there's plenty of historic examples of bent barristers.'

'Yeah, not surprising if they spend their working lives with criminals. Just like us.' Knowles chuckled.

'But it's usually financial,' Gillard said. 'Never using shooters. You just can't imagine it. No precedents in the UK.'

'I had a word with the CPS,' Knowles said. 'Ran exactly that scenario past the lead lawyer on the NCA case. She laughed so much she had to put the phone down.' He sighed. 'Look, Craig. I know you're up to your eyeballs in this beheading case, but seeing as she's in your manor, if you could spare one of your team to look in more depth at the barrister that would be appreciated.'

'That shouldn't be hard, we can do it under the cover of a burglary investigation. I'll start with some checks to see if she is a member of a gun club.'

'If she is, I'll eat my hat,' Knowles said.

Either way, Gillard thought, this is a woman I'd definitely like to meet.

–

Gillard spent the next few hours finding out everything he could about Julia McGann. Unmarried, no kids, no criminal record, and seemingly an unspectacular career at the bar, too. Unsurprisingly, not a member of a gun club. There were no mentions of her name in any of the online barrister journals, except for small snippets about her recruitment to the chambers she now worked at. Her name turned up here and there in crime stories in the local press across the south-east when she was defending some miscreant or other. A middling, law-abiding, indeed law-upholding, life. There was really nothing to get his teeth into.

He filled out a production order with a request for a financial inquiry into her and sent it to his boss. Radar Dobbs, being a detective chief superintendent, needed to sign it off. Gillard had no expectations of finding paydirt here either. The woman didn't seem to have an extravagant lifestyle, quite the contrary, judging from what Michelle said about the state of her car.

Forensically, she was also in the clear. There was absolutely no evidence linking her with the crime he was investigating. Her DNA did not match the unknown sample from Adam Heath's Jaguar, her fingerprints – which had been taken for elimination purposes by Kirsty Mockett as well as by Nottinghamshire Police – were not there either. Her presence at Woolwich Crown Court when Heath was murdered was an unimpeachable alibi. Yet for all that, Gillard could not shift a nagging suspicion.

Her presence at Bonner's apparent suicide so soon after the burglary at her home, was perhaps simply luck. But add in the prints from the same pair of gloves as had been used in the murder of Heath, it was just too much of a coincidence to ignore.

Everything depended on the gloves. Just two faint impressions from fingertips at the burglary linked that crime to the killing of Adam Heath. DC Karen Desai was the expert, and she was sure. Certainly cases had been decided on much thinner forensics. But if the gloves were wrong, then there was much less to explain.

Endlessly recycling conjecture can be corrosive without extra information. Instead Gillard focused on trying to establish other links between the burglary and the murder. The aged BMW whose registration number Julia McGann had supplied had been flagged as a clone more than a year ago. The actual owner of that licence plate lived in Bradford. The vague description of the two men in the car was not good enough to do anything with. But the man who came to Ms McGann's door, well maybe. She had described him as dapper, a shortish, light-skinned black guy. That narrowed it down a bit, but there were still thousands on the criminal records database. He needed to look at this from a different direction.

Was there a direct connection between Adam Heath and Terrence Bonner? If Adam Heath had been a drug user, there would be a certain credence to the idea. But careful swabs of bathroom and bedroom surfaces in his home had come back negative. Their paths would not normally have crossed, except perhaps in Heath's secret life. Bonner was such an animal that Gillard could not imagine he would have been the meat in the sexual sand-wich between Adam and Stella Heath. Just the thought of it made him shudder. But Bonner was suspected of a side hustle running vice rings, so maybe Adam Heath had been a customer. It was an idea. Certainly it was the only possible connection he could think of.

Then there was the elusive Destiny Flynn, mentioned by Ms McGann. A missing person, hanging around the barrister's home and allowed to stay for a couple of days. Her name had cropped up before. When a brothel in Merstham had been raided in 2017, one of the girls found there mentioned that someone called Destiny had escaped the previous year, and the description matched. The boss of that particular establishment had not been caught in the swoop. Janille Murdoch was to turn up several months later in pieces along the M25, with dabs of Terrence Bonner's DNA on him, for which he was about to be tried when he met his untimely end.

These were tenuous links, perhaps. But the best he had.

Where on earth could Destiny Flynn be hiding now?

Perhaps it was time to go and see if she was back again with Julia McGann, the supposedly brave barrister who tried to save Bonner's life.

–

Gillard saw from PC Geraint Howlett's records that following his advice, Julia was once again staying with a local friend called Rachel Meadows. He wouldn't have been surprised if she headed home to Weldon Road from time to time. It was only a five-minute drive between the two places. Six o'clock found Gillard at Julia's flat, darkened and seemingly unoccupied. Her saw no sign of her distinctive car. He tried the front door, locked, then prowled the garden, noting the French windows and garden shed were secure. His torch illuminated nothing indicative of recent activity. He emerged into the street in time to surprise PC Howlett, who had just arrived in a patrol car. Howlett had seen no sign of the dark BMW, but agreed to patrol a bit more widely on the area's residential streets before finishing his shift. He told Gillard that a few reporters had been seen knocking on doors, including Ms McGann's neighbours.

The detective then drove on to Rachel Meadows' address, arriving shortly before seven. When he rang the doorbell of the Victorian terraced house, he could hear the sound of a young child racing around. The child ran up to the front door and looked out at Gillard through the letterbox.

'Are you a burglar?' he asked.

Gillard crouched down so he could see the boy. 'No, my job is to catch them. I'm a detective!'

This was enough to set the child off running back into the kitchen, from which his mother was emerging. 'Mummy, Mummy, there's a detective at the door.'

An attractive but harried-looking blonde of about forty opened the door. Gillard introduced himself, asked if she was Rachel Meadows, and said he was looking for Julia McGann. The woman affirmed her identity and confirmed Julia was staying with her.

'Has she been naughty? Are you going to arrest her?' the boy said, poking his head round from behind his mother's legs.

'No, I just want to ask her some questions,' Gillard said with a smile, ruffling the boy's hair. Beyond Rachel, a petite dark-haired woman had appeared in the hallway. 'I'm Julia.'

Rachel directed them to the dining room, where Gillard sat at the table opposite Julia. With the door shut only the distant sound of toddler noise penetrated, until silenced by parental hushing. Gillard spent the first few minutes asking how she had been since the Bonner suicide and whether the process of giving a witness statement after such a shocking event had gone smoothly.

'I am a bit shell-shocked to be honest,' she said. 'I'm quite glad not to be staying at my own flat for now. I just hope that you can catch the burglars so I can feel safe to return.'

'We're doing all we can,' Gillard said. 'And it's on that subject you can probably help us.'

'Of course.' She smiled.

'The statement the uniforms took was rather sketchy but referred in passing to a young woman called Destiny Flynn. It seems to indicate that she had been staying at your flat.'

'Well, yes, briefly. I found her camped in my garden, cold, wet and destitute. She put me in quite an awkward position – I wanted to call social services, but she begged me not to. So I allowed her to stay for a couple of nights.'

'What were the dates?' Gillard asked.

'I'd have to check in my diary,' she said. 'But it was only a couple of days, then she seemed to disappear.'

'Do you have a phone number for her? Or an up-to-date photograph which could help us identify her? The last one we can find is of her at thirteen, when she still had all her teeth.'

'No. I'm sorry.'

'We're obviously relieved that Destiny has turned up, however briefly. We always worry about those on the missing persons register for that long, particularly vulnerable young women. Are you sure she said nothing about where she was intending to go?'

Julia shook her head. 'She said she had learned not to trust anyone. And I can believe it.'

Gillard nodded. 'She's been pretty elusive. I've made a point of ordering extra patrols right across Guildford, asking amongst the rough sleepers, looking inside derelict buildings, that kind of thing. We have indications of her continued presence. A bit of shoplifting locally, and an elderly woman reported that her purse had been stolen while she was in a cafe.'

'Oh dear,' Julia said.

Gillard got out his iPad and flicked through to a video which he enlarged to full screen size. 'This is CCTV from an off-licence in Stoke Road, not far from here.' He showed Julia the footage, which showed a young woman wearing a distinctive white coat with a hood pulled low. The face wasn't visible from the high angle of the camera, but it clearly showed a girl ask the Asian male at the till for something from the shelf behind him. While his back was turned, she slipped a large bottle of Strongbow cider into her backpack. She then refused the proffered bottle of Smirnoff and walked coolly out of the shop.

'Is that her?' Gillard asked.

'Well, it's certainly my coat,' Julia said. 'So I suppose it is.'

'That same coat was also described by the pickpocket victim. So, Ms McGann, can you categorically assure me that you haven't allowed her to stay at your home in recent days?'

'No, of course not. She is a thief, and I want nothing more to do with her.'

Gillard nodded. 'We do of course remain very concerned about her safety. I'm thinking of the man who came to your door, and the two who were waiting in the car outside your home. Do you think you could identify him again?'

'The one who came to the door, definitely,' she said.

'Okay,' Gillard said, and turned back to his iPad. He had already set up a series of twenty-four mugshots, and now set them to run in slideshow mode, before turning the device towards her. 'If you see him on this list just shout.'

He watched as the barrister scrutinised each picture carefully. It was on picture nineteen when she said: 'That's him, definitely.'

Gillard stopped the slideshow and turned the iPad back towards him. The face she had chosen was Lyron Smart, a small-time dealer from south London who had no known links to Bonner's crew. Gillard didn't tell her the name but made a mental note to look further into Smart's background. So far Ms McGann had seemed coolly in control, answering each question crisply and without much delay. He decided to ruffle her feathers a little.

'How long was it, Maggie, that you were Adam Heath's secret lover? Was it twelve years or fifteen?'

She looked stunned, and her mouth hung open, ready to speak, no words selected for several seconds. 'I beg your pardon? What name did you call me?'

'Maggie. It was the nickname he used with his lover. You're Maggie, aren't you?'

'I think you've made a serious mistake, detective chief inspector.' She had recovered her *froideur* quite quickly and was holding his gaze. 'I can categorically assure you that

I had never even heard of the man until the tragic news made the papers.'

Gillard nodded. 'So if we get a search warrant for your home, we won't recover a huge stack of his love letters to you?' This was a threat he thought might shake her.

She laughed. 'Help yourself. You'll find nothing incriminating in my home except a heap of dirty washing and a stack of unwashed dishes.'

The detective nodded. There seemed real confidence in that response. If she was a liar, she was a pretty good one. He decided to call her bluff.

'In which case I hope you won't mind if I send in a couple of forensics officers. I know that there was origin-ally a bloodstain, which was inadvertently damaged—'

'—that stain was from some liver, as I've already explained to your crime scene woman.'

'Nevertheless, if as you say you have nothing to hide, you won't object if we do a chemical bloodstain analysis. That will show up any spots, however small, even if they have been cleaned.'

'Will it damage my carpets or soft furnishings?'

'No. But until that is completed, I have to ask you to stay away from the flat.'

She smiled. 'All right, it's a deal.'

Gillard thanked her for her time and made his way back through the house to the front door. As they passed through the lounge, the little boy left his mother's embrace and raced up to him.

'Are you Himself?' he asked.

Everyone stopped moving. You could hear a pin drop. Gillard looked at the two women, neither of whom appeared to be breathing at all.

'I'm myself,' Gillard said to the boy. 'But who is himself?'

Jack, clearly picking up that he might be in trouble, looked at each of the grown-ups in turn.

'Oh, it's just a bit of childish nonsense, isn't it Jack?' Rachel said, scooping up the toddler.

'Himself was a naughty man to Aunty Julia,' Jack said.

'I told him about the burglar who came to my door,' Julia said hurriedly.

Jack said to Gillard: 'He made her cry, didn't he Mummy? Will you lock him in prison?'

Gillard smiled at the boy. 'Well, Jack, there are lots of bad men who do many things which make people cry. My job is to catch them, and yes, put some of them in prison. Now, is Maggie here?' he asked the child.

Jack laughed and ran away. 'Moggy! Moggy!' He grabbed Julia's leg, and hid behind it, peering at the detective between her knees.

'Next door's cat,' Julia whispered, with a smile.

When the detective had closed the door behind him, alarm bells were screaming inside his head. He replayed in his mind the interview with Julia McGann as he drove along the residential streets of Guildford towards the A25. He'd get CSI in the morning to search her flat again, and to do the BlueStar test. He had nothing to offer in the way of evidence for her involvement, simply a hunch. That gut feeling merely told him that something didn't sit right. The child had really had his finger on something, at least from the perspective of those two paralysed women. Are you Himself? No one would call a burglar that. It would be Mr Bogeyman or something, in front of the child.

Who was Himself?

The fact that he had spotted Julia's friend watching him drive away, her hands cupped over her face, proved his point. Whatever Julia McGann was up to, Rachel Meadows was in on it too.

—

Julia and Rachel peered out of the window until the detective's anonymous grey Vauxhall had slid away from the curb. 'Oh my god,' Rachel breathed into her hands. 'Out of the mouth of babes.' Seeing that Jack was now playing with his red tractor, Julia followed her friend back into the kitchen and closed the door. She closed her eyes and leaned against the door. She was convinced the room was swaying.

'How was the interview?'

'All right at first, he just asked about the burglary and everything, but then right out of the blue, Rachel, he asked me whether it was twelve or fifteen years I'd been with… you-know-who.' She turned to the kitchen door, as if convinced Jack was still listening.

'What did you say?' Rachel asked.

'What could I say? I said I'd never heard of him until the news about the crime. Now they are going to go over the house with a fine-tooth comb, testing for tiny specks of blood.'

'Oh, God. But didn't you clean up?'

'Yes, I scrubbed everything. But this stuff they use, it came up in one of my cases. BlueStar, I think it's called. They just spray it on a surface and if there's ever been blood on it, even a microscopic speck, it lights up like a bloody Christmas tree.'

'What are you going to do?'

287

'Well, if they do find anything, they might think it was brought in on the gloves by the burglars.'

'Did you burn the gloves?'

'Not yet.'

'Julia! For goodness' sake.'

'Look, I could hear that Briony was in when I wanted to do it in the garden, and it just seemed too suspicious. They are sealed in a plastic bag here with my luggage, together with the correspondence and photos that Adam sent me over the years. There's also Destiny's knife, and the wire she used to...'

'You've got to get rid of all of that lot, and quickly!'

'I will, don't worry. It's pretty funny, actually. Gillard asked if he searched the flat would he find sheafs of love letters from Adam. As if! Six birthday cards in fifteen years, two postcards, and one scrawled note on the back of a Sainsbury's receipt. It's all upstairs in my bag, and I'm going to put it into your log burner.'

'Yes, but don't put the gloves in there. The rubber will stink. And you've got to dump the other stuff.' Rachel embraced her friend. 'You can beat this, Julia. None of it is your fault, remember that. But don't delay, get on with it!'

'I will. But there's a lot happening. Did I tell you that the *Daily Mail* has asked for an interview and a photoshoot?'

'Wow!'

'They want it for Thursday's paper. I wasn't sure, to be honest. I'd rather hide away until it's all over.' Julia's smile vanished. 'The thing that most worries me, Rachel, is Destiny. I didn't let on I have her new number now. The police are looking for her, and when they catch her, she'll probably tell them everything.'

'Will she?'

'Well, I don't know. I mean, she is so selfish. She's probably still got that video. If she is accused of killing Adam, I have no doubt she'll drop me in it. Co-operation might mean a lower sentence for her. The police would be banging on about making a deal in every interview with her. With the video, she could easily claim that I paid her or threatened her.'

'Shame you don't still have the gun,' Rachel said, with a grim smile.

Julia stared at her friend.

'Don't look at me like that!' Rachel retorted. 'You've got us both on this slippery slope, haven't you? I realised some days ago that I'm effectively an accomplice, so I'm simply being logical. She's part of the evidence you need to get rid of. That *we* need to get rid of.'

'No, it doesn't have to be like that. I've bought a burner phone,' Julia said. 'Because I think I have to ring her. I've done what she asked for, she should be delighted.'

'Until, as you say the police track her down, as they will. Once they find the phone with the video on it, we're toast.'

The two women sat at the kitchen table as Julia unpacked the newly acquired phone. Julia turned to her friend. 'Actually, I can't even use it in here, because if the police ever get Destiny, they'll get the burner phone's number from her call record, and then go to the service provider to get a triangulation of where the call was made from.'

'Bloody hell, we are having to think like criminals,' Rachel said, head resting in her cupped hand. 'Look, I don't want to be dragged in any further, so would you drive out somewhere if you have to call her?'

Julia nodded. 'I'm really sorry, Rachel, that it's come to this.' She reached out for her friend and they briefly hugged.

'We can get through this together,' Rachel said. 'But you've got to follow the logic. We've got to deal with Destiny, otherwise we'll always be wondering, for years and years, even when Jack is all grown up and gone to uni we'll still be worrying. I'm not going to live my whole life like that.'

Julia packed up all the items she had to dispose of. She had delayed and delayed, but she couldn't leave it any later. Her precious MacBook Air, on which Destiny had made all those incriminating searches, the plastic bag with the gloves sealed inside, the bag with wire and knife. The letters from Adam she left with Rachel to dispose of. She felt a pervasive sense of melancholy, not just about the irreplaceable letters, but about her changing friendship with Rachel. She felt she was being nudged along a path that she did not wish to travel. Julia headed out into the cold, shadowy street, and loaded everything into the car.

–

No sooner had Julia got out of the street, she was rung by a TV producer inviting her onto a breakfast show the next morning. She pulled over to give her full attention to the call. At first she demurred, feeling that making her face recognisable would make it more difficult to dispose of the remaining evidence. On the other hand, the producer was so flattering about her attempt to save Bonner's life, she thought it could help bolster that very important heroic narrative, one that was already in the public mind. It was exactly what the *Daily Mail* guy had said.

So she agreed.

It would mean going up to London, but she didn't have a case that day, and it would allow her to get to the *Daily Mail* interview on the same trip. The one tricky element was dealing with Hogarth. It was hard to predict how he would react, so she made the decision to risk calling him at home.

'What do you think?' she said, after describing the various press approaches she had received.

'Well, well, the great Julia McGann has arrived.' To Julia's ear it sounded sarcastic and she was about to interrupt when he continued: 'You are soon going to be in much greater demand, you realise that, don't you? Our clientele sit in Wormwood Scrubs and elsewhere watching daytime TV. Once they see your mug on there, our phones are going to be ringing off the hook.'

'But that doesn't make me a star in court.'

'Doesn't matter. Only a few are going to take the trouble to really research your results. So long as you sound like you know what you're talking about, and dress up for the lads, do a bit of an Edwina, we'll have you booked up till next Christmas.'

Julia got off the phone feeling something of a fraud. She rang Rachel and told her about it. Rachel agreed with Hogarth's conclusions.

'I don't know if I've got the brass neck,' Julia said.

'You're a barrister, for God's sake. You know better than anyone that if you're going to tell a lie, you have to make it such an enormous whopper that everyone will be taken in.'

—

After she hung up, Julia surveyed her precious laptop and the bags with gloves, wire and knife. She had dithered for days and her latest idea had been to drive out to the reservoir to dump them, but now there was something she wanted to do first, before her face became known, which might give her a clue to Destiny's whereabouts. She took a detour to the off-licence in Stoke Road, the one whose CCTV Gillard had shown her an hour ago.

LK Stores was the classic convenience store, open all hours, like tens of thousands right across the country. She made her way inside, past the crowded drinks-laden displays to the till, where an upright Asian man was watching her. Julia took a deep breath and said: 'I'm a lawyer working with Guildford social services. I'm very anxious to trace a young woman in a white hooded coat who was seen in here earlier this week. The police say she was shoplifting.'

The man gave a snort. 'She was. Now it seems everyone is after her.'

'Apart from the police?'

'Yes. Two guys came in here earlier this evening, asking about her. Offering money if I ring them.'

'How did they know she'd been here?'

'The CCTV footage has been on the local TV news.'

'Of course. Can you describe them?'

'The little one did the talking. A light-skinned black guy with short dreadlocks, the other was a well-known local tearaway.'

'So you know him?'

'Not socially. But I like to know who the trouble-makers are, in case they come in drunk and threatening, you know. His name is Vardy, I think. Gary Vardy.' The man pointed to a stack of local newspapers. 'I read this cover to cover, especially the court reports. Know your customers!'

'They left you a phone number?'

He shrugged and passed across a notepad in which a mobile number was written. 'Here it is. But I'd leave it to the police if I were you. The small bloke looked a nasty type.'

'Thank you. If you see the girl again, would you ring me?'

'I know you, don't I?'

'I don't think so.' She smiled.

'Definitely. I never forget a face.' He shrugged. 'Anyway, the girl won't be back here again, now it's been on the local news.'

'Well, just in case.' Julia wrote her burner phone number on the man's pad.

As she left the off-licence she wondered how long it would be before the shopkeeper recognised her. Breakfast TV tomorrow, probably. She wondered how much the hooligans had offered him. The shopkeeper looked a decent sort, clearly aware that the girl was likely to come to some harm from the two men chasing them. She supposed it depended how annoyed he was at being the victim of shoplifting. Suffering changes who you are. Sometimes a little, sometimes a lot.

Once she was back in her car, Julia sat with her fingers steepled over her nose, wondering what to do with this fabulous piece of information. Gary Vardy. He sounded just the kind of petty criminal she often represented, though the name wasn't familiar. She abandoned her plan to visit the reservoir and drove back to see Rachel. There always seemed to be one more incriminating search to do on her precious laptop before she dumped it.

It was nine p.m. Jack was already in bed asleep, and Julia and Rachel sat with the laptop and strong black coffees in the front room. Julia searched for 'Gary Vardy' and 'Guildford court'. There were two identical reports in local newspapers from nine months ago, which underlined the accuracy of the shopkeeper's memory. Class 'C' drug possession charges, a guilty plea and a fine. The crucial information that she hoped would be there came in the second line. 'Vardy, of Welwyn Court, Farnham Way, Aldershot, pleaded guilty to two counts...'

'Fantastic, good old court reporters. They always give an approximation of the address. We could ring the police anonymously and let them know,' Julia said.

'Why hasn't the shopkeeper done that?' Rachel asked.

'Why would he? The shoplifting was nothing to do with them, it was Destiny. Besides, the police don't even know they went to the off-licence and haven't got a link between Vardy and the other guy whom I described. All they have is the car registration number, which is a clone.'

Rachel shook her head. 'Okay, I'm with you so far. But let's fast-forward. Why are you doing this at all?'

'Because I never want to see them at my flat again, obviously. I would sleep so much better at night knowing they were in custody, but it would also mean Destiny would be safer, wherever she is.'

Rachel screwed her face up. 'I'm not sure about this, Julia. I mean they weren't actually the burglars of your flat, were they? It was Destiny who broke in to deposit the head in your freezer. Okay, so they were after her to retrieve Bonner's gun. Once they are arrested and tell their story, she is linked to the gun. The very same gun that you used.'

Julia conceded that her friend had a point, then added, 'For all that, we should let Destiny know. They'll kill her if they find her.'

Rachel rolled her eyes. 'Julia, I really, really think you need to be less worried about Destiny and more worried about yourself. Or should I say, us. You've got to get Destiny's phone, and smash it, chuck the pieces away, destroy that video.' She leaned forward and grasped Julia's wrists. 'Look, that's safest for us and safest for her.'

'Exactly how am I going to do that?'

'Give her your new phone, as a gift in exchange for the old one.'

'She's a taker, Rachel, she probably won't give up the old one. She's very suspicious.'

Rachel gave a shout of frustration. 'For God's sake, Julia! We have to be *rid* of her. Don't you see? There's no other way.'

'Look, it's bad enough already. I'm not doing anything else illegal, well, not as illegal as that. Besides, we don't even know where she is.'

'Sometimes, Julia, you are impossible. This isn't court, you know. It's real life.' Rachel looked angry and turned away.

'I've got another plan,' Julia whispered, but Rachel didn't want to hear it. She stalked out to the lounge and slammed the door.

–

Rachel went to bed at eleven, uttering just a terse 'good night'. Julia waited in the lounge at her laptop, pretending to work, until she could no longer see a light under the bedroom door. Once she was certain that her friend was asleep, Julia slipped upstairs into the guest room, quietly changed into her running gear and grabbed a woolly hat. Downstairs again, she picked up Rachel's car keys and slipped out of the house. She had with her the plastic bag containing the gardening gloves that Destiny had used, which she tucked inside her shoulder bag.

The street seemed deserted.

So far none of the press had discovered which friend Julia was staying with. There would almost certainly be a renewed effort to track her down tomorrow after the breakfast TV show. Now might be her last few hours of anonymity, and she had to use them well. She unlocked Rachel's work van, got in, pulled her hat down low, and drove off towards Aldershot. She had researched the route carefully on her Mac, not wanting to insert an incriminating destination into Rachel's satnav.

She didn't get back until two a.m.

Chapter Twenty-four

Wednesday morning

Breakthroughs in intractable cases often come from the least expected sources, neglected evidence well down the pile. DC Rainy Macintosh had been working on and off for five days reviewing statements. Three hundred and eighteen pupil interviews, forty-six school staff, seventy-three from residents in the area, nineteen other potential witnesses. She and Carl Hoskins had already viewed sixty-one dash cams, five cyclist helmet cams, fourteen domestic CCTV systems, and 116 hours of footage from pedestrian crossing and traffic light cameras.

Nothing.

When there are a nearly a million evidence numbers on the database, the little stuff is easy to miss. A witness who had answered questions, but had never been asked the right ones. Ryan Watkins was one such. On the Thursday afternoon of the killing, the twenty-nine-year-old builder had just finished repairing a garden wall in Badgers Walk. That was the road behind Adam Heath's house. It was less than sixty yards from where Watkins was working to the back gate into Heath's garden. His statement said the light was going and he was just clearing up, hosing down the cement on the pavement before heading off in the works van. He hadn't seen any adults come down that path in either direction from 3.30 p.m. when he'd finished the wall until he departed for home at 4.45 p.m. He'd only seen schoolkids.

The questions asked of him reflected the fact that he was one of the first to give a statement. Rainy realised they reflected an assumption, prevalent early on in the case, that an adult, probably a male, would be the perpetrator. Now they were not so sure. She rang him up and caught him as he was just beginning another job.

'I've got your statement here, but I just wondered if I could ask you a couple more questions about what you saw.'

'Yeah, if you want.' He didn't sound enthusiastic about it.

'You said you saw a few schoolkids, but no adults.'

'That's it.' There was the sound of tools being shifted in the background.

'Were they all in school uniform?'

He blew a sigh. 'Well, I don't know the schools, like, but it looked like the kind of stuff kids wouldn't wear if they didn't have to.'

'Did any of them have any heavy-looking bags?'

He thought for a moment. 'Yeah. There was one girl with a sports bag that looked too big for her.'

'How old would you say?'

'Dunno. Thirteen, fourteen? I'm crap at guessing. I assume they're all underage.' He chuckled to himself.

Rainy ignored the stupid joke. 'How was she dressed, Ryan?'

'It's really hard to remember. A skirt I think, definitely not trousers. Yeah, she had bare legs. There's only one thing I really remember about her. I turned the hose away, where I was washing down the pavement, so I didn't soak her. When she looked up at me, I saw she didn't have any top front teeth.'

Bingo! Rainy made time to visit him at home that evening to take a formal second statement.

–

When Gillard heard about it, he was overjoyed. Julia McGann had mentioned Destiny's distinctive dentition, and this sighting could well be the girl. Rainy said that the builder hadn't noticed any bloodstains. Watkins said she had gone up to a vehicle parked at the far end of close, a small white van, which had been driven away shortly afterwards. The witness confessed he hadn't actually seen her get in the van.

'I think she's got an accomplice,' Rainy said.

'That would make sense,' Gillard replied. 'Let's concentrate on the vehicle.' The builder hadn't noted the van's number but had noticed that it was an old and noisy Renault diesel.

Gillard knew the sure way to find the van was to re-examine all the pedestrian safety and traffic light camera footage from the area, a mighty task. The sixty-two CCTV cameras had been installed by the local council following the death of a child in a hit and run in 2016 and covered all crossings within a half mile of a school. For that afternoon alone, more than 8,000 registration numbers had already been noted, spread over nineteen sets of lights and crossings. None of these cameras were ANPR, so seven officers had been involved in the boring task, and it had taken four days to manually note them and input them to the inquiry system. The vehicle type, which wasn't always apparent from the camera, had not been noted. The thinking was that, if required, it could be done on the DVLA computer and later cross-referenced from the registration number.

'Let's make a wee assumption, that the van was stolen,' Rainy said. 'It won't take long to check the list of missing Renault diesels. Then we can crosscheck the registration numbers against the numbers we've already noted from the safety cameras.'

Gillard admired the brilliant time-saving idea. It took less than an hour for Rainy to come back with a result. 'We've got a dozen Renault vans on the list, but only one which went through any of the pedestrian crossings in Byfleet on the day of the murder. It's a 1999 Renault Kangoo, reported stolen in Reading four months ago,' she said, passing across a couple of fuzzy enlargements from a pedestrian crossing camera. The small van was rusty, missing the passenger-side wing mirror, and had a taped-up headlamp.

'There's a female driver,' Gillard said, peering at the photograph. 'But I see no signs of a passenger.'

'Aye, I'm actually now thinking the wee girl was the driver. So maybe no accomplice.'

'Well, there's no driving licence on record for Destiny Flynn. But of course that means nothing.'

Rainy pulled up an electronic map of the area around Adam Heath's house. 'The van crossed the nearest lights to the school on Whipsnade Avenue twice on the day, and on Worplesdon Lane four times, here.'

'Ah, and that connects to Highgrove Crescent,' Gillard noted, tracing the link to Heath's home.

'I also looked up the same wee rust bucket on ANPR to see where else it had been. It's been up to Nottingham on the motorway, but mainly it's been around Guildford.'

'Anything in the last week?' Gillard asked.

Rainy shook her head. 'A big fat zero.'

Gillard swivelled in his chair and tapped his teeth with a biro. 'I tell you what, let's look at the safety camera footage on the three crossings nearest to the crime scene for the two previous days, to see if she did any reconnaissance. This was a well-planned attack, and it would have taken a while to figure out what she was going to do.'

Over the next two hours it became clear how much preparation Destiny Flynn had put in to the attack, with numerous previous appearances by the van. One of the safety cameras showed the girl clearly on the day before the attack, apparently dressed boyishly in a boiler suit or overalls and a woolly hat.

Uniformed officers were dispatched to some of the Heath's near neighbours to ask whether they had seen the van in the days leading up to the assault. There were a couple of vague recollections, but nothing that really added to the sum total of the intelligence they had.

It was late that afternoon when Gillard went back to see Stella Heath and asked the same question. She had seen no sign of the van, but she had something else to show him. An enormous pile of love letters from the woman known as Maggie.

'Are these any use to you?' she said. 'I found them on Saturday but didn't know whether you wanted to see them or not.'

Gillard glanced through the many letters. 'When is the most recent?'

'About five years ago. It at least bears out what Adam told me about when the relationship ended.'

'It's hard to say whether they will have a bearing on the case or not, but I'd like to take them, if I may. We will of course return them to you at some point.'

'Don't worry about returning them, I'll only burn them.'

–

As Gillard pulled up in Weldon Road outside Julia McGann's flat, he saw a couple of male reporters interviewing her upstairs neighbour in the street. As he descended the steps to the basement flat, they abandoned Briony Winters to shout questions to him. 'Is Ms McGann a suspect now?' one of them called out.

He made no comment and signed in with the female officer posted at the door. He was let in just as Kirsty Mockett had finished treating the kitchen with BlueStar. Gillard donned gloves and booties and stood with her with the curtains closed, letting the reagent do its work. After five minutes, there were just a few tiny pinpricks of light.

'Well, not very spectacular,' Kirsty said.

'Maybe not. There's still something on the seal of the freezer door,' he said, pointing it out. 'If we can get a sample you can check whether it was liver, as she claimed.'

Kirsty leaned forward with a cotton bud and stroked the tiny speck. 'We'll be lucky if there's enough to be sure whether it's animal or human. But we'll give it a try.'

Gillard sighed heavily and looked around the kitchen. There was a tiny speck on the edge of the kitchen table, and another couple in the grouting between two kitchen tiles. Kirsty worked her way round taking separate samples from each location.

Finally she stood and turned to Gillard. 'I know that we're looking for a pair of gloves to link this crime scene to the one at Adam Heath's house, but are you thinking of this as anything more than a burglary by the same people?'

'It's a great question. Julia McGann picked out a guy called Lyron Smart from some ID photographs. This isn't his manor, but I suppose it could be relevant if he was looking for Destiny Flynn and had somehow tracked her here. The trouble is, we only have Ms McGann's word that either Smart or Ms Flynn were ever here.'

'I saw an interview with the woman on *Good Morning Britain* today,' Kirsty said.

'I saw that too. She played it all down, intervening to stop Bonner's suicide.'

'Quite the media star, isn't she sir?'

'Unfortunately, yes.'

–

Gillard was halfway through meeting with Christina McCafferty when the next breakthrough came. Christina, the PR chief for the Surrey force, was putting together a public appeal to find Destiny Flynn that would go out that evening. Due to the lack of a recent photograph, an E-fit was being used partially based on Julia McGann's description. Gillard wasn't really happy with the image, but the description of a young woman missing her two front incisors didn't need to be too precise. The PR spin was that it was a missing persons case. She was described as petite and vulnerable, and likely to flee. The public was therefore urged not to approach her but to inform the police. That seemed to cover all the bases.

The campaign would need the sign off from DCS Dobbs, Gillard's boss, as well as Chief Constable Alison Rigby, but he didn't expect that would be a problem.

A bigger problem, hinted at by Dobbs, was the Crown Prosecution Service. Senior lawyers apparently didn't like what Gillard had sent them so far.

The knock on the conference room door came from a young PC. 'We've got Crimestoppers on the phone, and it's urgent.'

Crimestoppers was set up as a charity for anonymous reporting by phone or email of crime anywhere in the UK. It was an enormous help to the police, even though it sometimes added hugely to the workload. Gillard asked Christina to excuse him while he took the call, which was simply to bring to his attention an email message left on the site. It said: 'Gary Vardy of Welwyn Court, Farnham Way, Aldershot, killed Adam Heath. The stolen black BMW is round the back.'

Surrey Police had received hundreds of messages through Crimestoppers about the Heath murder, with a majority either blaming Muslims in general, or citing the name of someone who sounded Islamic. The Vardy tip-off was more interesting than most because of the mention of the BMW, which was not public knowledge. That vehicle had seemed to disappear since it was first reported outside Julia McGann's flat. If found, it could potentially unlock the case. However, Gillard was aware that many Crimestopper reports this detailed were simply score settling amongst the criminal fraternity.

After taking down the details, Gillard rang a local uniformed officer who had dealt with Gary Vardy. Though he wasn't aware of an association with Lyron Smart, the officer had been tipped off the previous day by the shopkeeper in the shoplifting incident with Destiny that Vardy and an accomplice who matched Smart's description had been asking about Destiny Flynn.

'Why didn't you flag it up for CID?' Gillard asked.

'Sorry, sir, I was seconded to the West Oakham unit doing door-to-door follow-ups and hadn't got round to writing it up.'

–

An hour later DC Carl Hoskins and DC Michelle Tsu were sitting in an unmarked white van outside Welwyn Court, Aldershot. It was a tidy 1970s low-rise block. They had established that Gary Vardy lived in one of the two ground floor flats, easily identified by the West Ham United stickers on the window and the claret and blue colour scheme of the front door. The curtains to his flat were drawn, and there was no sign of life. The two detectives left the vehicle and made their way around the back of the block to a parking area within a perimeter of lock-up garages. They had established from the landlord that lock-up number nine was allocated to Vardy's flat. Outside that garage was a vehicle covered by a mildewed tarpaulin. There was nobody around, and Hoskins drew up one edge of the car cover, enough to reveal the distinctive grille and paintwork of a dark BMW. They couldn't tell whether it was the actual vehicle they were seeking because its number plates had been removed.

The two officers then approached the rear of Vardy's flat, one of just two in the block that boasted a garden, though backyard might have been a better description. Over the rotting ranch-style fencing they could see a rusting barbecue, broken plastic outdoor furniture, all surrounded by weeds. As they watched, a tousled head appeared at the kitchen window, filling up a kettle from the sink. It was Vardy.

Vardy was arrested without drama and was taken to Aldershot police station and put in a cell for the night while a crime scene team took his home apart. The arresting officers found no sign of Smart. Gillard arrived the following morning after basic forensics had been undertaken, and the suspect was taken to an interview room. DC Michelle Tsu and a duty solicitor joined them.

Gillard sat down and looked at the prisoner, a raw-boned individual in his early twenties, with a face set in a permanent scowl which distorted the West Ham tattoo on his neck. The muscle of a gang perhaps, but clearly not the brains.

After going through the formalities of describing who was present for the tape, Gillard said, 'All right Gary, where were you on the evening of January fourteenth at around eight o'clock?'

'No comment,' he said.

'Isn't it true that you were sitting in a stolen BMW outside the Weldon Road home of Ms Julia McGann?'

Vardy made no reply but looked at the ceiling, as if there was something of interest there.

'The same BMW that is currently parked around the back of your flat, minus its number plates. The BMW that has your fingerprints all over it, along with those of a certain Lyron Smart.'

Vardy's eyes flicked up at the name. 'No comment.'

'Do you know Mr Smart?'

'No.'

'We think you do. When was it you first met him? Was it before the burglary of Ms McGann's home? Yes or no?'

Vardy scratched the back of his thick neck and examined his fingernails afterwards. 'No comment.'

'Do you want to reconsider that answer? Your phone records show a series of messages between you and Smart, going back a couple of weeks.'

Gillard opened a file in front of him and produced a photographic enlargement of some gardening gloves. 'Recognise these?' he asked.

Vardy shook his head and returned to inspecting his nails.

Michelle intervened: 'For the tape, the interviewee shook his head.'

'We found them in your garden,' Gillard said.

Vardy shrugged. 'So what.' He clearly didn't believe that the rubbish-strewn garden was anything to do with him. Gillard had sent off the gloves for DNA and other forensic checks. He looked at Vardy's hands. They were, in fact, average to small, like the gloves.

'What about this?' he said, passing across a picture of a bloodstained serrated knife.

'Not mine.'

'Do these all belong to someone else?'

'Yeah, guess so.'

Gillard smiled to himself. 'To Lyron Smart?'

'Maybe, I dunno. They ain't mine.'

'If you don't know him, how do you know they might be his gloves?'

Vardy stared Gillard. 'Dunno. You're just saying that to try and make yourself look clever, aintcha?'

'Certainly not an accusation that could be levelled at you, Gary.'

Vardy scowled at the various subdued smiles around the room. Gillard could tell he was aware he'd been insulted, or disrespected, as he would prefer, he just didn't quite know how.

'All right, Gary. Lyron Smart was arrested about an hour ago in London and is being transported here for questioning. This is your last chance to tell us the truth before we start comparing your version of events with his.'

'Whatever.'

'One final point for you to consider, Gary. These gloves and the knife are stained with the blood of Adam Heath, the school principal who was murdered earlier this month.'

Gillard finally had his attention. 'That's bullshit,' Vardy said, his brows knitted even more deeply.

'I think you'd better start talking.'

'I ain't got nothing to say.'

After another ten minutes with no progress, Gillard terminated the interview and left Vardy to his own thoughts. Something wasn't right here. The reappearance of the gloves and knife in a place where they could have been planted was just a little too convenient. DC Karen Desai, the glove expert, had told him that no DNA had been recovered from inside the gloves, and for one good reason: they had been swilled out with bleach. However, the bloodstains on the outside of the gloves, and in partic- ular the unusual shaped stain on the tip of one thumb, were still there. And that blood had been confirmed as Adam Heath's. If Lyron Smart or Gary Vardy had been involved in the murder of Heath, why wouldn't they have disposed of the evidence? In particular, why would they leave them in the garden of Vardy's home, where anyone could find them? It just didn't make sense.

He left Aldershot unhappy with the trajectory of the evidence. That afternoon he was going to have to account for it to a senior lawyer at the CPS.

Chapter Twenty-five

Gillard felt he was on trial. He was sitting in the large conference room at HQ, between Chief Constable Alison Rigby, to his left, and his immediate boss DCS Brian Dobbs. Opposite him was Christine Baddeley, a senior lawyer for the Crown Prosecution Service, who had descended on Mount Browne with a team of seven to review the evidence that Gillard had so far submitted on the Heath killing. Mrs Baddeley, once a leading QC, was an imposing fiftyish woman with a hint of faded glamour. Gillard had dealt with her before and found her intimidating but fair.

'DCI Gillard,' she began. 'I have reviewed the Adam Heath homicide file so far, and I have to say it's incomplete, confused and entirely unpersuasive. On the one hand, you seem to have just stumbled upon two well-known criminals in possession of highly incriminating evidence, with all the forensic connections that one could hope for, yet you are still looking elsewhere. Here we have the blood of the murder victim, found on gloves and a knife in the possession of one of the suspects. The other of the suspects was picked out by a key witness, Ms Julia McGann, whose house was later burgled. Identical glove prints were found at this crime scene. Is that not a correct summary?' Her eyes flicked up to him over the top of her glasses.

'It's an incomplete summary, ma'am. There is no evidence to put either Vardy or Smart at the scene of the Heath killing, and they both deny any involvement, and claim the evidence was planted—'

'Well, they would, wouldn't they?' muttered one of Baddeley's male associates, to the evident delight of some of his colleagues.

Gillard continued: 'As I mentioned, traces of bleach were found inside the gloves, so we cannot say for certain who wore them. But the bloodstains on the outside, surely the most incriminating element of the evidence, were untouched. That to me says they have been tampered with.'

'These were gardening gloves, were they not? I know that when I have used mine, and they have come into contact with dog or cat mess, I wash them in disinfectant. There is nothing to say that this cleansing process did not occur before the gloves were used in the crime, is that not true?'

'It's possible, ma'am. And in that case there might still have been DNA left within subsequently. But the main point is the implausibility of the two suspects deciding to leave such incriminating evidence in a place where it could so easily be found, or indeed could so easily have been planted.'

'So, let me get this right, detective chief inspector. Your argument is that these criminals would not be stupid enough to do such a thing?'

'Yes, that's part of it.'

Baddeley then turned to a female colleague, who had a great stack of files in front of her. 'Sarah has been looking in detail at the previous criminal records of both these individuals, which as we have already discussed is extensive.'

Sarah started reading from one of the documents. 'In 2014 Gary Vardy was convicted of stealing a Ferrari roadster from an address in Aldershot. According to the evidence, much of which was submitted by your own DC Carl Hoskins, Mr Vardy was caught on three CCTV cameras as he broke into the vehicle, was caught on two ANPR cameras as he drove the car at double the relevant speed limit, and to crown it all, posted on Facebook no fewer than four selfies of him sitting inside said vehicle.'

'I was aware of that, yes,' Gillard said.

'The actions of an intelligent man, keen to cover up his crime, detective chief inspector?' Baddeley said.

'On that occasion, no, obviously.'

'Well, I would contend that on this occasion too, he has been a tad dim.'

'He had no motive to kill Heath, and neither did Smart.'

'My goodness, detective chief inspector. You know, probably better than I do, that a huge proportion of British violent crime is perpetrated by one drunken, drugged-up section of the population, against another, for motives that do not bear any logical scrutiny.'

'I contend, ma'am, that the Heath killing was carefully planned and executed—'

'Yes, you do, but seemingly not by these two individuals. The trouble is, detective chief inspector, that we have a reasonable prospect of conviction of Smart and Vardy on these charges, but you prefer to put your faith in some other, speculative, may I say even fantastical, notion for which there is no evidence whatsoever.'

'I am working to produce the evidence, ma'am,' Gillard said through gritted teeth.

Baddeley re-read Gillard's submission. 'Reading between the lines, you are suggesting that a barrister by the name of Julia McGann was the frustrated ex-lover of Adam Heath, and arranged for the killing of this beefy ex-rugby player, and chose for this difficult task a vulnerable, drug addicted child runaway, height five foot one, who no one has seen for several years. Is that correct?'

'Once again ma'am, it's a partial and skewed summary. She is no longer a child—'

'Indeed. I should also have mentioned that there is no forensic evidence whatsoever to back up this claim. Ms McGann denies having even heard of the murder victim until his name appeared in the press.'

'Well, she would, wouldn't she?' Gillard said drily.

She fixed a glare on him. 'I suppose I should also mention that you suggested verbally to one of my colleagues here your view that Ms McGann, far from trying to save the life of Terrence Bonner when he shot himself at Nottingham Crown Court, was in fact trying to kill him. And had been given his gun in order to do so.'

'It's not my case, but it's a damn sight more plausible than Bonner killing himself.'

'DCI Gillard. It is my job to put firm and compelling evidence in front of a jury of twelve good British people. Why are you making it more difficult for me than it already is?'

'Because I believe in the truth.'

'But the truth also has to persuade. And this,' she lifted and let drop the files in front of her. 'This is entirely unpersuasive.' She turned to the chief constable. 'Alison, please can we have a rethink on this?'

Gillard's eyes swivelled left, to watch Rigby's affirmative nod. She'd left him high and dry.

The CPS posse swept out, pausing only to hobnob in the foyer with Rigby and some of the other higher-ups. DCS Dobbs kept a restraining hand on Gillard's arm.

'I'm sorry, Craig. You're off the case. I'm taking charge. This has gone on long enough. We are going to charge Smart and Vardy. Murder, burglary and car theft.'

–

Furious, Gillard strode out of the police headquarters to his unmarked Vauxhall. He drove to Weldon Road and stopped outside Julia McGann's flat. There was no one around. A wave of impotent rage swept over him. He knew she was involved, he just couldn't prove it. He thought about breaking in, but what kind of evidence might he find? He was missing a DNA sample from Destiny Flynn, which would be useful to compare to the one so-far-unidentified trace inside Heath's Jaguar. Maybe there was one in the barrister's spare room. It was tempting, but it would be stupid, illicit and above all legally inadmissible. Still, perhaps there was something he could do. He drove back to the V&I legal chambers in the centre of Guildford. He parked right outside on double yellows, leaving the blues on, and stepped inside the hushed wood-panelled entrance. He asked the posh receptionist if Julia McGann was in, to which the answer was another question: did he have an appointment?

There was a few minutes' wait before he was shown into a reception room with an antique leather settee and bookcases full of legal tomes. On the coffee table in front of him was a copy of the *Daily Mail*, open at a half-page interview giving an account of Ms McGann's intervention to save Bonner, illustrated by a fetching full-length studio picture. It was another five minutes before the woman herself arrived.

'This is a pleasant surprise, detective chief inspector, how can I help?'

'It's about the Adam Heath murder.'

'Really? I'm a tad surprised, seeing as you have apparently been removed from the case.'

Gillard tried to conceal his shock. *News travels fast. Very fast.*

'This is informal. I just want to let you know, Julia, that you may have fooled them, but you haven't fooled me. You're deeply involved in this. You know, I know, and Rachel Meadows knows too.'

She looked shocked. 'What an extraordinary accusation, detective chief inspector.'

He smiled. 'Just so you know: I never give up.'

She smiled indulgently. 'I don't know what you mean. I was recently burgled, and then caught up in a very distressing shooting incident. I really don't need this. As you have no official business being here, you make yourself vulnerable to any of a range of allegations that I could level against you. So if you approach me again, I will have no option but to report you for harassment.'

Gillard said nothing.

'Do we understand each other?' she asked.

Julia McGann had doused his anger, but it was replaced by a cold, hard understanding.

After Gillard left, Julia sat in her office to let her heart rate return to normal. She then picked up the phone and returned a call from a senior lawyer at the CPS. She was put through quickly, and said: 'Thanks for the tip-off, Christine, Gillard has just come round making accusations against me.'

'Really! Do you want to make a formal complaint?'

'No. Not yet. But I told him I could if he does it again.'

'That's probably the right way to do it,' Baddeley said. 'I know we've never met, Julia, but many years ago I was in pupillage with your father, and his guidance was instrumental in my being called to the bar. He would be horrified to see the kind of accusations that Gillard is making about you, and I just wanted to let you know the latest development. Anyway, with two arrests made of the burglars of your home, and those incriminating gloves found, that will hopefully be the end of it.'

'Let's hope so,' Julia said. 'And Christine, thank you so much.'

Chapter Twenty-six

Destiny Flynn was sitting on the settee watching TV when she saw on the local BBC news that a public search had been put out for her. Mr Edwards, the elderly man whose home in Reading she was sharing, pointed at the screen with his walking stick, as he saw the CCTV footage of her shoplifting in Guildford. 'Another young tearaway, they should bring back the birch.'

'That's right,' Destiny said. The report said she had last been seen in Guildford, nearly forty miles to the south.

Running into Bill had been a piece of luck. After more than a week living on a mattress in the stolen Renault van, she had finally abandoned the vehicle a week ago in a side street in Reading. It was becoming a liability. The more she tried to move around, the more certain it was she would eventually be found. She had already altered the number plate with black electrical tape, turning a five into a six and a one into a four. She had also swiped the 'police aware' sign off an abandoned vehicle she'd found on some waste ground and put it on her van when it was parked. But still she worried about being found. She had already cut her hair short and then dyed it blonde in the ladies' toilet at a local Wetherspoons, and bought some cheap reading glasses to aid her disguise. When she went out she always kept her mouth closed. The white coat that Julia had given her was lovely and warm but it was too distinctive, so she had gone into a branch of Edinburgh Woollen Mill and switched it for a similar coat in maroon when the staff weren't looking. She had put each coat on and taken it off so many times, she was sure they wouldn't know which one she had actually arrived wearing.

That was the day she discovered that Terrence Bonner was dead. Caz had texted her from her mum's phone to tell her, and Destiny had gone into a branch of WHSmith to read the papers. Suicide, they said. Amazing. The barrister woman had actually done it. Destiny had assumed it wouldn't happen. It was the revenge she wanted, but it didn't necessarily make her safe. Bonner's henchmen would be furious, desperate to find her. She knew the threat of 'the chemist' was real. It made her blood run cold, as cold as she was that day when Big Tel had poured petrol on her, standing with his lighter above.

She needed somewhere really secure. Not a vehicle.

As luck would have it, it was as she came out from WHSmith that she had spotted Bill. He had been struggling to carry his shopping from the local Co-op, and she'd offered to help him with his bags. It was only a few hundred yards to his run-down terraced house. He had invited her in for a cup of tea to thank her. Her initial inspiration for this charitable act had been robbery, as she was going hungry again and didn't dare use any of the cards that she had stolen any longer. But once she got inside his tidy little house, which was a lot nicer than it appeared from the outside, she felt a little sorry for him, and realised she could do something far better than simply take a few pounds. He had an old caravan in his back garden, which would make a nice base for her. She had no worries about being identified. Bill certainly wouldn't have a clue. He was partially sighted, a bit deaf, quite confused and very lonely. When she asked about the caravan, Bill said that he and Edith used to go on holiday in it years ago.

Destiny had given her name as Mary, but even during their first conversation he asked: 'Why don't you come down and see me more often, Edith?' She realised from their subsequent conversation that Edith was his younger sister. There were several photographs of her around the house, and he then said she had died, though he could no longer recall the year. He cried a little at that realisation, which made her want to put an arm around him. A few minutes later Bill asked another question of her, again as if she was Edith. So Destiny decided she would become her. Bill asked about her children, and she made up stories saying they had left home. Bill seemed quite happy even when the details were not consistent. Destiny in turn asked about any family he had nearby. There were none. 'There's only Edith, who lives up in Newcastle,' he said.

Bill was utterly delighted to have some company, and Destiny in turn was happy to do odd jobs for him, reaching for things in the kitchen, folding up the washing when it came out of the tumble dryer, and doing the drying-up when he washed. She ordered in takeaways using his landline, and paid for them with his cash, and they shared them while watching TV. Only one point of concern came up. On Tuesdays, he said, the home help came. She arranged to be out that day and hid her few possessions from prying eyes. If Bill told the home help that Edith was staying with him, it would hardly raise any eyebrows. Just him imagining things again. In the meantime, Bill was more than happy to let her to stay in the caravan with bedding from his airing cupboard.

After she'd got the text from Caz, Destiny had kept her phone turned off for days. It was the only way to be sure that neither the cops nor those after her would find her. It was hard, as she hadn't been able to speak to Caz or her few remaining friends. But she was certain they would be under the thumbscrews to tell where she was.

Which was okay, because nobody knew.

Staying with Bill was all right for now, but Destiny knew that for the long term it was impossible. She needed to be somewhere that they couldn't find her. She needed a new ID, a new life. So it was that Thursday evening, when she ventured into the centre of Reading, she risked turning on her phone. There was a message on it she had long expected to receive, and when she returned the call it led to an offer she felt she could accept. It would, eventually, meet all her requirements. And for once in her life it might mean an end to running away.

Chapter Twenty-seven

Six months later

Gillard was sitting at home on a Friday night with Sam when the BBC TV ten o'clock news reported that Lyron Smart and Gary Vardy had been convicted of the murder of Adam Heath. The correspondent described how as the life sentence was read out Smart had bellowed at the judge that he was being 'fitted up', while Vardy looked expressionlessly into the distance.

'They're innocent,' Gillard said. 'Criminals they might be, but they didn't do this.'

'They can appeal, I suppose?' Sam asked.

'At some stage, but they'll need new evidence.'

'What kind of new evidence?'

Gillard sighed. 'Forensic, ideally. I've no idea where we would get any now. I had Kirsty Mockett go back to Julia McGann's flat on the quiet back in February and see if she could find any DNA trace of Destiny Flynn there.'

'Were you allowed to do that once you were off the case?'

'Not really, but at the time they were still looking for more evidence in the burglary, so CSI had an excuse to be there, and Yaz Quoroshi turned a blind eye. I was hoping she'd get a hair or something like that from Destiny to match up with the unknown trace in the Jaguar. But it turned out the flat was up for sale, and when Kirsty got in there, it had been completely stripped of furniture and carpets.'

'And this missing girl hasn't turned up anywhere?'

'No. Destiny may be hiding, she may even be dead. She has certainly turned out to be pretty elusive for a girl missing her top two incisors.'

'I suppose you just have to let it go and move on, Craig,' Sam said, looking pointedly at his hands. He had been flexing his fists in frustration. 'I know you hate to let go when you feel there has been a miscarriage of justice, but sometimes you have to do it just for your own sanity.' She leaned over and embraced him. 'That's what I had to learn to do in the last year. And I've done it.' She kissed him on the forehead, and he smiled.

'Yes, you're right,' he said.

An hour later, as they were just getting ready for bed, Gillard's phone rang. It was DC Michelle Tsu, on overnight duty. 'Sir, we've had a potential sighting of Destiny Flynn, thought you'd like to know.'

'Where?'

'Bakewell, in Derbyshire.'

'Hmm. A long way away. Might be a long shot. Is Radar Dobbs chasing it up?' Gillard asked.

'I don't think so. It's been on the case system since Wednesday, and I'm the first person to look at it according to the log. Of course, the case was formally closed today when Smart and Vardy went down.'

'But she's still a missing person!'

'That's why I'm letting you know, on the quiet. I've sent you the witness statement. It's a good one, because it's from a retired cop.'

'Thank you.' Gillard ended the call, and after reading the email and perusing the attached photos, looked up at Sam.

'Something interesting?' she asked.

'I'm off to the Peak District tomorrow, first thing. There's been a sighting of Destiny.'

'Craig, let it go. You'll only get into trouble.'

He smiled tightly. 'I'll give it twenty-four hours, Sam. I'll be back tomorrow evening, I promise, whether I find her or not.'

—

Gillard set off before seven on Saturday morning, and was past the M25 and heading up the M1 by eight. He drove close to the speed limit where there were cameras, and beyond it where there were none. Traffic was unusually heavy, presumably prompted by the recent removal of lockdown restrictions. It was all eating into his available time, which might make him less careful. If he was caught investigating this case, it could mean dismissal. He had no official excuse to be investigating Destiny Flynn as a missing person. Radar Dobbs had made that clear when he was removed from the Adam Heath murder case. He was barred from investigating any of the principal connections to that case, especially anything involving Julia McGann. He couldn't cross the line, as he was sure Dobbs would be checking for his electronic fingerprints on the case files. But something inside him felt that this was important. There was a miscarriage of justice with Smart and Vardy, of that he was certain. He could only put it right if he could find the girl and get her to talk. If he failed to track her down, but found something else important, he'd feed it in to either Michelle or more likely Claire Mulholland to pursue. A detective inspector like Claire would have the rank to open a case on her own initiative.

As Michelle had noted, the statement was a good one. The retired Warwickshire detective had been very sharp-eyed to spot the facial resemblance of the girl with the short blonde hair to that of Destiny Flynn, last seen with long dark hair. His photographs, taken from a parked car on Tuesday, showed Destiny in conversation with an elderly woman. It was definitely her. The body language seemed to indicate they knew each other well. This wasn't simply a casual conversation with a passer-by. This still left many questions: what was Destiny Flynn doing in this small tourist town? Who was the elderly woman she was walking with? Most vital of all, was she still in the area?

After getting the call last night, Gillard had spent an hour trying to find some historic family link between Destiny and Bakewell. The nearest connection was via Adam Heath. The late headmaster had, according to his widow's statement, been a regular walker in and around the Peak District National Park, encompassing parts of Derbyshire, Cheshire and South Yorkshire. But as far as Gillard could see, Destiny herself was a city girl. She had no reason to be in Bakewell, and no family links what-soever outside the south-east. He had logged onto the ANPR system, and taken the risk of checking whether Julia McGann's Dacia Duster had come up north in the last two weeks on either of the two main routes, the M40 or the M1. As of Friday night, it hadn't.

Past Nottingham, he took the turning to Mansfield, continuing onwards to Matlock and the A6. Tourist traffic heading to the Peaks was heavy, and often slowed to a crawl. It was just gone ten when the satnav reckoned he was an hour away from his destination, but as Gillard got caught in long queues, he knew that was optimistic. It was turning out to be a warm and sunny day, and Bakewell would inevitably be heaving with visitors. That could be a problem, because Gillard was intending to ask shopkeepers and cafe owners if they recognised Destiny or the other woman from the photos on his iPad.

It would have been so much easier if the witness report was fresh. The sighting had been on Tuesday morning, and was reported the same day to local police. According to the evidence log, no one in Surrey Police had even looked at it until Thursday afternoon. By Friday, Smart and Vardy were sentenced, so the matter became moot. When you had a fixed idea, as DCS Dobbs certainly had, you wouldn't start digging into evidence that might force you to change your mind.

Gillard crawled into Bakewell to find the pretty town as packed as expected. He located the bakery-cum-cafe outside which the pictures had been taken, found somewhere to park half a mile away, and after donning his face mask, waited in a long queue to get in. It was noon by the time he got to speak to the harried staff, none of whom recognised anyone in the photos. He tried another half dozen shops over the course of the afternoon.

Nothing.

–

At the same moment, less than seven miles away, Destiny Flynn leaned back on a folding chair and opened the ring pull of another can of ice-cold cider. The green dales of Derbyshire stretched away for miles, threaded with dry stone walls and scattered with flocks of sheep. The day was warm and bright, with just a few puffy clouds, and she could smell the new-mown grass from the field across the way. For the first time in her life she felt happy. Something very special was going to happen today. The caravan she lived in now was modern and clean, much better than Bill's musty, mouldy one. Mrs Meadows, Rachel's aunt, had been very kind to her, and gave her fresh eggs every day along with milk from a neighbouring farm. Mrs Meadows owned the farm, although a tenant farmer did most of the work. Mrs Meadows must be nearly eighty years old, widowed for almost twenty years, but she was very sprightly and friendly. She had even taught her to cook, starting with how to make an omelette.

Destiny had gone straight now, since the middle of winter, helped by the two £20 notes that arrived every week by post from Julia. Since the shooting of Bonner, she had warmed to the woman for keeping her side of the bargain, and helping keep her safe. The crowning glory, completely unexpected, was that the two gangsters pursuing her had been put away for life. She didn't know quite how that had happened, but assumed Julia had something to do with it. Destiny was proud of herself for keeping her own side of the bargain. She hadn't stolen anything since coming here, even though she knew that Mrs Meadows kept a lot of cash in a silly little cuckoo clock on the wall. She was gradually becoming the completely reformed character that Julia insisted she must be. She had even stopped lying, except for the essential untruths she was now committed to. The false name that Julia and Rachel had given her so that Mrs Meadows wouldn't realise who she really was.

Jo Robinson, from Chelmsford in Essex.

The given reason she was there wasn't actually a lie at all. She was trying to recover from childhood sexual exploitation. That was what Rachel had told her aunt. It was enough to ensure that there weren't too many nosy questions.

It didn't matter. There were very few visitors to the farm, and the only people she saw were lines of cheerful middle-aged walkers who marched past on the public footpath to the moors. She had even started to read books, a lot of the old horror thrillers that Rachel had left in the caravan. She began to think about the kind of stories that she could write one day, about all of the suffering she had endured and had now put behind her. It might be cathartic.

Rachel and Julia were coming up late this afternoon with Jack. That is what she had so been looking forward to. One day she hoped she would become a mother herself, and put all the terror behind her. She would be a good person, a kind person. Jack was lovely. He somehow brought out a soft caring side in her. It was the promise of regular visits from Jack that had finally swung her into taking Julia's offer on trust.

–

In Bakewell, Gillard was close to giving up. He'd fruitlessly shown the pictures to dozens of people, and even taken the risk of making contact with the duty DI at Derby. There had been no follow-up to the witness statement from their end, and the DI made it clear that there were no resources whatever to spare today. He'd also rung the ex-copper witness, who'd been able to add very little to his comprehensive statement. He certainly hadn't spotted a yellow Dacia Duster, filthy or otherwise, when he was in Bakewell, and the photo of Julia McGann that Gillard sent him provoked no recognition. Finally, at five, Gillard sat on the steps outside a bank with an ice cream and wondered what else he could do before turning round and going home.

And it was then that a Duster just like Julia's drove past on the main road no more than fifty yards away. He was so surprised he dropped the ice cream off his cornet in his hurry to get a better look. He couldn't see the number plate, which was obscured by a van close behind. The colour was right, and a glimpse of the roof confirmed it. Bird crap everywhere. It couldn't be a coincidence, surely. By the time he got to his own car, the Duster was long gone, and the ice cream had melted into his trousers. Cursing his luck, he got into the car and headed off blindly up the road where the car had gone. He stopped and rang Carl Hoskins at home, to ask him to do an ANPR check for him. He quickly returned with the news that the Dacia was hers, it had been recorded at Matlock this afternoon, but nothing since. Camera coverage was thin here. Gillard used the enduring evening light to drive around Bakewell and the surrounding villages. Pub car parks, holiday cottages, caravan parks, village halls, National Trust parking areas and mile after mile of illegal roadside parking. Not a single yellow Duster. Those he stopped to speak to at the roadside all turned out to be tourists rather than locals. No one had noticed the car, or recognised the two women on his iPad. The task was becoming hopeless, particularly without the resources that he would normally be able to call on. He left a message for Claire Mulholland, summarising what he'd discovered.

Finally, just before eight, he rang Sam, and told her he was coming home.

–

At that point he was less than two miles from Destiny. Two hours earlier, she'd heard the sound of an approaching vehicle, grinding its way up the lane.

'That'll be the filthy Duster,' Mrs Meadows called out from the kitchen window. 'I'll go and get the kettle on.'

Mrs Meadows had been talking non-stop about seeing Jack again. Destiny smiled, recognising in the older woman the same affection and excitement that the boy stirred in her. She was also, she had to admit it, looking forward to seeing Julia, to thank her for everything she had done to turn around her life. When she'd come up here originally, it was Rachel who had given her a lift from Reading. Julia had said that it was too risky, given the press interest in her, for them to meet in public.

In fact, Destiny was so grateful, she wanted to give Julia a present. A much better one than the previous unwanted object she had dumped at Julia's home. She looked down at her mobile phone. It was the reconditioned one Julia had bought for her on their one shopping trip together in Guildford. It had been her insurance and leverage, in a time before trust. She had always refused to give it up, even for a brand-new phone, though Julia had offered her one. She swiped through to the video of her and Julia, drunk together on that Saturday night last December. She didn't play it, because she knew every second of it. It was the one link to that terrible past that she and Julia shared.

She looked up at the sky, where the clouds had just parted. A patch of blue, lined with dazzling sunlight, lit her up. And as Julia's car rumbled through the gate, her finger hovered over the video, then hit delete. A welcome gift for Julia.

–

The rest of the weekend was sociable, the most fun Destiny had enjoyed in years, despite the weather being terrible. Horrible driving rain caused mud to cascade down the farm tracks, and water to gurgle in the gutters. For all of Sunday they stayed indoors, entertaining Jack inside the farmhouse, chasing him around, playing hide-and-seek with lots of laughter and giggling, while Mrs Meadows went backwards and forwards to the kitchen bringing home-made cakes and scones, and cup after cup of tea. And though the weather had not improved by Monday morning, there was much to look forward to.

Rachel looked out of the window, and said: 'Julia, we've got to go. Ten o'clock appointment, remember?'

'Yes, of course,' Julia replied.

'Where are we going?' Jack asked.

'Sorry, Jack, you've got to stay with Mrs Meadows,' Julia said. 'We're taking Jo to the dentist, to get her some new front teeth.'

Jack turned and looked at Destiny. 'Going to the tooth fairy!'

'Yes, that's right, except to get teeth back we have to pay *her*,' said Rachel.

'And then some,' Julia added.

They raced through the rain to Julia's car, Destiny sitting in the front with Julia, and Rachel in the back with a heap of coats and luggage. They rocked and rolled up the rough path back into the village, en route to Bakewell.

Destiny chatted away happily about all of the recipes that she was learning to make.

'Mrs Meadows has been so nice to me,' Destiny said. 'Like the granny I never had.'

Julia gave her a very kind smile, and in her eyes Destiny could see tears. Late last night, when she was lying in the caravan, Destiny had overheard an argument between Julia and Rachel as they went backwards and forwards to the car. She couldn't catch what was being said between the slamming of the car doors, but the tone was clear. Rachel was angry and insistent, and Julia was upset. Destiny hadn't yet mentioned deleting the video. That would certainly cheer her up. She'd pick her moment, when she and Julia were alone.

They had been going along the main road for twenty minutes, when Rachel leaned forward from the back, and pointed. 'It's a right turn here.'

'Where are we going?' Destiny asked.

'There's a really lovely waterfall I want to show you both, and it will be fantastic in all this rain,' Rachel said.

'Great,' said Destiny, and looked at her phone. 'I hope it won't make us late.'

'No, we've got time,' Rachel said.

They went up a steeply climbing road, which later narrowed to a track. Between the arc of the wipers, Destiny could see only windswept moorland under a brooding sky. 'Where's the waterfall?'

'Just a bit further on,' Rachel said, her head leaning forward in the gap between the front seats, so close Destiny could smell the apple shampoo on her hair.

Julia drove on, bumping the car over a cattle grid between slabs of broken dry stone wall. It was wild country, acre upon acre of rough grass and bog, dotted with dead trees spotted with lichen. The track became more rutted, and the Duster bounced through potholes. Hail and sleet began to ping off the roof and passenger side window. They were fifteen minutes off the main road now, and Destiny began to worry about the appointment. 'I don't want to be late,' she said, looking at her phone. 'Can't we come back here after my teeth are done?'

'Nearly there,' crooned Rachel into Destiny's ear. 'There's a shortcut into Bakewell, a much faster road just over the other side, near the falls.'

'But I can't even see a river or stream,' Destiny said. 'How can there be a waterfall?'

'That's what makes it so unusual,' Julia said, sniffing and wiping her eyes with the back of her hand. Destiny sensed Julia's continuing upset, and leaned forward, but Julia turned away. 'What's the matter?'

'Hey, Destiny,' Rachel said, resting a hand on her shoulder. 'Look on this side.' She pointed through the passenger-side windows. 'Can you see the signs?'

'No.'

'Well, the Romans used to mine lead up here. The whole place is still littered with narrow mine shafts and sinkholes. Every so often a sheep falls in, but you can't get them out. They get eaten by rats.'

Destiny heard a sniff, and looked back at Julia, catching an anxious glance before she turned away. A tear was tracking down Julia's face.

'It's only a sheep,' Destiny laughed. 'Bloody hell, you are so soft!'

'We stop here,' Rachel said firmly.

Julia braked and turned off the engine. Suddenly there was silence.

'Where's the waterfall?' Destiny asked.

No reply. Julia's head hung forward, hair draped around her face like a curtain. Something wasn't right. She seemed really upset about something. Destiny's first thought was that she and Rachel had argued about the cost of the teeth. Destiny knew it would cost hundreds. Maybe they weren't going to take her to the clinic after all. 'What's the matter?' Destiny asked.

'Destiny, I'm so sorry, so very sorry,' Julia replied.

'Sorry for what?' It's the teeth, Destiny thought. I knew it. There was such an atmosphere in the car. They'd promised her, and now they were going to let her down. 'Sorry for what?' she repeated, more angrily now.

She saw Julia's eyes flick left, over her shoulder to Rachel. Destiny felt the hand from behind flick across her throat, the impact like a knife. The wire, so thin so tight around her neck, from behind. Instantly immobilising, getting tighter and tighter. Can't breathe. She looked at Julia, and as her throat constricted, the words came to her head. *I deleted it. It's gone. I trusted you.* But she couldn't say them. She couldn't say anything, her voice just an unearthly gasping, barely audible above the pattering of sleet on the windows.

Afterword

I am indebted to several sources who checked key sections of the book or gave me information that would otherwise be difficult to access. Hester Russell, head of crime at solicitors GWB Harthills in Sheffield was an invaluable source of advice for the working lives of barristers. Further reading in this area was provided by *Confessions of a Barrister* by Russell Winnock and *Defending the Guilty* by Alex McBride. I would also like to thank former prison governor Andy Clarke who assisted me on aspects of prison life, Bridget Campbell for steering me on the complexities of running a secondary school, and Bethan Hodges at the website *Missing People*. Retired detective inspector Kim Booth was as always a great fund of knowledge. All remaining errors are my own. As usual, I have invented a few locations in Surrey, such as West Oakham, for the purposes of the plot.

Michael Bhaskar and the Canelo team as always were enthusiastic about the book. Miranda Ward did an excellent editing job. I would like to thank my readers circle, Tim Cary and Sara Wescott. Above all is my wife and first reader, Louise, to whom this book is dedicated.

CANELO CRIME

Do you love crime fiction and are always on the lookout for brilliant authors?

Canelo Crime is home to some of the most exciting novels around. Thousands of readers are already enjoying our compulsive stories. Are you ready to find your new favourite writer?

Find out more and sign up to our newsletter at canelocrime.com